SEDUCED BY A DEMON KING

ETERNAL MATES BOOK 17

FELICITY HEATON

THE ETERNAL MATES SERIES

CHAPTER 1

Tegan's battle plan was sound.

A simple feint. Trick the eye. A stroke of genius.

With a dash of the fates smiling upon him, he might escape this prison tonight.

This castle had been his cage for a thousand years, since the night his brother had been murdered, the throne beneath him a shackle that held him fast, unbreakable except through death.

He ran a steady hand over his right horn, feeling the smoothness and the slight bumps where the enchanted gold had been inlaid into the grooves he had carved himself. Some of the bumps were barely noticeable, a sign of how many times he had performed this act since Edyn had died.

The plan was sound.

But still a trickle of nerves ran in his blood.

Or was that excitement?

It had been so long since he had experienced that emotion that he was unfamiliar with it now. He pondered that as he swigged from his pewter mug, the brew sweet on his tongue. One of the few pleasures he had left in his long and tedious life.

Excitement. Fear. Pain. The high of victory.

Everything he had loved had been stolen from him the night he had been thrust into a role he had never wanted.

Although perhaps he would have lost it all anyway, even if his brother had survived.

Peace.

He cursed that word.

He cursed Edyn.

He cursed the throne.

He cursed his kingdom.

Tegan mentally took that one back.

As much as he despised the truce with the First Realm of the demons and the elf kingdom, as much as he despised his throne and his advisers who sought to keep him tethered to it, safely holed up in his castle, he couldn't blame his people for what had happened to him.

Perhaps he was the one who was cursed.

Cursed to lead a dull and *peaceful* life for the rest of his days.

Tegan leaned to his right, dropped his chin on his upturned palm as he planted his elbow against the arm of his black throne, and huffed.

He had been born for war, not peace.

Yet here he was, presiding over a feast celebrating the anniversary of the truce his brother had formed with the neighbouring demon realm and the elves.

Celebrating peace.

He could practically feel his life draining from him, one grain of sand at a time through an hourglass that was shielded by layers and layers of steel designed to keep it *safe* from harm.

What sort of demon wanted to be safe?

Peaceful?

He craved battle, adventure. A glorious war or two every decade wouldn't go amiss either. But here he sat, his backside stuck to a throne he wanted no part of, doomed to rule a peaceful kingdom while the other demon kings indulged in lavish wars, were out there on the frontline spilling blood and breaking bones.

He lifted his cup to his lips again and took a deeper draught of the mead.

Gods, he was bored.

Cursed.

It was Edyn's fault.

His older brother was meant to rule while Tegan did all the fighting as commander of their Royal Legion, not broker a damned peace treaty and then die, leaving the Second Realm in Tegan's hands.

He growled low in his throat.

A few of the warriors celebrating at the long feast tables that lined the grand hall of the castle paused to look his way, their brew or their females forgotten as they checked on him. Tegan glared at them all, tempted to flash his emerging fangs as his mood took a sharp dark turn, plunging him into the mire of thoughts that had been his own personal hell since the night someone had placed a crown upon his head.

The warriors returned to their drinks, laughter spilling from their lips as they toasted him and cheered, as if that would lift his mood. He drummed his short claws against the layer of stubble on his cheek as he surveyed the room, dark gaze passing over the towering carved black columns that supported the vaulted ceiling high above him.

The candles in the middle of each long black wooden table illuminated the faces of his warriors, playing over their dark hair and horns, flickering over their bare chests as they shoved and laughed, caroused with the females he had brought in for the celebration.

At least someone at the feast was enjoying themselves.

Edyn had always said the people came first.

Something he and his brother had agreed upon. Although Tegan liked to place his warriors first, a hang up from his days serving in the legions, leading them and witnessing the toll battle took on them. Now peace took its toll on them instead.

So he had agreed to tonight's feast.

His men needed to blow off some steam, and if drinking and females could supply them with an outlet for it, he would gladly sit through a thousand boring feasts. He couldn't give them war after all.

He had once contented himself with feasts, mead and females. It had worked for a while, taking the edge off, but now he found them dull.

What he wanted now was a battle. A war. It was the only thing that could improve his mood. The news from the other demon realms wasn't helping. Several of them had gone to war recently, and although he had lobbied his advisers and made a valiant attempt to let the Second Realm join the Third Realm in their battle against the Fifth, their answer had been the same as always.

He must maintain the peace.

Tegan huffed again.

Maintaining the peace was exhausting. It went against his very nature.

He went to take another mouthful of his brew and frowned at the bottom of the large pewter mug when he found it empty. He held it out to his right and the male standing there refilled it for him. He nodded, lifting his mug to thank the male, and drank deeply, emptying half the tankard in one go.

A few of the warriors in the room tugged females away with them.

Almost time to put his plan into action.

He just needed to be patient for a little longer.

But patience wasn't his strongest virtue. It lacked a little.

He tapped his foot, jiggling the female seated on his left thigh. One he had completely forgotten about, even though she was about to become a key factor in his battle plan.

She immediately went into action, fawning over him, running fingers over his shoulder, shifting the material of his loose white shirt as she murdered his language so badly, he struggled to interpret her meaning. "My lord, your muscles. You are strong."

Tegan slid her a look he hoped conveyed how irritating she was. It didn't stop her. She prattled on, all smiles as she flicked blonde hair over her shoulder to reveal a hefty amount of cleavage. Unsurprising given how tight her red leather bodice was.

He wasn't sure what species she was, and he didn't care.

He tuned her out as he surveyed his warriors. Were they really content with feasting and females? He wasn't.

How was he meant to continue like this?

He was a warrior at heart, but every day he had to pretend to be something else. Worse, he had to *be* someone else. He no longer recognised the male who obeyed the wishes of his advisers even though he was tired of hearing them all tell him he had to place the peace of the kingdom above all else. He no longer recognised the male who sat on the throne, listening to the complaints of his people.

They were not content, not as they were meant to be anyway. Many came to him to complain about everything from their neighbours to the travelling traders he permitted to roam through the kingdom to sell their wares.

He settled his gaze on two males, both close to his seven-foot height, both packed with as much muscle as he was. Commanders like he had been. Demons born for war. They weren't content. They stood to one side, had been there all night, deep in discussion and ignoring the advances of the females.

Talking of war? Of glorious days long past but not forgotten?

He wanted to speak with them, to relive the days they had fought beside each other, the great battles they had witnessed in their years and the close shaves that had brought them dancing dangerously with Death.

The female seated on his knee showed no sign of moving though and the two guards who flanked his throne, standing slightly behind it as if he wouldn't notice them there, would stop him if he tried to speak with them. No doubt they had strict orders from the court to keep him from talk of war and battles tonight.

The two males glanced his way, lingered and dipped their heads, raising their tankards at the same time. He could see the weariness in their eyes, as if they were a reflection of him. The inactivity grated on them as viciously as it did on him.

If he could give them war, he would do so in a heartbeat.

Tegan mentally took that back too.

As much as he hated the peacefulness of his kingdom, as much as he craved doing battle, he couldn't just go to war. The majority of his people had become accustomed to this dreadful peace. They enjoyed it, finding pleasure in having a land dominated by stability and peace.

He was their king, whether he wanted it or not, and he couldn't deny them that which they desired—a kingdom not at war.

More of his men left with females in tow. Soon.

The night was growing older, the feast becoming louder, the merriment infectious as the gathered warriors consumed mead by the barrel and sampled their females, selecting the one who would pass the night in their bed.

Soon.

He had successfully managed to pass the day evading his advisers, which had lifted his mood. Or that might have been the punishing training routine he had indulged in, competing in mock battle with four of the finest warriors in the Royal Legion. They were always kind enough to help him fill the tedious hours of the day and grant him some escape.

Tonight, he had meant to carry out his usual method of filling the dark hours.

A long time ago, that would have meant bedding one or more females, living up to the rumours that he had a harem of them at his disposal. He had quickly grown bored of females after ascending to the throne though.

Females were too compliant, always too willing to throw themselves at his feet in a grand effort to please the king.

So now he filled his night hours with a different sort of entertainment. A guilty pleasure he found himself indulging in more and more often recently.

Reading.

His aide called him voracious. He had a thirst for knowledge that kept the male constantly teleporting back and forth to the mortal world to bring him more books. Since becoming king, he had learned twelve languages, both written and spoken. He had studied the culture and history of every mortal country, and every fae and immortal realm. He had learned about music and art, and as much as he could about the modern human world.

He had read books on almost every subject imaginable.

He had a library in his private floors of the castle, a sanctuary few knew about, one he was adding new shelves to and expanding every year.

That was where he had intended to pass the night after managing to escape the feast.

Only he had finished his last book while dressing for the feast.

So his plans had changed.

Had grown more thrilling.

He meant to escape more than the feast.

More than the castle.

He meant to escape Hell for the first time in a thousand years.

Just the thought of seeing the modern human world with his own eyes had adrenaline surging through his veins and he couldn't contain the smile that tugged at his lips as his heart soared. He turned it on the female as she sidled closer, attempting to conceal the true reason for his excitement in case the guards were watching him.

She fluttered long black lashes, her grey eyes sparkling at him as she stroked the horns that curled from behind the top of his ears, her fingertips lightly tracing the curve of them down to his lobes in a way that did nothing for him.

She leaned in closer still and murmured in his ear, her use of the demonic tongue leaving a lot to be desired as she mangled his language in an attempt to seduce him. "Your horns are so *big*."

He supposed she meant to use the old adage about a demon's horns having a correlation with the size of his manhood.

Some part of him felt that he should be enjoying her attention and the feast, but he wasn't.

Something wasn't right, and it hadn't been for a long time.

The female pressed against him, her breasts threatening to spill from her corset as she leaned her side against his chest and her arm came to rest along his shoulder. She pushed her fingers through the longer lengths of his black hair and skimmed them over the shorn sides to tease the more sensitive base of his horns.

He still felt nothing.

He swigged his mead as she traced patterns on his chest, working her way over to the lacing on his shirt. She toyed with the ties, curled them around her fingers and tugged, clearly intending for him to move closer.

He took another mouthful instead.

He wasn't interested in the female. He hadn't asked for her company, had given her no indication he desired her attention, yet here she was, fawning over him.

"You have masculine beauty," she husked, and he gritted his teeth. Whoever had taught her to speak the demon tongue had done a bad job of it. "Strong male."

Did she think her praise would rouse his interest and make him want her?

It had quite the opposite effect.

He had lost interest in carousing with females when he had realised they were only interested in one thing—his throne.

He despised the fact every female he met viewed him as a throne, not a male. They wanted the power he could give them, the status. They didn't really want him. Of course, he could sleep with them and discard them, slaking some of his hunger on them, but where was the fun in that?

He preferred a challenge, something that would appease his hunger for battle. If he couldn't do battle physically, he would do it mentally. He wanted a female who would be that challenge for him, one who would make him fight for her.

His warriors and his younger brother Ryker, the current prince, weren't complaining about his lack of interest in the females. All the more for them.

Gods, Tegan envied Ryker a little. He had freedom, came and went as he pleased, while Tegan was locked in his castle, only allowed out with an entire entourage of advisers and bodyguards, and even then it was only to official functions where the kingdom needed to be represented by its king.

Ryker had everything Tegan had lost, and Tegan would give anything to return to that life.

His dark eyes scanned over the feast. Edyn would have lapped this up. He would have loved sitting on the throne with a female on his knees, soaking up her praise and that of his people.

Tegan hated it.

A thousand years he had endured this dull and unsatisfying life.

That changed tonight.

His battle plan was sound, everything was in place. His strategy had been checked from all angles, every little thing accounted for and covered. All that was left was to put it into action.

He signalled the male to his right, who eagerly bustled over, his jug at the ready. Rather than allowing the male to fill his cup, Tegan placed it on the tray in the male's other hand and nodded.

Tegan grasped the female's slender wrist, pulled it from behind his head and pushed her forwards, forcing her off him. She tottered a little, giggled and swayed against him as he stood.

The two males guarding him immediately moved forwards.

Tegan turned on them. "I do not require an audience."

Both males dipped their heads and pressed their right hands to their bare chests.

He cut them off before they could mention standing guard outside his rooms. "You are done for the night. Enjoy the feast and the females."

The two exchanged a glance and then looked beyond him, to the males who were still celebrating, pawing at the females on their laps and calling out to the others that wandered around the room, seeking a partner.

The younger male on his right looked as if he might mention the orders the court had given them, but the other male grabbed him by the back of his neck and pushed him forwards, guiding him towards the nearest females.

Phase one of his plan successfully completed, Tegan tugged the blonde female towards the side door of the grand hall, one only he could access. She stumbled along behind him, still throwing compliments and things he supposed were meant to sound seductive. He paid no attention to her as he mounted the spiral steps, eager to reach his rooms and move on to phase two.

The female slowed him down, so he turned and scooped her up into his arms and took the steps two at a time instead, making swift progress towards his private floors. She stroked his chest and shoulders, even went as far as pressing kisses to his throat as he kept his focus ahead of him.

Almost there.

Light chased back the darkness ahead of him and he quickened his pace, his heart pounding harder as he thought about what he was going to do.

He set the female down as soon as he reached the broad torchlit corridor at the end of the stairs and pulled her along behind him as he stormed towards the door of his apartment. She continued to twitter, babbled words that were lost on him as he went over his plan again, ensuring everything was perfect.

He shoved the wooden door open with the flat of his hand and pulled her inside, shoved her aside and released her as he closed the door behind him. She moved around his drawing room, saying things he didn't hear as she studied the paintings that hung on the black stone walls and ran her fingers over the glass that covered the long low display cases that lined them, eyeing his collection of weapons, helmets and other things from all the regions of Hell.

His trophies of war.

She fell silent, her eyes landing on him as he pulled his shirt off over his head and discarded it on the wooden floor.

Her throat worked on a hard swallow and she sidled towards him, heat kindling in her eyes as she approached. She raked them over his chest and stomach and that heat became a fire.

"You are beautiful, my lord."

Tegan turned away from her, grabbed the black shirt he had laid over the back of his wine-red wingback armchair before leaving for the feast and donned it. Disappointment flared in her eyes.

He ignored her and tackled the buttons on his shirt. *Buttons.* They were fiddly small things, irritating him as he fumbled with them, trying to close the shirt of mortal fashion that Ryker had given him as a present.

He wasn't sure how his younger brother could wear such things.

It was tight and restrictive, made his back itch as his wings pushed for freedom. He focused to keep them hidden as he adjusted to the confining feel of the shirt. If he attempted to swing his sword arm, he would rip the damned garment to pieces.

But then, he supposed it hadn't been made for fighting in.

When he had first tried it on at Ryker's insistence, his brother had assured him it was all the 'rage' for males to wear such tight clothing in the human world, an apparent attempt to reveal their physique whilst still being dressed.

Tegan glanced at himself in the mirror above the fireplace behind him when he was done with the buttons. He arched an eyebrow at his reflection. He supposed the cut of the cloth was rather complimentary. It stretched across his broad chest and tightly gripped his biceps, and even hinted at his muscular stomach.

"You look divine," the female purred in approval in the common tongue and he conceded that he did look rather good in human fashion. "Do I get to peel it off you?"

He flicked her a glare, stooped and picked up his coin purse from the table beside his armchair. She swayed towards him, her eyes on his chest, clearly intent on unbuttoning the shirt he had just put on. He moved around her, crossed the room to a set of black wooden drawers, and pulled the one on the right open. He picked up a smaller coin purse and hung it with his other one on the waist of his black leathers.

He turned back to the female.

He would get into trouble with his advisers if they got wind of what he had done, but he didn't care. He needed a change of scenery. He had been stuck in this castle for the last thousand years. It was time he got out.

It was only going to be for a short time. Everyone would think he was sleeping with the female in his quarters. He would be back before he was missed.

He just wanted a taste of the current mortal world to see if it was as exciting as the stories painted it to be, filled with marvellous technology that sounded like fantasy to him. He had heard tales of it from the Third King and his mate, glorious stories of a world that was vastly different to the one he remembered.

Electronic communication devices that could be used to speak with someone across the globe? Impossible.

Giant metal birds that carried mortals to far-flung destinations? Laughable.

But he had heard the stories coming from the Third Realm and the king himself had told Tegan all about the miracles of mortal technology. Thorne was using the technology to bring electricity into the demon realm he ruled.

Electricity.

Tegan glanced at the sconces burning on the black wall, at the dark wooden furniture of the office that adjoined his drawing room, and the paintings hanging on the walls. Mortals had things that took paintings. No, that wasn't right. They called them photographs. They displayed them on their walls rather than paintings now, and such photographs appeared on electronic devices too.

Thorne had shown him such a strange device when the demon king had brought his new queen to visit. The mortal queen of the Third Realm had one in her possession.

It had been magic.

It had awed him.

A flat rectangle no bigger than Tegan's hands side-by-side but it had been colourful and bright, and she had touched it and things had happened. His advisers had deemed it witchcraft of the darkest degree and warned him against it, but Tegan had been fascinated. He wanted to see more of these mortal inventions.

He wanted to possess them.

It wasn't as if he was committing a crime by leaving the kingdom. He was king. He only meant to go out to a place the Third King talked about and also purchase some more books. Small steps. If the mission was successful, perhaps he would go out again.

He grabbed hold of the female. She pressed closer to him, sliding her hands over his chest and leaning into his embrace. Tegan kept hold of her as he summoned his portal. The black abyss opened beneath them and the female squeaked as they dropped into it. They landed in the free realm, in the middle of the town he had once visited. People on the black cobbled street between the obsidian stone buildings stopped to stare as he pushed her away from him and distanced himself.

"This is as far as you go," Tegan said.

Confusion danced in her pale grey eyes and she tried to get closer to him again. He backed off a step, maintaining the distance between them, and the confusion turned to anger as he spoke.

"I am leaving now." He took the smaller coin purse from his belt and tossed it at her.

She caught it and he teleported before she could give him hell, nerves and excitement clashing inside him as he dropped back into the black abyss.

Heading to the mortal world.

That filled him with an unsettling, but thrilling sensation.

His life had been static for the last thousand years.

Now he was going to taste freedom.

And something told him his life would never be the same again.

CHAPTER 2

Suki regretted agreeing to come to Underworld tonight. She had regretted it from the moment her sisters had cajoled her into the trip, and she should have made her excuses and left. She wasn't in the mood for hunting tonight. She was tired, cranky, and absolutely nothing was going her way.

She had managed to steal one kiss from a nice guy who had moderately good looks and had fallen for her charms, but he had tasted like ashes and her fuel gauge was still on the red line. She needed a male who could fill her tank, didn't want to resort to the sort of feed her sisters seemed intent on getting tonight.

Allura openly fondled the man she had cornered, one who Suki had surmised was a shifter of some variety. Shifters often provided a good feed, but it would come at a high price. Chances were, Allura would kill him once they got busy. Shifters were strong, but not strong enough to handle sex with a succubus.

Suki had lost track of Vidia. The blonde female had been swift to ditch Suki's sorry ass as soon as she had spotted potential prey. If Suki had to guess, she had spotted her favourite food.

A nymph.

Nymphs were strong enough to handle a succubus if they were old enough, but the ones who were old enough were so damned conceited and egotistical that Suki couldn't stand them for long enough to get past the conversation stage of a hunt.

Vidia had once said that petting the ego of a nymph was worth it, even though it left a bad taste in her mouth. According to Suki's clan, doing whatever it took to get a good feed was worth it, regardless of how crappy it made you feel.

Maybe that was the reason they all thought Suki was a complete and utter failure.

She was starving but she still couldn't bring herself to sleep with a guy who wasn't strong enough to survive it or stoop to grooming a nymph's narcissism.

Suki tried to push all the niggling voices out of her head, the thousand jibes and taunts, and harsh words that had come from every corner of the clan, including the mistress who acted as the head of it. They went, but not before they took a few cheap shots at her already fragile mood, cleaving holes in her heart.

Why the hell had she bothered coming out tonight?

She looked at the pleasant man opposite her, one who scored an eight in most departments and who was talking her ear off about a subject she had no interest in and slowly looking more and more as if he was leaning towards ditching her for someone else.

Probably Allura or Vidia. He had asked about them more than once and she had caught the way he had drooled over Allura when the onyx-haired and violet-to-blue-eyed beauty had stopped to check in on her. She couldn't blame him. As always, Allura had somehow managed to squeeze her incredible body into a black rubber mini and a leather corset that barely contained her ample breasts.

Suki was beginning to feel she should have stayed at home. This night was going to go the same way they always did when her sisters dragged her out. She had started out thinking tonight would be different, as always, and she would finally get things right. A few unfulfilling kisses later she would end up screwing everything up and going home alone, still hungry and in an even worse mood.

The opinion of her sisters would only get worse and her future would only look gloomier, and her mood would only grow darker.

She smiled at the nice man and forced herself to move closer, tried to focus on what he was saying but it really was boring. She didn't really care what kind of car he drove, or that he owned his apartment rather than rented. None of that impressed her.

She had never been into material things.

At least not to the extent that her sisters were.

Sometimes, her succubus nature got the better of her and shiny cars and fat bank balances easily seduced her. The perils of living on a tiny allowance. When her money was in danger of running out, she fell victim to her nature, a strange sense of desperation gripping her that had her spending most of the days until her next payment walking around frazzled and in her own little world, seeking a male who might buy her something pretty.

A girl could dream about having money, enough to buy whatever she wanted, couldn't she?

Of course, normally allowing herself to dream like that only made the reality of her situation an even worse nightmare.

Her sisters could afford pretty things, nice clothes and jewellery, and expensive make up, because they preyed on more than the sexual energy of their hosts. They preyed on their bank accounts too, convincing the addled males to buy them things. Suki had tried that once or twice, or maybe a million times, when in the grip of her flat-broke-fever.

She was yet to succeed in convincing a male to buy her something.

Another thing that left a sour taste in her mouth.

Allura did a drive by and sneakily pressed her hand to her forehead, forming an L against it. L for loser.

Her sister meant the male was a loser and to ditch him, but Suki couldn't help but take it personally. Her entire clan thought she was the loser because she was forever having problems with men and feeding. The charm her mother had been famous for had apparently refused to be inherited by her.

Suki lacked the basic succubus skills so badly that a few of her sisters questioned whether she really was her mother's daughter and not some stray she had picked up in the fae town or a baby swapped at birth with her real daughter.

Sometimes, Suki wondered that too.

Most of the time, she wondered how she could make her sisters proud of her. She didn't want them to look down on her. She didn't want to lose them.

The world would be a bleak and lonely place without her sisters.

She struggled to fit in at the clan, but she would struggle even more to fit into a world without them in it. She belonged at the clan, with her sisters. She had lost her only blood relation, but every female in her clan was her sister, whether they were a daughter or a mother, an aunt or a grandmother. They were all her sisters.

The only family she had.

Before her mother had died, she had told Suki something that remained with her to this day.

One day, she would find her place in this world.

Suki knew what her mother had meant by that. One day, she would prove herself to the clan, would learn to use her powers and bloom just as her mother had always said she would, and she would become part of the family just as she had always wanted.

One day, her sisters would love her just as she loved them.

Solid Eight tossed her a flirty smile, one she returned as she sidled closer to him.

She brushed her arm against his, savouring the way his aura shifted, the colours that flared around him like an aurora changing to reveal the red of passion and arousal. He wanted her. She could bag and tag him, although there was a danger the tagging part might end up being one attached to his toe as they wheeled him into a morgue.

Why did Solid Eight have to be human?

She was sure that underneath his blue jeans and dark checked shirt he had a good body, one that would delight her, and that his desire and passion would provide a modest meal. Humans were off limits as far as she was concerned though. One slip and she would end up killing him, even if they were only kissing at the time. She didn't have the energy to focus on restraining herself. She was too hungry, needed a man who could get her off the red line through kissing before she dared to do anything saucier with him.

Allura strolled past again, tugging a handsome man along behind her. Suki was surprised her sister didn't plant another L on her forehead. The clan's favourite succubus just rolled her eyes instead.

Suki glared at her.

Fine, she was taking too long with the guy, but Solid Eight had her twisted in knots. The temptation to kiss him and see if he could handle giving her a little of his energy was great, but the thought of accidentally killing him was like a bucket of icy water on her libido.

Suki looked around the room again, hunting a stronger target, one who could handle a succubus and might be able to provide her with a good feed. If she could find a powerful man, not a nymph, she could probably fill her tank on kissing or at least kissing and a little fooling around.

An ache bloomed between her thighs and she rubbed them together in her tight black cotton mini, the thought of getting frisky with a man sending her temperature soaring and short-circuiting the part of her brain that constantly chided her, telling her not to go too far in case she accidentally killed her host.

A man flashed into her mind, his gaunt face and dull blue eyes hurling another bucket of ice down her panties, quenching the fire that had just started burning.

It had been more than a month since she had let her hunger get the better of her and had almost killed him, and although it had been a mistake on her part because she had been convinced he had been stronger than he had turned out to be, she still couldn't shake the guilt.

That night had left a bitter taste in her mouth.

And it had also cemented her clan's opinion of her.

Any one of her sisters would have gone ahead and given the man a pleasurable exit from this world in order to fill up her tank to the max.

Suki had panicked and teleported him to the emergency room of a London hospital instead.

Cyrena, the clan mistress, had hauled Suki into her office and had talked about the rules, reiterating them for the thousandth time, and had given her a look that left Suki in no doubt that her next mistake was going to be her last.

If she kept failing at everything a succubus was meant to be good at, if she kept tarnishing the hallowed name of their clan, she was going to be kicked out of it. She had been warned enough times that they wouldn't tolerate any black marks on their highly respected name, and Suki was a massive dark smudge right across the middle of it. If her mother had been anyone else, she would have been tossed out on her ass by now.

In the last month, she had doubled down on her training, more desperate than ever to prove herself worthy of being a member of the family that had raised her. She had hit fae clubs in Scotland and northern England, and even a few in America, practicing her charms on soft targets.

Tonight, she had come to practice on stronger marks.

But judging by the bored look on Solid Eight's face, she was failing dismally. If she couldn't charm a human tonight, how was she meant to charm a strong immortal?

A hot bolt of fire shot down her spine, lighting up her insides and cranking up her temperature, and she frowned as she swiftly scanned the room. Someone was looking at her and it wasn't the human.

She shivered, the delicious heat that curled through her threatening to rip a moan from her lips as she tried to keep it together. Her eyes darted over everyone, her limited senses stretching out around her in an attempt to pinpoint the one who was looking at her.

Because whoever it was, they had somehow fired her up with just a look, one she wasn't even reciprocating.

Her eyes locked with intense dark pools set in a stunning sculpted face and the room dropped away, Solid Eight's words lost on her as she fell into those fathomless depths.

Heat suffused every inch of her, fire flaring in her veins as she swallowed hard, bewitched by the spell this newcomer had cast on her with just a single look.

CHAPTER 3

Tegan rose out of the black pool of his portal, relief beating through him as the scent of nature swamped him. It had been centuries since he had last smelled grass, trees, the air of the mortal world. A thousand sounds assaulted him, a cacophony of noises he couldn't identify, and he turned in all directions in the park, seeking their sources.

The trees were thick around him, sheltering him from the sight of the mortals in the area, and he was glad this park still existed just as the map his aide had bought him had showed.

He breathed slowly to settle his racing heart and gave himself a moment to adjust to the onslaught of sensation. The humans were at a distance, far away enough that their weak mortal eyes wouldn't see him. As his pulse evened out and his ears adjusted, dulling the noise, he looked around himself again.

Now came the worst part of his plan.

Tegan closed his eyes and focused, hating himself for what he was about to do. It was shameful, ate away at him a little, but he put up with it. It wasn't the first time he had done this, and it certainly wasn't going to be the last if he had his way and visited the mortal realm more frequently.

He took a deep breath and focused on his horns. They began to shrink, disappearing into his head. If a demon saw him now, they would be disgusted with him. But it was better he dishonoured himself than reveal the existence of demons to the mortals he could sense in the distance.

Satisfied that his horns were no longer visible and his ears no longer pointed, he scrubbed his right hand over his black hair. The sides of his head felt strange beneath his palm without his horns, alien to him. He shook off the unsettling feeling and inhaled slowly, steadying and preparing himself.

He stepped out through the thick copse of trees into the open area of the park, tipped his head back and frowned at the dark sky, at the stars barely visible through the haze of light that hung above the city.

He couldn't remember the last time he had seen a sunrise or sunset. It must have been more than a thousand years ago.

He had squandered his freedom back in those days, more interested in waging war and fighting than he had been in seeing the beauty of the mortal world. Over the centuries, he had come to cherish a few of his memories of the mortal world, in particular ones of beaches, sunrises and sunsets. He was a warrior, a warmonger, was restless on his throne because he was trapped in a time of peace, yet oddly he craved the peace he had felt then.

That had been true peace.

He recalled watching the waves rolling against the shore, listening to them breaking, feeling the warm breeze as it kissed his skin, and smelling the salt that laced the air. He had never felt peace like that, and he felt sure he would never know it again.

So as he stood in the middle of a park surrounded by buildings that stood shorter than his black castle, he couldn't help but feel disappointed that the sun had already gone down.

He drew down a deep breath and sighed, trying to push away from the disappointment that ran through him and focus on his mission.

His first order of business was procuring more books. There were subjects he had been hungry to read about since a meeting with Thorne, the Third King, but Tegan's advisers had employed a dirty tactic in an attempt to control him and make him attend meetings with them.

They had refused to allow his aide to go to the mortal world to get more books for him.

It had worked. He had attended a week's worth of meetings, listening to their drivel about the Second Realm and his position as king. A week, and they still hadn't allowed his aide to go for books.

So Tegan was taking matters into his own hands.

If the aide couldn't get his king books, then the king would get them for himself.

He studied his surroundings as he moved through the park, crushing the grass under his heavy boots, heart pounding in eagerness as he approached the edge of the trees that enclosed the wide lawn that created the heart of the pocket of nature.

He frowned as he passed beneath two towering oaks, the loose stones of the path crunching under his weight. A wrought iron gate blocked his path. He grasped the two sides of it and pulled, attempting to open it. They moved, but didn't give. He lowered his gaze and glared at the thick chain that held the gate closed.

Tegan focused on the other side, on a swath of dark grey that resembled stone, and teleported there.

The street was quiet, the elegant white stone buildings around him illuminated by warm lights. Electricity? He wanted to approach them, to study them, but he didn't have time. Not this visit anyway.

He opened the dark leather coin purse hanging on his hip and took out a piece of paper. He unfolded and studied it, seeking the address printed at the bottom. According to the map his aide had procured him in the past, the bookstore was located close to his current position. He scanned the streets around him, seeking the one that bore the name at the start of the course he had charted, one that would lead him to his goal.

He had studied the mortal world enough to know that the humans liked to label their streets, giving them names to help identify them. He strode across the grey road to the far side where the buildings hugged it and moved around the square. He found one name on a dark placard supported by two posts, but it did not match the one he was looking for, so he kept on walking, reaching another road that branched off from the square. This one's placard bore the right name.

He tucked the piece of paper back into his coin purse, closed it, and focused on the far end of the road, where more buildings intersected it. He dropped into the black abyss that opened beneath him and reappeared there, directly in front of another sign. According to the map he had seen and studied, there should be another junction to his right. He turned in that direction and smiled as he spotted it.

Tegan teleported there, looked left and teleported again. In a few more short teleports, he was standing outside the store, looking up at the painted sign that spanned the length of the two windows and the door that stood between them.

The dark slashes of his eyebrows dipped low in a frown as he dropped his gaze to the doors and read the sign.

Closed.

He gripped the brass handles and rattled the wooden doors anyway. A growl curled up his throat as he found there were locked. Damn it.

He had wanted to do this the right way, cursed the feast for taking so long, delaying his arrival in the mortal world. Now he had no choice but to do this in a way that felt wrong to him. He huffed. He would be sure to make reparations for what he was about to do.

Tegan focused on the other side of the doors and teleported into the building. He landed in front of the register and fought to keep his focus as his eyes danced over the thousands of books around him. A veritable library. He wanted to pause and check every book, to see if there were any others he desired, but he couldn't afford to waste time. If the bookstore was closed, there was a chance the place King Thorne had spoken of might be closed too if he didn't hurry.

He strode through the aisles between the tables filled with books, dark gaze scanning the signs above the bookshelves for the one that would contain the volumes he sought. He found them deep in the back of the store, two entire bookcases dedicated to subjects close to his heart.

The fingers of his right hand danced over the spines of them, deftly plucking the tomes that interested him and piling them in his left arm. When he had gathered close to a dozen books, he forced himself to make a note of the others and turn away. He moved back through the dark store, working his way to the register. He plucked one of the pale cream sacks that bore the name of the store on the front and piled his hoard into them, before teleporting outside the store.

Not quite the way he had intended the mission to go, but a success nonetheless.

Now he just had to find the place Thorne had spoken of, which presented another problem. It was a long way from his current position, in an area he was unfamiliar with, which meant it was going to be difficult for him to find it. He made his way through the streets, pausing to admire the lamps that lit them, and study the vehicles that lined them. They were a myriad of colours and shapes, all different sizes, every one of them fascinating to him.

Tegan teleported to the end of the road, an attempt to avoid being distracted by the vehicles and everything around him. A terrible mistake. He rose out of the ground close to a female. She turned and shrieked, hit him with her bag, and fled before he could apologise for startling her.

A male on the other side of the street paused to look at him.

Tegan flashed fangs in his direction. Not quite kingly behaviour, and one that might land him in more trouble, but instinct had labelled the male as a potential threat, liable to attempt to apprehend him for what he had done.

The dark-haired male didn't leave. He remained standing on the other side of the street, staring across him. Tegan drew down a deep breath, catching the male's scent. An immortal if he had to guess, possibly a vampire since his scent carried a faint undertone of copper. Had the male been tracking the female, stalking her as prey?

Perhaps he could prove useful.

King Thorne's mortal queen had been most excited by what she had called a 'club', speaking of how many fae and immortals visited it, and that it was owned by a shifter. Now Tegan wanted to see what was so exciting about the place.

If the male was a vampire, he could perhaps point Tegan in the right direction so he could find it before the night was through.

Tegan crossed the road to him, or at least attempted it. He lunged backwards as a vehicle roared past him, almost clipping him in the process. It blared a warning he supposed was directed at him for almost colliding with it. He shifted his gaze to the vampire.

The male arched an eyebrow at him and sighed, shaking his head at the same time.

He turned to leave.

Tegan teleported, landing directly in front of the shorter male, who bared his fangs and swiftly leaped back, placing some distance between them.

"I mean you no harm." Tegan held his hands up, revealing his palms as his bag of books slid down his arm, showing the vampire he was unarmed. "I seek a club called Underworld."

The vampire's right eyebrow shot up again. "That place? Switch is nicer."

Tegan presumed Switch was another club. Was it also frequented by many different species? He added it to his list of things to see in the mortal world, ones that would have to wait for another visit.

Presuming his advisers didn't physically shackle him to his throne upon his return.

"This one comes highly recommended. King Thorne speaks well of it." He resisted the urge to growl when the vampire looked him up and down, his lip curling to flash a hint of fang and a lot of disgust.

"A demon. I should have known." The vampire folded his arms across his chest, causing the sleeves of his black jacket to pull tight across his biceps.

If the male meant it as a show of strength to intimidate him, he was going to have to do better. Tegan could easily take him. He wouldn't even break a sweat.

"Do you know where to find Underworld or not?" He was wasting time. He didn't know the particulars of clubs, wasn't sure whether they closed as early as a bookstore or later.

He frowned.

Judging by how the vampire had suggested a different club, he deduced such establishments were open late. Like a tavern?

When he had last visited the mortal world, taverns had been very popular, and they had remained open late into the dark hours, some of them even serving brew all night.

"You are a long way from it. Not even close. Switch is closer." The vampire jerked his chin to Tegan's left. "Just up that road there. I was hunting that female to see if she went there."

The female Tegan had scared off.

Judging by the calculating edge to the male's now-crimson gaze, the vampire believed Tegan owed him for that and was about to suggest a way of compensating him for his loss.

"Underworld does not exactly like vampires, but it is a good hunting ground. If you can swear to get me in, I will take you there."

Tegan wasn't sure whether he could get the vampire into the club or how the male meant to get him there considering he couldn't teleport and had admitted the club was a long way away, but he was swift to nod and accept the male's terms.

The vampire nodded too and stepped around him, giving him a wide berth. Tegan turned on his heel and followed him, not taking his eyes off the male and keeping all his senses trained on him, just in case he tried something. He settled his hand over his coin purse.

Ryker had spoken frequently of charlatans and thieves in the mortal world, people who would rob and murder you given the chance. His brother had made them sound as if they would take advantage of even the smallest slip in focus or awareness. Of course, normally those people were targeting humans.

Did immortals target other immortals in such ways?

The vampire glanced over his shoulder at him. "You can stop looking at me as if you want to murder me now. It is getting old fast."

Perhaps this male was not interested in robbing or murdering him for his coin.

Tegan relaxed, but only a little, and his entire body cranked tight again when they reached a busy road and the vampire stopped between two parked vehicles and raised his arm as he leaned out into the road.

He lunged for the male, caught his other arm and pulled him back. "What are you doing? You will get yourself killed."

The vampire's eyebrow arched again as he slowly swivelled his head towards him, his arm still raised. "I am hailing a cab."

The disbelief in his tone and the look that entered his now-ice-blue eyes questioned Tegan in ways he didn't like because they left him feeling lacking, as if he didn't measure up in this male's opinion and was an idiot.

He kept his mouth shut, refusing to ask what the hell a cab was and cementing the male's low opinion of him.

A black vehicle stopped in front of the vampire, a bright orange sign above the plate of glass near the front of it. The mechanical beast hummed, a low rumbling purr that gently settled as the human male in the front leaned towards the vampire.

The vampire said something Tegan didn't hear and then he was pulling on Tegan's arm, luring him towards the rear of the vehicle. He opened the door and Tegan swallowed hard. The male expected him to enter the belly of the beast?

This was far more interaction with the technology of the human world than he had anticipated. He swallowed his nerves, refusing to let them show, and clutched his bag of books to his chest as he slid his seven-foot frame into the cramped space.

The vampire eased in beside him and spoke with the driver, and Tegan did his best not to tense as the conveyance began to move. A cab. This was a cab. The vampire had raised his arm and it had stopped for him, and now it was taking them somewhere.

Fascinating.

Streets whizzed past him, flashes of light that he found difficult to take in as wave upon wave of them collided and crashed over him. Every one was different, every store front unique. His eyes darted around, managing to pluck small details from the blur. A shop filled with jewels here. A bustling food store there. He wanted to stop at every single one, but held his tongue, telling himself that he would return and explore this modern version of the city he had once known.

All too soon, they left the bright lights of the stores behind and entered darker roads, where houses and large brick buildings occupied much of the space along the streets. Interesting, but not as exciting or alluring as the brightly lit and colourful stores.

The cab stopped. The vampire offered coin and a polite word of gratitude to the human male, and opened the door. The second he did, Tegan flinched. A heavy beat resonated in the air, a thumping that was accompanied by a cacophony of noises, grating sounds and screeching.

"Out," the vampire said as he poked his dark head back into the cab.

Tegan reluctantly shuffled out of the vehicle, biting back a grumble as he struggled to get his feet over the lip of the door. Once free, he straightened and stared up at the dark red building in front of him. It was plain, a wall of brick that looked insignificant to him, lacked decoration and windows. Apparently, it was popular though. A stream of people lined the wall in the narrow street, pouring from the open double doors beneath the blindingly bright sign.

Underworld.

CHAPTER 4

The vampire pulled Tegan forwards, towards a large shaven-headed male dressed in black, bypassing the queue that lined the road outside Underworld.

The burly male looked them both over before settling a glare on the vampire.

"I am with him. He is a demon." When the vampire said that, the male shifted his dark gaze to Tegan.

Tegan shrugged, unsure whether being a demon qualified him for entrance or not. The vampire seemed to think it did. The way the guard was looking at him said it didn't grant him immediate entrance, but it did soften the hard edge to his pale eyes.

Tegan wasn't sure of the protocol in this sort of situation, and many of the people lined up outside the club were beginning to stare at him. One or two of the females were openly ogling him too. He was tempted to glare at them and flash some fang, but kept his focus on the guard instead.

Because he was waiting.

For what? Coin? His name?

It never hurt to name drop a little, but he wanted to keep his own identity private. He wasn't here as a king. He just wanted to be Tegan tonight. So he would have to drop a different name, one that was not his own. Besides, he doubted this male would know of him or be impressed if he mentioned who and what he was.

He would however know one of his acquaintances.

"I know King Thorne of the Third Realm."

The male grunted, unhooked a velvet rope and eased back a step as he grumbled, "Try anything funny, vampire, and boss'll slaughter you. Same goes for you, demon."

Tegan inclined his head. "Many thanks."

The vampire arched a final eyebrow at him and disappeared into the crowd, blending like shadows as he stepped through the open doors. Tegan supposed that would be the last he saw of him, unless the guard received word that he had been trying something funny.

He wasn't sure what that meant, but he would do his best to behave and be civil, because despite the irritating volume of the noise emanating from the doors, he wanted to stay and explore this place called a club.

He wanted to see what was so exciting about it.

Tegan pulled down a subtle breath to steady himself, not wanting the male on the door to notice his nerves. He lowered the hand he held the book bag in to his side and ran his free hand over the shorn sides of his head. The lack of horns disturbed him, giving his nerves a stronger hold over him.

He would let them out as soon as he was away from mortal eyes.

Those mortal eyes tracked him as he moved forwards and he didn't need to look to know it was females who studied him so intently. He ignored them and stepped into the dark embrace of the club. It took his ears a moment to adjust to the volume, but once they did, he found the beat less irritating, the screeching instruments less annoying. This was not music as he knew it.

The mixture of mortals and immortals packed into the large space jostled around him, bumping him at times as he ventured deeper, his nerves giving way to growing excitement as his dark eyes leaped around to take everything in. Ahead of him, the space opened up, the ceiling soaring so high it was difficult to make out even with his heightened eyesight. The black wall to his right continued, but the one to his left gave way, running at a ninety-degree angle to form a cavernous room that was packed with people who appeared to be carousing, drinking and dancing with each other.

It reminded him of the feast he had left at the castle, although this club seemed even more alive than that celebration had been. Everyone was in good spirits, many of the people pairing off with their choice of male or female, leading them away into dark corners or openly unleashing their passion in front of the watching eyes of the others. Intriguing.

The crowd was thickest to his right, where a colourful array of bottles lined the walls, bright lights dancing over them and the people who moved between them, filling glasses they then served to the patrons who waited at the black bar.

Tegan's gaze caught on the lights and he found himself staring at them as they whirled, sweeping over the room and changing colours. They hurt his eyes, but he couldn't stop staring at them. They were electric. They had to be, because he had never seen anything like them.

He had never seen such vividly coloured light before.

They constantly switched. White. Purple. Red. Yellow. Blue. Around and around they went, and the more he stared, the less aware of the world he became. The music dulled as his mind filled with questions and awe flooded his body with a strange urge to smile. Electricity. Perhaps if he moved closer, he could get a better look at them, could study them and decipher how they worked.

He lifted his foot to take a step forward.

Someone tapped his right shoulder, just above his pectoral.

A growl rolled up his throat as the world came crashing back and he sensed the presence of a strong male in front of him. He was tempted to make him pay for disturbing his study of the lights, but bit back his snarl as he lowered his gaze to the sandy-haired male who stood before him, a few inches shorter than Tegan's seven-foot height.

"You look like a kid at Christmas." The impudent male shot him a wide grin, flashing straight white teeth as his golden eyes lit up in a way that made it clear he was being mocked.

No male had ever mocked him and survived. This male would be no different.

Those golden eyes narrowed on him before he could even think about moving, warning that the male had sensed his rising intent to attack. The male folded his arms across his chest, his white shirt stretching tight across his honed muscles as he stared Tegan down.

"You should probably come with me before someone tries to mug you or something. It's pretty bloody clear you're fresh out of Hell." The male unfolded his arms and slung a black towel over his shoulder, and something dawned on Tegan.

The male worked at the club.

Those serving behind the bar had similar towels and wore a similar white shirt with their black trousers.

It didn't stop Tegan from wanting to flash fangs and snarl at him, even when the male was right. He had been dangerously caught up in something as basic as a coloured light, revealing to all present that he was new to this modern version of the mortal realm. He scanned the crowd, picking out a few immortals who were watching him with interest.

Tegan narrowed his eyes on them, making it clear he wasn't a soft target. If any of them dared anything, they would meet a bloody end.

The sandy-haired male jerked his chin towards his right shoulder and turned, making his way towards the busy bar.

Tegan followed, carefully working his way through the crowd. A few of the females stopped what they were doing when he brushed past them, turning scowls on him that morphed into looks of fascination as they trailed up and up to meet his gaze. He could understand their surprise. The immortals in the club were tall, but he stood at least four inches taller than the rest of them.

The male went behind the bar and gestured to a space on the other side of it when Tegan went to follow. "Patrons go that side."

"What've we got here?" A pretty blonde female offered a smile to the male and a glance at Tegan.

"A newbie. I think he fell out of a portal or some shit." The male grinned, his eyes lighting up with it again.

"I came because King Thorne of the Third Realm recommended this place." Tegan wasn't about to let them make him out to be some sort of greenhorn.

He knew he was out of place in this modern world, but he was experienced in many more things than the young immortal who seemed intent on mocking him.

"Thorne?" The male huffed. "Fair enough. I'm not going to complain if he sends business my way. Name's Kyter. I run this joint."

Tegan frowned at him. He dared to speak of Thorne with such little respect? The male was immortal, possibly a shifter judging by his scent, and clearly believed himself powerful because he owned this club, but that was no reason to speak of a king as if he was a nuisance and beneath him.

The blonde mortal just rolled her eyes and moved off to serve another patron, squeezing past a broadly built silver-haired male who looked between Tegan and Kyter, a concerned edge to his grey eyes.

Tegan had the feeling that if he attempted to put Kyter in his place and teach him to respect the demon kings, the male would have back up. Any fight that went down in this place wasn't going to be one on one. He could probably handle Kyter, but he wasn't sure he would be able to handle him and his companions if they all attacked at once.

He frowned at his line of thought.

He wasn't here to fight at all. He was just on edge, in a strange place where he wasn't sure of anything yet. It was bringing out his instinct to protect himself. He needed to shut that instinct down before it ended up overpowering him and getting him into a fight.

Kyter had been kind enough to notice him and take care of him. He wouldn't repay the male by attacking him, no matter how little respect he showed Tegan's fellow demon king.

The male scrubbed a hand over his tousled dirty-blond hair and poured something from a dark bottle into a tiny glass that was barely big enough to hold a sip of the black liquid. He set it down on the obsidian bar top and slid it towards Tegan.

Tegan took the pouch from his hip and opened it, selected a small gold coin and offered it to the male.

Kyter shook his head, disbelief colouring his golden eyes.

"It's on the house." He pressed his hand against Tegan's, pushing the coin back towards him, and smiled. "How about some advice for free too? Look into credit and debit cards if you're planning to leave Hell more than once a millennium. Plastic is king."

It was?

Tegan nodded and slipped the coin back into his purse. He had heard of plastic, but hadn't realised it was a form of currency. It seemed like such a worthless and trivial thing compared with gold, and he didn't understand how it had more value, enough to render it a king among other methods of payment, but he would look into it as soon as he returned to the Second Realm.

Kyter moved away to serve the person two seats down and Tegan watched as the female produced a small rectangle and offered it in exchange for her drink. Kyter lifted it and flashed it at him, his grin stretching wider as he pointed at it. Tegan presumed that was the plastic the male had spoken of so highly.

Oddly, the shifter didn't even keep it. He did something with it using some sort of device that the female also interacted with and then returned the plastic to her. The female went on her way with her drink *and* the plastic.

Tegan had a lot to learn about this world.

More than he had anticipated.

He looked down at the bag of books on his lap, a sense of urgency rising inside him. He had thought he had learned much in the last few years, but apparently it wasn't enough. He needed to learn more. That need was vital, seized command of him and had him pulling a book from his hoard and flipping it open, the desire to know more about this world so strong that it consumed him.

He flicked the pages, greedily devouring the information as he sipped the drink the male had given him, enjoying the fieriness of it as it warmed his tongue and burned his throat. The brew was good, stronger than demon mead. It would go down well with his warriors. He would purchase a bottle before returning and would share it with the officers of his legions first to see if they enjoyed it. If they did, he would see about buying more bottles and keeping a stock of the fierce liquor for celebrations and feasts.

When his glass was empty, Kyter returned for it and slid him another.

Tegan stared at the male. If he asked him the thousand questions ricocheting around his mind, would he answer them? Tegan felt sure that he would, but he was busy, was already hurrying back along the bar to serve another person, and he didn't want to impose on the male.

A shiver tripped down his spine.

Tegan ignored it, sure it was just the people around him looking at him and nothing to be concerned about. There were many different species in the club and his instincts were sure to label some of them as threats, even when they weren't a danger to him.

He glanced across his shoulders in both directions, meeting the gazes of some of the people surrounding him. None of them affected him.

His eyebrows pinched and he lowered his book, so the spine rested on the edge of the bar as he focused on his body, on that sensation that lingered inside him, a feeling he was being watched.

His skin heated, a flush sweeping across his face and around the points where his horns were hidden, and rolling down his back, spreading over his shoulders like a wave of fire that ignited his blood. That blood rushed faster in his veins as his pulse quickened, heart thundering against his breast.

He stared at the glass of black liquid.

Was this unsettling sensation a reaction to it?

Or something else?

He twisted at the waist, eyes scanning the crowd as he tried to pinpoint the source of the feeling that continued to hold him in its grasp, refusing to abate.

Was it someone watching him?

A threat?

The crowd just over his left shoulder parted, giving him a glimpse of a female who stole the breath from his lungs as his eyes landed on her.

His ears grew pointed, the reaction to the sight of her so swift and powerful that he couldn't stop the change from happening. His back itched, his wings pressing for freedom at the same time as his horns began to break through the skin above his ears. He absently raised his hands to cover them, some part of him, the only part of him not focused on the lovely female, aware that allowing his horns out would land him in serious trouble.

She laughed, her beautiful face lighting up with it, and his heart missed a beat before slamming hard against his chest, battering his ribs as if it wanted to break free of them.

He had never seen anything like her.

Her hair was like the ocean, a beguiling blend of blues, turquoises and greens with hints of purple. It tumbled around her slender bare shoulders in rippling waves, caressing skin as creamy as tropical sand, the tips breaking against a black bodice. He dragged his gaze over the ample swell of her breasts, up the smooth column of her throat that had his fangs itching to descend, to a face that was both lovely and delicate, and sinfully seductive.

She was a sylph. A siren. No. A *mermaid*.

A male fantasy made flesh and blood with her colourful hair that matched her striking green-to-blue eyes, her pixie nose and full rosy lips, and a body made for sin, petite and packed with curves.

The urge to go to her, tangle his hand in her hair and attempt to bend her to his will was almost overwhelming, had his hands dropping from the sides of his head as he went to stand.

Her eyes swept over the crowd, stilling him as they skipped past him, a hard edge to them that warned him that attempting to control her would be as foolish as attempting to tame the sea.

Her gaze suddenly locked with his and a million volts arced through him, lightning striking hard and fast, leaving him shaken as he stared at her, breathless and reeling. The world faded around him as the distance between them seemed to shrink to nothing and a question pounded in his mind.

Who was she?

Another followed it as she turned her cheek to him, and his gaze tracked the direction of hers and he saw she was with another male.

A growl curled up his throat, the rumble so low no one would hear it over the pounding music, and the tips of his horns broke through his skin as his fangs extended.

The urge to fight flooded him, so fierce and violent that he had to wrestle for control, had to force himself to turn away from her before he succumbed to it. His claws elongated and he dug them into the wooden bar, anchoring himself to it as the dark desire to tear the male away from her and utterly destroy the bastard blasted through him.

What the hell was wrong with him?

CHAPTER 5

Suki tried to tear her gaze away from the male who had captivated her so completely as she sensed her sisters nearby, felt one of them tug on her arm.

"Suki, you even listening to me?" Allura. She didn't sound pleased. "I'm out. Vidia is too. You'll be alright on your own?"

She nodded dumbly, not really taking in what they were saying.

Until Vidia spoke.

"*Ho-ly* fuck! Is that who I think it is?"

Allura sounded just as shocked. "Oh boy. If the mistress knew he was here, she would have a fit."

Why would their mistress have a fit if she saw this man?

Before she could ask, Vidia said, "To think... the one who got away is sitting right there. If I wasn't so full, I'd have a shot. I can't blame Cyrena for attempting to bang him."

Attempting? The mistress had failed to seduce this man?

Allura moved away from her. "Like you could seduce him? He's un-seduce-able. The succubus who bags and tags that trophy will be crowned queen."

Suki's eyes popped wide.

Bingo.

Suki was fairly certain that there was no such word as un-seduce-able, or at the very least it shouldn't exist in succubi language, but if she could succeed where Cyrena had failed, her clan would have to recognise that she belonged with them.

They would have to accept her.

She didn't want to be queen. She just wanted to be accepted. She just wanted to be one of the family she always felt as if she was looking in on from the outside.

All she had to do was bag and tag him. Given the way he was looking at her, his dark eyes riveted on her in an unblinking stare, seducing him wasn't impossible. She just had to make the right moves and her victory was assured.

Okay, that probably wasn't going to be as easy as it sounded in her head, but she had to give it a shot.

It didn't hurt that he wasn't bad on the eye either.

If the human had been a solid eight, then this man was a solid eleven.

He was huge, his black shirt like a second skin, stretched over powerful muscles and across the impressive breadth of his chest. And he was more than handsome. He was divine. A god made flesh.

No man on Earth, Hell or Heaven was like this one.

She canted her head, studying his intense dark eyes, tracking the straight line of his regal nose to a firm mouth that lacked laughter lines, and a solid jaw that was only made stronger by the black stubble that covered it.

Everything about him screamed warrior.

But she had never seen a warrior who also screamed Adonis like he did. He was so handsome, she might have mistaken him for an incubus. It would have explained her mistress's failed attempt to seduce him. He wasn't one of that vile kind though. Her senses would have been screaming at her to run if he had been an incubus and he certainly wouldn't have been looking at her as if he was interested in her.

He would have been looking at her like every other incubus she had met in her years—as if he wanted to kill her.

No, this man was something else. Immortal? For sure. A warrior? Definitely.

Panty-melting? Abso-fucking-lutely.

Even propping up the bar, he was commanding, a confident and alluring display of masculine perfection that had more than one woman taking note of him.

Suki focused on him, a need to know what he was thinking demanding she satisfy it.

His aura shimmered into being around him.

Only it wasn't colourful.

It rose as black smoke from his shoulders and head.

Was her damned emotional radar on the fritz or was he immune to her ability?

Was this the reason Cyrena had failed to seduce him?

Reading the aura of her target made it easier to charm him, acting as an early warning system that told her when she was doing something wrong and when she was doing something right. She glanced at Solid Eight. His aura was flashing a warning at her, all dark shades of blue-grey and red that told her he was annoyed and was definitely about to ditch her.

She couldn't blame him.

She was a little distracted.

Her gaze roamed back to Solid Eleven.

His gaze narrowed and he turned away from her, twisting on his stool so his back was to her. He ran a hand over the longer strands of his black hair, sweeping the tangled finger-length ribbons back before rubbing both sides of his head, as if he had a killer headache.

The heat that had been building inside her suddenly chilled, leaving her off balance as she ignored Solid Eight and tried to figure out what she had done wrong.

She frowned.

All she had done was glance at Solid Eight.

Was Solid Eleven a jealous type? She could probably use it to her advantage, but she didn't want to get Solid Eight killed.

Her frown deepened as she stared at the shadows rising off the warrior's back, attempting to pierce them to see his emotions. No luck. His aura remained as black as midnight.

She wasn't going to let it deter her. Her ability to read his aura might be useless, but she still had decades of training to fall back on. She would read his body language instead.

It was hardly a chore.

She raked her gaze down over his back, drinking in his wide shoulders that tapered down into a trim waist, and an ass that had to be grade A rump packed into his tight black leathers.

She bet his clothes hid a body she could spend hours studying without getting bored.

Plus, when she bagged and tagged him, her sisters would have to admit she was awesome because she would have done it without the aid of reading his aura.

Suki rubbed her damp palms on her short skirt and took a step forward.

"Are you even listening to me, Sucky?" Allura's sharp tone made her jump.

She had forgotten her sisters were still with her.

Suki brushed off the hurt that welled in her heart on hearing her clan's pet name for her and turned on her sisters with a smile, refusing to let Allura get her down. She was just a late bloomer. She was going to find her talent and then she would show them. It would be as her mother had said.

She would be the greatest succubus there ever was.

Although, apparently tonight had been an epic fail so far.

Her confidence took a nosedive as she looked at Solid Eight. He was all over Vidia, playing with one of her long blonde pigtails and eyeing her cleavage in her tight white shirt, and the handsome nymph was all over both of them. Damn it. She had taken her eye off the ball and now Solid Eight was caught up in the male and her sister when he should have been swept up in her. She blamed Vidia. The damned catholic schoolgirl outfit she was wearing was probably pushing the perverted fantasy buttons of half the men in the club.

Never mind. She had a better, bigger target in mind now.

"I'm listening." Suki tried to resist focusing on the male behind her at the bar.

He was still there. She didn't need to panic. She would get rid of her sisters so she didn't have an audience and then she would leap into action. He wasn't going to know what hit him.

Even the most powerful immortal could be seduced under the control of a skilled succubus. The leaders of her clan had fed from the mightiest warriors, from gods. Tonight, she was going to join their ranks. She was going to succeed where her mistress had failed.

Her tutors had told her countless times that it was her attitude holding her back. She feared killing and that affected her ability to charm men. Solid Eleven was strong, he could probably handle her. Scratch that. She was meant to be confident. Positive attitude. He *could* handle her. She was going to seduce him and then everyone would stop calling her Sucky.

"I don't need a babysitter," she said when Allura gave her a worried look. "I'll find another host."

She slid a pointed look at Vidia, who just shrugged and petted Solid Eight, twining her fingers in his hair as she offered Suki an unrepentant smile that was all 'you snooze, you lose'.

Suki waited for them to leave, her thoughts returning to the shadowed male behind her and the fact her mistress had failed at seducing him. According to succubus law, shadowed males were dangerous and forbidden because of it. That gave her pause, but only for a moment. Cyrena had targeted him, which meant the succubus couldn't be angry with Suki if she dared to do the same.

She glanced over her shoulder at his back. He certainly looked dangerous, but he wasn't ringing any internal alarm bells. He didn't register as a threat to her.

But then her senses and abilities were hardly top notch. Maybe he was as dangerous as clan law painted him and she just wasn't feeling it.

Although if he was so dangerous, why would her mistress have tried to seduce him?

When she was younger, she had read in a book for young succubi that certain males were more difficult to control, and some were even immune to a succubus's powers. Had that book been referring to shadowed males?

She wasn't going to let it deter her. She had set her sights on him and she was going to give it her best shot. It was now or never. If she didn't prove herself worthy of being a member of her clan soon, she was going to end up on the streets.

She just hoped her sisters weren't leading her on, setting her up to fail. It would be just like them to make up some crap about a guy in an attempt to get her to try her luck with him so they could see her screw things up. Apparently, watching her fail was entertaining. Suki didn't find it at all funny.

Suki cleared her throat, plucked her cheeks to redden them, and blew out her breath.

She could do this.

He glanced over his shoulder in her direction and an ache rolled through her, had her wanting to rub her thighs together and lick her lips as her hunger ratcheted up another notch. Damn, he was hot.

His dark eyes narrowed on her, sending a white-hot shiver dancing over her skin, and she adjusted her opinion.

With his silky black hair, square jaw coated in a fine layer of scruff, that regal profile and a broad firm mouth that had been made for wicked things, coupled with the intensity of his powerful gaze as it held her immobile, he was more than hot.

He was movie-star gorgeous.

She managed to drag her eyes away from his and a frown flickered on her brow as she noticed something.

He had tattoos.

They looked like tribal designs, inked in black and visible through the shaved sides of his head.

And if she wasn't mistaken, there was a hole in the design, a ring in just the right place for something.

Horns.

Solid Eleven was a demon?

She trembled at the thought he might be. Demons were exceptionally strong, and that meant he could probably handle her.

That ache grew fiercer, roused by the image building in her head as she pictured him with horns and found him devastating.

Heat flashed through her as she ambled towards him, a little sway to her hips. His eyes dropped to her body and she raked her gaze down his, over a torso packed with muscle. His shirt hugged it like a second skin, and damn she envied it and the black leathers that encased his powerful legs. Heavy black boots screamed biker bad boy, pressing all the right buttons in her.

Holy Hell, he was panty-wetting delicious.

Maybe her mistress had wanted him for that reason.

Her nerves melted away as she stopped beside him. "Can I sit?"

He stood with a roguish smile that had her heart fluttering in response, knees close to buckling as she found herself facing the impressive breadth of his chest. She slowly tilted her head back, her eyes widening as she had to keep going and going in order to reach his face.

A low whistle escaped her as she finally locked eyes with him.

Damn, he was massive.

He dwarfed her five-seven, had to be pushing seven feet, if not more. She had never seen a demon as tall as he was, and it felt so wrong that the difference in height between them spoke to the deeply feminine side of her, making her want to stake a claim on him.

Hell, she was a nanosecond away from climbing him like a tree despite their audience.

Only the feel of him studying her stopped her from doing it. She met his gaze again and confusion broke through the haze of desire, shattering its hold on her as cold eyes held hers, disappointment flickering in them.

What the heck?

He had looked interested before, his scent had even changed to reveal his hunger to her, but now he looked as if he was bored.

Suki struggled to muster her confidence again as it shattered into a million pieces, her mind filling with questions and doubts, leading her in circles as she tried to figure out what she had done wrong. She must have done something. He *had* been interested. She hadn't imagined that.

Had she been too confident in her approach? She had thought him a sure thing, had been convinced she could score with him and claim the victory she badly needed, but now it looked as if she needed a new plan.

He silently took his seat again and turned his side to her.

Went one better at driving a knife into her confidence by picking up a book and reading it.

A book was more interesting than she was?

That was a new low for her.

Suki slumped into the empty seat, racking her brain to figure out where she had gone wrong. She must have made a mistake somewhere along the line. Or maybe this was just a game he liked to play with women. He led them on, making them believe he desired them so they felt attractive and a little bit happy, and then he stuck his nose in a book and ignored them, wounding them and leaving them feeling as if they weren't beautiful after all.

She turned a glare on him, anger rising to the fore because she was damned if he was going to play with her like that.

The sight of him arrested her, silencing the jibe that had been on the tip of her tongue.

His dark eyes rapidly devoured each line of text in the book, the black slashes of his eyebrows knitting hard above them as he focused, losing himself in it. The corners of his broad sensual mouth quirked and faint lines bracketed it. He was genuinely enjoying the book. She didn't need to see his aura to know that.

She looked around them, at the busy nightclub, and then back at him.

He was an anomaly.

In a bar filled with revellers, he was sitting at the counter, a study in quiet and calm, lost in a book of all things.

How fascinating.

She peered at the book, trying to catch a glimpse of the cover or something that would tell her what he was reading about. Although it wouldn't answer the most prominent question pinging around her head.

Why was he reading it in a bar?

Was her hot geek shy? Maybe she had come on too strong and flustered him, and that was why he was now hiding in a book. How adorable.

Her confidence zipped right back up.

Time for attempt number two.

"What are you reading?" she hollered over the music, aware his hearing was probably sensitive enough to hear her if she had spoken at a normal volume but not wanting to give him a chance to pretend he hadn't heard her.

The way his fathomless black eyes came to land on hers told her she was mistaken.

This demon was in no way shy.

The intensity of his look, the way his gaze drilled into her with a commanding air, flustered her and she made an awkward lunge for the book, pushing it up so she could see the cover. That earned her an arched eyebrow from him.

She was too busy staring dumbfounded at the cover to notice.

A book on wind turbine construction?

In her head, it had been a novel, perhaps a thriller. She wasn't sure how to compute this. The fact he had been reading in a bar had been incomprehensible. The fact he was reading the geekiest book imaginable was just… well. Her mind felt as if it was about to short-circuit.

"What's a guy doing reading a book in a nightclub?" The words had left her tongue before she could consider his reaction, and the fact she might be on course to offend him and drive him away.

She was sure men who read books were somewhat sensitive about that subject around women, presuming they were going to be ridiculed or perhaps the woman would think less of them for being bookish.

Suki found it rather alluring. Here was a man who wanted to better himself. After the number of men she had encountered who thought themselves perfect, he was a breath of fresh air.

He muttered, "I could not read at home, and I required space, so here I am."

Suki's brain blew a fuse after the second word and she could only stare at him, blood heating from the low purr of his delicious baritone. She blinked, struggling against the devastating effect of his voice, trying to piece together what he had said so she had a shot at not making him think she was either stupid or rude because she hadn't taken in what he had said.

When she had gathered the scattered remnants of her brain and had reconstructed what he had said, two things struck her.

His accent was odd. She had met demons before, but none with his accent. The ones she had met sounded a lot more like the humans of this world. Which led her to the question, did he spend more time in Hell than on Earth?

The second thing that hit her was she liked his bass voice. It was gruff, yet regal. His English was good, but a little antiquated.

Her panties would have melted more, but they had burned away long ago.

"Why couldn't you read at home, and why did you need space?" She leaned closer, hoping it wouldn't drive him away.

Rather than fleeing or burying his nose back in his terribly educational book, he eased his massive frame back on the stool and rested the book on the bar top, his large hand draped across the pages to keep them open as he twisted slightly towards her.

Before he could answer, she added, "Are you in the doghouse with your missus and that's why you're here?"

"I have no female." The remark was casual, but carried a boat load of juicy new information she stored away.

He was single.

He was old, and definitely didn't get out of Hell much. Modern demons who spent most of their time in the mortal world or the fae towns hidden within it had adapted to call females women.

She eyed him again, casually so he didn't get jittery, not lingering too long on any part of him. Excitement thrummed in her veins, and this time it wasn't because he was hot. It was because she was enjoying this game, unravelling the mystery of her gorgeous geek.

And she was enjoying the fact he was relaxing around her again.

"Are you an engineer?" She wasn't sure Hell had engineers like the mortals did, but why else would he be reading a book about wind turbines?

"No."

A little abrupt. She dialled back her ogling in case it was triggering his mood change, lifting her eyes back to his and giving him an innocent smile.

"Why are you reading a book on wind turbines of all things then?" She prodded the book.

He visibly stiffened and drew the book towards the edge of the bar top, towards him, a protective gesture if ever she saw one.

He glanced down at it and murmured, "It seemed interesting."

How amusing. "More interesting than getting drunk and rowdy, and dancing up a storm?"

A frown flickered on his brow. "I have no interest in those things, which is why I am here."

Suki filed that away too. Was there anything about this demon that wasn't fascinating? He had come to a nightclub because he didn't want to drink and dance. Was that what he had escaped at home?

"Most men come to bars to pick up women, not read books." She planted her left elbow against the tacky bar top and leaned her chin on her upturned palm, giving him the whole of her attention.

"I am not most men."

She could see that.

Someone stopped on the other side of the bar to her. She glanced at him.

Kyter jerked his chin towards her, his golden eyes on the demon. "She bothering you?"

Suki hit the shifter with her best glare. Annoying prick. She was a regular here. The hot geek wasn't. Why was he getting deferential treatment?

"The female is no bother." Solid Eleven added a graceful dip of his head, his eyes never leaving Kyter.

Suki added polite to his list of qualities.

When the irritating shifter had moved on, Solid Eleven turned to her.

"What know you of wind turbines?"

What know she? She barely stifled her smile. He had to be at least a thousand years old if he was speaking like that.

"What do I know about wind turbines?" She pursed her lips, wriggled them a little to get his eyes on them, and satisfaction hummed in her veins when his dark gaze fell to them and narrowed. "Not much. Less than you, I'd imagine."

The heat that had been building in his eyes turned to disappointment, but he rebounded quickly, his gaze coming up to meet hers as interest flared in it once more.

"Do you know of anywhere they are installed?"

He was more than interested in the subject. He was fascinated by it. A little like she was fascinated by him. What did wind turbines have that she didn't? By now, she had expected him to be enthralled by her.

Not that she was disappointed. He was proving more and more fascinating, and for the first time in a long time, she was enjoying herself. She was enjoying herself so much that she kept forgetting she was meant to be seducing him.

His near-black eyes glittered with keen intelligence as they lowered to the book and he sneakily read a few lines. She couldn't remember the last time she had met a man who seemed so educated, was refined and intent on pursuing intellectual goals. Normally, the men she met were interested in only one thing.

They wanted to let their bodies do the talking, not have an actual conversation.

"I've seen a few in the countryside. There's a farm in Scotland near a mortal town I often visit." She wanted to smile when his eyes lit up and leaped back to her. "It's charming how much you care about silly windmills."

His expression sobered, losing all warmth. "They are not silly. They are important to—"

To who? To him? To others? Was he something similar to an engineer after all? Perhaps demons had a different term for it. Or maybe he was talking about them being important in other ways.

"Are you some sort of eco-warrior? Looking to save the planet?" She cracked a grin. "It all seems a pointless waste of time to me. Renewable energy isn't going to save the world when human and immortal corporations are pumping crap into the air nonstop."

He closed the book and tucked it close to his chest as he turned his side to her, as if it was precious and she had just attempted to destroy it. She had certainly destroyed the moment.

Solid Eleven toyed with his shot of Hellfire, his eyes fixed on it as he turned it this way and that.

Way to wreck things, Suki.

She waited at least two full minutes, the seconds trickling past as slowly as a glacier, and just as chilling. He wasn't going to talk again. He was making a point, shunning her until she left. Damn it. She really needed to learn to think before opening her mouth.

She was on the verge of leaving when he finally spoke, his eyes still glued to his drink.

"I thought perhaps you would be different."

Wow. She wasn't sure what that meant, but the fact he sounded bitterly disappointed had her feeling bad, both about herself and about not being whatever he had expected her to be.

It dawned on her that wind turbines might seem silly to her, but they were important to him. They meant more than he was letting on. This wasn't just a subject that interested him. This was a subject that was close to his heart for some reason.

Because he wanted to build one?

As far as she knew, Hell didn't have electricity. No power plants. No running water. No real sanitation to speak of. Everything she took for granted, his world lacked. He wanted to change that, and she had poked fun at him for it.

Damn, she was such a screw up. She was starting to see why her sisters called her Sucky.

"You are like the others," he grumbled.

She glared at him for that one. She had never been like others. That was part of her problem. So, he had that all wrong.

She huffed and turned her side to him. It looked as if Solid Eleven was a lost cause. Now she had to return to her clan as hungry as she had left it and looking like the failure she was. She had lost her appetite. Or rather he had wrenched it from her.

Sherry walked past and Suki flagged her down, because if she was going to be miserable, she might as well drown her sorrows in a cocktail or two. Maybe it would help her find her mojo again. A little liquid courage and she would be right as rain and ready to find another target, one who didn't think she was like every other woman out there.

"Something tall and strong?" Sherry beamed at her, her long blonde ponytail swaying across the shoulders of her white shirt as she reached down behind the bar.

Suki nodded, trying to ignore the delicious slice of tall and strong sat beside her at the bar. The whole thing was a bust, which was surprisingly disappointing. For a brief moment, she had been having fun, had been a world away from her worries about her clan and losing her family, and whether or not she was going to succeed in seducing Solid Eleven.

She couldn't recall the last time she had felt that way, and she doubted she was going to feel it again anytime soon.

She closed her eyes and cursed herself. Why couldn't she have kept her stupid mouth shut? It was rare she found a man she actually enjoyed looking at, one she wanted to spend time with and get to know. It wasn't how her kind were meant to be. Her mother and her family had drummed that into her head. Succubi weren't meant to form attachments with anyone outside the clan. Men were for feeding, or the occasional breeding when the clan allowed it.

But she had never been like the others. She had never been one for convention. Sure, she believed that succubi couldn't experience relationships like others, that love was impossible for them because of what they were, but that didn't mean she liked forced seductions and killing someone by feeding from them.

Maybe her father had been a saint or something.

She reached into her black boot, fished out a folded ten pound note, and held it out to Sherry as she finished mixing the hurricane for her.

Solid Eleven suddenly leaned in close, his earthy masculine scent invading her senses and freezing her on the spot as he deftly plucked the money from her fingers. He unfolded it and eyed it, lifted it towards the light and then lowered it again, bending his head to closely inspect it.

"What is this?" His dark eyes leaped to her, a furrow between his eyebrows as he held the note towards her, stretched tight between his fingers. "This is not credit or debit card."

Damn, he was so cute. Why did he have to be so awkwardly adorable? She had never imagined she could find a man who was drop-dead-gorgeous, brash and masculine, yet so innocent and naïve about some things.

"I thought you were done talking to me? I'm like the others, right?" she snapped and tried to take her money from him, but he leaned back, folding the note in his right hand as his left went to the side of his head.

He scrubbed a hand over that side. "I apologise. I have been... on edge recently... and something about you unsettles me."

Suki wasn't sure whether to take that as a compliment.

Solid Eleven turned the ten pound note in his hand over, looking for all the world as if he was hiding in studying it.

She sighed.

"It's called cash." She reached over and took it, carefully brushing her fingers across his as she slipped it from them. His gaze remained rooted on his fingers as she handed the note to Sherry. "I don't roll with plastic."

His eyebrows pinched hard, he blinked and locked eyes with her. "The shifter said plastic is king. It is not king?"

He definitely didn't get out of Hell much, if at all.

"The fae towns don't accept it." She took her change and didn't miss the glimmer of interest in his eyes.

Suki reached down into her boot again, pulling a different note from the small pocket on the inside, and a few more coins.

She slipped him the five pound note.

He was quick to take it and study it, his dark eyes taking in every small detail about it.

"That's a fiver. The other was a tenner." She weathered his frown as he glanced at her, because she was enjoying herself again. Educating a demon with a voracious appetite for knowledge was certainly a new one for her, and she found she liked it. "A tenner has twice the value of a fiver."

His frown returned.

"But they are not much different. How does the orange parchment hold more value than the blue? The blue one is not half the size of it." He huffed and muttered, "I do not see how parchment or plastic is as valuable as coins."

Suki plucked five pound coins from her change and set them on the bar top in a line. "Their value is the same as the note you hold."

His gaze flickered to them and she didn't miss that he looked more comfortable with the golden coins.

He handed the note back to her, his voice a low belly-heating purr as he said, "Thank you."

She was about to tell him it was her pleasure when he spoke again.

"I expected you to throw yourself at me."

Suki was tempted to hit him with her best glare now, but she couldn't quite bring herself to do it. She had planned to hurl herself at him after all. The bite in his tone told her that she had been wise not to go through with it. She supposed a gorgeous guy like him probably got a lot of women throwing themselves at his feet.

If she wanted to conquer him, she was going to have to work a little harder, she could see that now.

"Why did you assume that?" She slipped the money back into her boot.

He rolled a thickly hewn shoulder. "Because you are a succubus."

She muttered, "Typical."

She felt it too.

She was so tired of men thinking she was an easy lay because of her species, as if she would screw anyone who bought her a drink or just entered her orbit. Some of her sisters operated that way, taking any opportunity to feed. Not her.

She could have her fill of men who did nothing for her, the ones who didn't present a challenge and flocked to her despite her dysfunctional ability to charm and her not-so-stellar glamours. She knew beggars shouldn't be choosers, but over the years she had lost interest in kissing men who weren't attractive to her. Feeding from them was hardly going to prove her abilities to her sisters and clan. They would probably think worse of her for picking the easiest possible targets.

Her sisters who snacked on such targets filled their quota of hot guys and challenging men too. Maybe once she had her skills down and was steadily feeding from men like that, she could take a few easy meals, but not when she was out to show everyone she was worthy of being a member of the family.

Although easy targets often meant weak men and that usually meant they ended up dead, killed by the succubus in the throes of passion, when it was difficult to control themselves and hold back the hunger for more.

The thought of taking a life like that made her want to be sick.

Her mistress had once questioned whether Suki had been born into the wrong species. Sometimes she wondered that too. She had never really felt comfortable in her own skin.

"My apologies again," Solid Eleven murmured close to her, his breath washing over her bare shoulder, sending a sharp thrill through her.

She shrugged it off. "You're not the first guy to think that and you won't be the last. I saw a free seat and figured you'd have a date or a fuck buddy with you, so I just checked to see whether the seat was taken. It wasn't a come on."

It had been, but she wasn't in the mood to tell him that. Right now, she wanted him to feel bad for judging her based on her species.

"You have a strange way of speaking." He looked as confused as he sounded when she snuck a secret glance at him.

"You're one to talk. You're the odd one out here." She pulled the tall curvy glass towards her, swung the black straw around and sucked on the fruity concoction. Hurricanes were the best, and no one made them quite like Sherry. The mortal bartender really amped up the alcohol and alcohol was one of the few mortal things Suki could enjoy without being irritated by the fact all food and drink lacked taste to her. "You sound like an antique."

He loosed a deep, delicious sigh that had her wanting to look at him, and stared at the bar and then at everything around them. "I suppose that I am."

New to Underworld or more than this club?

She bet he was new to everything given that he was definitely new to the money of the mortal world. Her eyes dropped to his left hip and the leather pouch on it that looked heavy. She would bet her left tit there were shiny pure gold coins in it.

"I have not visited the mortal realm in a long time."

Suki read between the lines. A very long time.

Her ass vibrated.

She frowned, reached around into the pocket on the back of her tight mini, and pulled out her phone. The screen lit up. A message from Allura. She tapped her thumb against the screen and slowed as heat rolled through her, awareness of the man seated beside her drawing her focus away from her phone.

She slid a furtive look at Solid Eleven.

The light from the screen reflected off his black eyes as he followed every move her thumb made. He had definitely never seen a phone before. She forgot about checking the message and waggled the device at him.

"I take it you don't have digits?" She smiled when his dark eyes shot up to hers.

"Digits?" His brow crinkled. Adorable!

"A phone number."

Those intense eyes dropped back to her phone. "It has a number?"

Gods, he was so damned cute that she wanted to eat him.

"They all do." She cursed as the music grew louder, drowning her out.

47

And then cursed for a different reason when Solid Eleven lifted his face towards the speakers and glared at them.

Because a faint purple-red glow lit his irises around his pupils.

And his ears went a little pointy.

And damn, he was even sexier like that, looking as if he was about to go into a rage and wreak bloody havoc on the nightclub's sound system for disturbing their conversation.

He leaned closer, his masculine scent stirring the heat in her veins again, a fire that refused to abate while she was near him. His shoulder neared hers and she could feel his heat as it rolled off him, ached to lean closer to him so they would touch again.

"Is there somewhere quieter we might go?" he rumbled over the music, that sexy purr tearing at her control.

Suki managed to hold it together. "For what? I'm not going to screw you if that's what you think will happen."

Something briefly blazed in his eyes, something fierce and exciting, intoxicating. She hadn't been wrong about him. He wanted her. She was hungry for a taste of him too, but she wasn't about to let him see that.

Not when he seemed to be enjoying her rejecting him.

He liked that she wasn't an easy conquest.

Her new plan was in effect. Her way of claiming victory here was taking it slow and making him burn for her.

No bad thing as far as she was concerned. She was enjoying being around him, wanted to get to know him better and spend more time with him. There was something about him that drew her to him, had her falling under his spell whenever she looked into his eyes, and part of her felt it had nothing to do with his good looks and everything to do with his personality.

He intrigued her.

"I wish to know more about your... *phone*." He nodded towards it.

Suki couldn't deny him, not when she wanted to see his eyes lighting up again, that fascination shining in them as he spoke with her and learned new things.

She held her hand out to him.

He stared at it for a few seconds before slipping his into it. A million volts whipped through her as his fingertips swept over her palm, the heat of him branding her and melting her bones, filling her with a need to move closer to him.

To surrender to him.

She pulled herself together instead.

And pulled him into a teleport that tore a vicious growl from his lips.

CHAPTER 6

Tegan ripped his hand free of the female's grip as they landed in a new location, cool air kissing his skin, the scent of salt hanging heavily in the moonlit darkness.

He snarled and backed off a step, his guard swift to rise as he quickly took in his new surroundings, preparing himself for an attack. His wings itched for freedom, his shoulders writhing beneath his tight black shirt as he turned in a fast circle, eyes scanning the darkness as they adjusted to it.

"Where are we?" he growled through his fangs, flashing them at her as he rounded on her, came to tower over her, breathing hard as he fought to keep himself from lashing out at her. "What are your intentions?"

Her hands were swift to rise between them, her palms facing him as she shook her head, causing the colourful waves of her hair to caress her creamy shoulders.

But it wasn't fear that lit her enormous eyes.

It was desire.

Need that beckoned him, had him breathing faster still as his blood surged hot and heavy, an urge to drag her into his arms and kiss her flooding him and tearing at his control.

It hit him that she liked him like this. She liked his fangs. His rage.

"You wanted somewhere quiet and this is the quietest place I know," she whispered, voice barely there, a hint of fear in it as it trembled in the still air. "I come here to think sometimes."

He looked around, slower this time, taking in the details rather than scanning for warriors who were liable to attack him.

He was on a beach.

The moon was high, casting veins of silver over the rippling black water to his left. To his right, dunes rose to obscure the horizon, the moonlight reflecting off their faces. Heat drifted from the sand beneath his boots, the lingering warmth of a day long over.

His eyes roamed back to the sea.

Gods, he loved the ocean.

There was nothing like it in Hell.

His last memory of the mortal world was of a beach like this, a tropical shore where the sand had been snowy white and the water an enticing vivid turquoise. He had been there on business, had forgone watching the sunset so he could get on with meeting his contact.

He slowly turned towards the waves, watched them gently roll and lap against the shore, carrying a cool breeze and the scent of the water onto the land.

As fleeting as that memory was, he had come to cherish it and a few others over the years since his brother's untimely death. They were all moments like that, sunrises and sunsets, crisp snow and verdant green forests. Things Hell lacked. Things he had taken for granted.

Things that made him feel the true depth of what he had lost.

He craved the peace he had felt in those times, a sensation he had thought he would never know again.

But here, in this place, he felt it.

And it was deep, comforting as he watched the waves breaking, their white foam bright in the moonlight.

But it wasn't only because of the scenery.

It was because of his company too.

He found the sea relaxing and enchanting, but it was the succubus who enchanted him this time, kept pulling his focus back to her as if she was magnetic and he was powerless to resist.

She turned towards the sea and sat on the sand, her fingers playing in it as she stared at the waves.

"You can let it all out now." Her words were casual, perhaps a little teasing.

He didn't follow. His eyebrows dipped low when a meaning to her words came to him. She wanted him to get naked.

She glanced up at him and waved at his head. "Your horns. You don't want to let them out?"

She did not mean for him to get naked.

Interesting little female.

51

She intrigued him at every turn.

He brushed his palm over the side of his head, tamping down the urge to unleash his horns. He wanted to let them out. Gods, did he want to let them out. It was so shameful to hide them, but it was necessary in this world. He couldn't risk letting them out though. His sharp senses said they were alone, but he couldn't be sure a human wouldn't pass by or see him from a distance in the strong moonlight.

"Trust me," she murmured, voice a husky and tempting whisper. "No one will see."

"I cannot risk it." He paused and looked at her. "Unless you mean to veil us with a glamour?"

He knew the tricks succubi could employ. They could charm a male if they wanted, luring them under their wicked spell, and they could teleport, but the most interesting skill at their disposal was their ability to cast a veil on themselves that rendered them invisible to all eyes.

Her fine eyebrows dipped and she lowered her gaze to the sand as she played with it, watching the grains slip through her fingers like a waterfall. It was as if all the light had suddenly flooded out of her. What had he said to cause such a drastic change in her mood?

She gave a small shrug that barely lifted her shoulders. "I'm not good with glamours. Seventy percent of the time, my veils fail and people can see me. I don't even want to talk about the times I accidentally cast them. Being invisible for days on end isn't exactly fun."

Apparently, the topic of glamours caused her distress. He made a mental note to avoid talking about them. He didn't want to upset her. He liked it when she smiled, when her striking eyes glittered like a tropical sea, warm and inviting.

She tipped her head right back, so her colourful hair fell from her bare shoulders, exposing her throat. "So many stars."

As little as he wanted to take his eyes from her captivating beauty, he lifted them to the sky.

A backbone of diamonds stretched across the inky heavens, stealing his breath from him.

Another memory to cherish.

He had never seen anything so beautiful and mysterious.

He lowered his focus back to the succubus. Or perhaps he had.

Her eyes were on him again, heating his blood, quickening his pulse as they locked with his and pulled him back under her spell. What was it about this female that had him lost whenever he looked at her, but left him feeling as if he had been found too, as if this was where he belonged?

Normally, females fawned over him, but she was different. She looked at him with desire in her eyes at times, but it was tempered with other feelings. He had angered her more than once, had upset her too, and had made her turn cold towards him. She didn't simper and coo, hadn't paid him one compliment, false or true. She spoke her mind and cared little about how he might react.

And he liked it.

She held her phone up. The bright screen illuminated her face almost as easily as the moon did.

He sat beside her, the sand warm beneath his backside, and took the phone.

He wasn't sure what to do with it so he stared at it, no doubt looking like a complete idiot to her and hating the thought she might view him in such a way.

She leaned close, her enticing sweet but warmly-spiced scent teasing his senses, and planted her left hand beside his hip. She reached over with her right and her fingers danced across the screen.

"This is an app." She pointed to several small pictures on the screen and he growled when she made the entire lot of them shift to the left and he got a clearer view of the image that sat behind them.

A nude male.

Her cheeks darkened but she didn't sound at all apologetic as she spoke.

"And that's a hottie. A girl needs a hottie in her life." She lowered her voice to a whisper so quiet he barely caught it. "Even if he's just a picture."

So that male wasn't hers?

Relief swept through him, so startling in its intensity that he missed several things she pointed out about the device. He was glad she had no male?

He wanted to growl, barely managed to bite it back as the thought of her with another male crowded his mind, throwing images at him that stoked the fire in his blood, turning desire into rage.

"You're not listening," she snapped.

Chiding him?

He couldn't remember the last time a female had dared to raise her voice at him. His mother had probably been the only one to do it. He fondly remembered her scolding him whenever he had run amok in the halls of the castle, causing pandemonium with a wooden sword.

"You're not listening and now you're smiling like you don't give a fuck that I'm peeved." She snatched the phone from him.

He scowled at her and tried to take it back, but she held it out to her right, away from him where he couldn't reach it, and hit him with a glare that had her irises brightening. He stared at them as they swirled, the green and blue beginning to glow in the moonlight as gold flakes shimmered around her pupils.

Apparently, he had angered her again, but he couldn't bring himself to care this time, was too fascinated by this change in her. He had thought her eyes striking before, but now they were incredible. He could look into them forever, watching the way the colours shifted against each other.

"My apologies," he muttered, his voice distant in his ears as he fell deeper into her eyes, the world dropping away again, narrowing down to contain only her.

"My apologies," she parroted, mocking him in a snide tone. "I can leave you here. I don't have to play teach the dumb demon."

He growled and flashed fangs, intending to put her in her place.

It only made the colours in her irises glow brighter and her pupils dilated, reminding him that she liked it when he revealed his fury to her.

"I'm sorry." She shrugged and toyed with her phone, stealing the pleasure of her beautiful eyes from him. "I'm a bit hangry."

"Hangry?" Her vernacular was a steep learning curve for him. He had studied the common tongue of English over the centuries, but her way of speaking it left him confused at every turn.

"Hungry angry." Another little shrug.

He was beginning to find that habit of hers bewitching.

"You are hungry?" He resisted the urge to frown when she looked at him as if he was stupid for needing to ask that question.

"I went to the club to hunt. Lost my prey to my sister and ended up needing a drink. Which is where I met you, and you might have noticed I haven't been sucking face with any guys since we started talking."

Tegan thought he had the gist of what she had said. She had gone to feed and had lost her quarry to a fellow succubus, or sister as they liked to call each other, and had opted to drown her sorrows with brew. She had met him then.

He pondered what 'sucking face' could mean. The only thing that sprang to mind was kissing. He knew from his time at court celebrations that a succubus could happily feed from a host through kissing, not that he had experienced such a thing himself.

The thought of her kissing another male filled him with an urge to snap the neck of whatever male she chose.

He stilled, staring at the waves as that sank in. This female had utterly bewitched him, roused a side of him that had lain dormant for centuries. No. He wasn't sure this side of him had ever existed before tonight.

Before he had met her.

She awoke something fierce in him, something possessive and vicious, that had him wanting to growl whenever she so much as mentioned a male, made him want to flash fangs and take hold of her to bend her to his will so she would feel his strength, his power, and know his prowess as a male and want no other.

His gaze drifted to her, to those rosy lips that tugged at him, pulled him towards her and had him drowsy with a need to claim them. He could kiss her. That kiss would feed her.

Would she welcome it though?

She had told him that she hadn't brought him here to lay with him, had made it clear anything intimate wasn't going to happen, but she was hungry. Surely, she would accept a kiss from him.

It had been centuries since he had actually wanted to kiss a female. What was it about her that had him aching for a taste of her lips? Was it just because she was a succubus and her natural ability to charm was affecting him? Or was it something more?

Because she resisted him at every turn, held him at arm's length and wasn't throwing herself at him?

No. It wasn't that. There had been females in the past who had treated him in such a manner, and it hadn't roused such a powerful need inside him.

He felt as if he might die if she didn't let him sample her lips, or feel the softness of her skin beneath his fingers.

She pulled her knees up to her chest and fidgeted with her phone, a pout making her lips all the more alluring.

He was on the verge of offering a kiss to her when she did something on her phone that had his focus whipping to it.

It played music, a soft melodical piece that filled the night air with the warm sound of string instruments.

The succubus twisted the phone onto its side and the image on the screen flipped with it, growing to fill the entire space. No, it wasn't an image. It was a series of images. They were moving, as if the device now contained a tiny orchestra trapped within it.

He leaned closer, unable to hold himself back as curiosity got the better of him.

"It's a video." She angled the phone so he could see it more clearly. "Not my sort of music but I figured I would break you in gently. Mortals and modern immortals love videos."

When she held the device out to him, he took it from her and watched the video. The trapped orchestra disappeared, replaced by a soothing scene of a lake and birds, and then mountains. How was it doing this?

He risked a look at her.

She smiled. "No need to look so horrified. I can almost hear your thoughts. Oh no, what happened to the tiny people?"

She was mocking him again, but he didn't frown at her for it this time, because she took the phone and the music stopped as another app filled the screen. His eyes widened and leaped between her and the phone as she held it out in front of her and swept it slowly side to side.

The image on the screen matched that of the scenery around them.

When she pointed it at him, a light burst from it and he squinted against the sudden brightness of it.

"Don't be all frowny. Make love to the camera," she said with a laugh in her voice. "Be a good demon and tell us more about yourself."

He wasn't sure what making love to the camera meant, but he had heard of cameras. Although, as far as he had known, they took still pictures and it sounded as if she was somehow capturing him in motion, much like the video of the musicians.

He cleared his throat and failed to find something to say.

She sighed and startled him by twisting to face away from him and leaning back. The moment her spine made contact with his arm, lightning struck hard inside him, shook every nerve and lit him up. She was warm against him, soft despite her corset, and she smelled divine. He leaned closer as she raised her arms, brushed his cheek against her green and blue waves and breathed her in.

"This is Solid Eleven. He's a demon. I think he just scented me, but I'm cool with that." She slightly turned her head and he wanted to groan when her cheek brushed his, her lips achingly close to his. "Tell the camera where you're from."

"Hell," he grumbled, wanting to leave it at that so she didn't probe any deeper into things he didn't want her to know, not yet anyway.

He was enjoying being himself and the fact she found that enough for her, was interested in him as he was. All that would end if she discovered who he was.

"As you can see, Solid Eleven isn't very talkative. He's the strong silent type, but I'm not going to complain. He's easy on the eye after all." She pressed closer and he bit back a groan as her lips edged nearer to his.

"Why do you keep calling me Solid Eleven?" His gaze flickered between the phone she held pointed at him and her lips.

She twisted her head towards him and her lips brushed his jaw as she said, "Because you're more than a ten?"

"I do not know what a ten is." He hated admitting that, but he wanted to know what she meant by it and she wouldn't tell him unless he confessed that he didn't understand her.

"Most guys are maybe a four or five. Sometimes I meet a seven or an eight. Sometimes, I meet a solid seven or an eight. That means they're well rounded. Ah, have all their qualities at that number I guess."

So the number was a judgement of their quality as measured by her.

"Men can lose points for failing in different areas. So a guy who was a ten in looks might drop to an eight because he has a sucky personality."

"And ten is the usual maximum?" He thought he might be starting to understand her, although he still wasn't sure which attributes she judged males by other than looks and their personality.

She nodded and moved the phone, picking a higher angle.

"And I score eleven?" Which meant what exactly?

"A *solid* eleven." She turned a dazzling smile on him. "Although, you were in danger of losing a couple points back at the club for being rude."

He opened his mouth.

"My apologies," she said before he could, a regal dip to her chin that grated on his nerves. Her smile returned, wider than before, her eyes glittering with it. She enjoyed mocking him.

He didn't particularly enjoy it.

Although, he did enjoy the effect it had on her, brightening her mood.

"If I were to ask of your method of scoring, would you tell me about it?"

She shook her head, pushed up into a sitting position and turned the screen of the phone towards her. "It's a secret scoring system."

"Could I go higher than eleven?" He watched her fingers as she did something on the device and peered closer when an image of him appeared on the screen.

She pressed a button and the image moved, she spoke and then he did. It replayed everything that had just happened, and gods, the sight of her nestled close to him had his blood pounding faster, that hunger to pull her into his arms growing stronger.

Her lips had been so near to his.

"You probably could. I wouldn't put it past you." She stopped the video on an image of them pressed close together and stared at it, a crinkle forming between her eyebrows.

Meaning that no other male she had met could achieve a ranking past eleven. That pleased him greatly.

She shuffled closer to him and angled the phone so he could see it again. He tried to pay attention as she taught him more about apps, showed him that she could use the device to send messages to other people who also owned one, and could make a voice call to those people too, talking to them over an unbelievable distance, as if they were right next to each other. She introduced him to something she called 'the interweb', bringing up some of her favourite sites, many of which appeared to be focused on shopping.

Apparently, a person could by anything online.

She even admitted that plastic was king when it came to this form of shopping.

He lost track of time as he sat back and let her talk, soaked everything in and asked questions whenever he didn't understand something. She always smiled when he found the courage to voice them, revealing that she was a kind soul. That pleased him too. Admitting he lacked knowledge left him feeling vulnerable for some reason.

He frowned. Because he didn't want her to believe he was stupid?

"Is intelligence a quality you measure males by?" That question slipped from his lips and he regretted it when she looked at him, her incredible green-to-blue eyes bright in the dim light.

She stared deep into his, causing that unsettling sensation of the world dropping away again, stealing his awareness of his surroundings. He was vulnerable like this, his senses so focused on her that he wouldn't notice any danger until it was too late. A small voice deep inside him roared at him to be more careful, to guard himself better, but he couldn't bring himself to heed it.

She nodded slowly.

Intelligence. Personality. Looks. What other things did she measure a male by? Wealth? Skill? What sort of skills? Strength? Abilities?

He wanted to know.

A delicate sigh escaped her rosy lips as she turned her cheek to him.

"Gods, that's *beautiful*." She softly breathed the words, awe lacing each of them, pulling his focus away from her for a moment so he could see what she found so beautiful.

Warm light spilled over the ocean, turning the white caps of the waves gold and lacing the fingers of cloud in the lightening sky with that precious metal and shades of pink and orange.

A sunrise.

He had longed to see one for centuries, but now that it was right before him, he found his eyes drawn away from it, to the female on his right. She pulled her knees up to her chest and rested her chin on them, her dazzling eyes sparkling and the colourful waves of her hair bright in the morning light as she watched the sun rise over the ocean.

Gods, she was beautiful.

With the first light of day warming her skin, she was breathtaking.

His heart beat harder. Beat for her. He was sure it was purely her charms as a succubus luring him under her spell and he wanted to tell her not to use them on him, because he felt as if he was on unstable ground when he was around her. He needed to know if this desire he felt for her, this pressing need to hold her close and bend her to his will, was real and not a product of a glamour.

A glamour she had admitted she wasn't good at using.

Was it real?

Why did the thought it might be make the ground feel even less stable beneath him, had him afraid it would crumble and give way at any moment?

He stared at her.

Because for the first time in his life, he wanted a female. Truly wanted her, with every drop of blood in his body and every fibre of his being that roared at him that he had to make her belong to him, that he needed this delicate, seductive and teasing little female more than anything else in this world.

He swallowed hard at that.

"I must leave." Those words rang hollowly in his ears, issued by his head even when his heart rebelled against them.

He had to stay. This was where he needed to be.

She smiled up at him as he shoved to his feet, pushing back against that alluring voice because if he didn't return now, his aides would discover he was missing from the castle. He wanted to return to this world again, to explore it more, and that wouldn't happen if the court learned he had left the kingdom without telling anyone.

Yet he still couldn't bring himself to leave.

He wanted to stay.

He *needed* to stay.

That unsettled feeling that had been growing inside him from the moment he had set eyes on the succubus reached a crescendo and he stood there staring down at her, trying to put his finger on what it was about her that caused him to react in this way.

Because it troubled him.

She stood, brushed her backside down and then smiled. "Wait here."

She disappeared before he could say anything and reappeared a heartbeat later, gripping something in her hand.

When she took hold of his right one, a hot jolt coursed up his arm, a hit of pleasure that filled him with a deeper ache to stay, to draw her into his arms and kiss her and forget about returning to his kingdom.

A dangerous way of thinking.

He tried to take his hand back, but she held firm, her strength surprising, and pulled his arm towards her. His heart thundered, beating loudly in his ears as his gaze fell to her lips and anticipation swirled through him, had his mind racing ahead to imagine how she would feel in his arms, her skin against his.

All softness against his hardness.

"Do not charm me," he growled and tried again to take his arm back.

She lifted her eyes to his, a crinkle forming between her fine dark eyebrows. "I'm not. When I said I never perfected the basics, I meant it. Failure, I'm afraid. Practically dropped out of succubus school. My tutors are perpetually disappointed with me."

His eyebrows dipped low. "You have no glamour?"

She shook her head, her green, blue and purple waves brushing across her bare shoulders. "Not a drop. Well… that's a lie. I do have it, but it's so unpredictable that I never use it on men… and it seems so dishonest."

He canted his head and sought the truth in her eyes, and when he saw no trace of a lie in them, his frown deepened.

He had the feeling she was far more complicated than he had imagined and that only made him want to stay even more, because he wanted to unravel everything about her.

"You are not like other succubi," he murmured, piecing together what he already knew about her.

She arched an eyebrow at him.

"Known a lot of them, have we?" She held her free hand up between them and shook her head. "Actually, don't answer that. I don't want to know. I can quite imagine and I don't want to ruin what was a nice night with you."

Tegan didn't want to ruin it either. He enjoyed spending time with her, doing nothing but talking and learning from her.

Unfortunately, his mouth had different ideas.

"I have never *known* a succubus."

"Known. Fancy way of saying sucked face or fucked?" She looked him up and down as he nodded. Surprise shone in her eyes as they finally locked with his again. "Never? Because I figured you'd had a heck of a lot of lovers."

He wasn't sure whether to be offended by that or not. He felt offended. Mildly. But still offended.

He tried to take his hand back again, but she had a strong grip on it, too firm for him to break without hurting her.

"It's not my business." She severed his line of thought as she unbuttoned the cuff of his black shirt and shoved the sleeve up his arm.

She used her teeth to open the slim black tube she held in her other hand and he frowned as she leaned over and scrawled on his skin with the offensive smelling pen.

When she recapped it and stepped back, finally releasing him, he stared at his forearm, his eyebrows rising.

She tiptoed and pressed a kiss to his cheek that had his ears going pointed and his claws curling. She had moved out of his reach by the time he had gathered his wits enough to attempt to take hold of her and steal a taste of her lips, leaving him grasping at thin air.

"It was nice meeting you, Solid Eleven. If you're ever in the mortal world, dial my digits."

She slid her fingers down his forearm in a maddening way, sending another bolt of lightning striking along it, and then she was gone.

Tegan stared at his arm.

There were eleven huge numbers inked on his flesh.

Her digits?

The sun broke the horizon, warming his skin, and he looked at it. Why did the sunrise seem dull and lifeless to him now when a moment ago it had been glorious?

Why did he feel so uneasy?

He looked back at his arm.

And why was he filled with a powerful urge to roar in rage?

CHAPTER 7

Tegan did his best to listen to his advisers as they droned on about the practicalities of the project he had put forward, a thousand excuses that blended in his ears. It was always the same whenever he came up with something new. Something they didn't understand.

In order to retain some sliver of power, they cited every reason imaginable as to why they couldn't condone it in the kingdom or why it wouldn't work. Some of those reasons weren't even applicable to the project he had set forth.

Their current route of protest being one of them.

"But the mountains would render such equipment unusable." The oldest of his advisers, a male of six thousand years seated to his left nearest him, preened his black horns, something he always did whenever he was nervous.

Tegan stared Balkan down from his position on the elevated platform at the end of the long dark wooden table in his war room. If any male among his four advisers would break, it would be Balkan. Eryt would be against everything that sounded even mildly dangerous and would stand firm about it. Sylas, seated just beyond Eryt on his right, would bend a little, but not break, especially if Tegan made it clear he greatly desired this project was put into action.

Raelin, who occupied a seat on the far left, one he had pulled around enough that it almost appeared as if he sat directly opposite Tegan at the other end of the table, a clever power play by the male, had been against every single thing Tegan had ever proposed.

Mostly because Raelin had despised him ever since the day Tegan had accidentally hobbled him with a wooden sword in the middle of an important meeting. Tegan had been a child at the time, barely three hundred, but Raelin had reacted badly, daring to cuff him for his insolence. Tegan's father had been furious, sending Raelin to the cells for a lengthy stay in one of them.

More than once, Tegan had attempted to remove Raelin from his council. The other three members always voted against it. That had led Tegan to attempt to disband the entire council, which had led to the court intervening.

Which had led to him backing down, because at the time he had only been on the throne for a season and had needed his court behind him, guiding him in the ways of being a king. Looking back, he should have pushed onwards to disband the council and form one consisting of males of his own choosing. By backing down, he had given the four males seated before him power over him, and they had been stealing more of it from him each season that passed.

Perhaps it was time he took that power back.

If he tried to disband this group of merciless demons who were intent on pointing out every flaw in his plans now, there was a chance the court might side with him.

Because as far as he was concerned, they were standing in the way of progress.

"The Second Realm needs power in order to advance as the other demon realms are. You desire us to remain behind them?" Tegan stared Balkan down as candlelight danced over his features, turning his black eyes even darker.

"No, my king. It is only that it seems—" Eryt started from his right.

"Dangerous?" Tegan barked and the candles positioned in a row along the centre of the table flickered, causing the warm light they cast to dip and shadows to flicker over the faces of the four males.

They settled, brightening and struggling to illuminate the large room on the ground floor of the black castle, their light barely reaching the columns that stood on either side of the table, and not making it as far as the bookcases that lined the walls. The tomes they contained, bound in dragon leather, recorded the history of his kingdom.

At least one book for each king.

His father had made it to two tomes before he had been slain. Edyn had barely filled the first few pages of his own book.

How far would Tegan make it before his ended?

He wanted to change his life before it was taken from him.

He toyed with the sleeve of the loose white shirt he wore. His right one.

The one that concealed the numbers the female had written on his skin.

Numbers he couldn't bring himself to wash away, even though he had written them down.

A female he couldn't stop thinking about.

"Expensive," Raelin put in and adjusted the gold embroidered collar of his black tunic, the uniform of the council. "This project would be too expensive. The people cannot afford what you are proposing."

Tegan's mood blackened and he narrowed his gaze on the male who was two thousand years his senior at close to five thousand years old. A weak male, physically at least. His scrawny build had led him to develop other strengths.

Such as his vicious cunning mind.

Tegan could see his fiendish line of thought shining in his black eyes.

He meant to make the people pay for the construction of the wind turbines and creating farmland that would become a village project, one Tegan had hoped would provide them not only with food but possibly with income too, improving their lives in many ways.

"Strange, I thought we were one of the richest of the demon kingdoms. I recall being told that many times as a youth, and remember hearing those words spoken to my father by this very council." He shifted his gaze to each of them in turn, reading their expressions. "Perhaps I should have been informed if the kingdom's finances are that dire? I presume they are dire?"

Balkan swallowed. Hard.

"You seem to want to speak, Balkan." Tegan waved his left hand, urging the male to find his voice. "Does the kingdom have coin or not?"

Raelin shot the male a black look. Eryt fiddled with his ledger. Sylas didn't know where to look.

Balkan finally spoke. "We have a plentiful supply of coin, my king."

"So the cost is not an issue. The funds needed to fulfil this project in the first seven villages are covered." Tegan leaned back in his chair, fingers stroking his right arm as he tried to keep his focus on the meeting now that he was beginning to feel he was getting somewhere.

"My king, we cannot just go ahead and pay for such expensive projects. There is a precedence to be set here." Raelin didn't back down when Tegan turned his glare on the male.

Nor when he stood, the scraping of the wooden legs of his chair against the stone floor loud in the heavy silence.

He leaned over and planted his hands against the table top as he stared hard at Raelin. "This project is *for* the people, not a method of extracting more coin from them. It is meant to benefit them, not bankrupt them."

He curled his right hand into a fist and slammed it into the table as fury got the better of him, causing Eryt to jump and scoot back in his chair to a safer distance. The male tucked his ledger close to the breast of his tunic when Tegan growled at him.

Every damned thing Tegan did was questioned by these buffoons. They had far too much control over his life and his kingdom. Testament to that was the way they had lectured him for a full day about the fact he had left Hell, scolding him as if he was a child, not a grown male.

As if he was beneath them.

Not their damned king.

He had been an idiot for putting up with it rather than putting them in their place.

But he had been distracted, thoughts of the female filling his mind and that strange need to snarl and roar keeping him off kilter.

He stroked his arm, almost feeling the numbers hidden there. Digits he ached to call so he could hear her voice again. He didn't care if she teased him, poked fun or mocked him. He had been slowly losing his mind over the past few days, sinking deeper and deeper into thoughts of her, into that need to see her again. If he could just hear her voice, he was sure the ground beneath him would feel solid again.

He had thought it unstable when he had been with her, but now it felt as if it was pitching and bucking, attempting to throw him to his knees.

He needed to see her.

The spell she had cast on him wasn't a glamour, he was sure of that now. If it had been, it would have faded by now, the distance between them and the time they had been apart destroying it.

"Where is the kingdom's money kept?" He splayed his right hand out and stared at it as he planted it against the wood, a thousand thoughts colliding in his head to keep him only half-aware of the other males in the room and what he was asking.

Someone stared at him. He could sense their curiosity, and the concern of everyone present.

"I asked where the kingdom keeps its coin." He lifted his head and fixed his gaze on Balkan, singling out the weakest in the group, the one most likely to answer him.

"In many places. We make use of the mortal banks, have accounts established in several countries there. We also have a reserve here in the castle, and two smaller reserves in our most heavily fortified garrisons." Balkan swiped the back of his hand across his forehead, his fingers trembling.

The male never had liked being openly challenged. He had been born of weak stock. Not one of his living family or his ancestors had ever gone to war.

None of these males had set foot on a battlefield.

Yet they were meant to advise him.

It was little wonder he couldn't bring himself to trust them.

"Accounts in the mortal realm." Tegan pursed his lips and frowned at Balkan as he considered that.

Kyter had mentioned debit cards. Did they perhaps debit such accounts of their funds? He recalled the device the male had used for the female's plastic card and felt he was on to something, finally figuring out the machinations of the mortal world. He narrowed his eyes on Balkan and carefully picked his words, not wanting any of the present males to see how little he knew of the modern human realm.

"And we have debit cards for these accounts?" He braced himself, and felt vindicated for doing so when all of their gazes turned suspicious.

"My king, we spoke at length about your foray into the mortal world and how dangerous it had been to venture there alone." Raelin sounded far too happy about how that lecture had gone too, had evidently enjoyed berating and belittling him.

Tegan slammed his fist into the table again, shaking the goblets that stood before each of them and toppling the one nearest him.

"You spoke, and you all spoke out of turn," he snarled and pinned Raelin with a hard look. "Answer my question. A recent discussion with King Thorne of the Third Realm revealed the male has access to such cards."

A lie, but one that spurred Balkan into action.

"My king, we have far more coin in our accounts than the Third Realm, if that is your concern."

Tegan sneered at him. "My concern is that I do not have such a thing, while my fellow kings do."

"Why would you need one?" Raelin said calmly, his tone the one Tegan despised the most because it was meant to calm him and make him believe the male was on his side, wanting only the best for him.

This time, Tegan wouldn't go along with it.

He was tired of this realm and their games.

"I mean to purchase more books with one, along with several other things from the mortal realm that have caught my eye, and the items my research indicates I will need in order to proceed with my projects." Tegan waited, holding Raelin's gaze, aware that the male was going to attempt to shut him down.

"Whatever you desire, we can arrange it for you." Raelin smiled, one meant to placate him but one that irritated him instead.

Never had he seen such a hollow, false smile.

"What I want is to visit some windfarms." Particularly one in Scotland, just in case the female lived in that locale.

Eryt held both of his hands up, dropping the ledger into his lap, his black eyes enormous as he shook his head, causing his wild black hair to tangle on his horns. "My king, we will send people to them and they can report back to you about these things. It is not your place to concern yourself about such visits and research. Others can take care of it."

So they could keep him under lock and key in the kingdom.

Tegan leaned towards him and growled, flashing fangs right in his face. "I am king. I demand to know more about our accounts and other important things, not less. It is my duty to know everything and be prepared. It is my duty to lead my people and this kingdom. You will bring me debit cards and you will not question my need of them. Or must I run everything past you all?"

He looked at each of them in turn.

"Who rules this kingdom, you or me?"

All four males bowed their heads and answered as one. "You, my king."

"Then I will hear no more on this subject. I expect debit cards to be delivered to me immediately." He took his seat again, slumping into the tall-backed wooden chair. It creaked under his weight and he stretched his legs out under the table. "What other business do we have to discuss?"

Because he wanted to get moving on his plans now that his advisers looked as if they weren't going to interfere. He needed to find males who would be able to visit the villages and choose the ones where the wind turbines and new farmland were most likely to succeed.

"The celebration, my king." Sylas managed not to flinch when Tegan's gaze snapped to him.

Tegan huffed. He had forgotten about the celebration. Sitting through the one for his finest warriors had been painful enough. He didn't want to suffer another one.

"The invitations for the public feast were successfully delivered to the heads of the noble houses across the kingdom," Sylas continued, an almost apologetic note to his voice as he looked to his right, directly at Tegan as he sank lower in his chair.

Another feast. Another reminder of the godsdamned truce that ruled every aspect of his life.

A truce that made his kingdom look weak, projecting an image of vulnerability when his enemies should only witness the might of the Second Realm. He was sure the other five kingdoms viewed the Second and First as weak, many of their warriors untested in battle now that a thousand years of peace had passed, liable to easily fold and fall during combat.

He was sure it was only a matter of time before someone dared to test them, believing them an easy target, a kingdom ripe for plucking.

Gods, Tegan longed for that day.

He would prove the might of his kingdom—his undeniable strength.

"We must honour the truce," Raelin said, as if reading his thoughts.

Or perhaps his desire to end it was written plainly across his face.

He had never hidden it from them, had never concealed how much he hated it. They were all old enough to have seen how vehemently he had been against it when Edyn had proposed it all those centuries ago.

The only thing that kept him from breaking the truce was the fact he would dishonour Edyn's name and those of his ancestors if he went through with it.

Although many of his warriors argued that being a peaceful realm dishonoured them in a more despicable fashion.

Hell, if Valdaine were present, his old friend would tell him to remove his advisers by force, seize true command of the kingdom and rip the truce to pieces.

Where was Valdaine?

The male had never been away from the castle for this long before. It had been almost a season since Tegan had seen him.

Eryt pulled him out of his thoughts. "There is word the Fourth Realm is moving warriors close to our borders, establishing a new fortress near the western lands."

Tegan perked up. Was it finally happening?

Adrenaline poured through his veins and he sat straighter, leaned forwards and watched one of the candles as he gathered his thoughts, putting together a plan.

"We will dispatch two legions, one to the north and one to the south of the position of this new garrison, and I will go with the Royal Legion and oversee things at the closest point to it." He had to bite back his grin as his mind leaped ahead, already picturing the battle that was liable to break out once the Fourth Realm got wind he had moved his legions to face their threat.

Raelin flatly said, "The Royal Legion has already been dispatched. Prince Ryker is leading them as usual."

Tegan's mood soured, the corners of his lips dipping sharply downwards as he frowned at Raelin.

His brother was getting all the glory again.

Gods, he wished he was as free as Ryker, as free as he had once been. He wasn't sure when he had started to feel as if he was locked in a cage, but he felt it more keenly each day.

He paused.

Except for when he had been with the succubus.

When he had been around her, he had felt free. He hadn't needed to be what everyone expected him to be, and it had been exhilarating, refreshing, and fun. He couldn't remember the last time he'd had fun.

He certainly wasn't having it here in this damned meeting.

He stood, waved his hand and turned away from the four males.

"My king, we still must discuss the celebration." Eryt made a valiant effort to stop him, leaping in front of him.

Tegan bared his fangs. "You do it. You all like controlling every little detail of things. Here is your chance to do that. I have things I must attend to in my quarters. I expect the debit cards I requested to be delivered before dinner."

He swept past the male and out of the door, not waiting to see if anyone was going to voice a protest about his leaving. He had sat in that damned hard chair for five hours. He was done with it and his advisers.

He made his way through the black corridors, nodding to anyone he met as he moved up through the building to his private floors. A glare hurled at the two guards outside his door was enough to send them on their way. He pushed the heavy wooden door open, entered the drawing room, and closed it behind him.

His boots were loud on the wooden floor as he crossed the room to the open door in the opposite corner and turned right beyond it, heading up the winding stairs there to the next floor. He banked right again at the top of them, picking up pace as he neared his destination.

He passed the open door to his bedroom, his focus fixed on the closed one at the end of the wide corridor.

His sanctuary.

The door stuck a little as he pushed it open, the metal hinges squeaking and cutting through the silence. He closed it behind him and moved to his left, found the oil lamp and matches his aide had bought him last year from the mortal world and lit the wick. He placed the glass over the flame and turned the tiny dial, pulling more wick from the oil so the light brightened. He carried the lamp with him, over the plush furs that lined the wooden floors, to the tall green leather wingback armchair that stood by the fireplace.

Tegan set the lamp down on the low wooden table beside it and stooped in front of the grate, stacking logs and tinder in a uniform pattern before setting fire to them. He waited for the flames to catch and spread, devouring the offering of black wood, before he eased into his armchair. The leather creaked beneath his weight, a sound he had come to love over the years.

He leaned back and looked at this side of his library, only a small section of the entire room. Beyond the wall where the fireplace stood was another room, filled with wooden bookcases that were crammed with books. The ones he had already devoured were kept there. The bookcases that lined the walls in this smaller side of the library held the books he was yet to read. Hundreds of them.

Only Valdaine and Ryker, and his advisers knew of this place.

Tegan knew the image a demon king needed to project, and it wasn't the one the succubus had witnessed last night. Few in his kingdom would understand his love of learning, even though he often read subjects with the intent of finding some way of using them to benefit his kingdom.

Even in this time of peace, his people still expected him to be savage and just, a powerful male driven by a thirst for bloodshed and a fierce need to protect, not a thirst for knowledge and a fierce need to improve the lives of his people.

He picked up the book on the side table and opened it.

Familiar guilt flared in his gut.

How many hours had he spent in this armchair, reading books when he should have been attending meetings with his advisers or doing other things? Reading had become an escape for him, but it didn't lessen the feeling that he was shunning his duties as king.

In the early days of his rule, he had taken days at a time off, shutting himself away in this room, passing every hour reading in order to escape the hell that had become his life.

Sometimes, he still stole a day or two for himself, locking himself in his quarters and ignoring anyone who came to his door, losing track of time as he wrote down his thoughts and came up with plans, ways of improving the lives of his subjects.

He had drawn up thousands of blueprints over the years and hundreds of plans, outlines of projects that had never seen the light of day.

Yet.

Wind turbines to generate electricity and farms to provide sustenance and income weren't the only projects he planned to put in motion. Education was just as important. Many of his people couldn't read or write. Even some of his commanders lacked such basic skills, things he took for granted.

Things that made him feel like a spoiled bastard.

He had been educated by the finest tutors and had left his people and his warriors uneducated.

What sort of king was he?

One who intended to change that, although it wasn't going to be easy. Demons were notoriously stubborn. If he announced his plans to establish schools in every village, his people would think he had been influenced by the elves, a species many of them still didn't trust. He only wanted to improve their lives, but so many of them would resist him.

Tegan wanted to laugh at that.

His burden as a king wasn't the constant threat of war, it was the pressing weight of wanting to improve the lives of his people.

Part of him would have preferred war to this. War he understood. War came easily to him. This was difficult. It required more strategizing, more study and cunning than the greatest battle.

A lunar cycle ago, when he had been shut away in his library attempting to find a way to bring education to his people without them resisting it, he had hit upon an idea, one that might just work.

He would enlist the help of the females who called the villages home. Since his kind couldn't produce female offspring thanks to a curse placed upon them by the Devil when they had broken from him millennia ago, all of the village females were from outside the realm, a mixture of mortals, immortals and fae. Many of them were already educated to a degree and many of them had children with their demon mates. They would want an education for their offspring and Tegan didn't know a demon male alive who could deny his fated mate something she wanted.

He grabbed the notepad and a device his aide had called a *biro* from the table beside him and scrawled a few ideas for locations where he could start implementing an educational programme. Once the other villages saw the project working, they would be less resistant to it, especially if he made sure the teachers in the schools pitched that an educated warrior was a better warrior and played up the swordsmanship and combat lessons he wanted to include.

Something he could personally attest to since he had been a damned awful warrior as a youth. It was only once his mind as well as his body had been trained that he had become the warrior he was, honed and skilled, using knowledge as well as physical strength to his advantage on the battlefield.

Tegan stared at the pen he gripped, mind whirling back to that night that seemed like a forever ago now.

He felt as if he needed to use all of his formidable skill as a warrior to claim her. She had been cunning, wily, led him on a merry dance that kept him on his toes.

Gods, he had loved it.

He set the pen down and tried to focus on his book, but windmills made him think of her now, and the black shirt he had draped over the back of his favourite armchair smelled of her. He shifted in his seat, a vain attempt to get comfortable, as if that would help him concentrate on reading.

There was little chance of it happening, he knew that deep in his heart. Normally, he could sit and read for hours, lost in whatever book he was devouring. Since meeting her, he had only been able to read in short bursts, his focus shot to hell.

Because he was restless.

Ached with a need to see her again.

His little succubus.

He growled at himself for the millionth time, rage curling his horns, causing them to grow past the lobes of his ears.

He should have asked for her name.

It plagued him, made him even more restless if that was possible. How many hours had he lain awake, wondering what her name was? She hadn't even asked his. Had he meant that little to her? Was she truly not interested in him?

He rested his book on his knee. She had been interested. He had seen it in her eyes, smelled it on her, and felt it in the kiss she had pressed to his cheek. She wanted to see him again, had even given him her digits so it would be possible for him to speak with her.

Tegan pulled the sleeve of his loose white shirt up and rubbed his thumb over the numbers.

They were fading now.

The numbers weren't the only thing that was fading. Her scent on his black shirt was too, and the weaker it grew, the fiercer the need to see her again became.

And his temper shortened too.

He reached over his shoulder and pulled the shirt from the back of his armchair, brought it to his nose and closed his eyes as he inhaled her sweet yet warmly-spiced scent. Calm rushed through him, easing the fire that had been building in his veins, and he sank into her scent, using it to smooth the edges of his temper.

It was no use.

He needed to see her again.

He stood and forced his horns away as he set his book aside and discarded the shirt. The moment they were hidden, a black hole opened beneath him and he dropped into it. Cool air rushed over him, comforting and soothing his ragged nerves, and then the scents of a thousand different things hit him.

The mortal world.

Tegan lifted his head, his eyes locking with the golden-brown ones of the brunette female behind the black bar of Underworld as she whipped to face him. The gasp that left her lips morphed into a growl as she shifted, transforming into a sleek silver feline with dark rings in her fur. She leaped onto the bar and hissed at him, her ears flicking backwards as her fur stood on end.

The door to the left of the bar area burst open and the huge silver-haired male he had seen when he had visited before barrelled through it, took one look at the female as she swiped claws at Tegan, and launched at him on a feral snarl.

Tegan dodged backwards, evading the slash of the male's claws. They raked through the air just inches from his chest. He bared his fangs, matching the shifter's snarl, and kicked off, slamming into him and knocking him backwards into the bar. The male hit it with a low grunt and Tegan drove forwards, bending him over it as he grappled with him, attempting to grasp the male's throat.

The male's bare chest strained, every muscle flexing as he shoved at Tegan's shoulder and face. His eyes brightened, turning silver as he bared fangs and fur rippled over his skin, revealing he was the same breed as the female on the bar.

She loosed a vicious growl and kicked towards Tegan, her right paw a blur as she batted it at him. He pushed away from the male and leaped backwards, evading her and the male as he quickly took advantage of his freedom, gripping the brass railing that ran the length of the black bar top and leveraging himself up with it to kick at Tegan with both feet.

The door shot open again, a flare of bright light that had Tegan covering his eyes so his sight didn't dull and give the shifters an advantage over him.

"The fuck is going on?" Kyter's familiar voice was a low growl in the dimly lit room as the door swung shut behind him.

Tegan felt Kyter's gaze land on him and then shift away. He flicked a glance at the male, unwilling to take his eyes off his opponents for more than a second.

"Cav?" Kyter frowned at the bare-chested male, a flicker of concern in his golden eyes as he checked him over. "You alright?"

"Eloise," the one called Cav breathed, his chest straining as he stared at Tegan, his irises a vivid silver now. "He attacked Eloise."

"I did no such thing," Tegan countered.

The female on the bar hissed and growled low, her eyes locked on him.

"I may have startled her," he offered with an apologetic smile that didn't stop her from hissing at him again.

Cav looked over his shoulder at her and her gaze leaped to him and then away, down to the counter she was standing on.

"Get her out of here. I'll deal with our uninvited guest." Kyter scrubbed a hand over his tousled sandy hair and yawned, the look on his face screaming of the anger Tegan could sense in him.

While the two pale felines, snow leopards he believed them to be, were not a threat to him, Kyter was. The male was unusually strong for a jaguar shifter.

Tegan shifted his feet apart as Cav led the snow leopard away and Kyter stepped forwards, closing the distance between them. While he had been confident he could best the male snow leopard, he wasn't confident he could win a fight against Kyter.

Partly because he was strong.

Partly because battling him would destroy whatever tentative friendship they had and would wreck his chances of getting the male to help him.

Kyter stopped a few feet from him, dropped his hand to his bare chest and absently scratched his left pectoral as he yawned again.

Tegan slowly took in the club as something dawned on him.

It was empty.

The female he had frightened hadn't been wearing much other than a small top and shorts. Cav had only been wearing a loose pair of black trousers. Kyter was similarly dressed, his soft trousers a pale shade of grey.

"You can't just teleport into someone's club when it's closed. It's rude." Kyter slumped onto one of the stools that lined the bar.

"I did not realise it would be closed." It hadn't even crossed his mind. He had presumed it was like some of the taverns he had known centuries ago, and operated all hours of the day and night.

Kyter leaned his elbow on the bar and propped his chin up on his palm as he drawled, "That's probably worse. You planned to teleport into a club that would be filled with humans as well as immortals?"

Tegan considered that, but concluded that he wouldn't have cared if anyone had seen him.

He took a step towards the blond male. "It is a matter of utmost importance."

Kyter sat up straight and twisted towards him. "Lay it on me."

Tegan presumed that meant the male wanted to know his reason for coming.

He pulled back the sleeve of his white shirt to reveal the number. "I have digits."

"Congrats, my man," Kyter dryly muttered. "You pulled the other night then."

Tegan wasn't sure what *pulled* was. When he said nothing, the male rolled his eyes and sighed as he shook his head.

"If you have her number, why are you here?" Kyter gave him a look that made him feel like he was an idiot.

Too many people outside of his kingdom looked at him like that and he was coming to greatly dislike it.

It didn't help that the male had every right to look at him as if he was an uneducated fool or that Tegan was about to reinforce the male's low opinion of him when he revealed the reason he had come.

He hesitated.

Looked at the number and battled with the urge to leave rather than make himself look like the idiot Kyter believed him to be. He couldn't. He needed to see the female again and Kyter was the only one who could help him with that.

So he swallowed his pride.

"I was hoping you would know how to use them."

CHAPTER 8

Suki's phone ringing came at the best moment possible, silencing her sisters in the middle of their in-depth comparison of their most recent conquests. She thanked the gods as she pushed up from the oversized jewel-tone pillows and fished it from the red velvet cover of the daybed in front of her crossed legs.

She had been trying to find a way of escaping for the last thirty minutes as she had stared at the colourful swathes of silk and satin that hung between the beams that crossed the expansive courtyard of her clan's mansion house. She had gotten sick of hearing her sisters as they attempted to one-up each other and tired of the taunts they tossed her way as she remained silent, unable to join in because her list of conquests was empty as usual.

It was only the collective power of her clan that was keeping her ticking over, her gauge on the red line but in no danger of falling below it thanks to the steady trickle-down effect of her sisters' feeding. Another reason her family were so important to her. Without this link to them all, she would have starved decades ago.

Or been forced to kill to remain alive.

She wriggled off the daybed, one of three that formed a semi-circle in this particular section of their outside lounge area, ignoring the way her sisters all watched her, curiosity sparkling in their colourful gazes.

Suki flipped the phone towards her and frowned. She didn't recognise the number.

She swiped her thumb over the screen anyway, bracing herself for another irritating sales call.

"Hello?" She pressed the phone to her ear, hyper-aware of her sisters staring at her, expectation written across all of their faces as they lounged on the mounds of pillows on the daybeds, looking every bit the cliché image of succubi in their tiny shorts and skirts, and revealing tops.

Silence greeted her.

She huffed. Great.

"Look. Whatever you're selling with this bullshit automated call, you can fuck off."

"Female?" The lush deep baritone that rolled through the receiver rolled right over her like a warm wave, the intense heat that followed it in danger of melting her bones.

As it was, her knees went a little weak.

"Solid Eleven?" She couldn't quite bring herself to believe he was calling her as she stared beyond the daybeds to the square stone fountain in the centre of the courtyard, but no other guy she had met had her number.

She had never been one for booty calls.

Her sisters instantly perked up.

"Who's calling?" Patrina leaned towards her, draping herself over a pillow, as if she could hear better by doing that. Succubi senses weren't that good.

Suki covered the phone with her hand. "No one."

Allura gasped, her violet eyes wide as she grabbed a smaller pillow from her daybed and launched it at her. "Don't tell me Sucky is finally going to bag and tag a guy?"

Suki swatted the pillow away before it could hit her, flipped her sisters off and quickly escaped. She hurried from the courtyard lounge, passing areas where the colourful material draped over the beams had been lowered, forming a barrier between the rest of the lounge and the succubus on the other side. Low murmured comments and sensual moans emanated from them and her belly heated, her head growing a little hazy as she caught a hit of the pleasure the succubus's host was experiencing, a sliver of energy that lit her up inside.

She pushed onwards, because she didn't want the second-hand energy they were offering. She wanted to hear Solid Eleven's voice again, because it lit her up inside like the light of a thousand suns, an experience far more delicious than feeding off someone else's pleasure.

She worked her way through the ground floor of the mansion, her boots loud on the pale marble floor of the enormous grand foyer, her eyes on the open double doors opposite her.

Freedom.

Well, relative freedom.

The street outside the imposing three-storey sandstone building was busier than usual and as soon as she had ascended the wide steps that led down from the entrance, she had to fight her way through several groups of men. Their gazes tracked her as she rushed past the basement level of the building, heading to the right side of it, and ducked into the alley there.

Even then they ogled her, some of them moving so they could still see her.

"What is that noise?" Solid Eleven didn't sound happy.

"I'm outside now." She flipped off the guys who were staring at her too and smirked when they went on their way. "The town is busy today. Some sort of celebration that the witches are having, I think."

"Town?"

Gods, she had forgotten just how sexy his voice was.

In fact, she had done her damnedest to put him out of her mind when he hadn't called her by the second day, figuring him for another male she would never see again.

Another fail.

But here he was, calling her, and damn she was more than pleased.

She was absolutely thrilled.

"I live in a fae town with my sisters." She frowned. "Do you know about fae towns?"

She wasn't sure how much he knew about the mortal world or how long it had been since he had last left Hell. Long enough not to know about fae towns? They had been around for at least the last thousand years according to her clan's history lessons.

"Yes." A very brusque reply.

Was something bothering him? She had hoped he would sound happier to be speaking with her again. Maybe he was calling to tell her it had been fun and all, but he never wanted to see her again. Although, if that was the case, surely he could have just not bothered to call at all. She would have preferred that.

"What's wrong?" she said, risking a knife in the heart.

"I used your digits," he muttered, sounding disappointed now. "I thought I might see you... but this phone does not show me a picture. I would rather speak with you face to face."

So he wasn't calling to brush her off. He was just moody because he couldn't see her? How sweet.

"I still believe this to be witchcraft," he mumbled, his voice growing distant, as if he had pulled the receiver away from his ear to look at it.

She read between the lines. He wasn't comfortable with speaking on the phone. Her antiquated demon.

In the background, Kyter grumbled, "It's not magic."

"What is it then?" Solid Eleven was still distant and she could almost picture him glaring at the phone he held. There was that curiosity she had found so appealing.

Her hot geek.

Kyter hemmed and hawed over an explanation.

"Hello?" Suki hollered into the phone, a vain attempt to be heard judging by how Solid Eleven continued to question Kyter.

"There must be a logical explanation you can offer."

"Look… I'm not a scientist alright? It's something involving wires or radio waves or some such shit," Kyter snapped.

"Hello!" Suki shouted.

"Wires? *Impossible.*" Solid Eleven practically growled that word. "How can sound travel along a wire?"

"Same fucking way the internet travels through them," Kyter growled.

"You mean the interweb."

"What?" Kyter sounded confused now. "Interweb? It's called the inter*net.*"

"It is not." Solid Eleven didn't sound sure, probably because she always called the internet the interweb and had used that word when introducing him to it. Interweb sounded cute.

She sighed, checked herself over, making sure her hair looked killer and her jean shorts weren't riding up her ass any more than they should be, and teleported.

She reappeared in the middle of the nightclub, far closer to Solid Eleven than she had anticipated. He spun on his heel to face her, the telephone still gripped in his large hands.

Kyter looked at her too.

Which drew a stunning reaction from the demon.

He snarled and snapped huge fangs at the shifter, grabbed her around her waist and dropped into a freaky black abyss with her.

Cold rushed over her and she shuddered against Solid Eleven's broad chest.

Warmth kissed her skin as they landed.

She peered over his thickly muscled arm. He had taken her to the beach where she had brought him the other night.

Only it was morning here now, and the beach was already filled with humans, most of them sunbathing but some of them swimming.

And a lot of them were rather scantily clad.

Solid Eleven's gaze roamed over the mortals and she wanted to hiss at them all because she swore he was singling out the females in their thongs and skimpy bikini tops that barely covered their nipples.

She hissed at him instead and teleported, taking him to a private cove in a different location, one that was only accessible by boat. Normally, she came to this place to nude sunbathe. Her sisters did that on the more public beaches without breaking a sweat, but she couldn't.

The one time she had tried going topless on a busy beach, she had panicked so hard she had accidentally cast a veil on herself that had lasted three days and had left her exhausted.

Although, she might not panic that hard if she went topless in front of her current audience.

Solid Eleven stepped back, his black gaze raking over her, that deliciously alluring corona of violet-red emerging around his dilated pupils as he drank her in. She mourned the loss of his eyes on her as he dragged them away and turned in a slow circle to take in the cove. Steep cliffs surrounded it on three sides, giving it the privacy she loved, and the sea was calm as it swept against the pale sand, the golden light of afternoon rippling across it.

She loved this time of day, when the sun began to sink, and anticipation of a sunset built inside her. Once, she had teleported five times to catch five different sunsets, pinging around the time zones. She had watched one in a city, and then over some mountains, and then from a beach, followed by a lake and finally at another secluded beach.

Suki kicked off her black cowboy boots. One of them hit Solid Eleven in the back of his ankle.

The demon's focus shot back to her, sending a hot wave rushing through her as she removed the cerise checked shirt she had tied closed over her midriff, aiming for the cute-cowgirl look. His dark gaze devoured her as she dropped the shirt on her boots, leaning over to maybe intentionally flash a little cleavage at him. The white tank she wore was barely big enough to cover her breasts and just small enough to keep his eyes glued to her as she straightened.

Her skin prickled as that flicker of purple-red fire in his eyes blazed brighter, intense heat rolling through her from the combination of how he looked as if he wanted to devour her and the fact they were alone.

Nerves threatened to rise as that slapped her hard across the face. This wasn't the first time she had been alone with a man. Heck, it wasn't the first time she had been alone with him.

But something felt different this time.

She felt a little less in control of the situation.

"How did your book end?" she said in a light tone, attempting to fill the silence.

Or attempting to pull his eyes away from her hips and the tiny shorts she wore?

"I have been busy and have not been able to finish it yet." Solid Eleven remained serious, clearly missing that she had been teasing him. "I probably should not have come, but I wanted to spend some time with you, even if it is only a little while."

That touched her, because she could see he was under a lot of strain. It was written in every hard line of his face and in the depths of his eyes.

She ran a finger up and down through the air at him. "You're way overdressed for the beach."

His right eyebrow arched as he looked down at himself and then looked at her. He reached over his back, grabbed hold of his white shirt and pulled it off over his head.

Suki died and went to Heaven.

Her mouth watered at the sinfully divine sight of all that hard muscle packed beneath pale golden skin. She told herself not to stare but she couldn't tear her eyes away from him, couldn't stop them from roaming over every inch of him as he bent and removed his boots. Good gods. She swallowed hard when he straightened, coming to face her, hitting her with the glorious view of all that masculine perfection.

Wide powerful shoulders met the broad flat slabs of his pectorals, a dusting of short dark hair covering them that spread downwards over a chiselled set of abs that led her eyes down past the sexy dip of his navel to a black treasure trail of hair her fingers itched to follow beyond the low waist of his leathers.

He cleared his throat, awkwardly.

"Sorry, whaaaaa?" Suki fought to muster enough braincells to speak coherently.

They had all turned to mush the moment he had hit her with the sight of his magnificent body. She flexed her fingers at her sides, aching to trace every line of his muscles to see if they were as firm as they looked. She shook her head, hoping that might knock her ability to speak back online.

It helped her find the strength to lift her eyes to his face.

Beautiful red stained his cheeks and he scrubbed a hand over the right side of his head. Wanted to rub his horns that weren't there? Her mind hurled an image of him with horns at her. Her brain had another meltdown.

"I can't move and I can't stop gawping at you. I'm sorry." The words rushed out of her so fast she was sure he wouldn't be able to understand her.

A small smile teased his lips. "I appear to be having the same problem."

Well, that was good at least. He still wanted her; she was still on fire for him. Possibly even more on fire now.

About ready to burn to ashes.

"Maybe just let me stare a few seconds longer. I'm sure my eyes might get bored." She wasn't sure at all.

No, actually, she was sure she would never tire of looking at him.

If he looked that good half-naked, how devastating would he look completely naked?

With horns.

And maybe wings.

Oh *gods*.

Her face flushed as an ache bloomed between her thighs and his eyes darkened in response, his nostrils flaring as he breathed in.

"I need to cool off." She managed to tear her eyes away from his body again, forcing it up to his face and not missing that while he looked more relaxed now, distracted by staring at her, he was still tense and it had nothing to do with the fact they were locked in a battle of wills, a contest to see who could stop gawping at the other one first.

She held her hand out to him.

"You look like you need to cool off too."

When he didn't move to take it, she turned it palm up, showing him that she wasn't hiding anything in it and this wasn't a trick of any sort.

"Take it," she urged. "Trust me."

"I do not even know your name." The black slashes of his eyebrows dropped lower over his incredible glowing eyes and she could read in them that the fact he didn't know her name had been bothering him.

She could relieve him of that irritation at least. A first step towards relaxing him.

"I call myself Suki."

"Call yourself?" A furrow formed between his eyebrows.

"I'm not going to tell you my real name." Cold crashed over her as she swallowed hard.

His expression softened. "Forgive me. It has been a long time since I have met a fae. I forgot the power your true name has over you."

She loosed the breath she hadn't realised she was holding and shrugged stiffly, trying to let her momentary panic roll off her. "I shouldn't have reacted like that. I'm sorry. It's like an instinct... I just presume anyone who wants to know my name wants that power over me."

Her clan teachers hammered it into every member that giving anyone their true name would have a horrible ending. She had seen it happen once. A young succubus had foolishly offered her true name to a man and that man had enslaved her with it, had been able to call her to him at will and had made her do things.

In the end, the succubus had killed herself.

Suki had learned her lesson that day.

Never give a man your real name.

"You chose a pretty name for yourself," Solid Eleven husked, the warm purr of his voice melting the ice that had formed in her veins.

A positive sign? He liked her name and he was still looking at her as if he wanted to devour her.

"You do not wish to know my name?" He took a step towards her.

She did. Oh gods, she did. But knowing his name was probably as dangerous as giving him her true one. She never bothered to ask men their names. They were hosts and nothing more.

But Solid Eleven was so much more than that.

He was the first man she had thought about before going to bed at night. The first man to make her fantasise about him. The first man she had given her number to. The first man who had used that number to call her.

He was the first man she had brought to this place, her own little sanctuary.

The first man she ached for.

So she slowly nodded, because denying her desire to know his name was like denying herself breath.

Impossible to do without dying.

He opened his mouth and snapped it shut, his expression turning guarded. "How much do you know of the demon realms?"

Funny question. She shrugged. "Not much. I know there's like six of them."

"Seven," he said, and seemed pleased that she didn't even know how many there were. Or maybe he was pleased he had managed to teach her something for a change. He held his hand out to her. "My name is Tegan."

Tegan. A strong name. A warrior's name.

She slipped her hand into his. Electricity leaped up her arm, turning her blood to liquid fire that had her heating to a thousand degrees in an instant as her breath caught in her throat. Her eyes leaped to his, a need to know if he had felt that too rushing through her. They were stunning, no longer black with a faint corona around his pupils.

Now the whole of his irises were a reddish shade of purple.

So alluring that she had to force herself not to jump into his arms and kiss him, part of her remaining aware of what a tremendous mistake that would be. He didn't like females who threw themselves at him. He didn't exactly make it easy not to do that.

"You didn't bring your book with you this time," she murmured, lost in his eyes, her mouth working on auto-pilot to fill the heavy silence.

"I left home in a hurry." His smile was rakish.

Absolutely devastating.

Who was this male who was charming her, sweet in some ways and dangerously alluring in others? An enticing combination that had her wanting to know more about him. She instinctively focused, wanting to see what he was feeling as he stared down into her eyes, his hand firmly clasping hers. Black tendrils rose from his shoulders rather than the colours that would reveal his feelings to her.

She had viewed his shadowed aura as a challenge before. Now she wanted nothing more than to be able to pierce it, to see that the desire he felt for her ran as deep as what she felt for him.

Suki gathered her wits and lured him to the edge of the water, where the sand was cool and firm beneath her bare feet. She released his hand and crouched before him, trembling as his gaze landed on her, sending a hot thrill through her and stirring awareness of him, until her skin felt too tight and she itched with a need to stand and press against him, to beg him to ease this need she felt for him.

She reached for the hems of his black leathers instead, working to roll them up his legs.

"What are you doing?"

Suki paused at her work and looked up at him. Big mistake. What a view. He towered over her, chiselled abs and pecs kissed by the sun that played in the sculpted lines of his face and cast golden highlights in his black hair. It was hard to resist skimming her hands up his powerful legs to touch all that perfection, but somehow she managed it, finishing rolling up the hems of his trousers.

"You need to loosen up." She rose to her feet. "I find paddling relaxing."

She took hold of his hand and walked into the water, and jerked backwards when he didn't move but his grip on her hand remained firm.

"How do you know I need to relax?" he bit out, all that warmth she had been enjoying draining from his face, leaving his eyes black again. "A succubus trick?"

She resented the way he called her abilities a trick, was tempted to give him a big piece of her mind, despite the fallout it might cause.

But the guarded look in his eyes had different words rising to the tip of her tongue, because she couldn't blame him for being wary around her. He wasn't the first man and he wouldn't be the last one to think she was out to play him just because she was a succubus, and apparently that was what succubi did.

"It's written on your face." She released his hand and let hers fall to her side. "You look worn down. I don't need any *tricks* to be able to see that."

The bitterness in her voice surprised her, rattled her feelings and had her questioning why she was even here. Tegan was just going to turn out to be like every other man she had ever met. It wasn't going to end the way her stupid fantasies had.

He rubbed the right side of his head again, fingers scrubbing at his shorn hair and the tattoos inked beneath. "My apologies. You are right and I have been under more pressure than usual recently."

Suki pivoted on her heel and strode into the water without him, needing the space. The cool water lapped at her shins and then her knees, and she stopped when it reached her lower thighs, the depth far more than just paddling.

Far more than his rolled-up leathers would allow him to reach.

She stared down at her legs and watched the tiny fish gathering around them, trying to wrangle her feelings into submission. So what if he thought she was just like all the other succubi? He was meant to be a trophy hunt, one that would secure her place in her clan and erase the pet name she hated with all her heart.

So why did her chest ache when she thought about using him like that?

Shock rippled through her and her eyes widened when his bare feet appeared next to hers.

She stared at the section of his black leathers that were beneath the surface. "You're going to ruin them."

She tensed when his palm brushed her cheek and he lowered it, smoothing it along her jaw.

"I do not care. Ruined leathers are the least of my problems." His gruff tone did strange things to her insides, lifting the weight from them and making her feel light, as if she was floating, and warm all over.

"Is it the windfarm stuff that has you stressed out?" She kept her eyes on his feet, his wrecked leathers, watching the fish that nibbled at them, clearly curious about whether they could eat the black material.

"Among other things," he murmured and the intense heat of his gaze left her.

When she looked at him, his eyes were on the horizon, reflecting the golden light of the sun as it gradually edged lower.

"If you're so busy, why did you call?" A dangerous question for her to ask, because a man as clever as he was could easily see through it to the compliment grab it was.

His focus remained fixed on the horizon as he rocked her entire world with a handful of words.

"Because I wanted to see you again."

CHAPTER 9

Suki's heart fluttered and beat a little faster, and she resisted the smile that wanted to curl her lips as she let his words run around her head. They wreaked havoc on her at the same time as they offered her a slice of comfort because she felt as if they were on even ground with each other.

She hadn't been the only one thinking about their time together.

She wasn't the only one who had wanted to meet again.

"You are right." He slid her a look that warmed her from head to toe. "Paddling is relaxing."

"Um, this isn't exactly paddling." She lifted her right leg and swept it side to side through the water, disturbing the fish. "Paddling is strolling the shore where the waves meet it, so the water breaks over them. Like ankle deep. About as high as I rolled your leathers so you wouldn't ruin them."

He grinned, almost knocking her on her ass with it. "Well, whatever this is, it is nice."

It was nice.

She let her gaze drift over him, charting every sensual dip and swell of his torso, and frowned as she noticed something. "You have scars."

They were silvery, visible in the sunlight, and there were a lot of them.

She raised her eyes to his face. "I thought demons didn't scar?"

Another thing she hadn't known about his kind.

His smile widened and his black eyes sparkled, and whatever he was thinking about, it lifted his mood, had all the tension melting from him before her eyes.

"We do not retain scars if we gain them after we have matured. These scars are from when I was young." He lowered his gaze to his body, that stunning smile holding, gaining a boyish edge that had her heart beating harder in response. "I was a bit of a brawler."

She grinned now. "A ruffian. You don't strike me as someone who had been a right little sod as a kid."

He shrugged. "I was different then. A little out of control. A brat."

Bratty Tegan was an adorable image as it formed in her head.

"Lots of feet stomping and such?" She wanted to build the picture more clearly.

He shook his head. "Try a different sort of brat. I was not a good child at all. I was mean and elitist."

"Oh." Not so attractive.

His grim smile said he was well aware of that. "My father enrolled me into the army at the lowest rank possible to beat it out of me. He wanted to teach me humility by making me see how most demons lived."

"I'm guessing it worked." She swept her hand through the clear warm water, enjoying the feel of it cutting between her fingers. He arched an eyebrow at her and she arced her hand up and flicked water at his chest. "You're not so bratty now."

He raised both eyebrows at his wet stomach and sighed as he brushed the droplets away, lifted his hand and looked at the water on it, a thoughtful edge to his expression. "It taught me more than what my father expected. It completely changed me. I fought in brutal wars, forced to battle on the frontline. Every fight I engaged in, I picked up new scars and learned new skills and tactics as I fought for my life... as I fought to become the male I was meant to be."

She had thought she had been through a lot, but he sounded as if his life had been far worse. He had survived things that would have been the end of her.

"I can't imagine fighting." She studied a larger fish as it swam past, some sort of wrasse that reminded her of the colourful green and blue ice cream lollies that the witches sold at their fayres. "I normally freeze up when anyone tries to attack me or if I see a fight breaking out and feel it might head my way."

His gaze landed on her again, sending another delicious shiver through her. "Where do you live that fights regularly break out?"

"A fae town near Fort William." She made a grab for the fish, but it was too fast, put peddle to the metal and was gone before her hand had even neared the spot where it had been. All she got for her effort was water splashed up the front of her shorts and across her bare midriff. "The demons there are always rowdy."

She looked across at Tegan.

"What realm are you from anyway? I don't see many like you around there."

That guarded look filled his eyes and she was surprised when he actually answered her question. "The Second Realm."

He watched her closely, although she wasn't sure what he was looking for. Or was he expecting a reaction to that? She thought about what she knew of the Second Realm as she watched the sun tracking lower, turning the sea a deeper shade of gold and lacing the sky with beautiful warm colours.

She might have met one or two from his realm over her years, but she didn't remember them. The last demon she had met had dirty cream horns and blond hair, and she thought he had said he came from the First Realm.

She glanced up at Tegan.

Would his horns be black if he let them out, matching the colour of his hair? She wanted to see them, but she knew if she asked, he would deny her the pleasure, just in case a human witnessed them too.

When she finally tore her gaze away from him, the sun was close to the horizon, and a heavy weight settled in her stomach, dragging her mood down.

She didn't want Tegan to go.

"You kinda made out you were busy," she whispered, unable to say those words any louder because she didn't want him to hear them, because she feared he would go if he did. "You've been here for hours… with me."

He gave her a blank look. "It has been hours?"

Gods, she felt the same way. It felt like only minutes since he had called and she had teleported to Underworld to see him.

His gaze drifted back to the sunset, darkness washing across his features as they tightened, relaying just how little he liked whatever he was thinking.

His voice was hollow as he said, "I should return."

But he didn't want to, and that made her want to take hold of his hands and convince him to stay, even when she knew he wouldn't enjoy the time they spent together as much because his mind would be on whatever work awaited him at home.

His deep sigh spoke volumes as he turned away from the sunset, coming to face her, and she looked down as he slipped his hand into her right one and brushed his thumb over the back of it. For a heartbeat, he looked as if he wanted to say something, and then he released her hand and waded back towards the shore.

Suki watched him go, her heart growing heavier as the distance between them grew, rousing a need to follow him.

To remain close to him.

She couldn't deny that need, found her feet carrying her towards him as he picked up his shirt from the sand and pulled it back on, and shoved his feet into his boots.

She stopped close to him, wrestling with the words she wanted to say, rebelling against the part of her that kept telling her she had to let him go. She couldn't, because she wasn't sure she would see him again. She felt that if they parted now, they would part forever. Her sisters would laugh at her for that. Her tutors would berate her.

Because she was getting caught up in this demon.

He straightened to his full, impressive height, and took hold of her hand again. She didn't resist him as he drew his hand towards him, luring her with it. The heat of him rolled over her, his earthy masculine scent soothing her as it filled her senses.

"Would you like me to take you home?" He lowered his face towards her, his eyes holding hers, keeping her captive in a way she never wanted to break free from.

She slowly shook her head. "I might go for a swim and then I'll head home."

His face twisted in agony and his voice dropped to a low husky growl. "Do you mean to swim… *naked*?"

Suki nodded.

He groaned. "You slay me."

She laughed at that. Now who was being all melodramatic? He paused and looked at her, a strange light in his eyes, as if she was brightening his world with her laughter and he liked it. She slapped his chest, shivering as the solid steel of it met her palm.

"Get going, before you get into trouble."

"I feel I already am in trouble," he rumbled sexily, the slight tilt to his lips almost slaying her. "I want to watch you swimming."

"You just want to see me naked," she countered. "You haven't earned that privilege yet."

His eyes darkened a full shade and the tips of his ears flared, growing pointier. Desire. The demon wanted her. She didn't need to be able to read his aura to see he was hungry for a taste of her, as hungry as she was for a taste of him.

It hit her that she had him right where she wanted him.

So why wasn't she seizing the chance to bag and tag him?

Why had she forgotten that she was meant to be doing such a thing?

She stared up into his fathomless eyes, mesmerised by that corona of shimmering purple light, and something else hit her.

She was enjoying herself.

When he had called, she hadn't thought about her plan. She hadn't seen it as a chance to seduce him.

She had been genuinely thrilled that he had wanted to see her again.

He pulled his arm back behind him, luring her closer, and she didn't stop him. She stepped into him, planting her palm against his chest, feeling the thunderous beat of his heart against it as he lowered his head towards her.

His eyes fell to her mouth.

Suki tilted her head back, every inch of her aching for that kiss his eyes promised her as her heart pounded faster, blood racing in her veins.

His breath caressed her lips and she swallowed hard, silently urging him on, to take what he wanted from her because she wouldn't resist him this time. She needed this as fiercely as he did.

Their lips touched and she tensed as heat rushed through her, turned her blood to molten lava and had her burning for a hard kiss.

He swept his lips across hers, his kiss so achingly soft and tender that she melted into him, lost herself in the slow play of his mouth over hers, how the barely-there caress of them lifted her inside and made her feel as if she was floating, flying in his arms.

It was the opposite of what she had wanted, but gods it was everything she had needed.

He broke away before she was ready for him to stop and was a little breathless as he spoke, surprise lacing his words. "You did not feed from me."

She stared at his mouth, starving for the feel of them against hers again, sure that she would never be able to bring herself to kiss another now. They would all taste like ashes compared with his honey and whisky flavour, that masculine sweet and smokiness of him the most addictive thing she had ever tasted.

"A kiss doesn't always have to be about feeding a hunger, does it?" Although the kiss had fed another of her hungers, the one that had been riding her harder than her need to feed since the night they had met—the hunger to kiss him.

"It does not," he murmured, voice dropping low as his eyes drilled into her mouth. "But if you need it to be..."

His heart gave a hard kick against her palms that told her how much he liked the idea of her feeding from him, and she couldn't miss the impressive bulge that pressed against her stomach. The succubus in her said to take more from him, more than just a kiss. She could feed on him and be sated for days.

She pushed aside that desire and focused on him, on the need she could feel in him. That was enough for her, gave her a trickle of energy that brought her tank off the red line for the first time in months.

"I'm good for now," she said, a lie she hoped he wouldn't see through but one that had clearly been as plain as day judging by the way he looked at her.

"I am not the only one who looks tired." He gently stroked the backs of his short dark claws across her cheek, a beautiful look of concern in his eyes.

He didn't give her a chance to respond to that.

His mouth descended on hers, harder this time, and gods, his kiss was delicious, as intoxicating as the rest of him. She didn't want to feed from him though, partly because she didn't want to scare him away and partly because she feared hurting him.

He was strong, but was he really strong enough to handle her? If she lost control, would she kill him?

The thought she might had the urge to feed falling away, so shock swept through her when energy flowed into her through his kiss, with every sweep of his lips across hers. It was strong, had her head swimming and body heating, everything growing hazy as his energy filled her.

But a single thought, a startling realisation, pierced the clouds and hit her like a thunderbolt.

She wasn't stealing his strength.

Somehow, he was giving it to her.

Tegan clutched her upper arms more tightly, his blunt claws pressing in as he deepened the kiss, destroying her ability to think and all her fears with it. She leaned into the kiss, her heart drumming as fast as his was against her palms, and sank into his embrace as he wrapped his arms around her, caging her against his powerful body.

She tried her best to remain focused and in control, fear of hurting him rising each time their lips touched. She had seen what her abilities could do if she didn't keep them on a tight leash and the thought of accidentally killing Tegan had ice forming in her blood despite the heat he poured into her with every brush of his mouth over hers.

He groaned.

Suki shoved against his chest and shot out of his arms, a prickly chill sweeping down her spine and over her arms, and her breath seizing in her chest.

She had hurt him. She cursed herself, picking the vilest one imaginable, fury sweeping in on the heels of it as she tossed a panicked look at Tegan, afraid of what she would find.

He looked so pained, his eyes glittering with it as he pressed one hand to his chest and reached to her with the other.

Her right hand flew to her mouth as her eyebrows furrowed.

What had she done?

"Come back," he husked and stretched for her. "I need you back."

It hit her that it hadn't been a groan of pain.

It had been a moan of pleasure.

Suki released the breath she had been holding and smoothed her shorts and tank with trembling hands, her knees shaking beneath her, threatening to give out as relief crashed over her.

"You really should be going." She hoped he bought that as the reason she had broken away from him and couldn't see how shaken she was.

His dark eyes reminded her that fooling him was no easy task. They fixed on hers, so intense and focused that they rattled her as much as his kiss had.

She averted her gaze, stared at the sea and the sunset, not really seeing them as she gathered herself. Her nerves settled as he closed the distance between them, and she couldn't stop herself from leaning into his soft caress as he ran the backs of his claws over her cheek.

"You are beautiful, Suki," he whispered and her cheek blazed beneath his fingers, the solid one-two punch of his compliment and hearing him say her name for the first time in danger of knocking her out. She had never heard a man say her name before, and gods, she liked the way he said it, how it rolled off his tongue in a soft yet masculine way. His gaze drilled into her, as intense as ever, as if he was peeling away her layers, stripping down her defences to leave her weak and open to him. "I thought that the moment I saw you. You looked like a mermaid."

She frowned and turned her face to him, needing to see what had made him think that.

He half-smiled as he shifted his fingers back, skimming them over her ear and sifting them through her hair. "It looks like the ocean."

"It costs a fortune." She grimaced. He was paying her compliments that had her heart turning to slush in her chest and all she could say in response was that the colour of her hair had her burning through her allowance each month? She gave him a tight smile. "Sorry. I'm not used to men saying nice things about me. At least not genuine things."

His face remained soft, but his eyes darkened, a possessive light entering them. "Good. I do not like the thought of other males telling you that you are beautiful."

He more than didn't like it. He looked as if he wanted to murder anyone who dared to try it.

Which sent a thrill through her, one she knew she shouldn't be feeling because it felt as if she was wading into dangerous waters and she might drown. Only she couldn't bring herself to care. She wanted to drown in Tegan. With every small thing she learned about him, she fell deeper under his spell, felt more drawn to him than ever.

But there was so much she didn't know about him, and what if those things were truly dangerous, liable to get her killed?

She had never heard of a man being able to give energy to a succubus before and he had done so against her will.

In that brief moment, he'd had total control over her.

And that terrified her.

He looked off to the horizon and growled low, clearly not pleased that the sun was nearing it now. She didn't want him to go either, but maybe it was for the best. She had a lot to think about, and she needed some answers, and she could do neither of those things with him distracting her.

Although he was a beautiful distraction as he glared at the sunset as if he had the power to stop it from happening, to freeze time so they could remain together for longer.

"May I call you again?" He slid his gaze to meet hers.

She couldn't help smiling at how formal he still was as she nodded. "You have to come and see me again."

The black slashes of his eyebrows dipped low, forming a crease between them and narrowing his eyes on hers. "Why?"

Suki stepped up to him, tiptoed and whispered against his lips, "Because I'm already craving our next kiss."

He reached for her, but she evaded him, twirling out of his grip and beyond his reach, stopping facing him.

"Next time." She grinned at him and blew him a kiss.

He growled, the low wicked sound reverberating through her in a delicious way, frustration rolling off him as he stared at her. For a moment, she felt sure he was going to grab her and kiss her, her heart leaping into her throat in anticipation of another toe-curling kiss from him, but then a black abyss opened beneath him and he dropped into it.

She watched it as it rapidly closed, leaving perfect pale sand behind, and then twisted and sank to her ass. Her heart pounded, blood rushing. What was it about this demon that had her tangled in knots and flushed all over whenever she was near him?

What was it about him that allowed him to give her energy in a kiss?

Suki watched the sun as it reached the horizon, bathing the world in amber light, and brushed her fingers over her tingling lips that still tasted of him.

He was branded on her soul now, and she felt as if she was never going to be the same again. She already craved his kiss, ached for the feel of his strong arms around her, and the lush baritone of his voice in her ears. She was beginning to believe the myths about his kind were true.

Shadowed males were dangerous.

Dangerously addictive.

CHAPTER 10

Tegan was standing on the beach again, in the same spot and at the same time when he had left it. Only it wasn't the beach and it wasn't Suki cutting through the water with an elegant and captivating sort of grace.

It was a dream.

He was deeply aware of that as he watched her swimming, his gaze following her long strokes through the calm sea, her bare curves just visible beneath the clear water. Her colourful hair held highlights of gold in the tangled wet strands that were slicked back from her face, and droplets of water on her face sparkled like diamonds.

The urge to go to her, to strip off and swim with her, was strong, almost overwhelming in its force, but he couldn't bring himself to move. He couldn't tear his eyes away from her as she mesmerised him, enchanting him just as she had the night he had met her.

And when he had passed time with her on this beach in reality.

Her head swivelled towards the shore and a hot wave of need rocketed through his blood and lit him up inside as her eyes landed on him. His breaths shortened as she stared at him, holding him captive, a slave to her.

She rose from the water, her turquoise and blue hair falling in tangled ribbons over her bare breasts, teasingly concealing them from his eyes as they breached the placid surface. He groaned and rubbed a hand over his mouth as the need she ignited in him burned hotter, had his breaths coming faster now, his heart pumping harder as all his blood rushed south.

Suki was a mermaid made flesh as she walked towards him, a sway in her hips that lured his eyes down over her dangerous curves as they were exposed to him. Her eyes remained locked on him, demanding his do the same, as if he could stop himself from staring at her as she waded towards him, the water sluicing from the flat plane of her stomach, rushing over her hips, revealing the neat thatch of dark hair at the apex of her thighs, and then the slender lengths of her thighs.

The ache to touch her grew so fierce he couldn't breathe as he willed her to come to him, on the verge of begging her to put him out of his misery and let him kiss her again. He wanted to taste her again, had been thinking about that kiss all night, all through dinner and afterwards when he had been trying to read.

He had been thinking about it until the moment he had fallen asleep on his bed whilst reading.

And now she was here.

And he would give up his kingdom for a chance to kiss her again.

His cock stiffened, painfully hard in his leathers as she left the waves behind and sauntered towards him, every naked inch of her glistening with droplets of water that he wanted to lick and kiss away so he could taste the salt on her warm skin.

He groaned and palmed the bulge, trying to find some relief as she slowed her pace, taunting him just as he thought she would hurry into his arms. His breath stuttered as he imagined his hand to be her delicate one and rubbed himself, barely resisting the urge to grind against his palm as his need flared hotter, turning his blood to molten fire in his veins.

Her green-to-blue gaze dropped to his hand and darkened, the desire that shone in it beckoning him.

His female needed.

On a low growl, he closed the distance between them, swept her into his arms and seized her mouth in a hard kiss. She moaned softly, the sweet sound stirring the powerful need to please her that crashed over him, stealing control of him. His female needed and he would do all in his power to ensure she found the pleasure she desired.

He tucked her to his chest and scanned the beach, froze as his eyes landed on a smooth slab of rock near the shore, one that rose to waist height. He teleported there and leaned her over the rock, covering her with his body. A groan tore from his lips as her legs fell open and his hips slipped into the cradle of them. Her knees brushed his bare waist, scalding him with the heat of her, with the thought of where he was nestled.

The need he could feel in her grew, tugging at a part of him that demanded total obedience, had him aching to satisfy her, as if his life depended upon her finding the release she needed.

He broke away from her lips, loath to leave them but aware she needed him elsewhere. He swore he would kiss her again later, would take his time over it, savouring the way her lips brushed his and how she teased his with her tongue, tracing it over his lower one to drive him mad.

His hands shook as he planted them against the rock on either side of her waist, entire body trembling as need flooded him, an explosive combination of desire to please her and a desire to find some relief of his own. It had been too long since he had taken a female, and gods, he wanted to be inside her, but her pleasure came first. Every instinct he possessed demanded that.

Tegan lifted his right hand and brushed the tangled threads of her damp hair from her breast, groaned low in his throat as he revealed the dusky peak and it stiffened, dark against her pale skin.

He gently stroked his fingers over the pert bead.

She shivered and moaned, arched towards him as her face contorted, her breath leaving her in a sweet gasp.

He dipped his head and captured her nipple, suckled it slowly, swirling his tongue around it as he supported himself on his right hand and used his left one to brush her hair from her other breast. He pinched that nipple, eliciting another cry from her as her need rose, her breaths coming quicker.

He was the one who moaned as her hands tangled in his hair, twisting the lengths around it, and gripped it fiercely before releasing him. His entire body quaked as she skimmed her fingertips over the sides of his head, stroking the base of his horns. He tried to focus on what he was doing but it was impossible as she teased him, had thrill after thrill tripping down his spine, ratcheting up his need to find pleasure with her and pushing him dangerously close to the edge.

"Suki," he groaned, warning her that she was destroying him with that soft and teasing touch, was liable to push him over the edge.

She didn't repent.

She curled her fingers around his horns and gripped them, a brief flash of her strength that had lightning striking inside him and a growl peeling from his lips.

His female was strong.

Demanding as she steered him lower.

He gently removed her hands from his horns, because he wanted to pleasure her, to give her the relief she needed, and it was impossible to focus on that when she was driving him wild.

She huffed and pouted down at him when he looked up the glorious length of her body.

He chased it away by dropping kisses on her stomach, easing lower with each one.

A wicked smile replaced it.

Gods, she was incredible as she reached her arms above her head, draping them over the rounded rock, baring herself to him. Trusting him.

On a low growl, he pressed his palms to her inner thighs and opened them, revealing her feminine core. It glistened with the desire he could feel in her, need that pounded inside him, and he couldn't hold back the low snarl that rolled up his throat as he stared at her pink softness.

"My female needs."

He felt those words should shake him, but all he experienced was immense pleasure as he stroked his thumbs up her plump lips and scented her desire, felt her tremble beneath his caress and heard her gasp.

He eased her legs further apart, not wanting to hurt her with his horns but unable to stop them from flaring as he slowly closed the distance between them, as awareness of what he was about to do drummed in his blood.

The first stroke of his tongue over her flesh had her jacking up off the rock.

"Tegan," she gasped, thighs quivering against him.

He groaned and licked her again, unable to get enough of the sweet and warmly-spiced taste of her that continued here, drugged him and had him aching for another fix. He wedged her thighs apart and devoured her, drinking down her cries of supplication as she pressed her feet against the rock and raised her hips to meet his tongue.

The weather shifted as she strained for release, as her pleasure rose. The world darkened, the wind buffeting him as waves broke against the rock, washed around his knees where they pressed into the sand.

He didn't care.

Neither did Suki.

She rocked against his face, seeking more that he gave to her as he swirled his tongue around her pert nub, tasting her desire. He stroked it with the flat of his tongue, teased it with the tip, and caressed the length of her, from her core to her bead, relishing every cry that burst from her lips, every plea and demand for more. The scent of her desire grew heavier in the stormy air, the need he could sense in her reaching a crescendo.

He stroked a finger over her slick flesh and shuddered as he breached her core with the tip and pressed deep into her. Her heat scalded him, had his aching shaft kicking against his trousers as she gripped him, so hot and tight that he almost came just from the feel of her gloving him.

He growled against her and pumped her with his finger, careful not to hurt her with his short claws. She tightened, ripping another groan from him as she pushed her hips up, riding his tongue and his finger, a wanton and beautiful sight as he gazed up at her.

Lightning struck around her.

She flung her head back and screamed as her hips jerked upwards, body quivering and milking his finger, slick and hot around him.

Gods, his female was beautiful in the throes of release.

The image of her shattered, replaced with the dark canopy that stretched across the top of his four-poster bed, and he growled as he squeezed his eyes shut and tried to recapture the dream.

Fragments of it replayed in his mind, teasing snippets that had his already painfully hard length growing even harder.

On a low groan, he pushed the covers of his bed away and skimmed his hand down his shaft. He draped his free hand over his eyes to shut the world out as he thought about Suki, about how she had come apart in his dream, and stroked himself to a swift completion, spilling all over his bare stomach.

He breathed hard when he was done, remained laying on his bed for the gods only knew how long, his mind whirling with thoughts of Suki, his body still aching for more.

In the dark stillness, a seed of suspicion formed.

He immediately discounted it. It had been decades since he had bedded a female, and he was attracted to Suki. She was alluring, mysterious, and knew how to tempt him. She was the first female in centuries who hadn't thrown herself at him. It was little wonder he had dreamed of her, taking in it the pleasure she had denied him in reality.

But that seed remained, began to plant roots even as he tried to deny it.

The way he reacted every time she looked at him. The fact he wanted to hurt any male who so much as looked at her. The powerful need to be near her. To see her.

To please her.

It couldn't mean what he thought it did.

He shook his head. He wanted her and reacted the way he did because of it.

Not because she was something to him.

Something incredible. Special.

He would prove that to himself before he fooled himself into thinking she was something she wasn't.

He used his discarded shirt to wipe himself off, swung his legs over the edge of his large bed and stood. He padded across his bedroom, past the windows that overlooked the courtyard of the castle and the black mountains beyond. A cool breeze kissed his bare skin as he paused and looked out of the last one.

He had eight meetings today.

All of them were going to have to wait for another day.

He needed to see Suki and it needed to be now. He would prove that she was just another female, one more enchanting than the rest, but nothing special to him. She couldn't be.

Or could she?

He pushed that question aside as he tossed his soiled shirt in a basket below the window, near the door to his bathing room. The painted cream walls of his bathroom added a brightness fuelled by the row of arched windows to his right that allowed the light of the elven realm to flood into it. He had painted it himself with provisions brought by his aides from the mortal world, and although it was flaking a little now, it was still preferable to the drab blackness of the rest of the walls in the castle.

Tegan crossed to the stone sink mounted on the wall below a slightly crooked mirror, grabbed the pitcher of water that stood on a tray on the wooden cupboard beside it and poured it into the bowl. He splashed the water on his face and chest, washed himself off and dried using the black towel hanging over the railing opposite what passed as a toilet in his world. He curled a lip at it. One day, he would renovate the entire castle using technology from the mortal world.

He had heard of things called showers, a device for bathing standing upright. He intended to install one in every bathing room in the castle as soon as possible so his kingdom was the first to have such a luxury.

Demons loved war, whether it was done on a battlefield or not. Being the victor in beating other realms in the race to improve their kingdoms and make advancements through the use of technology or otherwise was almost as satisfying as beating them in a war.

Tegan intended to completely annihilate his competition in that respect.

King Thorne had beaten him to trialling the use of wind turbines as a possible method of producing electricity, but Tegan would beat him to implementing them on a widespread scale. Just as he would beat the male and every other king to improving education, sanitation and everything else.

He grabbed his latest book as he passed the small table that sat beside the black armchair near his unlit fireplace and tossed it onto the rumpled furs on his bed as he crossed the room to his wardrobe. A smile curled his lips. His aides had washed his black shirt and he had been irritated when he had discovered they had done such a thing, removing Suki's scent from it, but now he could wear it again. She had liked the sight of him in it and he wanted to see her eyes light up again, ached to have her gaze glued to him in a way that revealed her desire and how much she wanted him.

He tugged a fresh pair of black leathers on, tied them over his crotch, and pulled on his shirt. The buttons were easier this time. He was getting the hang of mortal clothing. He pushed his feet into his boots, wriggled his left one when it got stuck and growled as he bent to loosen the laces. He tied them again once his foot was secure and grabbed his book on the way past the bed again, a need to see his reflection carrying him back into his bathing room.

His hair was a mess.

He wetted the black strands and combed it with his fingers, slicking it back down the middle of his head to leave the sides clear. His right hand went to his horn and he preened it as he inspected his reflection, ensuring he looked good.

He looked damned nervous.

His left foot twitched as he picked up a cloth and rubbed it over his polished black horns, from the thick root above his pointed ears, down the curve to the sharp tip near his lobes. They flared a little as thoughts of seeing Suki drifted into his mind, pulling up images of her from his dream. His cock jerked and he pushed the thoughts back out as he focused on making sure the gold inlaid into his horns gleamed.

He would see her soon enough and he would realise that he was mistaken and was reading into the way he reacted to her.

She was just another female.

Not something special.

Because he wasn't that lucky.

CHAPTER 11

Tegan opened his portal and dropped into it, hugging his book to his chest as the dark engulfed him. When it receded, he stood on the cobbled road at the entrance of a fae town hidden inside an enormous cavern beneath a mountain range, one that had changed dramatically over the centuries since he had last visited.

The fae town where Suki lived.

His mood lifted but took a sharp downwards turn as he realised something.

She lived here, but he didn't know where she lived, and the town was far larger than he recalled, hundreds of buildings crammed into the space.

And he had no method of calling her.

He considered teleporting to Underworld and using the phone there, but now that he was here, he didn't want to leave. He wanted to explore this place Suki called home and while he was at it, he would ask around and discover her location.

Someone was bound to know where she lived.

His mood took another black turn at that.

Males would know where she lived.

He bared his fangs at a passing group of males dressed in white shirts and tan trousers, unsure what species they were or whether they even knew the succubi who lived in the town, and uncaring about either of those things.

The thought that the males in the town might know Suki had rage kindling in his blood, his horns curling around and growing, and a black need to kill every male present rolling through him.

That seed of suspicion buried its roots deeper.

Right into his heart.

Could she be his fated one?

He didn't want to get his hopes up, even when all the signs were there. He felt possessive of her, protective, and felt a powerful need to please her. He felt as if he was slowly losing his mind whenever they were apart and longed to be near her again.

Was it possible she was his one true mate?

Could he be so blessed to find his fated one in a female he found attractive, who pleased him at every turn, made him burn for her because she was beautiful, and interesting, and amusing?

He had never been lucky. Not on a battlefield, where he had come close to losing his head more than a hundred times, and not with his family, and not even as a king, a role he had never wanted and one that had felt like the worse sort of luck when the crown had landed on his head.

But if his years of poor luck had brought him to this, to Suki being his fated one, then they had been worth it. He would gladly accept bad luck in his life if she was his one piece of good luck. He couldn't ask for anything better than having her as his mate.

A group of female witches passed him, laughing and shoving at each other, their drab black dresses brushing the floor as they walked the cobbled road, heading towards a broad thoroughfare that cut through the town.

A vibrant artery that was busy with people, all of whom seemed in an equally jovial mood.

The celebration Suki had mentioned?

Curiosity gripped him and he found himself moving forwards, following the witches as they branched right, heading towards a district where the two and three storey houses were painted white and had roofs that looked like dragon scales. The green, blue and gold glazed tiles undulated over semi-circular windows in the roofs and followed a sweeping roofline, where the tiles were pointed or curved at the apex.

On the ground level of every house, a colourful canopy stretched out over the road, the space below it packed with copper stills and clay pots, and all manner of other things. Witches stood by some of them, calling out to people who were passing in both directions, attempting to lure them to see their wares.

"Love potion?" One elderly female muttered low as he passed and he glanced at her, his brow furrowing as he realised she was speaking to him. She jerked her chin a few times, an attempt to beckon him that he resisted. She grinned. "You don't look like you need one, but I see a glimmer of something in you. Like you want love."

Did he want love?

He paused, stopping facing her, causing the male behind him to almost bump into him. Tegan flashed his fangs when the male muttered something about watching where he was going. He had been watching, this male hadn't. His gaze returned to the device the male held as he hurried away. A phone. He was tempted to go after the male and ask to use it, but remained where he was.

The witch continued to grin, her worn pale face gaining more lines as her smile stretched a little wider, and her dark eyes revealed she thought him to be a sure bet.

Because he looked as if he wanted someone to love him?

If he purchased a potion from her, could it make Suki love him?

He immediately shoved that thought aside. He didn't want her to love him because a potion had made her feel that way about him, just as he didn't want her to love him because he was a king. If she could come to love him, he wanted it to be real. He needed to know she loved him because of who he was, not what he was or what he had given her.

He shook his head, went to leave and hesitated, staring at the cobbles beneath his boots.

He looked across his right shoulder at her again. "Do you know where the succubi live?"

It was safer to ask a female than it was to approach the males about it. He wasn't sure he would be able to keep his mood in check if he asked males where the succubi lived. Although many succubi lived within a clan house, and Suki had sisters, he would imagine every one of those males knew her intimately, that the succubus they called to mind when he asked about them was her and her alone.

His horns curled at just the thought of it, flaring past the tips of his ears and rising up towards his temples as his fangs emerged and claws lengthened.

The witch's eyes widened and she hastily pointed towards the other end of the curved road. He looked there, and when he looked back at her, intending to ask her exactly where in that direction the succubi lived, she was gone and the purple door of the white house slammed shut.

He cursed low.

He had forgotten that witches were always jumpy around demons for some reason, constantly viewed them as a threat even though he couldn't recall a time when his kind had ever been a danger to them.

Although, there was that rumour that a witch would lose her powers if a demon spilled betwixt her thighs.

Was that rumour true?

He shrugged and moved on, his thoughts shifting course as he took in the different wares on sale at each stall that lined the sweeping road, took in the varying scents that filled the air near each one, rising from the bubbling copper pots and stills. His ears twitched, the sound of merriment reaching them as he neared the end of the road.

It opened out into a square lined with imposing dark grey stone buildings, each at least three-storeys tall. To the right of him, a huge clock tower rose high into the cavern, the illuminated face of it revealing the hour was early, barely gone midday.

Or midnight?

No, he had left the castle during the daylight hours, and this part of the mortal world seemed aligned with the time in his realm.

His stomach grumbled, putting in that it certainly believed it to be time for food.

He sniffed, scenting the air, and his mouth watered at the smell of roasting meat and sweet brew. He followed the tempting scent, his stomach guiding him towards the source of it, and weaved through the thick crowd that had gathered at the entrance of the square.

A few demons glanced his way, their pale golden horns and cerulean leathers revealing they were from the First Realm. When their blue eyes widened, he stared them down, aware they knew who he was. The urge to hide his horns ran through him but he denied it. These males wouldn't dare bother him. The worst that would happen from this encounter was the First King would know he had been to the mortal realm, and that was of little consequence.

It wasn't forbidden for demon kings to leave their realms.

Although, his advisers and the court had made him feel as if it was.

The males wisely moved on and he moved deeper into the crowd, his focus shifting back to his hunt for food. Once he had filled his belly, he would search north of the square for the succubi house.

A groan threatened to peel from his lips when the crowd ahead of him parted, revealing a wooden stall with an entire animal roasting on a spit near it. The animal was small, only half his size, but it smelled delicious. He drifted towards it, lips parting, stomach grumbling, and stopped near it, staring at it as it rotated above the flames, the juices that dripped from it sizzling upon contact with the fire.

Someone had placed fruit in its mouth, a ripe red apple.

He pulled a face at that.

What sort of animals mixed fruit with meat?

"You want to buy some pork or just stare at it? Guessing you have money." A snippy female voice broke into his delicious reverie and he frowned at the owner of it, a portly female dressed in a stained white apron, her dark hair twirled into a bun at the back of her head.

"I will take some of this pork." He pointed to it, reached down to his hip and took his coin purse from it. He opened it as the female cut a chunk of the meat from the animal and studied his options.

Suki had said fae towns didn't take plastic.

He dug out a two gold coins, sure the portion of meat would be more than such a small sum, and showed them to the female. "Is this enough?"

Her eyes drifted down him, a flicker of interest lighting them. A smile teased her lips when she reached his hand and the coins.

"I do love a big man with an appetite." She plucked the two coins from his fingers. "This much, eh?"

He nodded, unsure what it would get him, but curious to see. When she went back to the animal and pulled off the entire back leg of the beast, his eyes widened and his stomach growled louder.

Now they were talking.

"I require brew too." He couldn't tear his eyes away from his hoard as she slapped it down in front of him, juices running over the wide flimsy tray she had placed it on.

Two coins got him almost a quarter of the pork.

If pork was a tasty animal, he would see about importing some into his kingdom once the farms were up and running. He was sure that they had to be cheaper alive than they were dead. He could have entire farms of pork at each village, enough to feed everyone.

With the selection of grains he had decided to invest in too, never again would his people have to starve.

"See Rod. He has the best brew in the town." She gestured to a bearded male two stalls over, nearer to a raised stone pathway that people were walking along, heading towards steps that led down into the square.

Tegan nodded, tucked his book under his left arm, took hold of his bounty and went to see the male.

He offered a gold coin. "I require brew."

The dark-haired male looked him up and down. "Demon, eh? I have just the thing. Your boys love this stuff."

He turned to one of the barrels stacked behind him, picked up the largest pewter tankard Tegan had ever seen and placed it beneath the tap.

As Tegan stared at the amber liquid running into the tankard in a seemingly endless stream, he realised something.

Gods, he loved fae towns.

Two coins for a quarter of a pork. One coin for a huge mug of brew that smelled sweet and strong.

Today, he truly feasted like a king.

The male slammed the tankard down on the wooden counter of the stall, causing the creamy foam to slosh over the sides, and Tegan handed him the coin and grabbed the brew, eager to taste it and the pork.

He moved to the wide raised walkway that lined the front of several towering grey stone buildings, placed his food and brew down at the edge of the path, and easily pulled himself up onto it. He picked up the leg of the animal and bit into it.

Gods, it was delicious. Juicy, sweet, tasting faintly of herbs and some spices. He swallowed it down with a swig of the brew and groaned. He needed to steal these people from this town and have them work in his castle kitchens. He would never complain about having to attend a feast if he could eat this pork and drink this mead.

He lost track of time as he ate and drank, watching the bustling square. Another group of demons passed him, their blue-grey horns marking them as from the Seventh Realm this time. Their eyes flickered to his horns and they spoke with each other in hushed tones.

The temptation to hide his horns rushed through him again, not because he didn't want these males to know who he was, but because he feared that somehow word that he was a king might reach Suki. He didn't want her to know. Not yet.

He knew he couldn't keep it a secret from her forever, but he needed to keep it a secret from her for now.

Guilt writhed in his stomach, a voice at the back of his mind hissing that he was lying to her, and that if she was what he thought she was, it was an unstable foundation for their relationship going forwards.

It wasn't a lie. It was a simple omission of all the facts.

She hadn't asked him directly what he did. She had offered suggestions as to his occupation, but he didn't recall her ever asking him to tell her what he did.

He set aside the bones of the pork, drank the last of his brew, and licked his fingers clean before crossing his legs and leaning his elbow on his bent knee. He watched the world go by, picking out people to follow and study, enjoying the festivities as the crowd grew louder and music began to play.

Everywhere he looked, it was colourful and vibrant, the people varied, their clothing all different to each other. It was a world away from his kingdom, where everything was black and sombre, and all he saw each day were demons.

It seemed like a dream, and gods, that made him realise how deeply he resented his brother.

He had never wanted to be king.

Edyn had promised him several times in their years together that it would never happen, that he was safe from the throne, the most recent time being the night he had argued with his older brother about the truce, speaking out against it.

Edyn had assured him that he would never have to take the throne, because the truce would mean an end to the fighting in their kingdom and therefore the king would no longer be in danger.

And then Edyn had let his guard down and gotten himself killed.

Tegan rubbed his right horn, agitated now as he recalled that night, how his entire world had shattered on storming into Edyn's bedroom and finding him bleeding out, beyond saving.

His gut clenched, familiar guilt stirring in it. He shouldn't resent his brother, but gods, he couldn't stop himself from being angry whenever he thought about Edyn. He was sure that resentment over the crown being placed on his head would have faded over the centuries if the method of Edyn's death hadn't propelled the court advisers into placing Tegan under strict guard and shutting down his ability to go anywhere without their consent.

Now that he was free of their rule, reclaiming his independence, would the anger he felt towards Edyn lessen, allowing his heart to heal?

He chuckled mirthlessly as it dawned on him that the one most able to answer that question for him was Edyn.

Edyn had been a sage king, and a good brother. How many times had he talked Tegan out of a mood, or convinced him that going to war over something trivial wasn't the way to do things? Ryker had always stoked the fire in Tegan. Edyn had always quenched it.

If he had ever needed Edyn's advice, it was now.

About Suki.

He was sure his brother would be able to tell straight away whether she was his true fated mate or not.

He scanned the crowd, his senses reaching out, seeking her familiar scent in case she was in the square, enjoying the celebration like the hundreds of people who moved from stall to stall, stood in groups and drank, or were enjoying the music.

It all fascinated him. He tried to take it all in, but so much was happening that it was impossible. Overwhelming. The last time he had come to this fae town, it had been far smaller and much bleaker, a place where fae and immortals had gathered to hide from the human world, lurking in the shadows to avoid discovery and persecution.

Now, it was alive, bustling with activity and all manner of species, filled with traders and families, and travellers. It was incredible.

He could see why Suki had chosen to live in such a place.

He had made his private floors in his castle comfortable, adding colour where he could and small luxuries, but he couldn't replicate this.

The earth and rock in his kingdom were black, the trees the darkest shade of green, matching what little grass there was. All the buildings had been constructed of the obsidian stone quarried from the mountains and his castle was an imposing fortress, one designed to strike fear and doubt into any invading forces.

Compared with the hotchpotch buildings in the fae town, and the colourful roofs and canopies of the witches' district, it was bleak and grim.

The clothes his people wore were black, with accents of white and some gold for the noble demons. The clothes these people wore, the clothes Suki wore, were a rainbow in comparison. A maelstrom of colours and styles, adding to the individuality of the people who wore them.

His mind conjured an image of Suki, no difficult feat since he couldn't get her out of his thoughts. He pictured her colourful ocean-like hair and her dazzling eyes, and her bright risqué clothes that hugged and revealed her curves.

What would she make of his world after living in this one?

Would it look like a dark, grim and forbidding place to her?

A place where she wouldn't want to live?

He looked around him, taking in his surroundings, and wanted to growl as something hit him and had his mood faltering.

After living in such a vibrant place, Suki would never want to live in his world.

CHAPTER 12

Suki ignored the catcalls of the men outside the succubus house as she headed towards the road that cut down past one of the shifter compounds, a high-walled affair in black stone that suited the panther pride on the other side. Growls and snarls came from within. The usual.

She wasn't sure there was a time of day or night when the panthers were quiet. They were always brawling over something. Sometimes, living in a house sandwiched between a panther pride and a werewolf pack was tiring. She was surprised she managed to get a wink of sleep most nights.

Especially the nights the vampires who lived on the western side of the town, beyond the werewolf pack's mansion, decided to stroll past the succubus house to reach the town square. They did it on purpose. The vampires seemed to think the werewolves were on their turf.

Stupid considering the werewolf pack had moved in shortly after her family had according to the clan's history books, and the vampires hadn't built their first dwelling until a century after that.

Of course, vampires were never in the wrong. She had met enough of their kind to know that.

A few more men called out to her and she scowled as one of them devoured her with his gaze. She hadn't exactly dressed for attention today. After putting up with several rounds of her sisters playing 'why Suki sucks', she had thrown on an old dark purple leather corset that covered her from hip to over her breasts and a black pleated skirt that reached mid-way down her thigh and revealed nothing, not even a hint of her dull black shorts she wore beneath, coupled with a pair of knee-high thick-soled violet leather boots. She hadn't even done her make-up and her hair had only been finger-combed to death, was still a mess in places where she had dozed on it during her morning nap.

Good gods, what a delicious nap it had been.

Her guard had completely dropped because of it and she had walked right into a group of her sisters as they returned from hunting, and all of them had let rip, detailing how they had seduced several men each to feed the clan and asking what she had been doing to provide for her family, and why it looked as if she had been holed up in the house just sleeping while the rest of them were busy working.

If she could feed in a dream, she would have fed well on the one she'd had of Tegan.

Her sisters were right though, and she wasn't doing anything to strengthen her family. She was sucking energy from it like a parasite, just as they had accused.

But soon she would pour energy into it. She just needed to figure a few things out first.

She shoved Tegan back out of her head, but it didn't stop fire from sweeping through her, devastating her ability to concentrate. She was meant to be finding out more about shadowed males before she dared see him again, but at the rate she was going, she wasn't going to last more than a few hours before the constant craving she felt for him had her searching for a way to get in touch with him.

It had taken him several days to call last time and he was busy. She doubted she would see him before the weekend, which meant she had time to focus on discovering more about shadowed males.

If they turned out to be as dangerous as everyone at the clan made them out to be, well, she wasn't sure which path she would take. She still wanted to fit in at the clan, and he was the best way of making that happen. Was she willing to take the necessary risks though?

Would it be worth it?

Some part of her screamed that the risk would be worth it if she could see him again.

She silenced that part, because she feared what it meant.

She tilted her face up to the ceiling of the cavern as she walked, let her eyes drift half-closed and breathed deep, attempting to push him from her mind and the other rebellious and confusing parts of her.

She savoured the smells coming from the direction of the square, filling the rest of the town with the aroma of meat, booze and sweets.

Sometimes, Suki wished she could taste sweets. Every time a celebration was held in the town, she roamed the stalls that sold confectionary and cakes, delighting in all the colours and shapes, and the smells. Oh gods, the smells!

Two years ago, she had convinced one of her non-succubus friends, Julianna, to taste as many of the confections as possible and describe them. The witch had taken to it with gusto, ending up with a stomach-ache she had said had been worth it and a diet that had lasted weeks to shed the pounds she had gained in that one day. Since then, they met up at every celebration, spending it chatting as Julianna ate her way through the stalls.

Suki loved the town's celebrations because of it.

Spending time with Julianna was something she badly needed right now, and not just because her sisters were driving her mad again, constantly quizzing her about the man she had called Solid Eleven.

Tegan.

He was the reason she needed to meet with Julianna, was hoping that the witch was in town given the celebration was run by her kind.

Julianna knew a lot about the world, far more than just witchcraft related things. They had talked about the history of some species, mostly whichever species was leading the event they were attending. Her friend had told her all about nymphs, had spun fascinating tales about the sirens, and had filled her head with stories of the shifters.

The witch even knew about incubi.

She was hoping Julianna knew just as much about succubi and could tell her something about shadowed males like the one she had been trying not to think about all night and all day.

She pushed through the crowd to break into the busy square, tiptoed and tried to spot her friend.

Keeping her mind off Tegan was proving impossible, but she was going to manage it.

Her gaze caught on something to the right of her and she froze.

It was the most arresting, alluring and bizarrely attractive sight she had ever beheld.

No, it wasn't the hot naked perfection of an amazingly cut and carved male body.

But a burly demon sitting on the edge of the raised path that led off to her right, his head bent and thoughtful black gaze locked on the open book he held in the hand resting against his black-leather-clad knee. His muscles flexed beneath his tight black shirt as he turned a page and crossed his legs at the knee, bringing the book closer to his face and almost kicking an unfortunate passer-by in the shoulder with his heavy black boot.

The man glared at him, but he didn't notice.

A hank of the demon's black hair fell down to caress his brow and a strange and startling reaction swept through her, had her hand twitching at her side.

She ached to sweep it back.

Suki lingered, doing her best to blend into the crowd and the shadows so she could observe him unnoticed. She had never really had a chance to watch him like this, when he was unaware of her. She wanted to see how he behaved when she wasn't around, was sure she could learn more about him if she could deny the urge to go to him.

His left hand lifted. He ploughed his fingers through his hair, brushing it back, and preened his horns.

Horns!

Good gods, they looked hot on him.

She stared, mouth gaping open as her eyes widened, mind growing hazy as her body heated.

They were black, and incredibly smooth for a demon's horns. Had they been polished?

Something glinted and she squinted, trying to make out what had reflected the light as he had lifted his head slightly, a furrow forming between his black eyebrows as his lips pursed thoughtfully. Something gold? She wasn't sure.

She tracked the shape of his horns, from where they started above his pointed ears, to the curve that swept down and the sharp tips near his temples. Normally, a demon's horns ended at the lobes of their ears when they were calm. Was he aroused or angry?

Her mouth dried out as a need built inside her, one she had to fight to deny and even then, she felt as if she might lose the battle. She wanted to close the distance between them and stroke her fingers down his horns to know if they were as smooth as they appeared, and whether it would affect him.

She had heard that demons liked having their horns touched.

Would it make him horny?

She grinned at that. *Horny.*

Suki lazily soaked up the sight of him as he turned the page, his black gaze scanning it. Heck, he was delicious. Her odd demon. He was so engrossed in his book, was seemingly oblivious to all the attention he was getting.

Her eyebrows pinched and dipped.

Attention from a *lot* of women.

That had her moving at a clipped pace towards him, pressing through the crowd whenever it closed in front of her, attempting to hinder her.

He stilled halfway through turning the page.

His nostrils flared and his head lifted, his black gaze locking straight on her to send an electric thrill bolting through her veins.

He had scented her.

The thought he already recognised her scent had fire rushing through her, turning her blood molten as she felt a little giddy. She chastised herself. She shouldn't be feeling anything close to that, she knew that deep in her heart, but for some reason he deeply affected her, far deeper than any man before him had.

He was dangerous, the tales of men with shadowed auras was right about that, but she just couldn't keep away from him.

There was something magnetic about him. It drew her to him and she was powerless to resist, found herself drifting towards him even though she wasn't aware she was moving, was only aware of him as he stared deep into her eyes, his beginning to brighten with that entrancing corona of purple.

"What are you doing here?" Was that her voice shaking like a mortal teen talking to her first crush in one of those awful made-for-TV movies her sisters watched?

"I came to see you." He lowered his book to rest on his knee and straightened, looking down at her as she stood on the cobbles below him.

He had?

"You came to see me?" She couldn't quite bring herself to believe it.

No man had ever come to see her before. Another first for her.

He nodded, his expression sober, showing her that he meant it. "You said you lived in this town. I thought I might surprise you."

He had certainly managed that.

"How long have you been here?" She glanced at the discarded paper plate and pewter tankard beside him and her eyes widened at the remnants of his food. That was a lot of bones. "Did you eat half a pig?"

"Pig?" He frowned at the bones. "Pork. I ate a pork."

She stifled a giggle, covering her hand with her mouth, and shivered when he scowled at her, hot from head to toe in a heartbeat. Heavens, he looked too damned handsome when he glared at her.

"You ate a pig." She gestured to the plate. "Pork is the meat that comes from a pig."

"A pig." He nodded, as if filing that word away.

She had forgotten there was a lot he didn't know about this world, although she had expected him to know what a pig was.

"Didn't visit many farms the last time you were here in the mortal world, huh?" She poked his knee, causing it to sway to his left, and wished she had chosen to walk up the steps that led to the six-foot-high path he was sitting on so she could sit beside him.

She felt tiny standing on the cobbles, didn't reach anywhere close to the height of the wall he was sitting on let alone his head.

"No." He looked down at the drop and then at her. He held his right hand out to her. When she didn't take it, he murmured, "You look as if you want a lift."

"I could just go around." She did want a lift, but the fact he could see it in her unsettled her for some reason.

Was she being too unguarded around him or could he just read her like the open book balanced on his knee?

Going around seemed the safer option.

He didn't give her a chance to move. He leaned towards her as she went to tuck her hair behind her ear, caught hold of her wrist and pulled her up as if she weighed nothing, lifting her high into the air to settle her beside him on the wall.

Damn, he was strong.

His gaze raked over her as she smoothed the pleats of her black skirt over her thighs to avoid flashing her panties at the crowd as they glanced her way, her fingers shaking as heat rolled through her.

She had known demons were strong, but something about the way he had effortlessly lifted her had every feminine instinct in her rising to the fore. She shivered from the onslaught as it filled her with the urge to palm his muscles through his black shirt and ask him to lift her again, or do something else to flash his strength at her.

Stupid biology.

She was nowhere near her fertile stage, something that only happened once every fifty or so years. There was no reason for her to be getting all quivery over being around a powerful male.

"You could have asked me out to lunch," she said to fill the silence as she pieced herself back together, shutting down her biological urges until only one remained, one she would never be able to switch off.

Partly because she wanted him so badly she was close to screaming whenever they were together, or tackling him to the ground and riding him until he surrendered to her, and partly because she was a succubus and she was hungry.

Which meant she was in a permanent skirting-the-edge-of-horny state.

He released her wrist and scrubbed his hand around the back of his neck, a beautifully awkward edge to his dark eyes that told her everything he wouldn't.

He hadn't known where to find her.

"You were waiting here." She couldn't stop herself from putting that out there, even when it caused his cheeks to pinken and he looked away from her, stealing the delicious sight of his face from her. "You were waiting for me."

He shrugged stiffly. "I asked a witch where you might live and she was vague, and I did not wish to ask anyone else who might know."

His voice pitched downwards at the end, becoming a vicious snarl that spoke volumes. He hadn't wanted to ask someone who might know where the succubi lived because that someone would be a man.

Had he been imagining the worst? What was the worst in his opinion? That the man he asked would know her personally?

Intimately?

The violet in his eyes flared brighter, pushing back the black, and his horns curled, drawing her gaze there.

She stared at them, seeing for the first time that it had been gold that had glimmered in the light. Patterns had been carved into the polished onyx of his horns, inlaid with gold that looked as smooth. The fine detailing in the design bewitched her, had her following each swirl to the point or onwards to the next graceful arc. She had thought his horns sexy before, but now she itched with the need to reach out and run her fingers down them, hungered to know whether he would feel it.

And whether he would find it pleasurable.

His hand lifted between them, he tensed, and dropped it to his lap, an awkward gesture that screamed at her that he didn't like her staring at his horns.

Silence stretched between them as she fought to find the strength to drag her eyes away from the temptation of his horns, because she didn't want him to feel awkward around her. She had enjoyed their easy camaraderie the previous times they had been together and she wanted to experience that again.

So she searched for something to say.

Her eyes fell to the book balanced on his black-leather-clad knee.

She cocked her head to one side, her wavy hair falling away from her violet leather-and-lace corset.

"Is that the same book, the one about windmills?" She peered closer, trying to read the title printed across the top of each page.

"No." He reluctantly revealed the cover, and it wasn't a different book about windmills as she expected.

It was a book about hydroelectricity.

"You're *really* into renewable energy." She tried to grab the book.

He closed it, pinned it to his knee and drummed his short claws on it. "It is the only viable sort of energy in Hell."

Suki took the plunge, sure she was about to get lost and make herself look like an uneducated idiot, but willing to take that risk. "Have you learned anything that might work for the Second Realm?"

Surprise flitted across his face as he turned it towards her. Shocked that she wanted to talk about his book?

"You don't have to," she quickly said. "I was just interested."

That hand went to the back of his neck again as he cleared his throat. Charmingly awkward. Devastatingly confident. A contradiction that she was starting to like about him.

"You don't like that I keep catching you reading, why?" She wanted to bring her knees up and hold them, but she also didn't want to flash her modest panties at everyone in the crowd, so she settled for slowly swinging her legs, letting the heels of her violet boots bang off the dark grey stone beneath her.

He cleared his throat again, looked down at the book in his lap, a myriad of emotions crossing his face, so swiftly she couldn't decipher any of them.

But she did get the feeling that he was torn. Between what? Telling her something and keeping it secret? Or was it that he wasn't really sure how she might react and it was unsettling him for some reason?

It struck her that he was awkward about the reading thing because he believed she was liable to tease him about it. Had others teased him? She could see why they might. He was a demon. They weren't exactly known for being bookish and educated. They were known for being warriors and warmongers, dedicated to battle not books.

She eyed him closely, studying his profile as he stared at the book, clearly conflicted. Was he ashamed that he enjoyed reading?

That softer part of her whispered to let it go, but the part that needed to know more about her sexy enigma pushed her to keep going, because she wanted to get to the bottom of him.

She glanced at his backside.

A fine bottom it was too.

"I am… I am not used to people wishing to talk about this kind of thing." He lifted the book and let it fall back to his knees.

So, his friends weren't bookish like him then. She jotted that down in her mental file about him.

"I'm interested." She didn't falter when he glanced at her out of the corner of his eye, his filled with disbelief. "Honestly. I've never met anyone who reads like you do."

He flinched. She cursed. She hadn't meant to make him even more awkward. She had wanted to make him relax about the whole reading thing.

"I just want to better the lives of those in the kingdom," he grumbled and then lifted his head, his awkwardness falling away as his dark irises gained a glimmer, a spark that had her relaxing as she realised she hadn't messed up. At least not badly. "Electricity would be a huge leap forwards, and although thermal plants are not feasible due to the lack of such activity in the kingdom, I believe it possible to harness both wind and water to bring power to many of the villages and towns."

There went her hot geek. She twisted towards him, lifted her left foot onto the walkway and rested her elbow on her bent knee. She propped her chin up on her palm and smiled as his pitch-dark eyes sparkled, deep purple stars flickering in them.

"After we met, I put forward a plan I had been working on for the last four seasons, and the court have reluctantly accepted the proposal. I am hoping to see work begin soon. We must gather all the necessary components and it is possible we will need to hire in contractors or at least send some men to learn in secret from mortals before we can build anything… but it is a start." He was engrossed again, talking her ear off, his eyes on her and only her, and damn she was loving it.

Being the centre of his attention was exciting, warming and downright wonderful, lifted her spirits like nothing else could and had her wanting to ask him a thousand questions to keep his gaze on her, even if she didn't understand the answers.

"How many places are you planning to build these electricity plants?" She tried to imagine how big a demon kingdom was and failed. Larger than the United Kingdom?

"Around a dozen or so at first. We have funding in place for the first seven, but I believe I can stretch the coin to cover twelve. Small ventures to see what will work and what will fail. King Thorne of the Third Realm has areas with wind turbines and they are working well, generating power for farms that allow the females to grow vegetables and fruit for themselves."

She frowned. "Females need fruit and veggies?"

He nodded.

"All females within the kingdom are from other species. The blood curse means all demons in our realms are male. Our fated ones are therefore always from outside the species and require sustenance of different sorts to us for the most part," he said in a matter of fact tone.

A chill tumbled down her spine.

All fated mates of demons were females from other species?

How the hell hadn't she known that?

She swallowed, a vain attempt to wet her suddenly parched mouth, and stared at him. It wasn't possible he was anything other than a conquest to her. Succubi didn't have mates. She was just being jittery. It was common knowledge that her kind couldn't have that sort of relationship with someone. Love wasn't possible for her species and neither was finding a mate. Her kind bred with suitable strong males infrequently, whenever the clan agreed they needed to increase their numbers. It was done systematically, not because of love or mates.

The relief that swept through her was short-lived.

Because it meant that somewhere out there was Tegan's fated mate. The woman he would probably drop everything for, would do anything to make belong to him.

Including ditching whoever he was with at the time she entered the sphere of his biological radar.

She reminded herself that succubi couldn't have relationships like others enjoyed, so it was a moot point anyway. Whatever poor sap was dumped by him when his mate rolled on by, it wouldn't be her. This was a seduction, plain and simple. It ended the moment she had bagged and tagged him, and her clan knew what she had achieved.

It was a means to an end.

She wanted her clan to accept her, and he was her method of achieving that. That was all he was to her.

So why was she having to think of a thousand ways to convince herself of that?

She struggled to tune into what he was saying as his mouth moved soundlessly to her ears, the ringing in her mind and the strange tight feeling in her chest stealing her focus.

Why did the thought of another female being held in his arms, kissed by him, hurt like a bitch?

CHAPTER 13

"Suki?" Tegan murmured, a frown furrowing his brow as he lowered his head to look into her eyes. "Your smile disappeared. Something is wrong? I am talking too much, aren't I?"

Suki shook her head, swallowed the lump in her throat and forced a smile. His frown didn't go anywhere. If anything, it deepened, and he looked as if he was considering touching her cheek. To do what? Chase away the tears that had that damned lump in her throat returning?

"Sorry," she muttered and shrugged. "I'm a bit tired today. Cranky too. My sisters have been winding me up and pressing my buttons."

A reasonable excuse for her shift in mood.

When his hand lifted and he looked in danger of touching her, she scrambled for something to talk about that would distract him from her mood, because she wasn't strong enough to handle him touching her right now. She craved him too deeply, and the unsettling thing was it wasn't sex she wanted from him, it wasn't his energy.

It was the tenderness that would be behind that touch.

She couldn't let him affect her like that. This was meant to be a seduction. He was going to be her host. The build up to that was just happening at a slower pace than a succubus normally moved at and that was his fault for throwing a spanner in the works the night they had met. He didn't want fast and flirty, and she didn't want to lose her quarry.

"I've never really thought about the lack of power in Hell." She lifted her other leg and crossed them, making sure her skirt draped in the centre of her parted thighs so no one would see anything. "What's it like? I imagine it's rustic... and very dark... and challenging. Sort of like this world centuries ago."

He took his hand back, planted it against the stone slabs beneath him and scowled at her, his voice as dark as the realm he hailed from. "I have witnessed changes in this world, and I have seen it grow in surprising ways. Progress is swift here, but it does not face the same difficulties as Hell does. There are no coal deposits there. No nuclear power is available. Things are changing, but it will take longer. It is not as dark and rustic as you and the people who lounge in luxury here imagine it. We are not dwelling in caves and rubbing sticks together. There is industry happening... progress. The wheels are in motion."

Way to poke a sore point, Suki.

She hadn't meant to upset him, or maybe she had. She wasn't sure what she was doing anymore. Had she wanted him to distance himself because she hadn't been strong enough to do it herself?

Did that make her a bitch?

Whatever it made her, she didn't like how it made her feel.

"So you chose to harness what's available, which is smart of you." It was a weak attempt at winning him back over, one that drew another scowl from him.

"Do not pay compliments you do not mean. I hear enough of those without them issuing from your lips."

Hold on a moment. Who the heck was complimenting him all the time? Her brain slapped her with the answer. When she had met him, he had said she was like the others and he had hoped she would be different. He didn't like women fawning over him.

"I'm sorry. I forgot you have a harem of women throwing compliments under your feet like rose petals wherever you walk." She dropped her legs over the edge.

He seized her arm, his grip firm and unrelenting as he held her in place.

"Where do you go?" he barked, a demanding edge to his voice that had her hackles rising.

"Wherever you're not." She twisted her arm, attempting to work it free of his hand. Her skin burned when he didn't release her.

He tightened his grip and his horns curled.

Definitely from anger this time.

Suki winced when her bones ached.

Panic flared in his eyes and he quickly released her. "My apologies."

"Yeah, apologise to your harem of bitches. Or I guess you don't have to apologise to them. They probably like it when you're a bastard to them." She rubbed her reddened wrist and turned her cheek to him.

"I do not have a harem." He sounded exasperated about that for some reason, but she wasn't going to probe into the why of it. "Suki... stay. I apologised and I meant it. There is no reason to be upset with me."

"There's probably a dozen reasons to be upset with you," she snapped and refused to apologise when he flinched. She was allowed to be angry about this. "For one, the compliment was genuine. You're probably the smartest person I know... and the fucking stupidest. A walking contradiction as always."

She pushed off from the wall, dropping to her feet on the cobbles below, her heart pounding in her ears as she battled her raging emotions.

He leaned down and stopped her with a light touch, a caress that whispered across her cheek as he cleared her hair from her face and gently tucked the waves behind her left ear.

"I am not good at this," he husked and she refused to look at him. So what if he was as pained as he sounded? He deserved it for doubting her. He sighed. "This is... new to me."

A thousand needles prickled over her skin and as much as she fought to deny them, his words echoed inside her in her own voice, rising from her soul.

It was new to her too.

Whatever this was, it was rapidly becoming something other than a game. He was rapidly becoming something other than a means to an end.

Something impossible.

She shook her head, causing his knuckles to brush her cheek again. "I get it. A succubus wanting to talk with you and apparently enjoying your company must mean she's up to something, right?"

She hated that she was meant to be up to something. At least that had been the plan, but then she had started getting to know him, and she had found herself just enjoying his company. She felt good whenever she was around him, warm whenever he looked at her, and light inside as the world and her worries melted away.

A perfect example of what a defunct succubus she was.

She couldn't even successfully seduce a man who wanted her without screwing something up.

In this case, it felt as if the something she was screwing up was herself.

"Suki." His low voice had warmth curling through her and it had a startling effect on her—it chased away the hurt that had been building inside her, born of the thought that whatever this was, it would end.

And it wouldn't be because she had gotten her wish and her clan had accepted her as a worthy member.

It would be because something would ruin it.

He twisted his hand, opened his palm and cupped her cheek, his tone soft. "Look at me."

She shook her head again. She wasn't strong enough to look at him right now. Not when down felt like up, and up felt like down, and everything inside her was jumbled. She cursed him and all shadowed males if they had the same power over other succubi as he wielded over her, twisting her in knots and leaving her shaken, unsure of anything.

He dropped from the wall, landing silently in front of her, and pushed his hand back, burying it in her hair to grip her nape. His other hand caught her jaw and she frowned. What was he doing?

She opened her mouth to ask him that question.

He claimed her lips and it came out as a squeak as he hauled her against him. A thousand hot shivers rolled over her as his grip on her nape tightened, holding her immobile as he waged war on her, stripping down her defences with a single, intoxicating kiss.

She tried to resist him, but the heat of his mouth as it brushed hers, his tongue as it breached her lips to tease the tip of hers, burned away all her fight and she melted against him. She gripped his hips, shuddered and moaned as his muscles flexed beneath her fingers, filling her with an itch to tug the hem of his tight black shirt up to feel the silken heat of his bare skin.

He broke the kiss, pressed his forehead to hers and breathed deeply, his hot breath caressing her tingling lips as she stared up into his eyes.

"I do not think of you in that way, Suki... although I do think about you constantly. I go mad when I am away from you." He sounded pained, as if he truly meant that, and the remnants of her anger faded away as she stood there in the square, pressed against every delicious hard inch of him, captured by his large hand against her nape and his honest words. "I came here because I needed to see you. I dreamed of you."

He croaked the last four words, a husky edge to his voice that left her in little doubt about what sort of dream it had been.

"I dreamed of you too," she murmured.

He stiffened against her. "You did?"

She nodded. "Hardly surprising. You kiss like a demon and I left wanting more. So did you. It's only natural we ended up dreaming the rest."

He relaxed a little but didn't release her. His fingers remained tensed against her neck, his hold possessive and speaking to that deeply feminine part of her that enjoyed the flashes of his strength. Apparently, it enjoyed him being in charge too.

A dangerous cocktail of pleasure.

One she wanted to get drunk on.

"Walk with me," she whispered close to his lips, bringing hers up until they were almost in contact.

His gaze lowered to them. "Why?"

She skimmed her fingers up his side and drank in the way his eyes darkened and heated, desire flaring in them that gave her a hit of energy as his hunger soared and made her bold.

"I could make up something about how I had been going above ground to get some air, but it would be a lie." She lifted her hands between them and traced patterns on his chest, trembling as the need she constantly felt whenever she was around him cranked tighter, driving her to fulfil it. A kiss wasn't enough this time. She needed more from him. "I want to get out of here because I want you all to myself."

His gaze heated further, drawing her deeper under his spell as it spoke to her, told her that she wasn't the only one who needed another taste of the passion that blazed between them.

"You already have me all to yourself," he purred, an edge to his voice that said he liked that she wanted him that way.

"I don't." She drew back, breaking contact with him, and he frowned. "I'm sharing you with at least a dozen women who are gawping at you and have been from the time I spotted you sitting on the walkway."

His right eyebrow lifted. "They are?"

She shook her head, couldn't believe he was oblivious to the fact most single women who passed tossed him at least a sultry glance, and some had taken to just openly staring at him.

"You seriously can't mean you haven't noticed them staring?" She looked around at the crowd and then back at him, a frown pulling at her eyebrows. "Are you that used to women trying to fuck you with their eyes?"

He rolled his thickly-hewn shoulders. "I spend most of my time in Hell, in the company of demons. I spend little time around females."

She muttered, "All the more reason for you to notice the women then, surely? You must be horny. I can't imagine being so starved of the company of the opposite sex."

All the heat washed from his eyes as he frowned down at her.

She met his scowl with a roll of her eyes. "Stop giving me that judging look. I'm a succubus."

He growled. "I do not need a reminder of that. If females are staring at me, then just as many males are gazing upon your curves."

Suki shrugged that off. "I don't mind. I can snack on the flicker of energy their dirty thoughts give off."

She braced herself for whatever snarl or grumbled words would leave his lips in response to that.

Instead of the gruff reply she anticipated, his gaze heated again, his expression deliciously intense as he asked in a rumbling voice, "Can you *snack* upon my thoughts?"

She sidled closer, aching to touch his horns, and murmured, "The way you look at me sometimes... it's like a five-course meal and it's delicious."

He slid his arm around her waist and tugged her to him, the corona of violet in his eyes spreading as his pupils dilated, that flare of hunger captivating her and pulling her deep under his spell as it cast black magic on her. Her hands lifted, drifting up towards his horns, anticipation curling inside her as she neared them.

He turned his cheek to her and glared at something.

She followed the direction of his gaze. Two demons stared at him, their dusky brown horns and wild chestnut hair telling her that they weren't from the same realm as Tegan.

A gasp escaped her lips when she was suddenly jerked forwards, his grip on her wrist firm as he pulled her into the crowd with one hand and stuffed his book into the back of his leathers with the other.

Apparently, he was taking her up on that walk.

She looked back over her shoulder at the duo of demons who were still watching them with curiosity shining in their dark red eyes.

Watching Tegan.

Why was he avoiding others of his species? Were they from a realm his wasn't getting along with right now, or was it something else that had him swiftly exiting the square and heading towards a quieter part of town?

The road that swept through the witches' district was packed as the entire town tried to filter into the square.

Now that they were moving, Tegan's focus was fixed on everything but her, which sucked because she had been enjoying having it all locked on her and her alone.

It also sucked for a lot of the men in the town.

Whenever he noticed one looking her way, he was quick to growl and bare huge fangs at them, and the further they progressed through the witches' district, the larger his horns grew, and she swore he was taller than before too.

Regret rushed through her as she looked up at the back of his head, sensing how tense he was through the point where he touched her. She had wanted to whisk him away from all the women, but now she wished she hadn't made him move. He had been so relaxed back in the square.

Now he looked as if he wanted to rip the throats off every man in the town.

She twisted her arm free of his grip and slipped her hand into his before he could notice she had escaped him.

He stilled and looked down at their joined hands as his nostrils flared, his chest heaving as his pointed ears flared against the shaven sides of his head. His horns had completely transformed, curled past his temples to twist around on themselves and flare forwards into vicious black daggers, resembling the horns of a ram.

Sexy, but dangerous. Appreciating how incredible he looked when gripped by rage would have to wait. Calming him seemed the more appropriate course of action right now.

Before he decided to kill every man in the town.

"This way." She tugged his hand and he followed her, not putting up a fight as she pulled him down a narrow alley between two of the white rendered buildings.

She didn't slow as they left the crowd behind, kept leading him deeper into the maze of houses. He slowly began to relax, and his eyes raked over her, sending a hot shiver rolling over her skin wherever his gaze landed. It settled on their joined hands and she smiled when he shifted his grip and linked their fingers, clasping her hand so tightly there wasn't room for a single molecule of air between their palms.

When she was far from the main road, she stopped and loosed a sigh. "Crisis averted."

She turned on Tegan.

His features set in a hard frown as he lifted his black eyes from their hands to rest on her face. "Crisis?"

She nodded. "You kept murdering every man who looked at me."

"I did not. I have not shed any blood."

"Maybe not in reality, but in your head, you'd torn apart the last twenty or so guys who looked at me, hadn't you?"

He averted his gaze, his cheeks darkening a shade, and muttered, "My apologies. I do not know what has come over me."

"No worries. I wouldn't have complained or fainted or anything. Just... it would have ruined our date." She started walking again but he didn't move, and she looked back at him over her shoulder.

"Date?" That adorable crinkle formed between his black eyebrows.

"Don't demons date?" Gods, that was a mouthful. "Like, arrange a time and place to meet a female they like and do stuff with them like shopping, or dinner, or just hanging out?"

"Not that I know of. Many demons just seize their fated one and bend them to their will. It is not a particularly romantic courtship."

It sounded delightful. And why did he have to keep making everything come back to fated mates, reminding her that somewhere out there, there was a bitch he would go gaga over?

She released his hand and his focus snapped down to the gap that appeared between them. His hand twitched, his handsome face darkened, and his lips flattened as he stared at her hand. He wanted to take it again. Well, he was going to have to work for the right to do that.

"Come on." She sauntered away from him, deeply aware of his gaze on her as she walked, a little sway to her hips that she couldn't help.

If he was going to keep talking about fated mates, she was going to punish him for it. A round of look but don't touch would probably work.

When he still didn't move, she looked back at him, and satisfaction swept through her when she caught the pained look on his face as he stared at her backside.

She wasn't going to beckon him again. Doing that would probably make her look desperate and that would give him power over her, and she was enjoying this small power she currently had over him.

Suki sashayed around the corner, breaking his line of sight.

An unholy growl rolled through the air and he was suddenly beside her, glaring down at her. Blaming her for disappearing on him?

She shrugged that off. It was his fault for not keeping up.

"Is this a *date*, Suki?"

Heat shivered over her, a glimmer of bliss that had her step faltering as it hit her. She cursed him. He used her name whenever she was in a mood with him, had realised the power it had over her whenever she heard it rumbling in his deep voice, even when it wasn't her true name. Damn him back to Hell for abusing it like that because she was powerless to resist him whenever he uttered her name.

"No. I take it back," she snapped, clinging to her mood like a petulant child. "This is a chance meeting."

"When I used your digits the other day and you came to spend time with me. Was that a date?" His deep rumbling voice had another blast of heat washing through her, each low spoken and cautious word hitting her hard.

Her curious geek. Always trying to figure out the why and how of things.

She shrugged. "I guess."

"How do I make this a date again?"

She tried and failed to hold back her smile. Persistent bastard. No man had ever been so damned persistent with her. All the other ones in her life would have given up by now and moved on to find an easier target.

Tegan enjoyed the fight for her.

Because she wasn't an easy lay like the other females he had known, the ones who had obviously complimented him too much and thrown themselves at his feet?

"You have to work harder." She looked across at him, weathering his frown. "You show up in my town but don't try to find me. You eat dinner without me. You insult me. I mean really, Solid Eleven, at the rate you're going, you'll hit single digits in no time."

He growled. "Any attempt to find you would have resulted in the bloodbath you barely avoided back in that street. Asking males if they knew you…" He didn't need to say any more than that for her to get the picture. He would have murdered them all. "As far as I know, you do not eat food. I did not mean to insult you and I apologised for that."

Why was she trying to push him away?

Because he was getting too close, getting under her skin?

Because she was afraid that one day, he would find his mate and that woman would steal him from her?

She froze as that last one hit her. Tegan wasn't hers, which meant another female couldn't steal him from her. She was a succubus. Succubi didn't do long term relationships. They didn't do relationships at all.

So why did she ache to have one with Tegan?

Why did she long for a taste of what it was like to be in a relationship like the ones she had watched on the TV or in the town or the nightclubs she frequented?

A hollow feeling opened inside her, carving out her chest, leaving her shaken as she stared up into Tegan's eyes because she wanted something she could never have. Her mistress's words hit her and they slammed into her with the force of a wrecking ball.

Maybe she had been born into the wrong species.

She wanted things she had no right wanting, failed at things that should have come naturally to her, and had faulty abilities.

"Suki." Tegan's eyebrows furrowed as he closed the distance between them and lifted his hand. The backs of his fingers gently brushed her cheek, that earnest and worried look on his face ripping at her heart as she tried to hold it together. "What is wrong? Is it something I have done?"

She shook her head, considered sweeping his hand away from her and stopped herself from doing it when she realised just how much his touch comforted her, chasing the storm clouds from her mind and bringing a flicker of light back into her heart to ease the pain that had been building there.

"Rough day," she whispered, drew down a deep breath and ignored the voice at the back of her head that said she would regret opening up to him. She mentally flipped it off, because she needed to speak with someone, and he was here, looking at her as if he would die if he didn't discover what was wrong with her and make it better. "My sisters were dicks this morning."

She wanted to leave it at that.

"Dicks?"

She nodded. "They were on fine form. Total bitches. I don't really want to talk about it."

Tegan evidently did. "They are mean to you?"

She couldn't bring herself to look at him, didn't want him to see that she was defective like everyone said she was, even when she had admitted as much to him before.

Because she didn't want him to look at her as her family did, seeing something worthless.

"It's nothing. Let it go." She went to walk away.

He caught her upper arm and spun her back to face him, the darkness etched on his handsome features saying he thought it was something and he wasn't going to do as she had asked.

His irises flared purple and his horns curled again, and his fangs flashed between his lips as he opened his mouth and snapped it closed again, the fury that had tightened his features melting away as his eyes darted between hers and his brow furrowed.

He released her arm and cupped her cheek, his gaze holding hers, softening in a way that warmed her from head to toe and had her leaning into his touch. Something about that look in his eyes made her feel as if she was worth something.

To him at least.

She wanted to reward him for it, for improving her mood without even knowing he had done it by making her see that her sisters were wrong about her.

She could charm a man, could make him want her.

She just couldn't use her powers to make that happen.

Which made it a hell of a lot more difficult, but gods, it was more rewarding.

"Wait here." She tiptoed and pressed a swift kiss to his cheek. "I'll be right back."

She teleported before he could say anything.

CHAPTER 14

Suki appeared outside one of her favourite stores in the witches' district as a roar cut through the air, silencing the street around her. She shivered. Angry Tegan was the best Tegan. She almost wished she had stuck around to see him roar like that, to witness his strength and raw fury. Maybe she could make him roar for her when she returned.

"Hello?" She walked between the cases of wares outside the white building, beneath the violet canopy, and leaned her head into the open door. "Agatha?"

Abigail popped up from behind the counter in the crowded room and tugged at something caught in her long white hair. Her green eyes widened when whatever it was fought back. The witch muttered something beneath her breath, a puff of dark blue smoke exploded from between her fingers and a screech filled the air.

"Damned beasties getting in the wires again. Chewing the whole bloody shop." Abigail beamed at her as she swatted the smouldering blue patch in her tangled hair.

"Agatha not here?" Suki crossed the cramped room, sliding around several rotating metal stands filled with phone cases.

"She's…" A pained look crossed the young witch's face as she twisted the front of her black dress in her hands. "The raid."

A chill skated down Suki's back and she shook her head. "Gods… she wasn't killed… tell me your sister wasn't killed."

It had only been a couple of months since the bastard hunter organisation, Archangel, had raided the town, killing a lot of people and stealing others, abducting them for the gods only knew what reason. The town had been a sombre place in the aftermath.

She hadn't heard of any witches being killed.

The ice in her veins grew colder. Although the alternative was worse than death.

"I think... I think they took her." Tears lined Abigail's eyes. "I-I'm not sure though. It was crazy. I was with her and everything happened so fast. She pushed me away when the hunters descended. Cast a spell on me to hide me. I tried to help her."

Suki sank forwards, pressing her hands against the counter as she struggled to take that in. The attack had been unwarranted and brutal. Normally, the mortal hunter organisation left them alone because they were peaceful, none of the people who lived in the town a danger to the humans they shared this world with.

Rumours had run through the town in the aftermath, speculation that someone they had been hunting must have come to the town, bringing trouble to them. Suki wasn't so sure. They had killed many from different species and taken several captives from various ones too. A few shifters had gone missing from different compounds, and there had been a demon taken when he had fought against the hunters, attempting to stop them.

"Isn't there something we can do?" Suki looked at Abigail, even when she knew there was nothing they could do for Agatha now.

If Agatha had been taken, her fate was in the hands of the gods.

"I'm keeping the shop running," Abigail said with a hollow smile and Suki's heart went out to her, because she was doing the only thing she could to help Agatha.

She was keeping hope alive.

"I'll ask around town when I get the chance, and I'm sure she'll make it back to us... so we'll have to make sure everyone has been buying at her store, so she'll be ridiculously rich when she gets back." Suki took hold of Abigail's hand and squeezed it. "I'll tell the clan that Agatha got the latest iPhone jacked into the magical network. You make it happen and you know you'll sell out in a heartbeat. If the succubi don't buy you out, the incubi will. You know they can't let us have anything better than they have."

Abigail nodded. "Thanks. If you do hear anything, let me know."

Suki jerked her chin towards the display case behind the witch. "I need a phone. One like mine. I don't think he's equipped to handle anything different to what he knows."

"A man? You're buying a phone for a man."

She shrugged stiffly. "Don't start."

Abigail's green eyes brightened. "You like him."

She shook her head and grabbed the phone that Abigail offered. "He's a host. Nothing more."

Abigail refused to release the phone. "Never seen a succubus buy a phone for a host before."

"Shut up." She tugged the phone free of her grip. "He'll need a few charging packs too. He lives south of here."

Abigail looked as if she wanted to probe and then bent over and lifted a box onto the counter. "How many?"

"Two should do it." She was quick to take them as Abigail slid them across the counter. She waved the phone at the witch. "Bill me."

She disappeared, landing in the alley beside Tegan.

He growled and turned on her, flashing fangs.

"Down boy!" She grinned when he eased back and scowled. "Didn't mean to startle you."

He took one look at her and immediately closed the gap between them, his gaze searching hers. "Something happened. You are upset."

This time, she didn't try to pretend she was fine or keep the truth from him.

"A friend of mine was taken in a raid a couple of months back and I didn't know." She looked down at her feet. "I should have checked on her. Some friend I am."

"A raid?" He smoothed his palm over her cheek, and she stole all the comfort she could from that touch, closed her eyes and nodded. "Do you know where she might be?"

His voice had changed, losing all softness and warmth. Now he sounded like a warrior, hard as stone and unyielding, ready to make someone regret what they had done.

"Archangel." She seized his hand when he went to withdraw it and her eyes leaped to meet his, her heart lodging in her throat. "Don't even think about looking for them."

"Why not?" He canted his head, his black hair falling to his right to brush his horn and forehead.

She wouldn't hide this truth from him either. "Because I'm afraid you'll get hurt."

His expression softened again and he reached for her, looking for all the world as if he was going to kiss her breathless for that.

She panicked and shoved the phone at him, wincing when she slapped him in the centre of his chest with it.

He arched an eyebrow down at it.

"Sorry. Just. I'm a bit hungry and I'll probably hurt you, and I refer you back to what I just said. I don't want to see you hurt." Her heart pounded, blood rushing as adrenaline jacked it up, and her hands shook where they remained planted against his chest.

What the hell was she doing?

He lifted his hands and gently covered hers with them. "If it worries you, I will not kiss you."

"But?"

"But what?"

She swallowed her racing heart. "What about Archangel? Don't go after them."

"I have no intention of doing that. I was merely going to suggest I ask King Thorne of the Third Realm to inquire about your missing friend."

"Oh." Her eyebrows lifted. "You know royalty?"

He nodded and grimaced. "It is a long story."

One he didn't want to tell her for some reason.

"How does this king know Archangel?" She wouldn't probe about how he knew the king. From his wind turbine project? She recalled he had mentioned this king had installed some wind farms.

"His fated one was a hunter for the organisation and they recently aided him in a war."

"Wow. Didn't see that one coming. A demon with a hunter for a mate." She couldn't imagine how difficult that courtship had been and she doubted the method Tegan had mentioned, one that sounded awfully as if the demon normally just grabbed his mate and claimed her with or without her consent, had worked on this hunter.

"What is this?" He took the phone from her fingers and peered at it. "It is not your phone."

"Well, you seemed to really like advancing, so consider this one hell of a leap forwards."

"It is for me?" He raised his gaze to meet hers.

"It's magically enchanted, which means it can work in Hell." She held her hand up before he could speak. "I know what's coming. Magic allows it to use the portal pathways into Hell as transmitters that relay the call to the phone network in the mortal world and connect you to the person at the other end, no matter where they are. It's all the rage right now. The latest greatest thing. Magic meets technology. That has to knock your socks off."

His dark eyes lit up. "It does. I never considered the two things might be compatible. The avenues this opens up are endless, Suki. What if I could somehow couple magic and technology in the Second Realm… or across all of Hell?"

"Well, Agatha would probably make a fortune since she patented the spell and she would make everyone buy the phones from her. Demand would go through the roof. She'd be the richest woman in the realms overnight." Suki thought about that as she stared at Tegan, enjoying that glimmer of curiosity mixed with excitement in his eyes and the idea that struck her. "If you did the footwork in Hell, convincing everyone to buy into this technology, Agatha would pay you and probably make you rich too."

His eyebrows dipped low. "I am rich."

Her eyes widened. "How rich?"

Did that come off as a little grabby?

It was still weeks until her monthly allowance hit her bank account and brought her back into the black, and that side of her nature she tried so hard to deny was rearing its ugly head, stealing control of her once again.

He tilted his head back, blankly looked at the cavern ceiling as his lips pursed and eyebrows knitted, and eventually rolled his shoulders in a shrug. "I do not honestly know. I have bank accounts in this world."

He handed her the phone and opened the leather pouch on his hip, fished around in it and proudly produced several debit and credit cards.

"I have plastic."

It was sweet that he thought plastic made him rich.

She looked closer at the cards, the two black ones in particular.

Her jaw dropped.

"Holy gods… I thought the black American Express was an eye-opener but is that a Coutts World Silk Card?"

He turned them towards him, his eyebrows pinned high on his forehead. She wanted to slap him when he shrugged. Every succubus worth her salt knew what to look for in a man's wallet, or leather pouch. Her kind found it hard to keep jobs and most of them didn't want to work to begin with, so they relied on taking as much from a man as possible—both sexually and financially.

If what she was looking at was real, she had hit the jackpot with Tegan.

"I think you just made it to twelve. Although, Solid Twelve doesn't have the same ring to it."

He inspected the Coutts card. "It is worth a lot?"

"You don't know? My gods… how do you not know?"

He was strolling around with every exclusive card out there, some even people uneducated in the best cards to look for on a man would know, like the black American Express, and he didn't have a damned clue what that meant.

"I merely asked for plastic and was given it. These accounts are good?" He flexed the black Coutts card in his fingers, bending it back and forth, and she nearly had a heart attack as she lunged for it, afraid he would break it and somehow destroy the account at the other end in the process.

She gripped both of his hands and looked up at him, finding him watching her with an arched brow.

"You like money." He spoke those three words slowly, a wicked light entering his eyes that screamed he was dreaming up ways to abuse this knowledge.

"Did I not mention how my hair colour bankrupts me each month because I'm a total failure and have to live on a meagre allowance?"

The smile that had been curving his lips faded. "You are not a failure, Suki. Whoever tells you these things... they are wrong."

They weren't, but it was sweet of him to think that.

He looked at all the cards he held. Among the pile was a gold metal one she recognised as a JP Morgan card. He noticed her eyes on it and pushed his thumb against it, edging it forwards in the group, looked as if he wanted to offer it to her and then closed his hand around all his cards.

"I should pay you for the phone." His fingers flexed around them.

She shook her head. "It's a present... and really, I don't want your money."

He looked as if he couldn't quite believe that. "At least allow me to pay for something. Your hair colour perhaps?"

She refused to read into that. It didn't mean he was thinking about sticking around, about them being together that long.

"Really, I don't want to be that girl." It hit her that she really didn't. Another failing. Her sisters would have charmed the JP Morgan card right out of his hands. She was refusing it.

Why?

That damned voice said it was because she had always thought what her sisters did tarnished the name of their species. Sure, succubi needed money like everyone else and it was hard to get that when they had a tendency to accidentally charm anyone they worked with when they were hungry and a lot of the times that got them fired or their bosses killed, but taking money from men they had pleasured?

It crossed a line in her eyes.

She stared at the card. But curse her, she did like money. Not because she wanted material things, but because she liked the security of it.

Another why.

Another answer that rose from within.

Because she feared that her clan were going to kick her out and if she had money, she would be able to find a place to live, would be able to rebuild her life and maybe survive without them.

"I keep upsetting you today. Perhaps I should go."

She shook her head. Stupid emotions. They had been running amok since she had met him and no matter what she did, she couldn't quite get them under control.

She needed a distraction.

She lifted the phone she gripped in her right hand. "You have your own digits now."

"I do?"

She nodded as she pulled her phone from her skirt pocket and brought them together, swapping their contact details. When she was done, she brought up his name in her phone book and flashed the screen at him.

"And now I have your digits."

He frowned. "I did not give them to you."

Suki refused to let them mean anything less to her because of that. "It's the least you can do since I bought you the phone."

He glared at his collection of cards. "Can I not pay you for it?"

"Nope." She held back a smile when he huffed and she focused on his aura, wanting to see what he was feeling as he grumbled something beneath his breath.

Shadows rose from his shoulders and head.

She peered hard at them, trying to penetrate them.

No dice.

He shoved his cards back into his pouch and her gaze roamed over him, drifting across his broad shoulders and down the impressive bulge of his biceps. He stilled. Looked at her. His gaze landed on her in a scalding rush of fire that lit her up inside, had her pressing her thighs together as a flicker of energy washed through her.

"What are you thinking when you look at me like that?" She bravely lifted her eyes to meet his.

They were dark pools of violet, flooded with desire that had her taking a slow step towards him so she could get another hit of pleasure and energy from him.

His voice scraped low, thick with the hunger she could sense in him. "The dream I had of you... you were swimming."

"Naked?"

He swallowed hard. Nodded. Blushed a little in a way she found sexy.

"Did you enjoy the dream?"

Another stiff nod. His gaze raked over her, giving her another delicious hit of energy. "It did not leave me satisfied though."

"Oh. Why not?" She edged closer, unable to resist the desire to press against him as her hunger mounted.

"Because now I yearn to know you in reality... to know if your taste is as sweet and heavenly on my tongue."

Good gods. She shivered, her knees almost buckling beneath her as his words rolled over her, bringing her hunger to boiling point.

She blushed now. Her hot geek had a wicked tongue and damn, it fired her up.

"It takes a strong man to withstand that sort of thing with a succubus, and I already said I don't want to kill you." She felt as disappointed as he looked and she couldn't stop herself from adding, "Not when I'm just starting to like you."

The words slipped from her before she could stop them, and he looked as if they had hit him as hard as they hit her.

His eyes blazed, flooded with arousal and need she had stoked with the simple confession that she liked him.

She was probably going to regret this, but resisting him was impossible, was a torment she didn't want to endure. He was strong, and wasn't she meant to be seducing him? He was right where she wanted him.

She eased up to him, skimmed her hands over the hard slabs of his chest, and murmured, "I can think of something you can give me as payment for the phone."

He lowered his face towards her, a serious edge to his expression. "What?"

She tiptoed, bringing them closer together, whispering, "A kiss."

His throat worked on another hard swallow. "A kiss?"

He choked on those words and heck, that was a major turn on. She had never managed to fluster a man like that before.

She nodded, deadly serious now. "That's what I want most."

He drew down a deep breath. "Do you intend to feed on this kiss?"

She shivered at the thought. She hadn't considered it, but now it was all she wanted. She wanted to taste him properly, even though she feared she would lose control and hurt him.

"A kiss it is then," he husked, voice a throaty rumble that heated her insides. "But not here. Somewhere private. I need to be alone with you… because I am not sure what will happen."

Oh gods, she wasn't sure either. Right now, she felt as if the entire world might detonate if he kissed her, exploding into a shower of stars.

She couldn't answer him. Barely managed a nod.

He gathered her close, banding strong arms around her that had her temperature soaring and need flaring hotter in her veins, cranking her tighter. His hard body met hers, sending a thrill through her, and she pressed closer as they dropped into the darkness.

She wasn't surprised when they landed in the private cove.

Just pressed closer still, looping her arms around his neck to keep him pinned to her as her hunger reached a crescendo and her eyes locked on his lips as words fell from hers in a desperate tone that she knew would leave him in no doubt of the need she felt.

A need of him.

"Kiss me now."

CHAPTER 15

Feeding a succubus was probably an unwise idea, but gods, Tegan could feel how much Suki needed it, how fiercely she craved his kiss as her soft curves pressed against him and her hooded gaze locked on his lips. Her irises sparkled in iridescent shades of emerald and azure blue, gold glittering in them in the warm sunlight as that need he could sense in her rose even higher, had her rubbing against him, her breasts teasing him as her hard nipples brushed against his chest.

The instincts she stirred in him awoke, a powerful need to please her rising inside him in time with the desire in her, driving him to obey.

He dropped his head and captured her mouth, her taste flooding him the moment their lips touched, that nectar sweet with a hint of spice drugging him in an instant. On the heels of it, a haziness swept through him, awareness that she was stealing his strength causing a momentary swell of panic that quickly subsided when she moaned, the sound of her pleasure almost as intoxicating as her kiss.

He gathered her to him, clutching her backside and fisting her black skirt, twisting it in his grip as his claws emerged and a new hunger blazed inside him, stealing control. He angled his head and deepened the kiss, plundered her mouth with his tongue and stole his reward.

Another sultry moan.

He could feast on those just as she feasted on the energy that crackled between them, craved them and wouldn't stop until he squeezed another from her, and then another. They were his addiction, together with this pleasure he could feel building inside her, desire he swore he would satisfy for her.

His instincts flared again as the drain on his strength grew more intense, but he refused to let it panic him. Suki wouldn't hurt him. She was in control.

Which sparked a different sort of instinct within him.

On a low growl, he kissed her deeper still, demanding more of her as a need shot through him.

A need to dominate her and wrest control from her.

An urge to make her submit to him.

She moaned and writhed against him, breathless as their lips clashed, tongues tangling. Her small fangs scraped over his lower lip as he did his best to keep his larger ones from harming her. They ached as he kissed her, throbbed with a need that he fought to deny and keep from his mind, struggling to focus on why he was doing this.

To give her pleasure. To feed her.

Not to steal control from her so she would be compliant when he sank his fangs into her, marking her flesh.

He pinned her harder against him at that thought, as if it had unleashed that desire, allowing it to slip beyond his control. He tried to claw it back again as the urge to kiss along her jaw and down her throat burned inside him, followed by a tempting vision of him bending his head and sinking his fangs into the delicate arch of her neck.

He shuddered, entire body quaking and heating at just the thought of marking her.

Suki broke the kiss, stealing his focus from the urge to bite her as she leaned back in his arms, her dazzling heavy-lidded eyes holding his.

His female was satisfied.

He had done that, had fed her and made her boneless.

He raked his own hooded gaze over her and groaned at the sight of her, so wanton and beautiful in his arms with her hair flowing like a waterfall towards the warm sand and her breasts threatening to spill from her violet leather corset as she breathed, sunlight caressing her wicked curves.

The low rasp of his voice shocked him as he uttered, "Did I taste good?"

She moaned, skimmed a teasing finger down the valley of her breasts and up again to trace the line of her throat up to her lips, and grinned. "Like the most expensive meal on the planet times one thousand."

His horns flared, hunger sweeping through him again as his fangs elongated and his ears grew pointier. "Do I taste better than every other male you have ever kissed?"

Her incredible eyes went a little wider before narrowing on his, her smile turning teasing as she whispered, "You're a jealous sort. First you don't like men looking at me, and then you want to be the best I've ever had."

He was jealous, but that wasn't where either of those things had stemmed from. He didn't like males looking at her because they had no right to gaze upon the curves of his female. He wanted to know he was the best she had ever had because he would go mad if he wasn't, because it would mean that someone else out there had managed to please her better than he could.

Noise shattered the silence.

Suki grimaced, pushed from his arms as she righted herself and plucked the phone from her skirt. She pulled a face at it and swiped her thumb over the screen, silencing it.

"I need to blow off some steam. Someone got me all riled up."

He assumed that someone was him judging by the pointed look she gave him.

"I can think of ways to blow off steam." Ways he shouldn't be considering. Not yet anyway. But gods, he wanted her.

She snatched his phone from his pocket and played with it, lifting it up in front of her. It made a noise and she frowned at the screen and repeated the action.

"What are you doing?" He tried to see the screen, but she turned her back to him, leaned it against his chest and lifted the phone again, pressing a button on the side.

When she turned it around, a picture of them filled the screen.

She nestled closer, took hold of his arm and draped it over her shoulder and chest, and took another photograph. She smiled at this one. He did too. He liked the sight of them together, holding each other like that. When she lifted the phone again, he wrapped his arms around her and rested his chin on top of her head.

She flipped the phone to face them. "Oh, I like this one."

She did something with her phone and his, and the image appeared on it too. She wanted a picture of them together? His heart warmed and he held her closer. The pleasurable feel of her body against his was short-lived. She wriggled free of his grip, pushed his phone into his hand and played with her own.

He flipped through the images, getting the hang of the device. She had taken a lot of them, but his favourite by far was the last one, the one she had liked too. She radiated warmth and light in that picture, as if she was happy, and she looked good in his arms, as if she really had been made to be in them.

Music started playing, a different sound to the video she had shown him before, but not as grating as the music in Underworld had been. It had a good beat and an interesting rhythm.

He glanced up when she started moving and froze, utterly enthralled by the sight of her as she began dancing, swaying in time with the beat, a sensual and alluring sight that arrested his heart and had his shaft hardening in response.

"I love dancing." She kicked off one boot and tried to keep dancing as she tackled the other one, sending it flying across the sand in his direction.

Tegan stared at her. Would she ever stop surprising him?

"What kind of music is this?" He listened to it as he watched her spin and twirl, kicking up sand as she lost herself in the rhythm and began singing along with the male.

"Country." She beamed at him. "It's good for dancing. Lots of guitar and great beats, and a dash of romance."

He wasn't sure what a guitar was. He presumed it was an instrument. There was so much about this world he didn't know. He felt it keenly as she rattled off a list of the musical genres that she enjoyed and the ones she despised, and he tried to keep up.

Did she think less of him because she had to explain everything to him?

She pirouetted towards him, stopping only when she was right in front of him, and grabbed his hand. He resisted when she tugged him towards where she had been dancing, drawing a pout from her that had him relenting. He swallowed hard when she placed the hand she held on her hip and swayed against him, an expectant look on her face.

He did his best to dance with her, but this wasn't dancing as he was accustomed to and he felt clumsy as he tried to figure out where to put his feet and what to do with his hands. The way she moved was so fluid while he was so rigid, stiff where she was sensual, awkward where she was confident, rubbing against him briefly from time to time to tease him.

Gods, she was beautiful.

She shone with life, with happiness and joy, taking so much pleasure from this simple act.

She spun to face him and he caught her, pulled her to him and met her gaze. She stilled in his arms, heat and surprise washing across her eyes, and then began swaying with him, a slower dance that was more his tempo, one that had him losing himself in the moment, another one he would cherish for the rest of his days.

Her sultry gaze lowered to his lips.

Tegan obeyed her silent command, dipped his head and kissed her, softer this time. His lips played against hers, each sweep affecting him deeply, until he was breathless, utterly lost in her, and on fire with need.

She was breathless too as she pulled back, as she stroked her hands over his chest, her eyes hazy as she murmured, "I've never kissed like that. It's never been like that. It was incredible."

Her eyes darted to his and away, leaping to the sand to his right.

She didn't need to fear. He wouldn't preen and puff his chest out because of what she had said. He had enough self-control to maintain some dignity around her.

Although, not all of it.

He stepped back and unbuttoned his shirt, stripped it off and tossed it onto the sand.

She gasped, her eyes enormous and ripping at his control as she raked them over his bare chest. "What are you doing?"

"I am going for a swim. I have not swum in a long time, and I need to cool off before I go too far with you." He toed his boots off, leaving them on the sand near the one she had practically kicked at him, and reached for the laces on the front of his black leathers.

"How long is a long time?"

He lifted his head, pausing at untying his leathers. "Worried I will drown? You will just have to swim with me then."

Disbelief coloured her gaze. "Who are you?"

He frowned.

"You're so different... change so damned often I can't keep up... but I like it." Her lips curled in a faint smile. "Playful demon is a new one for me."

He grinned and shoved his leathers down.

Her mouth gaped open, her focus dropping to take all of him in as he kicked off his trousers and turned his back to her, facing the ocean.

She muttered, "This side of you is shooting straight to the top of the list of my favourite personality traits."

His backside was on fire as her gaze drilled into it and his entire body heated as he heard her grumble.

"You have an ass that would make even the best sculptor weep because no one could ever do that justice. Words fail me."

That put a little swagger in his step as he walked towards the sea, the feel of her eyes on him rousing a fierce need to turn and let her get a good look at him, to show her what she was resisting whenever they kissed and he felt her drawing away from him, attempting to stop things from happening between them.

Things he wanted to happen.

He waded into the water, smiling as she cursed him in the fae tongue for stealing the lower half of his body from view. He could understand her concerns, but he was strong enough to handle her, and there was only so many times he could deny his need to please her, to give her everything she needed from him, before he cracked and his instincts seized command and took the choice out of her hands.

He turned to find her still standing on the shore, looking shell-shocked. The water was clear and calm around him, sunlight rippling across it as it lapped at his waist. He looked beneath the surface at the sand and the fish that began to gather, grinned and dove into the water. It stung his eyes, blurring his vision as he tried to capture one of the fish, and he broke the surface.

Tegan stood again, coming to face Suki where she stood on the damp sand near the water.

Water ran in rivulets down his chest as he brushed his hands over his hair, sweeping it back from his face.

Suki whimpered, "Dear gods."

Every inch of him burned in response, aching with a need of her that wouldn't be denied, not this time. He was glad the water was colder than he had anticipated, because it cooled the hot iron of his cock as it hardened beneath the surface. He waited, heart pounding, nerves beginning to trickle through his veins with the fiery rush of his blood as she lingered, just gawping at him.

What was he doing?

He was meant to be keeping his distance, making sure this female really wanted him. He stared at her, deeply aware of her gaze as it travelled over him, devouring every inch of his chest.

She did want him.

The female standing on the beach staring at him as if she was starved and only he could satisfy her wasn't looking at him that way because he was a king. She was looking at him because he was just himself, and apparently, she liked him.

She proved that by suddenly teleporting into his arms.

He caught her, a grin stretching his lips as he planted his hands against her ass and hauled her against his body. Her lips clashed with his, her chest straining against his with every panted breath she drew as she wrapped her arms around his head, cupped the sides of it with her hands and kissed him. He groaned and held her aloft, his head tipped back as he kissed her, every brush and sweep of her lips over his a wicked sort of bliss he never wanted to end.

She trembled in his arms, her petite body shaking as she kissed him deeper, sweet moans escaping her every time their tongues touched. He groaned and shuddered as her tiny fangs scraped over his lower lip and she sucked it into her mouth, her body working against his now, a desperate edge to her movements that had him kissing her deeper, because she needed more.

She broke away from his lips, her hands firm against his shoulders, scalding him and igniting a need inside him, a hunger to feel her fingers traversing his body, to see her delight as she explored it and feel how much she desired him.

Him.

Not a king.

Just him.

A warrior. A demon. A male who needed her more than anything in this world.

Her male.

She had stopped the kiss, but she continued to writhe against him, a pained edge to her expression as her face twisted, brow furrowing and tiny fangs tugging at her kiss-reddened lips. She needed more. Stopping kissing him hadn't stopped the fire that burned inside her, had her wild in his arms, restless with an ache that he could sense in her.

One that roused a powerful primal instinct within him.

His female was on fire and he would die if he didn't give her the release she needed.

Which made that seed of suspicion bloom swiftly inside him, startling him as he stared at her, unable to believe his luck as something hit home.

This slight, dazzling and vexing female might just be his fated one.

CHAPTER 16

Things were getting out of control and fast. Suki was meant to be seducing the demon, but the demon was seducing her. She couldn't get enough of him. He was naked against her, hard, and damn, she wanted to see him in all his glory, but she couldn't peel herself off him to get a good look. When she stroked his smooth horns, he bucked against her, grunting in a way that left her in no doubt that he liked her touching them.

She tried to curb her desire, but control was beyond her, no matter how fiercely she fought the needs running rampant inside her, hungers that had her fearing she would hurt him.

Hungers that were so intense she couldn't deny them.

He wanted her.

She wanted him.

Why deny herself the pleasure of learning his delicious body? He desired her, was hard for her. This was her chance to take things to the next level and prove to herself and the clan that she could seduce a powerful immortal, without needing to read his aura.

But what if he wasn't strong enough to survive it?

What if she lost control?

Cold swept through her but he didn't give it a chance to take hold of her, to dampen her desire for him and the deep ache in her belly, one that demanded satisfaction.

He kissed her again, the brush of his fangs against her tongue as his tangled with it sending a thrill through her, one that had all reasonable thought burning away, leaving only need behind.

She needed him.

She wrapped herself around him and teleported to the shore, to the rocks that spilled close to the water, ones that had featured in a naughty dream she'd had of him. He didn't stop kissing her. His mouth continued to master hers throughout the teleport, tearing down her defences, ripping apart her control.

Why deny herself?

Why deny him?

He wanted this, she could feel it in him, could taste it in his kiss, his desperation a heady drug that she revelled in together with his desire, passion that she had stoked with only a kiss and looking at him.

She didn't want to wait any longer.

She pushed out of his arms, earning a low growl from him as he reached for her, trying to get her back into them. She evaded him and planted her hands against his chest, shoved him backwards so he fell, his spine meeting the curved rock.

Her breath rushed from her.

"Sweet gods," she muttered, eyes wide as she took in the sight of him, every process in her body shutting down in response to the glorious vision of masculinity and divinity in front of her.

His eyes darkened, that corona of violet-red spreading across his irises as he stared at her, hunger etched on every handsome line of his face as he held his head up. His horns flared, curled around like a ram's and had her aching to touch them again.

But touching the rest of him took priority.

She slammed her palms against the wide hard slabs of his pectorals, brushed her fingers through the dusting of black hair on them, and leaned over him to lick the valley between them.

He was officially hers now.

She licked it, she owned it.

That was how mortals worked with food apparently and she was appropriating it for her own use.

Although the delicious slice of grade A male in front of her was more than just food to her.

More than a host.

He groaned and leaned his head back as she worked her way downwards, swirling her tongue around both of his nipples before tracing the peaks and valleys of his stomach. She counted the ropes of his abdomen. Two. Four. Six. Eight! She shivered and tongued his navel, earning another husky moan from him as he tensed, which tore a moan from her lips as his muscles bunched, hitting her with another fix of his godliness.

He was strong.

She told herself that on repeat as she travelled lower, following that trail of hair that had teased her from the moment she had first seen it, a path she had been itching to take ever since and one that had prominently featured in her dreams of him.

Heat burned against her, drawing her focus elsewhere, and she eased back and gazed down at his cock.

Good gods.

She fell to her knees before him.

He pushed himself up on his elbows on the rock, a concerned edge to his pleasure-addled expression as he rasped, "Suki?"

She stared at his erection where it rose from a nest of black curls, thick and long, the sight of it stealing her breath as a thousand hungers surged through her, demanding she sate all of them. It wasn't hard to pick one.

She wanted to suck on that lollipop and taste him as she worshipped him like he deserved.

Her hand shot to his cock, wrapped around it and gripped it hard as her belly fluttered, the heat pooling at the apex of her thighs soaking into her shorts as she rose to her knees in front of him. He groaned as she stroked him, his legs falling open, head smacking back against the rock. The clack of his horns hitting it was the most erotic thing she had ever heard, a reminder of their existence that had her squeezing her thighs together as pleasure pulsed through her.

She licked her lips, gripped his right thigh in her left hand, and shuddered in time with him as she stroked her tongue up the length of him. Velvet on steel, heat that met her tongue and had another thrill sweeping through her, a flicker of energy that lit her up inside. She groaned and swirled her tongue around the blunt dark head, shivered as she tasted his saltiness, and worked her hand on him as she licked, wringing another drop from him.

"Gods... Suki." He swallowed hard, every inch of him flexing as he gripped the rock beside his hips, his claws scraping over the stone as they emerged.

She moaned and took him into her mouth, heat and life buzzing through her as she suckled him, teasing him with her tongue and her teeth before taking him deeper. He groaned as he slid into her mouth, inch after inch, his thigh trembling beneath her hand, and she didn't stop him from rocking into her as she began to move, sucking as she worked up his cock and pressing her tongue into the ridge of his shaft on the way down.

He grunted and thrust into her mouth, muttered things in the demon tongue as she licked him, swirled her tongue and sucked harder as she tightened her grip on the base of his cock. He growled, barked something at her she presumed was a demand to keep going. His left foot planted against the rock, his leg bending at the knee as he tried to gain leverage.

She held him firm, only letting him thrust so far, keeping him skirting the edge of insanity as she soaked up his pleasure, savoured the energy pouring through her now as he reached for his release.

Her head grew hazy, his bliss a drug that had her dizzy and aching for more, desperate to wring it from him before she let him climax. She lapped at him, teasing him with light caresses, her tongue fluttering around the broad head of his cock, tasting him as he spilled another drop of seed.

He growled as he tried to rock his hips and she pressed down on them, gripped his shaft tighter so he couldn't spill as he wanted. When he settled again, she rewarded him and herself at the same time, taking him back into her mouth and sucking him again as she eased the pressure of her grip.

He shuddered and moaned, his energy rolling through her as he writhed, seeking that one lick or swirl that would send him over the edge.

She loosened her hold on him and he worked his hips, bucking into her mouth each time she withdrew. He needed more. It flowed through her with his energy, awareness of him imprinted on her as she sucked him, savouring his taste. She lowered her left hand to his balls. He jerked up into her mouth as she rolled them, and barked out a moan as she dropped her hand lower, pressing fingers into the spot beneath them.

His pleasure hit her hard, telling her that he liked that. She rubbed him there as she worked her hand on his shaft and sucked him harder, building him back up, sending him soaring again.

He grunted and thrusted, free to move now both of her hands were occupied. She wasn't going to deny him. His left hand shot to the top of her head and she shivered as he twisted his fingers in her hair, gathering it into his fist, and held her in place as he pumped his hips harder, faster, his breaths bursting from his lips as he began to tense beneath her, his cock growing thicker in her mouth.

He was close.

Deliciously close.

She shoved him over the edge with a hard suck and a tug on his balls.

He arched off the rock, bellowed her name and did something that had her head jerking up and a thrill striking like lightning in her veins.

His wings exploded from his back, black leathery dragon like ones that were enormous.

She stared up at him as he spilled in her mouth, his lips parted to reveal his fangs, his horns flaring and curling even further, and his wings spread wide.

Gods, her demon was breathtaking.

He worked his hips still, each buck weaker than the last as he throbbed inside her, his body slowly relaxing as his climax ebbed.

He sank against the rock and she released him.

Ached for more.

The urge to climb up his body, will him back to hardness with her hand, and ride him was powerful, had her rising to her feet in front of him.

Cold swept through her.

Tegan's chest heaved as he panted, sweat covering it and his brow as he trembled and shook. His dull eyes struggled to hold hers, a dazed edge to them that terrified her.

She had taken too much from him.

Suki leaned over him, her hand flying to his right cheek. He was cold beneath her palm.

His hand shot to the back of her neck and she gasped as he twisted with her and pinned her beneath him, pressing her spine hard into the rock. His claws dug into her nape as he kissed her, claiming her mouth with a ferocity that lit a fire inside her, had her shock subsiding as pleasure rolled through her. It was intense. Erotic.

She lost herself in the kiss for a heartbeat, until the heat rolling through her became an icy chill that had her pulse spiking, prickles chasing over her skin as she grew aware of something.

She was weakening.

He was stealing her energy somehow.

Full-blown panic crashed over her and she focused to teleport.

Nothing happened.

She tried again, fear flooding her as that attempt failed too. She couldn't teleport. Why? Tegan's grip on her nape tightened, becoming painful as he kissed her harder, a growl rumbling in his chest as he dominated her, keeping her pinned beneath him. Her eyes widened.

Terror flared inside her.

He was stopping her from teleporting.

He was taking her energy.

She shoved against his chest and lashed out with her legs, but he wouldn't budge. He snarled and kissed her harder, draining more of her energy.

"Stop!" She battered his chest and shoulders, fear gripping her as her head grew light and the world wobbled around her.

She put all her strength into one last attempt to break free, pushing against his right shoulder only, and scrambled away from him when she managed to tilt him off balance and he lost his grip on her.

She backed away from him as he twisted towards her, his eyes glowing violet, wings huge as they flared from his back.

Warmth trickled down her nape.

She pressed her hand to it.

Tegan abruptly changed, the darkness and hunger in his expression washing away. His eyes widened and he lifted his hand before him, a stricken look on his face as he stared at the blood on his claws.

"Suki... I am sorry." He swallowed, his brow furrowed as he lifted his head and looked at her, fear and anguish in his eyes.

She teleported.

Landed in her small room and sank to her knees, terror still gripping her as her mind spun, thoughts blurring.

Not only could Tegan feed her energy, but he could take it too, and he could keep her from teleporting, anchoring her to the world in a way that normally required spells or charms.

Her hands shook as she planted them against her knees and stared at the dark wine-red covers on her bed.

What did it mean?

She twisted and sank to her backside on the Persian rug, and hugged her knees to her chest.

It meant she needed to know more about shadowed males, and she needed to find it out fast, because she was way out of her depth, and even though she feared the things he could do to her, she knew it was only a matter of time before the ache to see him again became too strong to deny.

When she saw him again, it would be armed with knowledge of his kind, no matter what she had to do to get it.

The voices of her sisters passing in the hall had her revising that.

She would do whatever it took other than asking her sisters. If she asked them, they would bring up the fact she should have been listening in all of their classes and would make her feel wretched about herself just when she had started feeling good again.

Because of Tegan.

She pushed to her feet, dusted herself off and pulled her shit together. Moping wasn't going to get her anywhere, and resisting the attraction and pull she felt towards Tegan wasn't an option either because she was tired of denying herself the things that made her feel good about herself.

Right now, she was shaken, but it would pass, and then she was going to want to see him again. It had been good until she had pushed him too far. She wasn't sure why he had changed so dramatically, but there had been genuine regret in his eyes when she had faced him and he had grown aware of what he had done.

She believed that he was sorry.

He had lost control when she had been sure she would be the one to do that. He could feed off her, could give her energy, and that meant he had a connection to her. A power possessed by all shadowed males? What if that connection had caused his reaction? Maybe he had sensed how close she was to losing control and it had pushed him over the edge instead.

She clung to that, her mind working at a million miles per hour as she tried to unravel the answers.

The truth about shadowed males.

To discover that, she was going to have to take a leaf out of Tegan's book.

She stormed towards the door, a succubus on a mission.

Her destination?

A place she had never set foot in before.

The clan library.

For the first time in possibly forever, she was going to read.

Gods help her.

CHAPTER 17

Tegan growled low as he kissed Suki, tasting the mead he had drunk from the tankards scattered around his study, brew that hadn't been enough to drown his sorrows, only enough to send him to sleep in his armchair.

He had woken in this dream, clutching her bare curves to his chest as the fire to his left crackled and popped, warming the pale furs beneath their knees.

His succubus purred in his arms and deepened the kiss, as wild for him as she had been on the beach. His cock stiffened, painfully hard at the memory of her mouth on it, how warm and wet she had been around him. He grunted and rubbed against her belly, shuddering as bliss rolled down the length of his shaft to tighten his balls.

Her fingers skimmed down his sides, feathering over his muscles as she moaned, as if the feel of his body gave her the ultimate delight. He drew a deep breath and growled as he smelled her arousal, the need he could feel simmering inside her through the connection that bloomed between them as their mouths fused. She rocked her body against his, her kiss growing desperate, as hungry as it had been earlier.

He swept his palms down her spine, drinking her moan as she trembled in his arms and pressed closer to him. He covered the peachy globes of her bottom with both hands and gripped it, held her to him as he kissed her, taking command. She melted into him, mewled into his mouth and rose up on her knees, bringing her body up his so he was closer to where he ached to be.

Where his female needed him.

She didn't resist as he spun her away from him, leaned back when he gathered her to him so her spine was against his front, relaxing into him. He feathered kisses over her shoulder, careful to avoid hurting her with his horns as he skimmed his hands up her slender thighs. She spread them and he groaned as he dipped his fingers inwards, felt her damp heat against them, luring him higher.

She shook in his arms as he gently stroked the length of her, teasing her plush petals open, and wriggled, spreading her legs as she seated herself on his thighs. He groaned and lightly bit her shoulder with blunt teeth as he slipped his fingers in, felt how hot and wet she was for him, how much she needed him.

On a low growl, he lifted her from his lap, gripped his cock and guided her back. A shudder wracked him as the head filled her and she eased back on him, slowly taking him into her. Her core gripped him hard, threatening to wring a climax from him before he was ready. He claimed her hips and tore a moan from her as he plunged deep and hard, seating himself to the root, unable to take her torturing him.

He gripped her hips and pumped her hard and fast, rocking her forwards each time he filled her from behind, her moans filling the air as she trembled against him. The urge to bite her and hold her to him flooded him, had his fangs lengthening as he took her, the pleasure that rolled through him clashing with hers as it filled him, driving him on. He grunted and clutched her shoulder, pinning her to him as he thrust faster, ripping cry after cry from her sweet lips as she arched away from him. He sank deeper, growled and couldn't stop himself from driving deeper still, giving her every inch of him.

Her need seized hold of him, had his primal instincts firing, control slipping from his grasp as he gripped her and thrust harder, faster, his breaths sawing from him and sweat rolling down his spine as he pushed her higher and higher. She rocked and rotated her hips, bucked and pushed him on, demanding more that he gave to her, until the room was filled with the sounds of their pleasure as their bodies met and parted.

She bowed forwards, a hoarse cry fleeing her lips as she quivered around his cock, pulsing and gripping it, pulling him over the edge with her. He snarled and roared, arched backwards to drive as deep as she could take him as pleasure blasted through him, his seed exploding from him in waves that rocked him, had him breathless and frozen, his entire body locking up as release took him.

His fangs ached, the need to press them into her flesh and mark her rising to the fore as he marked her trembling core with his seed.

He stared at the back of her neck, at the smooth column of her bared throat, and sank back onto the furs, bringing her with him. Instead of biting her, he wrapped his arms around her and held her to him, feeling her breathing as her body continued to spasm, sensing her satisfaction and bliss as it swept through the growing connection between them.

He closed his eyes and loosed his breath, sinking deeper into the furs.

When he opened them again, the canopy of his bed greeted him.

Tegan stretched and groaned, a glimmer of the pleasure he had felt in his dream rolling through him, deep satisfaction that had him boneless on the four-poster bed.

He stared at the swaths of material, not seeing them as he recalled elements of the dream, ones that matched up with what he had experienced in the real world with Suki.

Signs that she was his fated one.

The one he had been born to love and cherish.

The one he had been made for.

His forever.

He let his head fall to his left and looked at the phone resting on the furs beside his latest book and a discarded tankard.

His hand felt heavy as he reached for it, his heart a weight in his chest that pulled him down. He fingered the device, slowly dragging it within his reach, nerves rising as he thought about Suki, mingling with the anger that refused to abate.

Rage directed at himself.

He grabbed the phone and lifted it, woke the screen with a tap of his thumb and stared.

Stared.

Fear gripped him, fiercer than anything he had ever felt on a battlefield. He breathed through it, his hand shaking as he worked his way into the contacts list. A list that held only one number.

One name.

Suki xoxo.

He wasn't sure whether Xoxo was her last name, or whether it had another meaning. He stared at her name, at her number, fighting another bout of nerves. She was angry with him and he deserved it. If she was still furious with him, he would take whatever harsh words she threw at him. He would let her strike him physically if it would make her feel better.

He would do anything to make her believe he was sorry.

He had lost control and he had hurt her, and he wanted to say it would never happen again, but the urges he felt when he was around her were only growing stronger and harder to deny.

But he would do his best to contain them.

For her.

He swallowed his pride and recited his apology in his head, practicing to get it right. To make it perfect.

He wasn't sure whether calling her now, before she'd had a chance to calm down and forgive him, would make things worse or better, but he needed to hear her voice. He needed to apologise again.

He needed to know he hadn't messed everything up.

He pressed the button, hesitated, and then brought the phone to his ear, a growl rising up his throat when his horns got in the way.

It rang.

And rang.

She wasn't going to answer. He couldn't blame her.

His hope faded, heart sinking as he listened to it ringing. Had he lost her?

"Yeah?" Her voice came over the line, sharp pants following her greeting.

Why was his female out of breath?

His mood took a dark turn as one answer came to him. "What are you doing?"

He braced himself, expecting the worst, waiting for her to say she was with a male, one who wasn't liable to hurt her or attempt to bite her against her will.

"I don't have time for pleasantries, Solid Twelve," she snapped, and he didn't miss that he had retained his rise in rank despite what he had done. "I'm in a spot of bother."

Bother?

She was in trouble.

His female was in trouble and he hadn't known. He bolted upright, his horns curling further, almost knocking the phone from his grip as he tried to keep it pinned to his ear.

"Where are you?" he barked. "What is happening?"

"The fae town," she breathed and then muttered a ripe curse as the sound of clay shattering filled his ears.

Was it a raid? His blood chilled.

He gripped the phone harder and the line crackled, distorting as the device began to succumb to the pressure. It was hard, but he eased his hold on it as he leaped from the bed and pulled his leathers on with one hand, fighting the damned things as he hopped around the room on one foot.

"Wait there," he gritted as he managed to get both of his feet into his trousers and wrestled them upwards.

"Can't really," she panted. "Fighting for... my life here."

That chill in his blood ignited into an inferno and his wings burst from his bare back.

His female was strong, but she had vulnerabilities, was not as strong as many immortals, and humans could use drugs on her to slow her, allowing them to capture her. If it was Archangel and they took her, he would bring the wrath of the Second Realm down upon London to take her back.

Her voice grew distant, as if she was holding the device away from her as she shouted, "Take that, you piece of shit incubus. Kiss my ass!"

A male voice replied. "Fuck knows what disease I'd get if I did that, you defective bitch. You put the suck in succubus!"

Tegan's blood boiled.

The male dared to insult his female?

His heart bled in his chest as he waited for her retort and none left her lips, and he could almost see how she would look, how deep those words would have struck her. She doubted herself, thought herself a failure, and this vicious bastard was playing on that to wound her.

"Teleport," he snarled into the phone as his horns flared, twisting around on themselves and his muscles ached, his rage snaring command of him and pushing him to transform into his other form, one where an incubus would be little more than an inconvenience to him.

"Can't," she panted. "They hit me with a spell. Can't teleport till it wears off. Bastards were waiting for me."

Plural.

He growled low as his body began to grow, bones lengthening and muscles expanding, and every instinct in him roared to go to her, because she meant everything to him. He would drop everything for her. If she ever needed him, he would be there for her. If she was ever in danger, he would run to save her.

"I am coming, Suki," he bit out and stoked the rage inside him, giving it free reign over him, even when he knew it was dangerous to do such a thing. Instinct would be at the helm and anyone who so much as looked at Suki would be labelled as an enemy, one he needed to kill, but holding back now was impossible. He snarled through his fangs. "I will tear the incubi to shreds with my claws."

The black abyss opened beneath him and he dropped into it, pinning his wings back as he emerged on the other side, dropping out of the teleport above the fae town, close to the ceiling of the cavern.

He twisted and plummeted, swooping down towards the buildings, his gaze sharp and scanning everywhere for her. He had heard clay shattering. The witches' district.

He banked in that direction and spread his wings, beat them hard and shot towards that area of the town. Undulating green-blue roofs zoomed towards him and he twisted hard to his left as he neared them, skimmed along the glazed tiles and beat his wings again, gaining elevation.

And a lot of stares from the street below.

His eyes scanned it, spotting the broken pottery and furious witches as they looked north. Towards the square.

His gaze leaped there.

His heart lodged in his throat.

Suki.

She was running towards the witches' district again, wild sea-coloured hair bouncing with each long stride as her bare legs pumped, sending her short crimson plaid skirt flapping around her hips. Her open white shirt fluttered behind her, breasts bobbing in the tiny black top she wore beneath.

She glanced over her shoulder and then ahead again, and something crossed her face, her expression going slack for a moment before her eyes darted up, locking straight on him as he shot towards her. He pinned his wings back to gain momentum as he fixed his gaze on the cobbles just beyond her.

Between her and the three blond black-leather-clad males pursuing her.

On a vicious roar, he slammed into the cobbles, sending several of them flying as a shockwave rushed out in all directions from his point of impact.

The three incubi skidded to a halt, their bright blue and gold eyes enormous as they reared back. One fell on his backside with a grunt. That one wisely scrambled away from him, placing the other two between them.

The scent of fear that laced the air was strongest on him.

Had he been the one to hurt Suki with those vicious barbs?

Tegan bared his fangs at the despicable male. He would die first.

He spread his leathery black wings, forming a barrier between the incubi and Suki as she stopped running. Her eyes drifted down his spine, the heat she ignited in him whenever she looked at him stoking his rage rather than his desire this time.

He drew down a deep breath and straightened as he continued to transform, as the three males dropped away from him, looking smaller by the second as he reached his full ten-foot height.

His horns curled again, twisting around into deadly points that matched his claws as they extended to resemble black talons. His lower canines sharpened as his transformation completed and he leaned forwards and roared at the three males, tearing a gasp from the few people who had gathered to watch.

And Suki.

She stood behind him, her shock flowing over him.

Did the sight of him as he was now frighten her?

Gods, he hoped it didn't.

It was the last reasonable thought he had as his mind darkened, his instinct to protect her rising to the fore. His gaze darted from one incubus to the other, assessing them. They were not a threat to him.

Puny males.

On a low snarl, he held his right hand out before him.

The most fearful of the males tensed, as if he was about to be struck. Not yet. Soon. Tegan was going to take great satisfaction from making that male pay.

He twisted his hand palm down and focused, haziness running through his body and his mind as he connected with the earth and power rippled through him, twining with his own. His eyelids drooped as that power spread and his strength rose.

The violet pommel stone of his sword emerged from the fracture cobbles in front of him.

All eyes left him, their focus shifting to the weapon rising from the ground before him. A weapon he hadn't used in combat in a thousand years.

His lips pulled back in a harsh grin that flashed his fangs as the black leather grip emerged and then the gold guard. The broad silver blade breached the earth and he stared at it, at the words inscribed on it in the demon tongue, an oath to keep all those who were dear to him safe with this mighty weapon the earth had given to him.

He ached to reach down and grip the hilt, to pull it from the earth and feel the weight of it in his palm once more as he upheld that vow, but he forced himself to be patient, to receive this gift of nature in a manner fitting of a king.

Plus, he enjoyed watching the incubi quake in fear and their eyes grow ever larger as they watched the sword continuing to rise, the blade three feet long and then four, and then five.

It tapered to a point at last and he twisted his hand and slid it down the hilt, curled his fingers around it and didn't hesitate.

The moment it was in his grip, he launched at the stunned incubi on a vicious roar, the need to protect Suki and destroy her enemies pounding in his veins, drumming in his heart, a beat that filled his head and commanded him.

The first male was swift to teleport and snagged the one who had remained on the floor. The remaining male roused himself at the last second and hurled himself to the left, hitting the cobbles in an ungainly sprawl. He scrambled away.

Tegan turned to track him and swung again, aiming his blade at the male's back, just above his hips. A blow that would sever his spine if it connected. He snarled as the male teleported just as his sword reached him, the fury burning in his veins blazing hotter.

His quarry were wily.

Infuriating.

He grunted as one of the males slammed into his back, a heavy boot hitting his lower spine and shoving him forwards. On a feral snarl, he pivoted, bringing his sword around at the same time. His wings battered the male, forcing him back, and he grinned, flashing fangs as he kicked off, launching after the incubus as he attempted to gain some space. His senses blared a warning and he raised his right arm, blocking the attack of the second incubus, a punch that barely registered on his forearm.

He swung his left fist, slamming it into the male's face. Blood spurted from his nose, the sound of bone shattering a pleasing sound as Tegan rounded on him. It wasn't the one who had insulted Suki, but it was a victory, one that had the hunger for bloodshed burning brighter, stealing more control from him.

He snarled when the remaining two incubi swarmed him and he tried to counter them, blocking their blows as they appeared and disappeared. Their comrade slunk away, clutching his bloodied nose with one hand.

Tegan opened his portal, dropping into it and out of the air just in front of the bleeding male, swinging his sword as he emerged from the teleport. The tip of it slashed across the male's chest, cutting through his leather jacket, ripping a satisfying bellow from his lips.

The one who had insulted Suki suddenly appeared before him, catching him off guard. His fist smashed into Tegan's jaw, knocking his head to his right. Tegan snarled as he shook off the blow and his blade was a silver arc as it cut through the air. The male teleported as it reached him and Tegan twisted on his heel, coming to face the male as he appeared behind him, unwilling to fall for that again.

The other incubus kicked him in the back, knocking him off balance as he swung his sword. He flared his wings and beat them, battering the bastard and lifting off the ground, stopping himself from falling towards his primary target as the male produced a dagger.

He slashed at Tegan with it and Tegan dodged, sweeping right and coming around behind the male as he swung his blade again, aiming it at the incubus's throat.

The male with the bloody nose grabbed him before Tegan's blade could reach him, teleporting him away.

Tegan was ready for them this time, his senses sharpened and attuned to their scent. He spun in the air as those senses flared, the smell of blood appearing behind him, and swung his sword, a roar peeling from his lips as it cut towards nothing but air.

And then cut down the back of the incubus.

He yelled and arched forwards, blood swiftly tracking down his back as he staggered, knocking the other injured male to the ground.

"This is your fault." The third male, the only one he had yet to wound, spat from behind him.

"Fuck you," Suki snapped.

Tegan teleported, his vicious growl echoing in the brief flash of darkness before he emerged in the fae town again, directly between her and the incubus.

His eyes widened as he saw her standing before him, facing the male, not safely tucked behind him. The world slowed as the male lunged forwards, the dagger he gripped flashing silver in the lamps around the square.

Tegan's heart seized.

He reached for Suki, desperate to pull her from the path of the blade as she merely stared at it, her eyes slowly widening as horror filled them.

His fingers closed over her shoulder.

The blade pierced an inch below them.

Suki screamed, the harrowing sound turning his blood to icy sludge in his veins for a moment before it burst into flames and he roared, unleashing every drop of his rage in it.

His error in calculating his teleport had cost his female greatly.

Anger surged through him, fury aimed at both himself and the incubus who had wounded her as Tegan pulled her to him, tugging her free of the blade, and shoved her behind him. His mouth opened on another roar as he spread his wings and lunged towards the stunned male as he stared at his dagger and the blood rolling down it.

Suki's blood.

The sweet honey and spice scent of it flooded the air, stoking Tegan's rage, and he gripped his broadsword in both hands and shoved it forwards.

Deep into the side of the bastard incubus.

He twisted the blade in his grip, determined the cut the male in two for his part in what had happened.

The other two incubi grabbed him and teleported before he could make that happen.

He roared again, frustration coursing through him, darkening his mood and giving his rage a firmer hold on him. He swept his hand through the blood that coated his blade and licked his palm, tasting the copper as his senses sparked, one of his demonic gifts triggering in response to the blood.

Allowing him to pinpoint the male's exact location.

He teleported and appeared outside what looked like an elegant Georgian country house in the corner of the cavern, near to the entrance and the demon district.

The three males froze and looked back at him, their faces ashen and fear colouring their blue and gold eyes.

They would pay for what had happened to Suki.

He wouldn't stop until death had come for them all.

The heavy doors of the mansion opened and more incubi poured out, several of them stronger than the males standing before him. They came to face him now, the fear ebbing as they sensed the same shift in tides as he did. He glanced at the demon district to his right, where several males had already gathered, some of them looking as if they might aid him in a fight.

It was a struggle when he wanted to rip apart every incubi with his bare hands, but he managed to calm his mind enough to calculate his odds of winning as his gaze skimmed over the gathered incubi, close to thirty of them in total. The three he had fought had proven wily adversaries, using their ability to swiftly teleport to their advantage, and the two-dozen-plus lining the front of the elegant sandstone mansion were armed with swords.

Awareness shot down his spine, ripping a growl from him, and he looked over his shoulder, beyond his black leathery wings.

To Suki.

She hurried towards him, her face stricken, fear shining in her dazzling eyes.

Together with pain.

His gaze fell to her right hand where it pressed against her shoulder, her clenched fingers lined with blood that tracked down the front of her white shirt and stained her skin.

A wound he felt partly responsible for. He should have been the one bleeding, not her. His delicate little female.

She halted, breathing hard, and her eyes strayed from his to take in the incubi. She slowly shook her head, her eyebrows furrowing as her gaze darted back to him.

"Stop. They learned their lesson," she said with another shake of her head.

One of the incubi was quick to speak. "We won't bother her again."

That didn't appease Tegan.

His blood screamed at him to slay the entire incubi clan, but his heart roared at him to take care of his mate.

It won.

He stabbed his broadsword into the cobbles, waiting for it to start sinking into the earth again before he turned and stomped towards her. His gaze flickered over her shoulder and his rage gave way under the weight of fear that flooded him. His female was hurt. Bleeding. The thought that he might lose her, even when he knew she was strong enough to survive the flesh wound, seized him in icy talons and squeezed the air from his lungs.

He gathered her to him, tucking her close, his hand on the back of her head as he guided it to his chest. She nestled against him, trembling in his arms, her fear flowing into him as he lowered his head and breathed in her scent, a vain attempt to calm himself.

Tegan wrapped his wings around her and roared at the incubi.

Suki winced, tensing against him, and the scent of her blood grew stronger, choking him and pulling at his heart.

He needed to take his female somewhere safe.

A black abyss opened beneath them.

He would take her to the safest place he knew.

CHAPTER 18

Suki's entire body went rigid against him as the darkness devoured them. Cold swept over Tegan's wings as he tucked them more tightly around her and held her closer. She was safe. She didn't need to fear now.

He had her.

"Calm," he grumbled and wanted to growl when it came out in the demon tongue rather than English.

He wasn't sure she knew his language.

His face twisted with the frustration that mounted inside him again as he wrestled with his rage, the anger keeping his body transformed, fury that refused to abate while the delicate scent of her blood laced his senses.

They landed gently, rising out of the black earth in the garden of his mansion, a building that resembled the Tudor country houses of England only instead of sandstone, it had been constructed from the onyx stone of his kingdom.

The mansion formed an angular C when he viewed it from the air and stood three storeys tall, the left and right thirds of the building set forwards from the others, allowing windows on the inner sides of their walls that faced each other across an open sort of courtyard.

The entryway was his most recent addition, with a broad flattened pointed arched doorway that housed the imposing dark double doors. On each floor, windows made of between nine and fifteen smaller rectangular panes of glass set into dark wooden frames allowed what little light there was in his kingdom to flood into the rooms, brightening them.

He had spent decades building this home for himself, remodelling it over the ages based on information brought to him by his aides and his brother, but had lost interest in renovating it around four centuries ago, when the weight of his crown and the captivity he endured had begun to take its toll on him.

He rarely visited now, but the servants who lived in the house kept it in order for him and his brother used it frequently.

Because Tegan wasn't the only one who preferred life away from the castle.

The hold his rage had on him began to ebb, fading as he looked at it, growing aware that Suki was safe now. No one would hurt her here, and incubi, like succubi, were born of fae origin, meaning they couldn't teleport into Hell using the portal pathways without assistance from one who could use them or a spell.

Even if the incubi could enter Hell, they would never find her.

They would never reach her.

He would make sure of that.

Suki moved in his arms, attempting to twist her head to look over her shoulder, no doubt curious about where he had taken her. She winced.

"Bugger," she muttered and the scent of her blood grew stronger.

"Be more careful, little female," he murmured softly in the demon tongue. "It kills me whenever I sense your pain."

She tilted her head back. "I don't speak demon. At least not well. I only know a few words I'm afraid. I don't know what you're saying."

He knew. His face crumpled again as he looked down into her green-to-blue eyes and he smoothed his thumb across her ashen cheek, his fingertips resting against her jaw.

"I apologise," he grumbled, in the demon language again. He drew down a slow deep breath and tried again to speak her language, but the words refused to line up on his tongue, so he spoke in his own language. "Until I calm, it is beyond me."

A failing he almost didn't want her to know about.

When she looked as if she might speak, he scooped her up into his arms and tucked her against his chest. She didn't resist him, had heat pouring through him to ease his tight muscles as she leaned her side against him, relaxing into his embrace.

Trusting him.

He was gentle with her as he carried her, aware of his size compared with her now, and how monstrous he probably looked to her. She peered around, not seeming to care about the change that had come over him or her pain as she took in her surroundings.

"Is this your place?" Her eyes didn't leave the mansion as they neared it.

He nodded.

"It's nice." She winced again and pressed her hand against her bloodied shoulder.

He gentled his grip on her, afraid he had caused her pain, and shouldered the door open.

Someone rushed from a corridor to his right as he entered the main vestibule, one that was the height of all three floors of the house. He bared his fangs at the young demon, his horns curling as the male skidded to a halt on the dark stone floor and his black eyes fell on Tegan's precious cargo.

The male swiftly averted his gaze, pinning it on the floor near the door. "Greetings, my king."

Tegan really hoped Suki had been telling the truth and didn't know enough of the demon language to understand the servant. He risked a glance at her. She was busily taking in the foyer, her eyes dancing over everything, including the huge gold chandelier that hung above them between the middle and top level of the building, the candles casting warm light over the dark wooden staircase that wound its way up to each floor.

"Leave us," Tegan grunted at the male. "Remain in your quarters until called."

Because he didn't want the male accidentally revealing things to Suki, and he definitely didn't want the demon looking at her, not when he was finally clawing back control. He was liable to lash out and hurt the male, the instinct to keep her to himself making him view the male as a threat, one liable to attempt to steal Suki from him.

"In fact, stay in the gatehouse." He turned away from the male and mounted the steps, taking Suki up to the first floor, and banked left, the wooden floorboards creaking under his extra weight as he headed towards the drawing room.

He sensed the male leave and another wave of calm washed over him, easing his mood.

His rage finally began to ebb enough that he could regain control, and Suki squeaked in his arms as he began to shift, his bones shortening again and muscles shrinking back to their normal state. He sent his wings away and rolled his shoulders, trying to ease the tension from them.

He carried her into his favourite drawing room, one at the rear of the house that had a view over what passed for his garden. The neatly trimmed shrubs in the elegant borders were almost black rather than green, and he had never gotten around to tapping into a spring in the mountains just beyond his estate in order to fuel the series of fountains he had installed along the path between each section of the garden, but it was his favourite view in the kingdom.

What would Suki think of it?

He set her down on the middle of three gilt-framed dark violet couches that surrounded the huge white marble fireplace.

She didn't pay attention to him as he carefully removed her ruined shirt and used it to clean the blood from her wound. Her eyes continued to leap around, swiftly taking in everything, fascination shining in them. He breathed a sigh of relief as he looked at her injury.

It wasn't as deep as he had feared.

The last remnants of his fury faded and he eased to his knees on the pale cream fur that filled the space between the couches.

"You live here?" Her gaze settled on the plum coloured walls with their gilt-framed panels, the oak sideboards with their delicate crystal decanters and glasses, and the bookcases filled with some of his favourite reads. "It doesn't look very demony."

Because it wasn't all black and grim like the Hell she imagined?

He moved to kneel before the fire, stoked it and then placed another log on it, waiting for it to catch before he pushed to his feet and lit the oil lamps on the mantel above it. He took one and placed it on the wooden table near to her that formed a corner in the semicircle of couches.

His gaze flickered to the wound on Suki's chest and lingered. She glanced down at it, frowned and prodded around it.

"It'll heal." She took the shirt he had discarded and dabbed at a drop of blood that cascaded from it, darting towards her small black top that hugged her breasts.

This time, when the words lined up, they came out in the common tongue, bringing a glimmer of relief to him and to Suki judging by the way her features softened.

"How quickly?" He sank to his knees before her again, the need to see her healed firmly at the helm as he stared at the wound and it felt as if someone had plunged a blade into his chest rather than hers, right into his heart. "I want you healed now. If I kissed you, would you heal faster?"

His eyes leaped up to hers, his brow furrowing.

"I will not lose control again. I swear it, Suki. I did not mean to frighten you... and I hate that I was so... *rough* with you."

Her soft smile struck him hard in the heart. "I know. I pushed a little too hard and took a little too much I think."

"I did not feel so weak after... after I—" He cut himself off, unable to think about what he had done let alone speak about it.

"I'll take a little kiss as an apology." She shuffled to the edge of the couch and he did his best not to stare at how her crimson plaid skirt rode up to flash dark lace panties at him.

Her boots hit the fur on either side of his thighs, she gently cupped his cheeks and leaned towards him, so slowly that anticipation stole his breath and had his heart thumping against his ribs.

When her lips finally met his, her kiss was gentle, soft in a way that lifted him from the mire of his thoughts and the bleak abyss of what he had done, had him filling with light inside as she drove all the darkness back. After his dream of her, the kiss was too restrained, too sweet by far, but gods, it was what he needed. This gentleness. This tender connection to her.

It told him that he hadn't ruined everything.

Reassured him in ways he hadn't even realised he needed.

He felt the moment she began to take energy from him, sensed the subtle drain on his strength as she moaned and moved closer, kissed him deeper, as if she couldn't get enough of his taste. He reached for her, aching to hold her close as he kissed her, but she pulled back, a sigh escaping her as her eyes slipped shut and she sank into the violet couch, a satisfied smile curling her rosy lips.

His female was sated, and gods, she was beautiful.

He drank in the sight of her, enjoying how relaxed she looked in his home, alone with him, and the fact she already looked brighter, some of the colour returning to her cheeks, and her wound had stopped bleeding. The skin around it was paling now, no longer red and angry. He had done that for her. He had given her strength in his kiss, boosting her ability to heal the wound. He had protected her and now he would keep her safe.

Here with him.

Her eyes slowly opened and she smiled lazily as she looked him over.

"Are we going to talk about this house?" Her gaze left him to take in the room again. "Because I get the feeling I have to amend my notes about you. You're not rich. You're filthy rich."

He shrugged that off, uncomfortable as a feeling ran through him, a fear she might probe about what he did for a living.

"It is my family's home." Would that be enough to convince her that his wealth was inherited and stop her from probing further? "My brother still visits from time to time, when he is not training those under his command."

"But you do live here?"

"When I am not at the castle." He hoped she didn't probe too deeply into that either, but he didn't want to lie to her. He just wanted to deflect a little until he was sure of some things.

Like she was falling for him as he was falling for her.

She frowned and pushed up, so she was sitting rather than lounging on the couch. "Are you often at the castle?"

He nodded. "My duty is there."

"Ah." She wriggled and pressed the soles of her boots to his thighs, and he didn't mind her stepping on him like that, quite enjoyed the strange intimacy of it because he had the feeling she liked being connected to him, in contact with him in a way. "Because you're planning all kinds of things for the kingdom, right?"

He nodded again. "That is part of the reason. I have other duties."

Duties seemed like an understatement.

"What are they?" She leaned towards him and winced.

Tegan took the out. "Did you take enough energy from me?"

He could feel that she was hungry, could see it in her eyes whenever they leaped to his mouth too, her irises brightening briefly before she dragged her gaze away again. Their chaste kiss hadn't been enough for her. She wanted more, but was denying herself. Why? Because she feared he would hurt her again?

"I could do with a top up," she murmured huskily, stirring his blood, and then tossed ice onto it. "But maybe a rest first. I want to know more about this place."

She dropped her feet from his thighs, pushed onto them and toed off her boots, leaving them in a pile on the fur beside him as she moved off. When he turned, he found her looking at the black leather wingback armchair he had moved beside the fire when he had visited a few years ago.

She sat in it, brought her feet up and twisted her knees to her left, her eyes on the flames that danced on the logs, the warm light flickering over her face and her colourful hair, brightening the shades of green and blue, and the hints of violet.

Gods, she looked good in his chair, all curled up as if she belonged there.

"It's not what I expected." She took in everything on the other side of the room to her, from the bookcases between the windows to the black grand piano that occupied a space near the door on the right of the room.

He hoped she didn't ask him to play it. He hadn't practiced in decades and his skills were a little rusty.

"Better or worse?" He wasn't sure he wanted to know as he stood and turned to face the fireplace and her where she sat to the left of it.

She smiled. "Far better."

Her tone said he was a fool for thinking her answer would be anything else.

She pointed to the windows. "You have glass and everything. I didn't expect that. I've visited a couple of towns in the free realm and it's mostly open holes for windows there."

Her gaze skipped over the room again, taking in the paintings this time. When they reached the painting hanging above the fireplace, she paused. Her eyes widened. She leaped to her feet on his armchair, using it as a stool as she grabbed the mantelpiece and peered closer at the seascape.

She whipped to face him. "You're shitting me, right? That does not say Van Gogh!"

Tegan looked at the painting, one that captured the sea and sailboats battling gentle waves near the shore. He had spent more hours than he could calculate staring at that painting, enjoying the drama and blend of colours, and the craftsmanship.

He nodded.

"So, it's a copy... right?" Her wide eyes searched his. "*Right?*"

He shook his head.

She whistled low. "Damn, when I said you were filthy rich, I meant like... normal filthy rich. This is billionaire playboy level filthy rich."

He didn't really grasp the difference.

"I liked it. I like the ocean." He looked at her again. "You must too. Your hair is like the sea and you took me to a beach."

She sank back into his armchair and crossed her legs. "I do like the ocean. There's something wild and untamed about it. It speaks to me."

He moved to sit on the end of the couch opposite her. "Strange. I find it calming and peaceful."

But he liked that they had something in common.

CHAPTER 19

Suki wanted Tegan closer. The sight of him battling the incubi for her and the fact he had come rushing to her rescue had roused a fierce need inside her, one she was barely keeping a lid on as she sat with him in his home.

Alone.

She was deeply aware of that as she studied the oil painting, shivering under the intensity of Tegan's gaze as it devoured her. Warmth spilled through her, but chills washed it away whenever his eyes landed on her shoulder. It throbbed, a constant reminder that she had been wounded.

It wasn't the first time she had been cut or been in a fight, but it was the first time she had been bone-deep afraid, had locked up so tight she had only been able to watch as the dagger had come zooming at her. Her heart had almost stopped in that moment. She had been so convinced her life had been about to come to a horrible end.

Just when it had been getting good.

That realisation had struck her like a thunderbolt, a million volts that had poured through her and left her reeling when she had survived.

Her eyes lowered to meet Tegan's, their dark depths drawing her deep under his spell.

The lessons she'd had as a youth had been a lie.

It was possible for a succubus to love.

It had to be.

Because there was no other explanation for how she changed whenever she was around Tegan, filling with warmth and light whenever they were together, or how she ached whenever they were apart, filled with a need to see him again, to call him and hear his voice.

She had watched enough movies and enough couples in the real world. What she was experiencing with Tegan was what those people went through.

She was falling for him.

Was he falling for her?

He had come rushing to her rescue, had fought in her corner. No one had ever done that for her before. Not even her sisters. Did that mean he liked her? More than liked her?

A flush darkened his cheeks and he looked away, frowned at the fire and moved to it, sinking to his knees before the grate. She was unnerving him. It was strange to have such a power over such a strong male.

She tried to think of a subject other than his enormous wealth, because it was clear she had unsettled him by asking about it and about the house. He had mentioned a brother, one who was in the military by the sounds of things.

"So the Second Realm still has an army?" She smiled when he looked across his bare shoulder at her and tried not to melt into a puddle over the way his deltoids and biceps flexed as he curled his fingers around the fire iron.

His eyes were guarded again. What had his barriers coming up this time?

She wanted to poke, but let it go, because the ground beneath them still felt unsteady after what had happened at the cove, and she didn't want to sour things between them. She wanted things to be good again, as it had been before he had gotten carried away.

Her study in the clan library hadn't turned up anything new about shadowed males. No explanation for the things he could do other than the usual labelling him as dangerous because of the abilities he possessed. But it had turned up a few interesting titbits about demons. Apparently, the First and Second Realms had some sort of peace treaty happening between them. A strange sense of relief had washed through her on reading that.

Tegan had fought in so many wars, was very obviously a warrior at heart, and the thought of him fighting in battles against hordes of enemies frightened her. She was glad his kingdom was a peaceful one. Although, she wasn't sure how he felt about it.

He finally nodded, set the poker aside and stared at the flames. They danced in his dark eyes, the sort of fire that she associated with this realm. Hell. From what she had seen of it outside, it was as black and forbidding in the Second Realm as it was in the free one. But the mansion had been beautiful, a gothic vision cut in obsidian stone, and the inside looked much like any other house in the mortal world.

Or at least the immortal part of the mortal world.

His taste ran the gothic route inside too, rich but dark colours paired with wood and elegant accents.

But it was a world away from the drab black basic home she had imagined he owned.

"What's it like to you?" she said and a confused crinkle formed between the dark slashes of his eyebrows. She probably should have picked better words. She had started the conversation in her head. It wasn't a surprise that he didn't know what she was asking about. "Being at peace. Demons like war, don't they? You fought in a lot of them and last I heard, the demon realms are always at each other's throats. It's like a game to you guys."

Tegan shot to his feet, his expression blackening as that corona of violet-red flared around his pupils. "War is no game. It is a serious affair and not to be undertaken lightly. Kings who enter wars without considering the consequences of their actions or while regarding them as *games* should not sit on the throne."

She had hit another sore spot.

She cringed at that and cursed herself for speaking so lightly of battles and war.

He had been forced to fight for his life in them as a youth, had been shaped on the battlefield into the warrior stood before her with fury blazing in his eyes, his muscular torso tensed and firelight chasing over his skin, revealing the silvery scars that hid beneath the fine dusting of dark hair.

"Sorry." She picked at the arm of the leather chair, doing her best not to shrink under his steady hard gaze. "I just meant that war seemed to be a fact of demon life."

His tone gentled. "It is something we are accustomed to. A part of our existence that has led to my kind becoming warriors at heart."

"It must have taken some balls for your king to pick peace over war." She lifted her eyes back to him, gauging his feelings on the subject as best she could without being able to read his aura.

He scowled at the fire and she didn't need to read his aura to know he didn't like it.

"The current king did not make that decision." He was silent for a minute that felt like an hour, his face etched in pensive lines, before he added, "It was the right decision to make though."

He closed his eyes, drew down a deep breath and sighed.

"The people were dying... starving. Famine was rife across the kingdom because a disease had destroyed the livestock. The kingdom could not provide for its people. The elves and the First Realm pledged aid in exchange for peace. Edyn would have been a fool to turn down that offer."

"Edyn?" She watched him closely, because from where she was sitting, it sounded a hell of a lot like he had personally known the king.

He stroked his horn, his handsome face shifting towards sombreness as he breathed another long sigh.

When he opened his eyes and looked at her, they were hollow and haunted, and she wanted to go to him and do something to comfort him, because she could read in them that he was in pain.

"We were close. As commander of the Royal Legion, I advised him on the treaty. I was against it, but it did not deter him. He went ahead with it and it was the right thing to do."

"What happened to him?" Because something had happened, it didn't take a genius to see that.

It took only a single look into his eyes.

The pain they held grew. "A courtesan… They were alone together and she claimed Edyn had been rough with her and it had been self-defence. I knew he would never act like that, and it did not take long in the cells before she confessed she had aligned with the Sixth Realm. The murder had been meant to halt the forming of the treaty. Her act came too late… Although the ink had barely been dry at the time."

His eyes darkened as they turned to the fire and narrowed as his hands clamped down on the mantelpiece and he leaned over, hanging his head between his arms.

"I wanted to go to war and make the Sixth Realm pay for what they had done, but the truce bound my hands," he gritted, his deep voice a black snarl that spoke of his anger and his hurt. "That truce had been Edyn's last act in this world, it had been important to him… I could not bring myself to break it. I failed him. I failed to save him and I will forever live with that weight on my heart."

She stood, unable to keep still any longer, and closed the gap between them. She settled her hand on his left arm and ducked so she could see past it to his face, and her heart went out to him when she saw the tears lining his eyes and the regret swimming in them. He twisted away from her on a low growl and paced towards the couch, his right hand tracing the patterns on his horns.

The way his fingers followed the gold inlaid into the black told her much.

He had been close to the king and the pattern engraved on his polished black horns was meant to honour the fallen male.

She stepped into his path as he paced back towards her, stopping him. He gazed down at her, his head bent, his fingers methodically following the lines and swirls of gold on his horns. When she lifted her hand and stroked the tips of her fingers over each arc, following them down from the root, his fingers stilled.

"Did it hurt when you did this?" She searched his eyes.

He nodded and swallowed thickly, the pain lingering in his steady gaze.

"Was this your penance?" She caught the sorrow that flooded his eyes before he averted them and brushed her arm away.

Gently.

Many men would have shoved her arm aside, but even in the deepest grip of his pain, Tegan was being gentle with her. He wanted to keep that vow not to hurt her again, and she appreciated that, more than he would ever know.

He didn't want to talk about this, but she did, because she finally felt as if she was connecting with him, as if there was a string that tied them together and she wasn't alone in this world.

He'd had someone he loved ripped from him too.

"You must have loved him dearly." She kept her voice gentle and soft, a bare murmur as tension bracketed his mouth and anguish flared in his eyes.

Guilt burned stronger inside her, but she needed this connection to him, because she had never felt this with anyone before him. It was more than kinship. There was a bond growing between them, and as much as it frightened her, it thrilled her too, brought light into her life and lifted her as it made her see she wasn't alone.

She really wasn't alone.

Tegan had fought in her corner, he had defended her, and now he had revealed he held a similar pain in his heart. If she had believed in soul mates, the ridiculous mortal notion that there was one person out there who was a perfect match for you, she might have thought he was the other half of her, the one piece that would complete her.

Ridiculous.

She tried to laugh off the idea, but it stuck, taking root in her heart as she gazed at him. Succubi didn't have soul mates. They didn't fall in love.

They didn't.

"I loved him like a brother." He pushed past her, sighed and sank into the chair she had occupied. She turned towards him. He closed his eyes and tipped his head up as he slumped against the back of the armchair, his horns catching the firelight and his black-leather-clad legs spread as he draped his arms over the rests. "I lost much that day a thousand years ago."

A gasp lodged in her throat when the black shadows rising from his shoulders flickered to reveal a hint of deepest blue and dark grey, a glimmer of his sorrow, and she felt bad for pressing him. The pain he felt had to be intense to have lasted so long without fading.

Or perhaps it had faded, and the intense hurt she could read in him was only a fraction of what he had felt the night he had lost Edyn.

He stroked his horn, thoughtful and distant as he stared at the fireplace. "My horns… it was not penance… or perhaps it was in a way. I did it to honour Edyn. The ink too."

His fingers reached the root of his right horn and drifted over the intricate swirls and arcs tattooed in black on the side of his head, a design that centred around his horn.

Suki swallowed her nerves. She wanted this connection to him, and to forge it between them, to make it unbreakable, she had to let her guard fall just as he had and let him in, beyond the barrier, a place where no one had ever touched.

"I know a thing or two about honouring people." She resisted the urge to clam up when he gave her a questioning look.

Instead, she turned her back to him, swept her fall of wavy hair forwards so it flowed over her breasts, and reached over her shoulder to grip the back of her black tank. She pulled it up, revealing the full length of the tattoo that ran down her spine.

She heard him stand and the heat of his gaze seared her, the intensity of it sending fire skittering over her skin. That fire burned deep into her bones when he brushed his fingers over her markings, gently tracing each of the interlinked symbols that lined her spine.

"They're beautiful," he murmured softly and then his voice gained strength, an edge of surprise to it. "They change colour."

She gasped as he grasped her hips and electricity arced through her, igniting the need of him that always simmered in her veins, a constant ache that was never sated. He turned her back towards the firelight and dropped to his knees behind her, his warm breath skating over her lower back.

She twisted to see him, was about to ask what he was doing when he leaned in and brushed his lips over the mark at the base of her spine, just above the waist of her plaid skirt.

That heat he stirred exploded into wildfire and she muttered a fae version of his name as she clutched her top to her breasts.

"You shouldn't do this." Because control was a fragile thing for her and had been since the cove.

Even when she had been angry with him, she had ached for him, had dreamed of them together, making love in front of a fire on a rug like the one beneath her feet.

"Do not focus on me," he rumbled between kisses. "Speak with me to take your mind off your fears, because this time, Suki, we are not stopping."

It was impossible to do what he had asked. He had to know that. The entire world had narrowed down to them, all her senses locked on him as he delicately swept his lips over the symbols, fogging her mind with desire and need.

"Why did you mark yourself with these fae symbols?" Apparently, speech wasn't difficult for him.

She desperately tried to focus, clawing it back even as he tried to dismantle it again with each kiss he pressed against her markings.

"It was for my mother." She pushed the words out and trembled as he stroked his tongue over one of the symbols. Her breath stuttered. "She was banished from the clan... forty years ago... died shortly afterwards. An incubus killed her."

Tegan drew back, his deep voice a low snarl. "Did you kill him?"

She shook her head. "No. Incubi are far stronger than I am. Cunning. You saw that. I'm no match for one. If I was... he would be dead."

She had thought that burning need to avenge her mother had died out years ago, but it blazed just as brightly inside her now as it did then as she thought about the man who had taken her mother from her.

Taken her world from her.

"I will kill the male for you," he growled, heating her by degrees, starting with her heart. She had seen him fight. The incubus would be no match for him, not if it was one on one. "Your mother should be avenged."

"Is that what you did?" She looked over her shoulder at him, catching him glaring at her back, his handsome face etched in dark lines that spoke of his anger. "Did you avenge Edyn?"

He kissed her back again, murmuring between them. "I killed the courtesan. It was all I could do."

But it hadn't been enough for him. He didn't feel his vengeance was complete because the truce had stopped him from leading his men to the Sixth Realm. She could feel it in him.

"If you could, would you go to war with the Sixth Realm now, all these years later?"

He stilled.

Growled.

"Yes."

There was menace in that word, anger that matched her own. He needed vengeance as much as she did, but the truce bound his hands and her lack of strength bound hers. If she let him avenge her, would that satisfy her?

She wasn't sure.

Killing never really had been her style.

Another growl rumbled from him. "What is this?"

She lifted her right arm and peered down at her side, at a long black bruise that was slowly and surely emerging above her hip. "The incubi. They got a few lucky shots."

They had been more vicious than usual, throwing insults like daggers and several objects too, all because she had seen them stalking a group of fae women the night before, when she had taken a break from the books, and had decided to tell the ladies to stay away from them because they were syphilis carrying incubi who would either kill them in the act or at a later date like the gross disease they were.

Tegan pulled her back to him by gently kissing the bruise, lavishing it with attention that warmed her and had all her focus narrowing on him again.

Whenever he found a mark on her back, he gave it the same treatment, but with each cut and bruise, the softness she had been enjoying began to disappear, his kisses growing firmer.

She glanced over her shoulder at him again, wanting to know his feelings. His aura was black again, rising and writhing, not giving anything away. If she had to guess, she would say he was angry.

Suki turned towards him, stopping him, and he tilted his head back, lifting his gaze to meet hers. She stroked her fingers through his tangled black hair, the silken threads of it slipping between them as she absorbed the sight of him kneeling before her, violet-red flames licking around his pupils and his black horns flaring.

"I like you like this," she whispered.

He growled. "Angry? Furious?"

She smiled saucily. "On your knees."

He pushed to his feet on a wicked snarl and claimed her mouth, his kiss demanding and delicious. She was sure that no man in this world or the mortal one kissed like he did. He had ruined her to all others.

She tried to hold back, but his kiss was a drug that ravaged her control and she couldn't stop herself from stealing a little of his energy, justified it by telling herself that she was injured and he probably wouldn't mind since he wanted her healed.

Damn, she was sure her wounds would heal in an instant if he just kept kissing her like this, so wild and desperate as his lips clashed with hers. He gathered her to him, large hands landing on her backside to lift her up his hard body, so her feet dangled above the floor. She looped her arms around his neck and locked them tight, showing him she wasn't going anywhere and earning a growl from him, one that sounded as if it was born of satisfaction this time. He teased her, his lips dancing with hers, firm one moment and hard the next, a kiss that drove her wild.

The door opened.

The world whizzed past her and she struggled to catch up as Tegan growled, his bare back a wall before her wide eyes as the fire warmed her bottom. His right hand held her hip, his grip firm as he pressed her close to his back, as if she needed protecting.

She peered around him, aware she was risking his wrath as she pressed her hands against his back and felt the tension in him.

He was a bomb ready to go off. Why?

Another demon stood near the door of the room, his hand still clutching the knob. His polished black horns were in a normal state, the tips barely passing the lobes of his pointed ears, and she frowned at the gold that capped the last third of his right one. His dark eyes were fathomless abysses too, no trace of emotion in them, and when she focused, his aura appeared, swirling in golds and violets, with hints of red, revealing surprise and love.

Who was this man?

Wild black hair framed a face that was oddly familiar.

She looked up at Tegan and then back at the newcomer.

His brother?

Tegan bared his fangs at the demon and held her closer still, pressing her painfully against him as his grip on her hip tightened enough that his short claws dug into her skin through her skirt. Why did he want to attack his brother? He hadn't made it sound as if they were on bad terms.

Maybe she was misunderstanding the situation and his brother had merely surprised him, causing this reaction because he had been swept up in her and he wasn't happy about the disturbance.

She tried to step out from behind him to introduce herself, sure it would ease the tension in the room.

It only made it worse.

Tegan snapped fangs at her and pressed his claws in deeper, enough that the points of them were in danger of piercing her flesh, forcing her to remain behind him as he growled low at his brother.

The demon backed off and slowly released the door handle, his hands rising before him in a submissive gesture as he spoke, the deep baritone of his voice matching Tegan's. She wanted to know what he was saying, but she hadn't lied to Tegan. Her demonic was a bit rusty and extremely limited, and the way this man spoke it, growling each word, made it impossible to understand him.

Tegan snarled a reply. She caught what she thought was a name. Ryker.

"Is this your brother?" She adopted a firm tone, one she hoped would leave Tegan in no doubt that she wanted an answer, because she needed to know what the heck was going on.

He glared at the demon and nodded as he bit out something in the demon tongue.

Ryker just stared him down.

Tegan bared his fangs again when Ryker attempted to look at her. She got the feeling this was about her. Although it didn't take a genius to figure that out since Tegan was intent on keeping her hidden from his brother. She knew when it was time to make a graceful exit.

She had been having a nice time with Tegan and she didn't want to ruin it, or his relationship with his brother. They clearly had some things to work out and her presence wasn't helping matters.

She touched Tegan's bare back between his shoulders. "I'll go freshen up."

He was tense for a moment, and she was sure he was going to growl and snap at her again, but then he eased his grip on her and turned with her, guiding her towards a door in the corner to her left, just beyond the fireplace, and she didn't miss that he was leading her out of a door as far from his brother as he could get.

She wanted to glance back at the demon where he stood on the opposite side of the room, but she didn't want to anger Tegan, not when he was calming down again, his hand slowly relaxing against her as she moved further from his brother.

"My rooms are up those stairs and straight on. The door at the end of the corridor." Tegan gruffly murmured the words, his voice strained, speaking of the tension she could feel lingering inside him.

Suki turned, careful to keep her eyes on Tegan alone, and tiptoed to press a brief kiss to his lips.

Regret flickered in his eyes and shame crossed his features as he nodded and tore his gaze away from her, turning back into the room and closing the door.

What had that been all about?

She got the feeling that Tegan wouldn't tell her even if she asked him. Her heart sunk a little as she turned away from the door.

They were both keeping secrets from each other.

CHAPTER 20

Suki wasn't two steps away from the closed door before Ryker moved into the room.

"What the hell was that all about?" Ryker's dark gaze shifted to the door behind Tegan.

Tegan growled at him, baring his fangs to warn him to keep his damned eyes off her. Every inch of him ached as his muscles strained, his control slipping as rage threatened to overwhelm him again.

When Ryker looked back at him, Tegan could see the shrewd bastard had figured it out before he could say a word.

"She is your fated one." Ryker looked him up and down. "Do not deny it. You still look somewhere between wanting to commit bloody murder and wanting to get between her thighs."

He flashed his fangs at his brother for being so damned crude about his female.

"Talk about something else," he grunted as he managed to convince himself to move away from the door and stop blocking Ryker's path to it. "Anything else."

Because he needed to get his mind off Suki for a moment. He was too swept up in her, could still taste her sweetness on his tongue and smell the warm spice of her scent, and thinking about her was liable to send him stalking after her to finish what they had started.

He needed his mate.

A sudden, fierce fear gripped him and he turned on his brother. "Do not mention to her that I am king. She does not know and I do not want her to find out yet."

Not when things between them seemed to be going so well again.

Ryker shrugged and headed towards the crystal decanter on the oak sideboard. "Fair enough. I will go along with it, but only because it is good to see you close to happy."

He poured two glasses of mead, drained one and refilled it before carrying both over to Tegan. He pressed one into Tegan's hand and hesitated, as if he wanted to say something, and then slumped onto the couch where Tegan had settled Suki on first bringing her into the room.

His brother kicked his feet up onto it and leaned against the arm as he swigged his brew, his expression growing more pensive the longer he remained silent.

If he didn't speak what was on his mind soon, Tegan was going to throttle him. His brother had a stubborn streak though, and pressing him would only make him clam up and refuse to speak at all.

While he waited out the inevitable protracted silence, Tegan stoked the fire and tried to keep his mind off Suki. Sitting in his armchair was a mistake. It smelled of her, had him remembering how good she had looked sitting in it, which led his mind to how sweet she had tasted as he had kissed her skin, studying the markings she wore to honour her mother.

She was no stranger to pain.

Seemed to have more than her fair share of it in his opinion.

If he could take that pain away for her, he would do it. He had meant what he had said to her. She only had to say the word and vengeance would be hers. He would slay the incubus for her.

"What is it like?" Ryker finally said and Tegan looked over at him, catching him staring at his mead as he swirled it in his glass. "I know what every demon is told about finding their mate, but what is it really like?"

Tegan tilted his head back into the seat behind him and considered that question. There was only one answer that encompassed everything he had experienced since meeting Suki.

"Unsettling."

Ryker looked as if he needed more than that one word.

"Expect to be vexed at every turn and to feel as if someone has tipped your entire world on its head. The urges are strong, Ryker. More controlling than I had expected."

Ryker pressed his elbow against the armrest behind him and sat up straighter. "And the dreams?"

Tegan shivered, heat coiling inside him at the memories that rose to the surface of his mind. There was only one word for those too.

"Intense."

Ryker didn't look satisfied, but Tegan wasn't going to expand. His dreams of Suki were private. He didn't need his brother attempting to imagine her in the throes of passion. Just thinking about his brother imagining it was enough to have his horns curling again, flaring forwards as his fangs sharpened once more.

His brother held his free hand up. "I will not ask."

Tegan appreciated that as he swigged his sweet brew, but it didn't clear the dark haze from his mind as he thought about Suki, about how close he had been to taking things further and how his brother might have walked in on them.

"Horns are curling," Ryker muttered into his mead. "Furious or feeling a little hungry?"

"Both." Tegan pinched the bridge of his nose. "I have little control over myself these days."

"Sounds fun." The glimmer in Ryker's dark eyes said that he meant those words. "Maybe one day I will find my fated one."

Tegan frowned as he recognised something else in his brother's eyes and his tone.

Envy.

He wanted to laugh at that, the notion so ridiculous that it couldn't be true, but the way his brother kept his focus on his brew and the awkward air that surrounded him said that it was.

All these years he had been jealous of Ryker because he had given his brother the freedom he had once enjoyed, placing him into his former position in the Royal Legion and allowing him to do as he pleased, never pressuring him as prince and heir to the throne. He kept Ryker away from the castle as much as he could, so the court couldn't wear him down as it did Tegan, because he wanted his brother to live and experience the world that had been taken from him.

So the fact Ryker of all people was jealous of him came as a shock.

"Talk about something else." Ryker emptied his glass, pushed up from the couch and disappeared behind Tegan.

Glass clinked, the sound of mead splashing against the goblet filling the silence together with the crackle of the fire. He wasn't surprised when his brother drank that glass in one go and poured another.

Tegan drained his and held it out to his right, dropping a not-so-subtle hint.

"You have servants for this," Ryker muttered as he refilled Tegan's glass.

"I sent him to the gatehouse." He shrugged when his brother arched an eyebrow. "I will send you away too if you look at her."

Ryker shook his head and sighed. "Her claws are that deep into you?"

He nodded and knocked the brew back, and Ryker topped him up again as he tried not to think about Suki. Had she found his rooms? He pictured her roaming around them, perusing his belongings, her dazzling eyes bright as she snooped, probably feeling a bit naughty for investigating without him knowing about it.

Would she like the paintings he had selected for his private quarters? He had a Rembrandt and two Monet's in his bedroom. The largest of the Monet's hung above the fireplace opposite the foot of his four-poster bed. His mind leaped to picturing her on his bed, curled up on the mixture of furs as if she belonged there and was waiting for him to come to her.

"She is definitely your fated one." Ryker toasted him as Tegan blinked himself back to his brother.

He hadn't even noticed that Ryker had moved away from him, was lounging on the couch again, his black leathers almost blending into the dark violet fabric in the low light. His brother rested his arm along the gilt frame that ran over the back of the couch and stifled a yawn.

It wasn't that late, and Tegan's company wasn't that dull.

It had been too long since they had done this, drinking into the night and talking about whatever was happening in their lives. He couldn't remember the last time he had been able to sit with his brother and just talk, without his advisers breathing down his neck or the court needing him for something.

He stood and walked over to the couch where his brother lazed, pushed his feet off and sat at the end Suki had occupied. He picked up her bloodstained white shirt and frowned at it, battling another surge of rage as the fight flashed across his eyes.

"What happened there?" Ryker jerked his chin towards the shirt.

"A fight. She was hurt. I brought her here to keep her safe." He bundled the shirt up into his fist and gave Ryker a tight smile. "Tell me what you have been doing. I have not seen you in months."

"I was travelling." Ryker swilled his brew and took another swig, his eyes glittering as he smiled. "It was good for a while. Valdaine and I visited the mortal country known as America, and then we ran into trouble with some bears in Canada. The prides are large there."

Judging by the grin that curled Ryker's lips, the trouble they had run into had been fun.

"Then we hit a few tropical beaches, met a lot of beautiful females." Heat filled Ryker's dark eyes, telling Tegan that his brother had done more than simply meet the females.

He'd had his fill of them too.

Had Valdaine also indulged in the females? If he had, it was about time.

His old friend had lost his mate almost two thousand years ago, but he still blamed himself for what had happened to her, still wore the thick torc around his neck to show other demons he was a widower.

What had happened to his mate hadn't been Valdaine's fault, but Tegan could never bring himself to tell his friend that. He knew how easy it was to feel guilty about things, and how difficult it was to convince yourself otherwise. He blamed himself for what had happened to Edyn after all.

"Things were going well." That had his brother's smile fading and Tegan frowned as worry swept through him.

"Did something happen to you?" He leaned towards his brother. "Is that why you returned?"

He shook his head. "Not me. Valdaine wanted a break from the mortals so we went to a fae town and he got a little twitchy. He was acting different. I do not know what changed, and I did not get a chance to find out. There was an attack or something—"

Tegan tensed. "A raid?"

Everything Suki had told him came rushing back.

"Is that what the bastards call it?" Ryker's eyes blazed with fury and a flicker of curiosity that said he wanted to know how Tegan knew about such things.

"It was the town near Fort William, was it not?" Tegan continued when Ryker nodded. "My female told me about raids that have happened there, ones orchestrated by a mortal hunter organisation."

He didn't like the way Ryker's expression darkened.

"You are not to even think about going after them, Ryker. Do you understand?" Tegan bit out, his voice hard and unyielding, hopefully firm enough to make his brother see he was serious and any attempt to go after the hunters would see him reprimanded.

"I lost track of Valdaine in that *raid*." Ryker shoved his fingers through the tangled lengths of his onyx hair, the action screaming of frustration that was enough to tell Tegan that he would obey him, although he would hate him for issuing that order. "One moment he was right beside me and we were about to teleport as soon as we hit a clearing, and the next he was in the air, flying back the way we had come."

Ryker curled his free hand into a fist and growled as he slammed it against the back of the couch.

"I should have gone after him."

Anger flared in his dark eyes, a shimmer of violet fire that quickly morphed into regret.

Because Ryker had been forced to follow protocol as the sole heir of the Second Realm and leave, abandoning his friend in order to remain out of the hands of a potential enemy.

As much as Tegan hated that Valdaine was potentially now a captive of Archangel, he was glad his brother had managed to escape. The thought of his friend in their hands was sickening enough. If they had taken Ryker too and realised they were in possession of a demon prince? He shut down that line of thought, unable to even think about what they might have done to him without losing his fragile grip on his temper.

"I will speak with King Thorne about Archangel, for the sake of Valdaine and also a witch who is a friend of Suki's. She was taken too." He stared at his mead as he recalled how upset she had been to hear that and his heart ached to go to her, to gather her close and hold her, offering her the only comfort he could right now. "These mortals sound troublesome. Thorne's queen was once one of them, as was Prince Loren's mate. Perhaps they could set our minds at ease about Archangel or could somehow arrange the release of Valdaine and Agatha."

"I think you would have more luck asking the remaining demon realms to sign a damned peace treaty," Ryker grumbled and toyed with the golden tip of his right horn, a sign of his frustration.

Whenever something wasn't going right in Ryker's opinion, he resorted to touching the gold that had replaced the tip of his horn after an enemy had cut it off to shame him.

Tegan leaned towards him and placed his hand on Ryker's thigh. "We will get Valdaine back."

Ryker nodded stiffly. "I came here because I was going to go over all the information I have gathered in the last month so I could figure out who was behind things and plan an attack, and here you are to talk me down as always. Although, I hadn't quite expected you to be here with company. Was she one of the courtesans? Did you meet her at the celebration?"

"No." Tegan scrubbed his right horn and grimaced as he realised he had missed the celebration. Suki had been in trouble. She had needed him. Ryker's eyes narrowed on him, that flare of curiosity becoming suspicion. Tegan debated not telling him, weighing the pros and cons, and gave up when he realised his brother wouldn't let it go until Tegan confessed. "I met her in the mortal world."

His brother's face darkened. "I always wanted you to go there again, to have some freedom, but I am guessing this was not a court sanctioned and escorted visit?"

Anger rolled off Ryker and Tegan tensed on instinct, bracing himself for a fight even when he didn't know why his brother was suddenly furious with him.

"You snuck out," Ryker spat the accusation.

Tegan admitted it with a nod.

"What if you had been caught up in a raid? You could have been hurt or taken." Ryker gripped the back of the couch so hard the wood creaked as he swiftly sat up and leaned towards Tegan, fire flaring in his dark eyes. "No one would have known where you were!"

Now the anger made sense.

"I did not think about the danger." At the time, he had been too excited to visit the mortal realm for the first time in a thousand years. "And I was not aware of the danger this Archangel represented."

"You are aware of it now." Ryker didn't relax, remained sitting upright and glaring at him.

Tegan was aware, but he had no intention of vowing to never return to the mortal world as his brother wanted. Suki was a fae, one of a breed that couldn't teleport into or out of Hell through the pathways. She could freely teleport once she was inside Hell, but in order to leave it, he would have to take her home.

Because he was damned if anyone else was laying hands on his fated one to transport her.

Ryker's long sigh said it all.

He knew Tegan was going back to the mortal world no matter what he said against it.

His brother slumped against the arm of the couch again. "At least tell me more about our future queen."

Tegan scowled at him. "Do not call her that. Gods, I wish things were different."

Ryker sobered. "Still?"

Tegan nodded and took another draught of his mead, stood when little more than a sip emptied the glass and went to the oak sideboard. He poured a healthy glass, turned and planted his backside against the counter.

"Wishing things were different does not change anything. It never has. You have to make things different." Ryker sounded far too wise, sage enough that

Tegan wanted to ask if he was really his brother and not someone masquerading as him.

"How?" he snapped.

"I don't know. You are king... do kingly stuff." Ryker shrugged.

It was definitely his brother.

He was more comfortable with this side of Ryker, the one who merely wanted to have fun and fight, feast and bed as many females as possible.

Tegan rolled his eyes. "If only it was that simple."

"Do you hate Edyn?" That question came out of the blue and struck Tegan hard, had him staring at Ryker as his mind leaped on it, seeking an answer to give his brother.

He mulled it over as he stared down at his mead, watching it chase around the sides of the crystal goblet as he swirled it. "Not hate. Maybe there is a lingering anger towards our brother... unjustified resentment. It was not Edyn's fault what happened, but for some reason I cannot not be angry about the change in my circumstances."

Edyn had saddled him with a kingdom and his life had changed in the blink of an eye. Everyone had expected him to rule a land that had been heading into a time of peace when his every primal instinct was geared towards war.

"I had been happy with my life." He sighed wearily, despising himself for being so focused on his own life when their brother had lost his and the lives of thousands had depended upon him for salvation from the famine. "I had been free to do as I pleased. I led the legions..."

He trailed off before he started sounding jealous of the fact Ryker had stepped into his life and it looked damned good on him.

"And now?" Ryker offered.

Tegan averted his gaze to the fire, seeking the answer in the flames. "And now?"

He waited for all the negatives to flood his mind as they usually did, but Suki danced into it, leaving footprints on white sand as she twirled, the golden light of evening playing over her skin and sparkling in her striking eyes as she smiled at him.

She had breathed life into him again.

He had been so weighed down before he had met her, shackled to his throne and bogged down in the daily business of running a kingdom. Suki was a break from all that. She invigorated him and he liked being with her. He liked that she challenged him and hadn't thrown herself at him, and he liked that she didn't know what he was.

She only knew who he was.

She didn't see a title.

She only saw him.

He could be himself with her. There were no expectations between them and no fear she desired him only for his throne.

He huffed, "Maybe it is not all bad."

Ryker cracked a grin.

"You are thinking about the female, are you not?" His brother's smile faltered, seriousness invading his voice. "Life with her might be good, but she does not know the real you."

Tegan barked, "The real me is *all* she knows. I have not lied to her or been false in any way. She knows me... not the Second King. I am more than just my damned throne."

He clenched his fists so hard the glass he held in his right one shattered, shards of crystal slicing deep into his palm as he bellowed.

"I am more than just this fucking kingdom."

His muscles tensed and ached, fangs elongating as his horns curled and he cast the remains of the goblet to the floor.

Ryker was on his feet and across the room in a heartbeat, his right hand pressing to Tegan's bare chest as it heaved.

"Calm, brother." Ryker eased him back against the sideboard. "I apologise. I was wrong. You are right. Maybe people do expect too much from you."

Tegan breathed hard as he clawed back control, desperate to maintain it as his bones burned, the ache in them fierce as he denied the rage Ryker had stoked in him. He had lost control once already today, and it always made it more difficult to keep hold of his emotions and not let them rule him.

Ryker breathed slowly, steady draws and exhales that Tegan followed, because he didn't want to shift into his more demonic form again.

Doing so would send him straight to Suki, and she had been through enough today without having to deal with him in his fully demonic state, driven by a need to claim her as his mate.

He didn't want to hurt her again and he feared he would if rage seized control of him.

"They expect me to be something I am not," he growled and breathed steadily, scraping together calm little by little as his turbulent emotions began to settle again.

"You are a good king, Tegan." Ryker's words offered comfort Tegan seized on.

He hadn't realised how much he had needed to hear such a thing from his brother, from someone. His advisers only told him what he was doing wrong, and his warriors blamed him for their lack of battle, and even his people complained about things to his face. The compliments were few and far between.

Ryker sighed. "You never wanted it, but you accepted the burden of leading the kingdom, and you work hard to better it. That is the mark of a good king."

Tegan lifted the remaining decanter from the silver tray and drained it, spilling mead all down his neck and bare chest.

Ryker chuckled. "You still drink like the male you were. Edyn would have ordered fresh goblets."

Tegan couldn't hold back the smile that rose onto his lips. "True."

He brushed past Ryker and slumped into the black leather armchair. "Sometimes, I do not feel like a good king... the times I want to turn my back on it all... even when I know I would never do such a thing."

"Everyone is allowed to hate their duties or their life from time to time." Ryker eased back down onto the couch. "The difference is whether you pick yourself back up and keep going, doing what you know is right in your heart."

"It is not easy with advisers like mine."

Ryker sobered again. "Are they still doing their damnedest to slow down progress in the realm?"

Tegan had complained long and hard into the night over a year ago, holding Ryker captive in his drawing room at the castle until his brother had looked as if he wanted to remove each of his advisers' heads.

He nodded, but then shook his head. "I have a feeling they will not be as much trouble anymore. I may have put them in their place."

"About time! What finally made you make a stand against them?"

"I wanted plastic." Tegan weathered the confused look his brother tossed at him and pulled the cards from the pouch on his hip. "A shifter I met told me plastic was king. Suki believes cash is king... It is a form of currency used in the mortal world."

"I know what cash is." Ryker frowned and waved his hand dismissively. "Repeat the important part again."

"Which is?"

"We get to have debit cards." Ryker's gaze lit up in the way Suki's had when she had seen Tegan's collection of plastic.

"Oh, no. I have seen that look on my female's face. *I* get to have plastic. *You* would bankrupt the kingdom." He hastily tucked the cards away when his brother looked as if he was considering attempting to seize one for himself.

Ryker huffed and relaxed into the couch again. "So your female likes money?"

He hiked his right shoulder. "Apparently. My wealth seemed to impress her. It increased my rank by a point."

"Rank?"

He rubbed his horn, feeling he had said too much, but the look Ryker gave him told him he wouldn't let it go until Tegan explained.

"She scores males based on a secret system." He puffed his chest out a little. "I ascended to a solid twelve."

"Out of what?" Ryker grinned mischievously. "A hundred?"

Tegan shot him daggers. "Ten."

Ryker was lucky he was his brother and he loved him. If anyone else had dared to insult him in such a manner, he would have had them thrown into the cells.

Well, anyone other than Ryker and Suki.

"She will find out you know." Ryker sobered again and Tegan wished his brother had kept the mood light.

He didn't want to think about what the future held. Not right now, when everything was so uncertain.

He loosed a deep sigh. "I know. I can only hope that by then she is so madly in love with me that it does not matter."

His brother chuckled. "What's not to love about you?"

Tegan shrugged.

Ryker tilted his head to his right and pursed his lips. "She is an interesting mate though. A succubus."

His brother swiftly raised his hands when Tegan snarled at him.

"I am not interested in her." Ryker lowered his hands to his lap again and frowned. "You do have shitty luck."

That earned his brother another glare.

"I am just saying. Your path is not going to be an easy one. Even when you are mated and bound, males will look at her."

Tegan pinched the bridge of his nose. Hard. "I know."

His only hope was that her faulty glamour and inability to charm males continued and he wouldn't have to execute half the kingdom for gazing upon his beautiful mate and lusting after her.

Maybe he could cover her from head to toe at all times?

No. He couldn't do that. He loved how she dressed, so colourful and differently to others. He would never do something to change her or demand that she changed for him.

"The upside is, you have her diet covered," Ryker put in, pulling him out of his thoughts of her. "No need to worry about our choice of food not suiting her. She looked ready to gobble you up earlier."

Tegan growled again. This time, Ryker didn't apologise.

His brother was right though. Suki fed exclusively from sexual energy. He found himself wanting to be the only male she fed from for the rest of her life, lost himself in that pleasing idea and plotting ways to break it to her that she was his fated one, and that he was falling for her and wanted to be her mate.

"Have you considered the other downside?" Ryker just wouldn't give him a moment to think about his female, would he?

"Another downside?" He frowned, trying to figure out what his brother might be speaking about.

"Well, you are the king. The kingdom and your court will expect you to produce an heir with your fated mate." Ryker swigged his mead and pulled a thoughtful face. "I can recognise a succubus when I see one, but I admit, I do not possess much knowledge of them. Can she even have male offspring?"

Tegan hadn't considered that. Normally, a demon's mate always produced male offspring, a way of ensuring the continuation of the species. What if succubi were a species like his and always produced female succubi offspring?

It troubled him as he thought about it, charting all the implications and how everyone might react as his brother silently watched him.

Tegan nodded when he reached a conclusion, one that stemmed from the deepest pit of his heart.

"I would not care. If Suki honoured me with a child, I would love it unconditionally, regardless of its sex."

That didn't go down well with Ryker.

"But that means I would be in line for the throne."

Tegan slowly smiled. "Oh dear."

Ryker threatened to throw his crystal goblet at him.

CHAPTER 21

Suki woke alone beneath the layers of furs on the sumptuous super-king-size four-poster bed in Tegan's enormous bedroom. She rolled to her left side and reached out, strangely expecting her big demon to be there beside her, even though she had never slept with a man before. She rubbed her eyes and looked at the empty side of the bed, her hand draped over the cold furs. She had been dreaming of him again and had fallen asleep in it tucked in his arms, sated and boneless, and warmed right down to her heart.

Where was he?

She sat up and glanced around the room, gaze drifting over the mahogany furniture that lined the deep green walls and coming to rest on the armchair near the fireplace. The wood had burned out, leaving only the slender light from the oil lamps to chase the darkness back, but her eyesight was good enough to see Tegan wasn't in the room with her.

How late was it?

She fumbled on the bedside cabinet for her phone and woke the screen. It was gone eight in the morning. It had been late afternoon when she had retired to his room, washed herself in his modest bathroom and nosed at his belongings. She was sure she had fallen asleep by nine, which meant she had slept for eleven hours. Had Tegan come to check on her at all?

She felt sure that if he had, he would have stayed, and he would have woken her. It wasn't possible he had come and slept beside her without her knowing. She was certain the feel of the hard length of his body pressing against hers, his heat rolling over her, and his arms around her would have roused her.

She would have wanted to snuggle into his embrace.

Which was odd and unsettling, because this whole affair was nothing like she had planned.

She was meant to be seducing him.

Now she was sure she was falling for him.

That left her cold.

She couldn't fall for him, even if love was possible for her. Falling for him meant turning her back on her clan.

Her family.

Succubi who decided to stick with one man, attempting to have a relationship like others could, were cast out of their clans. She had seen it happen. Her clan was everything to her and she was doing this so they would accept and respect her, and she would finally feel as if she belonged there.

She had to remember that.

She pushed the furs aside, padded naked around the bed, passing the three shuttered windows and then the fire as she rounded the foot of it, heading for the mahogany double wardrobe that lined the wall opposite the windows. She opened it, rifled through the white shirts that hung in it and picked one. She pulled it on. It swamped her, had her thoughts turning to the burly demon who owned it.

Where was he?

Suki looked down, making sure the shirt covered all of her. It reached to mid-thigh, long enough to conceal everything. Satisfied she wasn't going to flash her wares at the servants or Ryker, she left the room and walked down the lamp-lit corridor, listening at each door in case Tegan was in one of them. All of them were quiet.

She took the stairs down to the next level and worked her way back to the drawing room. The door was open a crack, allowing firelight to chase into the hallway, a bright streak of gold that promised warmth. Her toes were freezing. She had forgotten that it could get cold in Hell, as chilly as her home in the mortal world.

She pushed the door open and peered around it.

Good gods.

Tegan lounged in his onyx leather wingback armchair, looking far too damned sexy in a heavy black housecoat that hugged his broad shoulders. The thick material clung to his biceps and framed his powerful torso, gaping at his waist where it met his dark leathers. His muscles flexed as he turned the page in the book he was reading, delighting her eyes and holding her focus, stoking the heat that rolled through her whenever she looked at him. Firelight chased over his skin, turning it golden, and reflected in his dark eyes as he frowned at the book.

Something was wrong.

It shook her from her reverie and had her stepping into the room. Why did he look so worn down?

Was it her fault?

Had she taken too much from him when they had kissed earlier?

He noticed her, his head lifting but gaze remaining sombre and troubled as he set his book aside.

He held his right hand out to her. "I apologise for my earlier behaviour."

"Did you make up with your brother?" She moved towards him and took his hand, skimmed the fingers of her other one over his knuckles as she studied him. Now that she was near to him, in contact with him, she could feel his fatigue.

He nodded.

She was relieved to hear that. Family was important.

Suki leaned over and brushed the backs of her fingers down his cheek as her brow furrowed. "Haven't you slept?"

He shook his head. "Much troubles me."

His gaze dropped to take in her body and his eyebrows knitted hard as it turned heated.

"You wear my shirt."

She looked down at herself and shrugged. "It looked comfortable."

And for some reason, she had wanted to wear it, had been hit with a need to put one of them on when she had seen them last night.

She leaned closer, drew down a subtle breath and savoured his earthy masculine scent. It warmed her, offering the comfort she had thought she would find in donning his shirt, and she didn't resist him when he pulled her onto his lap.

He wrapped his strong arms around her and that comfort she felt increased one hundred-fold.

His palm cupped her left cheek and he turned her face towards him, slid his hand around the back of her neck beneath her tangled hair and drew her to him. His lips brushed hers, the tenderness of his kiss lifting the comfort she felt in his arms to new heights, one where she felt dizzy and wanted to cling to him. She focused on his kiss as he held her seated on his thighs, on the addictive taste of him and the feelings that came through more clearly as the connection between them built.

He was troubled, but her heart said it wasn't because of her.

He was strong too, and relief beat through her, eased the concern that had been growing inside her since last night and allowed her to relax into him and enjoy the feel of his lips brushing hers, a kiss meant for pleasure not for feeding.

When he moved away from her lips to kiss along her jaw, she found the courage to ask, "What's wrong?"

He leaned back on a weary sigh and skimmed his hand up and down her thigh, sweeping the shirt higher with each stroke. Any moment now, he was going to realise she wore his shirt and only his shirt. She could just imagine how he was going to react to that, and gods, it was delicious, gave her a hit of energy that had a shiver chasing through her.

"A friend of mine and Ryker's, Valdaine... I am worried about him." A crinkle formed between his eyebrows as they knitted again. "Ryker was in the fae town with him when the Archangel raid happened."

Cold slithered through her. "And you think he was taken along with Agatha and the others?"

He nodded, a troubled edge to his gaze as he lowered it to her legs. "Ryker was unable to search for him. He returned to the Second Realm after they were separated."

She studied his handsome face, reading it and the emotions that flittered across his eyes, feelings she could sense a hint of when they were this close to each other.

"You feel guilty because you're glad Ryker made it out." She framed his face in both palms when he frowned at her. "It's okay to feel that way. It doesn't mean you care any less about Valdaine."

"I worry," he murmured huskily, a strained edge to it that she found endearing because it revealed the size of her demon's heart and it was as big as the rest of him.

"We'll find a way to get him and Agatha back. You mentioned a demon king had connections to Archangel." She shifted her hands to his horns and stroked their lengths, from the root above his pointed ears down the curve that followed them to the points near his lobes, wanting to soothe him. "I'm sure he will help us."

Tegan's expression turned deadly serious. "I worry about you."

She swallowed to wet her throat as her heart lodged in it. Her demon's heart was bigger than she had thought. The look in his eyes revealed all his feelings to her, ones she was afraid of deciphering because it was all getting too complicated and her resolve was beginning to waver as a different path opened before her, one she wasn't sure she was brave enough to choose.

His face darkened before it crumpled and he held her cheeks, drew her to him and pressed his forehead to hers as he screwed his eyes shut. "I do not like the thought you might have been taken... that these fiends might return and capture you... or..."

His voice broke on that final word, melting her heart in the process as his feelings flooded her.

He genuinely feared for her safety.

That touched her and she found it hard to remember why she was there as she fell into his eyes, drowning in the feelings they revealed to her.

To prove herself?

Or fall for this man who looked at her as if she was the most important thing in his world?

No one had ever looked at her that way before.

It was as addictive as his kiss.

"I thought you were sleeping." His palm dropped to her legs and grazed her thigh.

Heat shimmered outwards from that caress, spreading through her as his gaze devoured hers, slowly darkening with desire she could sense in him.

"I woke alone and wondered where you were." She trailed her fingers down his bare chest, the dark hair that covered it tickling their tips as her mind ventured down wicked paths, ones that had an ache blooming in her belly.

"So you came to find me?"

When she nodded, he gathered her closer and kissed her cheek. Her eyes rolled closed and she tilted her head back as fire blazed through her blood, each brush of his lips stoking it as he swept them along her jaw and down her throat.

He stilled, tensing in a way that had his entire body going rigid against her.

"What's wrong?" She couldn't find the strength to look at him, not while his breath skated over her skin, sending a thousand achy shivers rushing through her.

"Nothing." That word was strained, hoarse, as tense as the rest of him.

His entire body shuddered as he licked her throat, tongue following the line of her vein, and she trembled as he flicked her earlobe with the tip of it. A ripple of heat danced down her spine. He licked again, harder this time, leaving her breathless and wanting more.

"You need," he rumbled sexily in her ear, a purr that had a devastating effect on her, had that heat he caused pooling between her thighs.

She moaned and twisted in his arms, wedging her knees in the gap between his hips and the sides of the armchair as she sat on his lap. She looped her arms around his neck and rocked forwards, trembling as the bulge in his leathers pressed against her core.

His black horns flared, the tips curling up to his cheekbones, and his ears grew pointier, and he was devastatingly sexy as he gazed up at her through hooded eyes that shone with a red-purple light.

"Kiss me." That demand leaving his lips had another achy shiver cascading down her spine to spread heat through her.

Heck, she could get used to him ordering her around in the bedroom.

But right now, she wanted to be in charge.

"I was dreaming of you in your bed," she whispered.

He groaned, his face twisting with it as he frowned and his nostrils flared, that shimmer of violet in his eyes growing brighter.

He lowered his hands to her backside and froze.

His focus zipped down to the apex of her thighs.

"You are naked," he growled, eyes wide as they burned into her.

She shrugged. "I was in bed. Your bed."

"Naked." He swallowed hard. "Naked in my bed."

The points of his horns reached his temples and began to curl back towards his ears.

He looked as if he wanted to scrub a hand over his face but couldn't bring himself to remove his hands from her bare backside.

"Naked... in your bed... dreaming of you," she murmured as she traced patterns on his chest and teased his nipples.

He shuddered beneath her, his breaths coming faster. Any moment now, her big demon's restraint was going to crack. She could feel the need pouring through him, a desire that rolled through her too. He wanted to draw the white shirt back to reveal her. She wanted him to do it so she could see the delicious look on his face when he gazed upon her for the first time.

He looked like a man starved as it was. She couldn't imagine what rapture would fill his face when he finally caught a glimpse of her.

On a low groan, he pulled her towards him. Her shirt rode up, but her knees hit the back of the armchair before it lifted high enough to reveal anything. He snarled and brought his hands around, chest heaving as he caressed her thighs, slowly inching towards the front of them.

"Tell me what you dreamed," he husked, voice scraping low as he stared down at her thighs.

"I dreamed you were touching me in your bed, that you woke me by kissing your way up my bare thighs and used your horns to wedge them apart as you pleasured me with your tongue."

His hands tensed against her. "No more."

"But it gets better." She rocked forwards, pressing herself against his caged erection and bringing her lips close to his. "When I broke apart, crying your name, you rose above me and filled me in one delicious, brutal thrust with this."

She dropped her hand between them and cupped him.

He swallowed and groaned, tilted his head back into the seat as his eyes closed. "Gods, Suki. Stop."

"Why?" She didn't want to stop so she pouted at him when he looked at her.

She stilled her hand when concern filled his dark gaze and that unease she had sensed in him more than once came back with a vengeance.

"What's wrong?" She raised both of her hands and stroked his horns, hoping to calm him and ease him.

He turned his cheek to her, towards the fire, and was silent for so long she thought he wasn't going to tell her.

"I am... demons..." He swallowed hard again. "I am a passionate and dominant male."

Not her cup of tea. Not before she had met him anyway. Now, she ached to have him taking command, even when she knew it was dangerous to surrender control to him.

He flicked a glance at her. "I fear I will scare you. I must keep these urges in check lest I frighten you away, but you do not make it easy."

Suki laughed.

Utterly threw her head back and bellowed.

He scowled at her when tears laced her eyes, still deadly serious. It took several attempts to stop laughing so she could speak, and when she managed it, he looked thoroughly unimpressed.

Possibly angry.

She wasn't mocking him. Not much anyway.

"I'm not some delicate female who is going to have a fainting fit or flee in terror if you let your true nature out." She grinned from ear to ear. "You don't see me hiding who I am, do you?"

He shook his head, looked so damned enamoured with her that she wished he would always look at her that way because it made her feel light inside, warmed and something impossible.

Loved.

She pushed away from the L word and teased his horns. "I'm strong. I can handle you. Even at your wildest, you won't be a match for me. Whatever you deal, it will feed my nature and I'll rise to match you, probably even surpass you in your wickedness. And besides, I can easily knock you out with a kiss if you do something I don't like."

His pupils dilated and the violet corona pushed out the black in his irises.

Suki lowered her hand, skimming it down his chest, grazing her fingers over the crisp trail of black hair that led down from his navel and teasing the waist of his leathers. He bucked his hips towards her on a low moan, rising to meet her fingers. She followed the lacing over his impressive bulge, devouring the way he shuddered and breathed faster, harder, that fire in his eyes flaring hotter as they silently demanded more.

She whispered, "If you're that worried, I can give you a safe word... in case things get too intense for you. I'll stop if you say it. How about *cotton candy*?"

Because it was sweet of him to worry about being too passionate for her and because it would be amusing to hear him rasping that at the height of arousal.

He smiled, a devastating and panty-melting half-grin as he rocked into her touch, rubbing against her palm. "You are the one who will need one of these safe words. Perhaps I shall gift you one."

She played along. "What will it be?"

That seductive grin stretched wider. "More."

She placed her hands on his arms and teased his muscles, stroking her fingers over his bulging biceps. "More isn't a safe word. I don't think you get how this works. How will you know if I really want more? I might say it by accident and then you'll stop."

And she really didn't want that.

Not this time.

She'd had a taste of him and now she hungered for more, needed all of him.

He brushed his thumb over her lower lip, gaze hooded as he stared at her mouth, and husked, "You could scream it and I would not stop, Suki. There are no safe words for you because once we start this, I am not stopping until you fall apart in my arms. I plan to make you beg... to make you wild... and then I am going to make you come."

She shivered, heat prickling over her skin in a blissful wave that rolled up on her, had her breathless and edging closer, unable to stop herself as a need to press against him flared inside her. His thumb continued to tease her lip, sensitising it, and a fantasy built in her mind as his eyes promised her that he meant every word.

She was sure it would be searing.

Would leave her changed.

He made it sound as if they were going to do more than kiss, despite the risks, and gods she wanted that. Her body burned with a wicked need, an unrelenting heat that only he could quench. One that was melting the sane part of her brain that chanted this was too dangerous.

He was strong, but how strong?

Powerful enough to survive sex with her?

She shook at the thought, another wave of energy hitting her, lighting her up inside.

Tegan growled low and gathered her to him, his large hands grasping her bare backside as he hauled her against his chest and pressed his hips up to meet hers. She gasped and he swallowed it in a kiss.

Mastered her with it.

His lips claimed hers, tongue teasing and demanding entrance that she gave to him. She moaned as their tongues met, as his fangs scraped hers and he battled her for dominance, driving her into sweet submission whenever she tried to take control. She shuddered and moaned as heat built inside her, stoked by him as he softened the kiss until his lips barely brushed hers, had her feeling light inside again.

Just as she felt sure she would float away, he deepened the kiss, his tongue tangling with hers again, teasing her fangs in a way that sensitised them and had her trembling against him. She rocked in his arms, unable to stop herself as he took more from her, his kiss so demanding and the pressure of it so intense that she couldn't breathe.

He pushed her right to the edge, a trickle of his energy flowing into her to drug her, to turn her mind hazy and her body compliant, hot and aching for him, and then relented, turning the kiss maddeningly soft again.

Gods, what was he doing to her?

Her head spun, body quaking as he palmed her backside and teased her with his lips, taking her higher again before he seized her mouth in another demanding kiss.

One that awoke something inside her.

Something powerful and overwhelming.

She hissed and clawed his shoulders, ploughed her fingers through his dark hair and held him to her, twisted his black housecoat into her fists and rocked against him, on fire with need and desperate to sate it. He softened the kiss again, driving her right to the edge of despair as the tightness that had been building inside her ebbed again.

As soon as her body began to relax, he seized her mouth in another fierce kiss, stroked his tongue over her fangs and pushed her higher. His right hand pressed against her back and she hissed at him again, unable to hold back her anger as he caged her, stopping her from being able to rock against him. Bastard.

She groaned and tried to kiss him deeper, forcing him to do as she wanted as the energy building inside her grew more intense, had her restless and writhing in his arms, moving as much as she could as he held her, his arms steel bands around her.

He kissed her deeper again, sending fire licking over her skin and sucking the air from her lungs like he stole it from the room whenever he looked at her.

Her head twirled faster, need spiralling higher as his kiss grew rougher, more demanding, and she realised he intended to keep that vow he had made.

Damn, she wanted him to do it.

The pleasure of his kiss, alternating hardness and softness, roughness and gentleness, was too much. She breathed harder, her heart thundering as the pressure built inside her and she could feel release rolling up on her, could almost stretch and reach it. She moaned and rubbed against him, shivered as he palmed her bottom and kissed her harder.

His tongue swept over her small fangs, one and then the other.

She cried into his mouth, the sudden force of her release as it crashed over her tearing the startled noise from her as she shook and quivered, trembled so violently she shuddered in his arms.

He tucked her close and held her as she broke apart, just as he had promised.

Suki sank against him, breathless and reeling, hot from head to toe as bliss hummed in her veins.

The books were right about shadowed males.

They had a dark power at their disposal.

She lazily lifted her head and kissed him, tasting his bliss in it, the pleasure he had taken from bringing her to release with only a kiss.

Tempting him into using his dark power on her again.

Because damn, she couldn't get enough of him.

Wasn't sure she ever would.

Not even if they had forever.

CHAPTER 22

Tegan was no longer falling for Suki.

He had fallen for her, and he had fallen hard.

He had never been in love with someone before, and the depth of what he felt for the female dancing in front of his fire, mesmerising him with each sway and dip of her hips as she lost herself in the rhythm of the music, was staggering.

He sat in his armchair, watching her, absorbing everything about her. The gentle curl of her lips that said she was enjoying herself. The gold sparks in her green-to-blue eyes that spoke of hunger as she shyly glanced at him. The way she moved so sensually, weaving a spell on him with each kick of her hips that caused her short crimson plaid skirt to flare upwards, flashing a hint of thigh and lace-trimmed panties. How her small black top hugged her breasts, her beaded nipples rousing wicked thoughts, a hunger to tug her to him and pull the material down so he could capture one of those tempting peaks with his lips.

Her sultry teasing smile said she knew she was affecting him. Gods, he wasn't sure he would ever get enough of just looking at her.

His stunning little succubus.

She tossed him a smile that had his heart beating harder as she sexily sauntered towards him, hips swaying just enough to keep his gaze leaping between them and her face. She wedged her knees between his spread legs and bent over him to stroke his horns and tangle her fingers in his hair.

He wanted to kiss her, and this time he didn't want to stop there. He needed to do more with her. He needed to taste her as he had in her dream and his, needed to be inside her. She worried that he wasn't strong enough to handle her, but he was.

She was his fated one.

He had been made for her, so he had to be strong enough to handle her when she was lost in the throes of passion.

She leaned closer still, her striking eyes falling to his lips and stealing his breath as he ached for a kiss.

The door opened.

Ryker walked two paces into the room, stopped and stared at Suki.

Where she was bending over Tegan, her plaid skirt riding up, in danger of flashing her panties at his brother.

Tegan pushed her aside, leaped from the armchair, and was across the room in a heartbeat. He grabbed Ryker by the throat and shoved him against the wall, snarling through his fangs at him, warning him to take his eyes off Suki.

"Stop." She skidded to a halt beside him and pushed against his shoulder, gripped his arm and tried to pull his hand away from Ryker's throat.

Anger surged through him, turning his blood to liquid fire.

His female was defending another male?

He roared and tightened his grip on that male's throat, a black need to squeeze the life out of him so he couldn't steal his female raging inside him. The male choked. His female pulled on his arm, desperate words leaving her lips. He didn't hear them over the thunderous drumming of his heart, couldn't focus on her as that need to kill the male tightened its grip on him as he had on the male's throat, squeezing all reason from him.

He unfurled his wings, knocking the female aside, and stretched them, using them as a barrier between her and the male.

"Tegan," the male rasped, his eyes watering as his face reddened. His horns curled, flaring past his cheeks, and fangs flashed between his lips as he grimaced.

Satisfaction rushed through Tegan, the male's response making his blood hum. He had wanted a fight, and it looked as if the male was going to give him one. He grinned, revealing his own fangs, and grabbed the male by his right horn.

The weaker, damaged one.

On a vicious growl, the male retaliated, bringing his head forwards so fast that Tegan didn't have a chance to block. The male's forehead cracked off his, sending pain splintering over Tegan's skull, and he reared back and blinked as his vision grew hazy, darkness encroaching at the corners of it.

The male grabbed his wrist and twisted, ripping Tegan's hand from his throat, and snarled low in the demon tongue.

"Pull your shit together. I do not want your mate. I will be at the castle."

Tegan swung his fist at the male.

It cut through thin air where the male had been, seconds too late as the black hole in the floorboards shrank and disappeared. Damn him.

The urge to teleport to the castle and finish the fight rushed through him, but a stronger need held him in place.

He folded his wings against his back and turned on his female.

"You defended him," he bit out in English.

Her eyes widened before they narrowed on him and she planted her hands on her hips, showing him no fear. "You were trying to kill your own bloody brother. I wasn't going to sit back and let you go caveman on him. Not this time. I don't know what the hell is wrong with you, but you need to sort your shit out."

"What is wrong with me?" he snarled and advanced on her, and the foolish little female stood her ground. "What is wrong with me is that you drive me mad, Suki. Insane. The thought of another male looking at you… makes me want to kill them. The thought of you looking at another male… makes me want to die."

Her expression softened and she bravely stepped towards him, lifted her hands and framed his face with them. "I know, but I don't know what to do to stop you feeling that way."

He did. He knew what he needed to do.

He pulled her into his arms and teleported with her as it drummed in his blood, burned in his soul.

He needed to claim her.

He rose out of the teleport in his bedroom and seized her shoulders, pressed her back into the corner post of his four-poster bed and kissed her.

Hard.

He moaned when she matched the fervour of his kiss, just as she had promised she would, growing wild in his arms as her lips clashed with his and she fought him for dominance he couldn't give her this time. Her need pounded through him, driving him on, a hunger that hadn't abated since he had brought her to climax this morning. His female needed more.

He would give it to her.

He would make her wicked dream a reality for her.

Tegan swept her up into his arms and laid her on the bed.

Her chest heaved as she spread her arms out, breasts straining against her small black top, her eyes locked on him and her colourful hair spilling over the furs. She looked wanton like that and he couldn't get enough of it, of how she gazed at him as if she was starving for his touch, for something only he could give to her.

He growled and pushed her knees apart, kept his eyes on hers as he skimmed his hands up to her hips and took hold of her panties. She shuddered as he ripped them away, a gasp fleeing her lips as her eyes brightened with need.

His gaze fell and he groaned at the sight of her exposed feminine flesh, her curls glistening with her arousal, beckoning him.

Tegan dropped to his elbows, used his horns to wedge her thighs apart just as she had dreamed, and stroked the length of her with his tongue, tasting her sweetness as he dragged it from core to aroused nub. He groaned and shuddered, entire body quaking from the intoxicating taste of her and the way her hands flew to his head, her hips arching up into his caress as she moaned.

He growled and licked her again, swirled his tongue and teased her as he curled his hands over her thighs and held her in place, refusing to let her move her hips. She gasped and shook, twisted his hair into her fist and clutched it tightly as he devoured her, relentlessly stroking her with his tongue. Hunger mounted inside him, a burning need that threatened to overwhelm him as he pushed her higher, closer to the edge. She desperately tried to rock her hips, her grip on his hair tightening as she panted, her breaths coming faster as he mercilessly teased her.

When she shattered on a loud cry that echoed in his ears, the hunger rising inside him reached a crescendo, tipping him over an edge of his own.

He pulled back and growled at the sight of her slick flesh, the need to thrust to the hilt inside her and claim her pushing all rational thought from his mind.

He needed to be inside her.

Tegan dropped from the bed, untied the laces of his leathers and stripped them off, aware of her eyes on him, how they devoured the hard length he revealed to her. It ached and kicked, as solid as stone as need spiralled through him.

Suki groaned and sat up, moved onto her knees and reached for him, her bright colourful eyes sparkling with gold fire as she stared at his cock. He hissed as her hot little hand closed tightly around it. She drew her hand down, revealing the crown, and sent him out of his mind as her thumb glided over it, teasing the blunt tip.

He shuddered and bucked, his breath stuttering as her need mingled with his, rousing his primal instincts back to the fore. His female needed him.

He needed his female.

He curled his hand around her throat and pushed her back onto his bed, pressed his hips between her thighs and covered her with his body. He groaned as he rocked against her, cock sliding along her hot flesh, the feel of her scalding him sheer agony, cranking him tight inside. He pressed his thumb to her jaw and forced her head back and dropped his lips to her throat, devoured it with rough kisses as he thrust through her folds, as he drank her sweet cries and savoured the feel of her beneath him and how she arched, straining for more just as he was.

He wanted to seat himself inside her, needed to take her until she was mindless with passion and lost, and then he was going to bite her.

Claim her.

His fangs itched at the thought, his lower canines extending as the primal instinct to mate with her seized him, darkening the corners of his mind to drown out all reason, until all he could focus on was the urgent need to make Suki his.

He licked her throat and ground against her, shuddering as deep pleasure rolled through him at just the thought of sinking his fangs into her.

Shock rolled through him on the heels of it, turning the fire to ice in his veins, and he reared back and stared down at her, at the faint marks on her pale skin.

His eyes widened as he realised how close he had been to biting her.

As he saw how he was holding her pinned beneath him, one hand on her shoulder and the other clutching her nape, pressing into her flesh just as they had the other night.

Horror flashed through him, sent him reeling, but it wasn't enough to stop him from wanting to bite her, to ease the pressing demand beating inside him that commanded him to claim her.

Instinct ruled him.

Swiftly destroyed his control, no matter how fiercely he fought to retain it.

Even when he knew he would lose her if he imposed a bond upon her.

He stared down into her eyes as they slowly opened, battling the urge to claim her against her will, cold to the bone and deeply aware that he wasn't strong enough to stop himself, that it was only a matter of time before the primal urge seized command of him again and he wouldn't be able to stop it next time.

Concern flickered in her bright eyes.

Fae valued their freedom, protected their true name to stop others from using it against them, forcing them to do something against their will with the power it held over them.

210

He couldn't take Suki's freedom from her.

So he uttered a prayer to his gods that she would listen to the plea that was about to issue from his lips and see that he needed her to do it, even when he knew it would hurt her, that it would scare her. She had promised she would obey if he spoke these words, and he was depending upon her to keep that vow, because if she didn't, the alternative didn't bear thinking about.

"Cotton Candy."

CHAPTER 23

"Cotton Candy."

Those two innocent words, growled with so much pain and despair by Tegan as he loomed over her, his eyes bright violet and horns flaring, filled her with fear and dread.

Suki tried to get up, but he snarled and pinned her by her throat, shoving her roughly against the bed as his eyes raked over her, glowing brighter still as he fixed them on her throat and bared his fangs.

His muscles shifted beneath his skin and she swallowed hard, could only stare as his shoulders broadened, body growing even larger as whatever darkness gripped him tightened its hold on him.

His eyes roamed to his hands where they held her and his face crumpled, pain flaring in his gaze as he raised it to meet hers. "Please."

She froze, terrified of what he was asking her now, more afraid of it than she was of him as he towered above her, on the verge of transforming into his more demonic state.

She shook her head, her heart hammering and breath rattling in her lungs as she realised what he was asking.

"Knock me out," he gritted and then changed again, darkness swamping his features as he dragged in a deep breath and looked down at the apex of her thighs.

Hunger lit his sculpted face, burned in his eyes and warned her that he was serious, that things were going to go south if she didn't do as he had asked.

But knocking him out?

What if she took too much energy from him?

Chills swept over her skin and her brow furrowed. Could she risk that?

"Now," he snarled. "Before I do something... make you hate me."

His horns twisted around on themselves.

"I can't. What if I kill you? What if I hurt you? I don't want to hurt you." Her face crumpled in time with his and his eyes pleaded her even as he mercilessly tightened his grip on her throat.

"If you... do not..." His chest heaved, his breaths turning laboured as he leaned over her, pressing more weight into her shoulder. "Pain I would feel if I..."

Enormous fangs flashed as he muttered.

"Want to bite you."

Her hand flew to her throat, clashing with his.

Agony shone in his eyes and she knew it was because of her reaction, her instinctive attempt to protect her throat from his fangs.

He rasped, "If I bite you... you will hate me... in turn it would destroy me."

She didn't want to hurt him, but it seemed pain was inevitable. If she didn't stop him, he would hurt her and that would drive him deep into despair, would end up wounding him too. If she did stop him, she would hurt him but spare him that deeper pain, and herself too.

So she would stop him.

And she would stop herself before she went too far and killed him.

His eyes darkened and his nostrils flared as he barked, "No."

She only had a split-second to register that he had sensed her intent to stop him from biting her by taking him down. She reacted swiftly, bringing her hands up to shove against his chest as he lunged at her throat, his fangs snapping together just short of it as she locked her elbows. He roared and snarled, grappled with her, his claws pressing into her skin as he tried to overpower her.

Clearly intent on not being denied.

Suki released his chest, allowing him to close the distance between them as he fell onto her, and captured his horns before he could strike. He bucked and twisted his head, tried to free himself but it was no use.

She held him firm, pressed her lips to his and said a silent apology as she kissed him.

His energy flowed into her like a dark and powerful torrent, lighting her up inside even as it chilled her, and fear clutched her as he thrashed against her, growling and fighting her, his desperation lacing the taste of his kiss.

He was far stronger than she had anticipated.

She choked when he managed to close his hand around her throat, tightened her grip on his horns and refused to give up, because even though he wanted to bite her, it wasn't what he needed.

He needed her to keep her promise.

She repeated that in her head as she deepened the kiss and heat flared inside her, unfurling through her veins as his energy poured into her once more and he finally began to weaken, his hand going lax around her throat as his struggles slowed.

Suki forced herself to keep going, ignoring the voice inside her heart that was screaming at her to stop, that was shrieking that she was hurting him.

Killing him.

Not yet.

He was stronger than she had thought. He was powerful. If she didn't push him right to the edge, there was a chance he wouldn't be down for the count. She couldn't risk him waking quickly.

Because there was a second part to her plan.

A method of ensuring that she had a chance to escape if he lost control again.

The ashy taste of his fury and the dark need that gripped him gave way to honey and whisky, a sweet smoky taste that warmed her and gave her the strength to keep going, because she was pulling him back from the abyss.

He groaned and slumped against her, his weight crushing her as his strength gave out. She endured it, dancing her lips over his, draining his energy more slowly now as she eased back on the throttle. The need to keep kissing him gradually abated, releasing her from the grip of her own instincts, and she was quick to break away from him and stop before her chance slipped through her fingers.

Tegan rested heavily on top of her, his skin clammy and cold beneath her fingers, his dead weight making it impossible to breathe.

She rolled him over with trembling hands, the fear rushing through her refusing to go anywhere as she looked at his ashen face, at the dark hollows in his cheeks and beneath his eyes.

She kneeled beside him and brushed the damp wild strands of his black hair from his forehead as his horns shrank back to normal, and gently kissed him, funnelling some of her energy back into him.

Satisfied that he had enough strength to survive the onslaught of her kiss, she sat back on her heels beside him and waited. His skin gained colour, but the dark marks beneath his eyes remained. She wanted to give him back more energy, but she couldn't risk him waking. Not yet.

She hopped from the bed, her legs unsteady as strength coursed through her, dizziness assaulting her as her body struggled to absorb it all.

Heck, he was far stronger than she had anticipated.

She felt a little drunk as she staggered around his room, hazy and warm from head to toe as she rifled through his wardrobes and found several blankets stacked in the bottom. She took four of them and unfurled each one, ripped it into pieces and braided them together, transforming each of them into thick make-shift ropes.

Her legs felt steadier beneath her as she crossed the room to Tegan where he lay on the bed, out for the count.

She started at the top of him, tying his left arm with the rope and securing it to the thick post at the corner of the bed, and then moving around him to do the same to his right. His legs got the same treatment. When she was done, she appraised her work, checking each rope was tied tightly and secure, and then crawled onto the bed beside him.

Suki settled her ear against his chest and reassured herself with the steady, powerful beat of his heart as fear tried to seize hold of her again. She closed her eyes and listened to it, breathed in time with him and savoured the warmth of him as it returned.

It wasn't quite the way she had expected to sleep with a man for the first time in her life, but he needed her there. She felt that deep in her heart. She twisted onto her other side so she could see his face and traced patterns on his chest, grazing her fingers through the short hairs, feeling his heart drumming.

What instinct had gripped him to make him so savage?

It had terrified him.

She had seen it in his eyes.

They hadn't hidden anything from her, had revealed his desperation and fear, and his pain, together with the dark need that had consumed him.

A need to bite her.

She lifted her hand and cupped his cheek, curled closer to him as her heart whispered that even if she asked what had provoked that need in him, he wouldn't tell her. He was keeping secrets from her after all. She didn't care. She had her own secrets. What mattered is that he had done the right thing. He had kept his promise not to hurt her and she had kept hers.

The steady beat of his heart soothed her as it gained strength.

She relaxed against him, buzzing from the energy she had taken from him but aware that after the high came the fall, and when it hit, she would get sleepy. When that happened, she intended to remain right where she was, tucked close to him where he needed her.

Because when he woke, he was going to feel like a dick, and she didn't want that.

So she would stay with him, would be there when he rose from his sleep, showing him that everything was fine.

As the minutes trickled past, a sensation built inside her, a notion that she seized and studied, fascinated by the newness of it.

Sleeping with him made her feel strangely vulnerable, but safe.

Stripped bare of her armour.

But protected.

Or maybe that was just how Tegan made her feel.

He surprised her at every turn, was never quite what she expected him to be. Yesterday, he had been a warrior, a savage warlord bent on making her enemies pay, and gods, he had been beautiful.

There was a darker side of him she was only just becoming aware of, one that had emerged again just minutes ago.

She didn't understand what had come over him, but she appreciated that he had fought to protect her from that side of himself.

She appreciated that he understood her and knew her well enough to see what would have happened if he had crossed that line. All succubi had a no-biting rule. Marking her throat was a type of claim, a sign to others meant to warn them away.

She didn't belong to him.

She stroked his broad chest and kept whispering that to herself even when she didn't really feel it.

She felt quite the opposite.

She was beginning to belong to him, body and soul.

And heart.

CHAPTER 24

Tegan's arms ached, his muscles stiff from cold and the position he held them in. He moaned and lowered them from above his head.

Or at least he tried to lower them.

His eyes shot open, panic sending adrenaline surging through his veins as he twisted his arms, attempting to break the bonds that cut into his wrists, holding them outstretched beside him.

"What the hell?" he looked up at his left wrist, fear trickling in to mingle with the panic as he saw his wrist was tied to the thick post at the corner of his bed and grew aware that it wasn't only his arms that were bound.

His ankles were too.

Someone had tied him to the bed, laid out and vulnerable.

His pulse shot into overdrive and anger surged, his horns flaring in response as his fangs descended and his claws lengthened.

Someone had him as their captive.

That someone moaned and he stilled, the fire in his blood becoming born of desire rather than rage as he grew aware of the female sleeping facing him with her head on his chest, her bare knees tucked up beside his armpit and her hand resting softly over his heart.

His eyes inched down to her, the panic and fear ebbing away as he saw his beautiful mate resting curled close to him, her face soft with sleep as she used him as her pillow.

As the darker emotions settled, he grew aware of something else too.

What he had done to place him in this predicament.

He squeezed his eyes shut and let his head fall back onto the feather pillows as he cursed himself in the demon tongue.

Fear returned, swift to claim him as doubts flooded his mind, every reprimand and angry word he hurled at himself giving it a stronger hold over him.

He had hurt Suki again.

She moaned, sighed and shifted against him, and he opened his eyes and looked down at her, watching her wake, putting it to memory because he feared it would be the first and last time he saw it happening.

Her nose wrinkled, she frowned, and then her eyes fluttered open, their stunning green-to-blue depths hitting him hard as he struggled for words, for the ones that would make things right between them again.

"Hey, sleepyhead," she murmured, her soft voice lacking the anger he deserved.

Instead of pushing away from him and giving him hell as he expected, she snuggled closer and drew patterns on his chest, and it tore down his defences, destroyed his strength and left him shaken.

Because his beautiful mate had already forgiven him.

"How are you feeling?" She yawned, covering her mouth with the hand that had been tracing tantalising circles and swirls on his pectorals, and he mourned the loss of her touch, ached for her to place her hand on him again because her caress was reassuring.

And he needed reassurance right now.

"Terrible," he grumbled and twisted his hands again, the need to wrap his arms around her utterly wrecking him.

It was all he could think about. He wanted to hold her to him and never let her go, because he wanted her to cuddle into him and show him again and again that she wasn't going anywhere.

He hadn't ruined everything.

"I am sorry." He searched her eyes, seeking any trace of fear in them, any sign that he had hurt her and she harboured resentment, her feelings for him diminished by what he had done.

"I know." She placed her palm over his heart again and stared at her hand. "Do you hurt?"

He shook his head, feeling like a bastard who didn't deserve this caring, wonderful female before him. He had been the one to harm her, to scare her, to attempt to do something terrible to her, but she was asking if he was hurt. He should have asked her that first.

Hell, she shouldn't have asked him that at all.

He didn't deserve this tenderness.

"Are you... did I... hurt you?" He tried to see her throat, but her hair obscured it and fear gripped him again, squeezing his heart in icy talons as he imagined the worst.

He could remember how tightly he had held her, how he had pinned her by her delicate neck.

A neck he had wanted to sink his fangs into and mark.

She shook her head and gently brushed her hair back to reveal her throat.

It was unmarked.

Relief rushed through him, so powerful that the strength he had clawed back together shattered again and tears threatened to line his lashes, burned in the backs of his eyes as he stared at her.

"I am truly sorry, Suki," he grated, throat tight and voice hoarse as emotions bombarded him, an overwhelming tangle of relief, fear, doubt and regret.

"You said that already." She moved onto her knees and grimaced as she looked at his left wrist. "I'm sorry too. I think I tied them a little too tight."

He didn't care. Her safety was more important than his comfort. He was glad she had tied him down and had done it tightly, protecting herself from him in case he was still filled with an urge to bite her when he came around.

She shuffled to his hand and untied his wrist, and surprised him by taking hold of it and bringing it up to her lips. His chest warmed as she gently kissed the deep indentations on his wrist and smoothed her thumb over them.

"They will heal." He could heal anything except the pain that would have destroyed him if he had hurt her.

She placed the rope down beside him and he frowned at it.

"Um. I owe you new sheets." She smiled sheepishly.

He added resourceful to her list of talents, one he was glad she possessed as she moved to his left ankle and untied it. He bit back a groan as she clambered over his legs and untied his other ankle, and then crawled up the bed towards his right arm, looking seductively sinful.

"Perhaps you should leave that one." He wanted to be free, but he didn't trust himself around her, not when she looked so tempting and his body was responding to her, was growing harder by the second.

She shook her head. "Nah. Now you have your strength back, I can just take you down again if you get a little too frisky."

She untied his right wrist and tossed the rope onto the pile to his left.

The light left her delicate features, her fine eyebrows meeting hard as she kneeled beside him and gazed down at him.

"What happened?"

He wasn't sure how to answer that question. He needed to explain so much to her, but he feared the outcome. He worried that she would bolt if he told her that she was his fated one and that was the reason he needed to bite her. He needed to be sure she was in love with him before he told her that she was his mate and that he didn't just work for the Second Realm, he ruled it.

"A demon thing?" she said, sending another wave of relief crashing over him.

He seized on that as the reason, nodding vigorously in response.

Her eyes narrowed and he expected her to say something as suspicion formed in them, but then she shrugged and twisted away from him.

A groan tore from him as she crawled away from him, her plaid skirt swaying and in danger of flashing heaven at him.

"Where are you going?" he croaked.

The little look she tossed over her shoulder at him said she was doing it on purpose. "I'm a little peckish. I gave you energy back to heal you and now I need a little taste of you."

"This is not a wise idea, Suki. Not right now." He still wasn't fully in control. It only took a look at her thighs to have him wanting to seat himself between them.

She stopped near his knees and pulled the furs draped over his lower half down, the brush of them over his sensitive cock sheer agony as he tried to keep his focus on stopping her.

"Don't worry." Her eyes devoured every inch of him that she revealed, growing brighter in that way that entranced him. "I gave you back enough energy to handle this."

"That is not what I meant."

She smiled again. "I know. But I don't want to stop. I want a taste."

She leaned over and licked up the length of his cock, ripping a groan from him as his eyes rolled back in his head and he collapsed against the pillow again.

He muttered, "Maybe you should tie me back up."

She giggled, and gods, the sound bewitched him. Stole his heart completely.

"And spoil the fun?" She stroked her tongue over him again. "I liked what we were doing last night… before you got a bit too fangy."

He sensed it as the light drained from her and looked down at her, meeting her deadly serious gaze.

"Keep your fangs in check or you're taking another nap."

He nodded stiffly, even though he wasn't sure he would be able to manage it.

He would try his hardest for her though, would cling to the thought that one day he would explain the reason he needed to bite her and that she would accept it from him that day. She would wear his mark.

"Would sex help curb your growly need to mark me?"

That question yanked him back to her where she sat beside him.

She feathered her fingers down the valley between his stomach muscles. "I was just thinking. This is a territory thing isn't it? I've seen men behaving in a similar way and you did want to kill every guy who looked at me in the fae town... because you haven't had me yet. I'm, um... it's like I'm not... yours."

A pretty blush stained her cheeks and she averted her gaze, following her fingers with it as she traced his muscles.

"Let's just pretend I didn't say that."

No. No way was he going to pretend she hadn't just said that and not only because it had revealed she already knew where his behaviour stemmed from and therefore there was a chance she would easily accept that she was his mate when he told her.

He wasn't going to pretend he hadn't heard her because she had just proposed being his.

And the look that had been in her eyes coupled with how awkward she felt now said that she wanted to be his.

He shot his right hand down, snagged her wrist and pulled her to him. She fell onto his chest with a gasp that he swallowed in a kiss. The sweet spiced taste of her flooded him, drugging him in an instant, and he groaned as he clutched her to him and kissed her deeper, needing more from her.

Needing all of her.

She was swift to catch up, shifting so she was laying half on him, her hands skimming over his chest and shoulders as she wrenched control of the kiss from him. She moaned and he felt the drain on his energy as she fed on his pleasure, on the bliss she had given him with only a shy look and a handful of words.

"Gods, I need you," she whispered against his lips between kisses and he groaned, dropped his hands to her backside and gripped it hard as he pressed her against him.

Her hip met his cock and he rocked against it as he claimed her lips, stealing back control from her. He drew her higher and dipped his hands lower, wedging his fingers between her thighs. She shivered and moaned as he pulled her thighs apart and stroked her, and he growled.

She was so wet.

"I was having naughty dreams." That soft confession floored him at the same time as it ignited his blood.

She had been dreaming wicked things while sleeping with him.

He skimmed his hands up over her bare bottom and her hips, followed the curve of her waist to the small black top she wore. He hooked his fingers beneath it and pulled it up, groaned as her breasts brushed his chest, skin on skin for the first time. She broke the kiss for only as long as it took for her top to pass between them, panting against his lips as she grabbed it and threw it away from them.

Her fingers danced down his chest and stomach, tantalising swirls that cranked him tighter. She moaned when he flexed for her, kissed his chin and then the space between his collarbones, and down his chest. He relaxed into the bed, closing his eyes as his focus fixed on her, on every place she kissed or licked, branding his flesh.

She traced her tongue around his right nipple and then lightly bit his stomach, circled his navel with kisses, and drove him out of his mind by briefly taking the head of his shaft between her lips.

He growled when she pulled away, his eyes flicking open. The growl died as he stared at her, watching her fingers as she kneeled on the bed beside him and worked on the fastenings of her skirt.

She peeled it open and his mouth dried out as he got his first glimpse of her bare curves.

"Gods, Suki, you're beautiful."

Another blush stained her cheeks.

"Shut up." She slapped his thigh, her admonishing look turning wicked as she glanced at her hand.

What was she up to?

He didn't have to wait long to find out.

She skimmed her hand up his inner thigh, cupped his balls and pressed her fingers beneath them. His hips jacked up off the bed as a wave of pleasure rolled through him and he scowled as she grinned at him, one full of victory.

He grabbed her arm, pulled her up and twisted her beneath him, kissed her breathless as he pinned her, her warm soft body cushioning his and their legs tangled. When he drew back, her gaze was glassy, her lips crimson and cheeks flushed.

"Stop trying to make me climax by kissing me. It won't work this time."

He smiled down into her eyes. It would work, but it wasn't what his female needed. He trailed his fingers down over her breast, gaze tracking them, the whole of his focus locked on her. He knew what she needed this time, and he needed it too.

She swallowed and trembled, arched into his touch as he swirled his finger around her nipple, the peak stiffening in response. He had bedded many females, but as he lay tangled with her, his right arm beneath her back as he explored her with his left hand, he couldn't recall any of them.

Because none of them had been her.

The first female who had shared his bed and slept with him.

The first female who had known him as just him, not royalty.

The first female he loved.

The only female he would ever love.

She was it for him, no matter what decision she made when she discovered what she was to him. He would love her and only her forever.

"Make love to me," she murmured, a tightness in her voice that revealed her nerves, fears that ran rampant in him too.

They would both be new to this too.

He lowered his head and kissed her softly, reverently, with all the tenderness and care that she deserved. She wrapped her arms around his shoulders and held him to her, her kiss as soft and light as his was, stirring warmth inside him.

He skimmed his left hand over her breast to her stomach and onwards, dipped it between her thighs and groaned in time with her as he cupped her, teasing her with his fingers. She rocked into his touch, her breaths coming faster as he felt the pleasure building inside her, could practically taste it in her kiss.

"More," she breathed.

He stopped.

Her eyes flicked open, she scowled and cuffed him around his head, hitting his left horn. "You dare stop again."

He grinned and kissed her, showing her that he had no intention of stopping. He just hadn't been able to resist it since he had used that word for her safety one.

"I'm picking... a new... word," she murmured between kisses. "Later."

He kissed down her jaw and her throat, moaned as he tasted her skin and felt her pulse fluttering against his lips. The urge to bite her returned but he tamped it down, focused on the need he could feel inside her, one that drove him to satisfy it. She sighed and tilted her head back, arching her breasts against his chest as he kissed her and fondled her bundle of nerves.

When he sensed she was close, he couldn't hold back any longer.

He grasped her hip and moved between her thighs, rubbed his aching shaft along her core and shuddered as the heat of her scalded him. She moaned and rocked to meet him, her face twisting as he ground against her.

She captured him around the back of his neck and drew him down, kissed him hard as she worked her body against him, threatening to have him spilling before he was even inside her.

He pulled back, breaking contact, and reached between them to grip his length. His nerves rose again but were quickly vanquished by the thought of filling her and fulfilling the need to claim her in the only way he could right now. She was right about him. He needed to mark her and make love with her, so he would know she was his. Hopefully then he would view unmated males as less of a threat and the urge to claim her would no longer be as strong, would be tempered by the fact she was his female now, giving him the strength and patience to wait for her to be ready before he claimed her properly and bound them as mates.

He eased his cock down, groaned as the head pressed into her folds, and then into her core, disappearing from view. She moaned and fisted the furs with one hand and clutched his horn with the other, her head tipping back further as he sank deeper, stretching and filling her.

Damn, she was tight and hot, seared him as he slid deeper. His breaths shortened, the urge to sink deep and fast into her riding him. He resisted it, savoured their first coupling and how well they fit as he eased into her.

"Oh gods," she whispered on a sigh that tugged at him, had him lifting his gaze to see her face as he filled her.

Pleasure flitted across it, bliss that had pride stirring inside him.

Her grip on the furs and his horn tightened as he reached as deep as she could take him and slowly withdrew before rolling his hips forwards to fill her again. She dragged him down to her and kissed him gently as he rocked into her, her grip loosening again as she breathed in time with him, as her lips played against his.

She wrapped both arms around his neck again and held him to her as he kissed her, as he gave her long, slow thrusts that had him withdrawing almost all the way before driving back into her. Her moans mingled with his as he broke away from her lips, as he buried his face in her throat and held her to him, pressing one hand into her back beneath her and clutching her hip with the other, holding her in place as he lost himself in her and the pleasure building inside him with each deep thrust, each joining of their bodies.

"Suki," he breathed against her throat, needs clashing inside him, pulling him in different directions as she began to move with him, restless beneath him, reaching for her climax.

The dark need to claim her rose again but he battled it, told himself this was more than enough for now. He was claiming her in a way. In a beautiful way. He wasn't sure he had ever made love. No. He was sure. Nothing he had experienced had ever been like this. He felt as if more than their bodies were entwined.

He felt as if their souls were entwining too, twisting together to become one.

He kissed her throat and lifted her hip so he could slide deeper into her, taking more of her. She moaned and arched, clung to him as she wrapped her legs around his hips and pressed her heels into his bare backside. She spurred him on, in danger of unleashing his darker needs as she drove her feet into his buttocks whenever he withdrew, stealing control from him.

He growled against her throat and resisted her, curled his hips and kept things slow.

She didn't relent.

She groaned and trembled, her skin on fire against him as she grabbed his horn and yanked his head up. Her lips claimed his, fierce demand in her kiss. He groaned and shuddered against her as she raked short nails down his shoulders and grew wild in his arms, the pleasure he could sense in her reaching a crescendo.

When she bit his lower lip, snagging it between her small fangs, the battle he waged with himself came to an abrupt end.

On a low snarl, he angled his head and fused their mouths, claiming control of the kiss as the needs he had been fighting to deny roared to the fore. He beat them back, focusing on his body as he thrust into her, joining them and claiming her in a small way, but he couldn't stop himself from shifting his right hand to her nape.

He tangled his fingers in her hair and clutched her nape hard, gripping it in his short claws as he kissed her, as he plunged into her faster now, the pleasure spiralling towards climax inside him seizing control and driving him to find release.

The urge to bite her faded as he grasped her nape and mastered her mouth. He spread his legs, driving hers further apart, and pressed his knees into the furs, pumping her harder and deeper as he held her hips off the furs. She moaned and arched, gripped him tighter as he thrust into her, making her feel every inch of him and what she did to him, how fiercely he needed her.

He flexed his fingers around her nape, tried to convince himself to be more gentle with her but it was impossible as she kissed him, matching him in the way she had promised. She rocked her body against his, clawed his back hard enough that the scent of his own blood hit him, and pleaded him for more.

He tightened his grip on her nape, the need to show her he was the one in control running rampant through him. When he realised what he was doing, he wrenched away from her mouth and pressed his forehead to hers, breathing hard.

"Sorry," he muttered and spat a dark curse as he fought to be more gentle with her.

"Don't be," she husked and reached down, grabbed his backside with both hands and dug her nails in. "There's something kinda sexy about the way you hold my neck when you're fucking me."

Gods, she would be his undoing, speaking like that.

She didn't know the fire she was playing with, how liable he was to burn her and everything they shared to ashes.

He drew back, sure she was teasing him, unable to believe she meant her words.

The heat in her gaze as she stared up at him said that she wasn't. She liked it when he held her in place, dominating her in a way, and that knowledge eased the grip his urges had on him.

Because she was submitting to him.

Satisfying his primal need to bend her to his will.

He growled and kissed her, lost himself in her as she rocked against him, dug her claws into his backside and clutched him to her rather than pushing him away. He curled his hips, driving into her, the entirety of his focus on her as she breathed faster, tightening around his shaft, and her need flooded the tentative connection between them, the growing bond.

Her lips broke away from his, her sweet cry filling his ears as she shattered, her body pulsing around his, drawing him to the edge with her. He gripped her nape as his seed boiled up his shaft and release took him, crashed over him so hard and fast that his head spun as he spilled, entire body quaking as he held himself buried deep inside her.

When he could breathe again, he rolled onto his back, pulling her with him and clutching her to him.

He gazed down at Suki as she settled on his chest, her eyes hazy and soft, and something struck him.

She hadn't taken any energy from him.

"You did not feed." He cleared her hair from her face, tucking the green and blue strands behind her ear.

Her lids grew heavy, shuttering her beautiful eyes as she murmured, "Couldn't."

He frowned. "Because you did not wish to hurt me?"

She smiled lazily and pressed a kiss to the spot over his heart. "Something like that."

He would have been convinced by that answer if he hadn't sensed the tension spiking inside her and the flicker of nerves that followed it.

There was something his fated one wasn't telling him.

Whatever it was, he would convince her to tell him about it, because it frightened her.

And he didn't want her to fear him.

He needed her to love him.

As deeply as he loved her.

CHAPTER 25

Tegan was growling as he emerged from the mansion, but he fell silent as his eyes landed on her where she stood by a pool in the middle of a rather formal garden, glaring at the water. Suki had been there for the last ten minutes, since a messenger had arrived and Tegan had bundled her off into his bedroom, teleporting her there and telling her to remain in his room until he had finished his business.

She didn't mind him being controlling in the bedroom when they were fooling around but she wasn't going to stand for him attempting to control what she did, so she had teleported outside.

Which had apparently infuriated him judging by how harried he looked.

"I could not find you." He strode towards her, long black-leather-clad legs devouring the distance between them. "I thought something had happened. I told you to remain inside."

She shrugged. "I was bored."

He frowned at her and then sighed. When she looked at him, he was staring over his shoulder at the black mansion, a troubled edge to his expression.

"What did the messenger want?" Cold trickled through her as she waited for him to answer, draining her of the warmth she normally felt when she was around him.

He scrubbed his right horn and glared at the house. "I must go to the castle."

And he didn't want to leave her.

She could read between the lines.

It was time for her to return to her world.

Her heart felt heavy in her chest even as she told herself it was for the best. Being here with him was making her lose sight of things. She was too swept up in him. She hadn't even thought about her sisters or her clan over the last day.

"I would let you remain here," he started and sighed again, pain flickering in his eyes as they finally landed on her. "I do not want to leave you unattended and I do not know how long this will take."

She shrugged, but it came off as stiff as the strange ache in her chest worsened and she had the oddest urge to throw her toys out of the pram and have a complete rage.

Her gaze drifted to the mansion beyond him.

It struck her that she had been playing house with him.

She hadn't realised it, but she had been living a relationship like the ones she had seen on TV and in the fae town and mortal cities.

She had taken walks with Tegan, had bathed with him and shared meals with him. Well, he had eaten and then she had devoured him. She had talked with him long into the night. Made love with him. Fallen asleep in his arms, tucked safely against him.

And now she didn't want to leave.

Things were getting too intense and she was way out of her depth. Succubi didn't do relationships. They didn't fall in love.

And choosing him meant choosing to leave her family.

Which was something she couldn't do.

Not for a man who she was now one hundred percent certain was keeping things from her. When they had first made love, she had tried to feed from the experience, from the intense emotions that had flowed through her and him, but something had stopped her.

Him.

Whenever she had begun to feel a trickle of energy pouring into her, he had shut it down, pulling that energy back into him, maintaining a strange sort of equilibrium between them. She really needed to learn more about shadowed males.

She needed to learn more about demons too so she could set her mind at ease and silence the voice inside her that kept screaming the oddest things at her, things she was sure were impossible.

"It's fine. I should probably go home anyway." So she could do that research and also so she could look all of her sisters in the eye and tell them that hit of energy they had been receiving the last few days was courtesy of her.

She had completed her objective. She had managed to seduce him. Or had he managed to seduce her? She wasn't sure, but either way, she had succeeded where the clan's mistress had failed.

She could return to her family with her head held high.

They were finally going to be proud of her.

So why didn't she feel good?

Why did it feel as if her entire world was crumbling around her as Tegan took hold of her hand and drew her to him?

As he gazed down into her eyes and spoke. "I swear, I will find time to come and see you tomorrow."

She nodded and wrapped her arms around his waist, settled her head against his bare chest and savoured the feel of him against her as he teleported with her. The silent darkness gave way to a cacophony of voices, the smells of the fae town swift to replace the strange scents of Hell, and she looked around her at the square, sure she should be glad to be home.

But all she wanted to do was ask him to take her back to Hell.

Suki stepped out of his embrace, stared at his hand and drew down a deep fortifying breath before succumbing to the urge to take hold of it. She slipped her hand into his, entwining their fingers and led him towards the northern exit of the square, past the clock tower.

"I should return," he murmured, not sounding as if he really wanted to leave.

She glanced over her shoulder and caught him staring at their linked hands, the beautiful look of surprise and satisfaction on his handsome face imprinting itself on her heart and her mind.

"Walk me home like a gentleman." She couldn't resist teasing him, smiled when he lifted his dark gaze to fix it on her.

He hit her with a devastating smile of his own and that ache to go back to Hell with him grew fiercer.

He fell into step beside her and she held her head high as they walked, squaring her shoulders and tipping her chin up as the women passing them shot her daggers when they saw he was holding her hand.

They rounded a bend in the road and the succubus house came into view, and her steps slowed. Tegan followed her gaze.

"Is that home?" he said.

She nodded, staring at the three-storey Palladian style sandstone mansion and the group of men hanging around outside it, calling to the succubi who entered and exited it. Some of her sisters grabbed one or two of the men, pulling them into the building with them, earning them hollers of abuse from the other men.

As they neared it, Tegan slowed further, and she looked back at him. She tracked the path of his wide gaze and smiled.

"It *is* a house of succubi." She had gotten used to the triangular frieze that formed the roof of the columned entrance.

When she had been younger, the erotic acts depicted on it had made her blush.

Now they looked tame.

One of the succubi lounging on the balcony that cut across the columns at the first floor leaned over the railings and flashed the men in the street. They whooped and jeered, and one of them pushed another forward, sending him stumbling across the cobbles.

"Is it always like this?" Tegan scowled at the gathered men.

She shrugged. "Like, twenty-five hours of the day."

He turned his frown on her. "A day has only twenty-four hours, does it not?"

She rolled her eyes, enjoying the moment of lightness as it lifted some of the weight from her heart. "That's the point. Saying non-stop would have been boring."

"You are anything but boring," Tegan husked, his deep voice doing funny things to her insides.

"I could say the same about you." She flinched when the sound of a man crashing into the flowerpots at the base of the stairs that led up to the porch hit her ears, his muffled groan causing an outburst of activity on the doorstep as men and succubi rushed to help. "We should probably say goodbye here."

She grew aware of eyes on her as Tegan pulled her into his arms and kissed her, one that would have melted her panties if she had been wearing some. Energy crackled between them as his lips danced over hers, power and strength that flowed through her veins and lit her up, filling her fuel gauge back up to the max.

He wanted her well fed and both of his reasons for doing so warmed her inside. He was taking care of her and making sure she wasn't hungry, and he was also making sure she didn't go chasing after another male while he was away.

Jealous demon.

She sighed as he reluctantly released her and stepped back, his hand still clutching hers.

"Tomorrow," he murmured.

"Tomorrow." She somehow managed to release his hand.

The darkness yawned beneath him and he disappeared into it, and she stared at the cobbles, heaviness settling in her chest again, a weight she found impossible to shift, no matter how many times she told herself that it was only twenty-four hours, maybe less.

It wasn't as if she would never see him again.

"Suki?" Allura called.

Suki jumped and whirled to face her sister where she stood on the steps with several other succubi, all of them gaping at her.

She swallowed the nerves that shot through her as she spotted a figure beyond them, in the shadows of the vestibule.

The clan's mistress.

Cyrena.

Allura shoved through the throng of men to Suki and grabbed her around her left arm, her violet-to-blue eyes bright as she pressed against her, the leather of her black corset cold against Suki's skin. "Did you just come home with a guy?"

The onyx-haired beauty tugged her towards the house, ignoring the way the men raked their gazes over her, and Suki couldn't remember the last time Allura had been so friendly towards her.

Vidia appeared beside her, her blonde pigtails swaying across the shoulders of her tight white shirt from the teleport.

"Not *a* guy, but *the* guy!" Vidia paused and her aqua-to-navy eyes slowly widened. "Don't tell me that hit of energy we've all been talking about the last few days has been you."

A blush climbed Suki's cheeks.

"Oh my gods." Allura turned a shocked look on her and then Vidia. "It totally was her."

Vidia shoved Suki in the back, pushing her up the broad sandstone steps towards the entrance. "Come on. Come on. We want to hear all about it. Every juicy deet!"

Cyrena stood there, towering on the top step, a formidable sight as she stared down at Suki, her brown-to-blue eyes bright with sparks of gold as she folded her arms across her chest, pushing her breasts together in her elegant figure-hugging crimson dress.

"Where have you been, Suki? We were all worried about you." The mistress preened her white-blonde to sky-blue hair, twisting the waves that tumbled around her bare shoulders, perfecting her image as a few of the men noticed her and stared.

Hard.

Suki waited to see if any of them were going to faint. Sometimes it happened when the mistress made an appearance. The power she emitted was strong, three hundred years of experience making her the most formidable succubus in England, one no man could resist.

Well.

Except one.

She squashed her nerves and straightened her spine, met Cyrena's gaze and held it as confidence flared inside her, a little drugging as it filled her up. "I was with a demon."

"Your first big trophy male!" Vidia slapped her on her back again, jerking her forwards, and Suki grinned at her as warmth flooded her.

Several other succubi joined in, congratulating her, and at first she enjoyed it, was overjoyed that they were finally accepting her, several of them wanting to make plans to go hunting with her, but as they ushered her into the house, she began to feel cold.

And worried.

"Congratulations, Suki," Cyrena said in a regal, icy tone as Suki passed her.

That sense of cold turned glacial inside her.

What was wrong with her? Her clan were finally accepting her. Her sisters were cheering her on for the first time. She was one of them at last.

She had expected to feel something more than this strange sense of dread upon showing her clan that she was one of them, that she was finally blooming and coming into her own just as her mother had said she would.

Suki looked over her shoulder, at Cyrena as she reached the bottom of the steps and turned to her right.

And disappeared.

That sense of dread grew heavier inside her, even as Allura and Vidia swept her up into their arms and pulled her towards the lounge area, both of them telling her on repeat that they wanted to hear every juicy detail.

Her thoughts turned to her mother and to Tegan.

And a thunderbolt struck her.

She had found her place in this world.

Only it wasn't where she had expected it to be.

It wasn't at the clan house with her fellow succubi, foolishly trying to make them view her as one of them.

Her place in this world was by Tegan's side, wrapped safely in his arms.

It was the only place she really wanted to be. He had made her see that she was striving for something that she shouldn't have to fight to achieve, because he had accepted her as she was, flaws and all.

He loved her for her faults, wanted her despite how different she was to him, and he valued her.

And she was in love with him.

CHAPTER 26

Tegan reviewed the maps and charts his aides had laid out on the heavy black wooden table in the centre of his war room. He studied the north-eastern border in the light from the lamps mounted on the thick stone columns that stood on either side of the table. His lands connected to the Fourth Realm and the First Realm in that region.

Word had already been sent to the First King warning them of the activity building in that area, and he had received a response. Frey, uncle of the future king, had been dispatched together with his legion to assess the threat and take immediate necessary action.

Tegan had dispatched Ryker and the Royal Legion to the border to meet him.

If the Fourth Realm wanted war, they would have to fight it against two realms.

He glanced at the bookcases that lined the walls beyond the columns, seeking the section where the history of the Fourth Realm was held. He would have to read the latest accounts. He wanted to be certain of the numbers each legion in the Fourth Realm contained so he could prepare his own legions, reinforcing them with more warriors as necessary.

"My king." A quiet voice intruded on his thoughts and he had to wrestle back the urge to growl at the male for entering his war room without knocking.

The male was young though, the newest recruit in his ever-growing horde of aides.

Tegan's advisers meant to weigh him down with so many of them that he couldn't move a step without one of them seeing it and reporting it to them.

"What is it?" He didn't take his eyes off the maps.

There were several settlements in the north-eastern region that might be in danger if the Fourth Realm did press into his lands and only one had a garrison of warriors.

The Royal Legion wouldn't be enough to shore up their defences in that region. He would have to dispatch more warriors. Perhaps another two legions would be enough.

"A visitor, my king." The male bowed his head and fidgeted with his black tunic.

"I have no time for this." Tegan waved him away.

The demon backed towards the double doors, his head still bent, and Tegan resumed his study of the maps.

"I will not leave until you have heard what I have to say." The voice was female and irritating, not the sweet feminine one he longed to hear.

He lifted his gaze from his charts, settling it on the intruder as she swept past his man, her short crimson dress and her scent telling him what he needed to know in an instant. She was a succubus.

"It regards Suki."

His entire body locked up as his heart lodged in his throat, his maps forgotten as he pushed away from the table and rounded the end of it to take a step towards her. "Is something wrong with her?"

Gods, the thought that it might be had him aching to teleport, a need to see her rushing through him that was so powerful he found it hard to remain where he was and await her response.

"No," the blonde-to-blue-haired female said, a regal edge to her voice that only enhanced the sharpness of it. "She is in good health. Due to you, I imagine."

The female looked around, curling a lip at the dusty tomes that filled the bookcases lining the black stone walls, accounts from his ancestors that covered thousands of years. Her brown-to-blue eyes fixed on the table to his left, or more specifically, the oil lamp that was being used to weigh down and help illuminate his charts. A look of disgust filled them.

This was how he had feared Suki would react to his world, but she had taken it in her stride, hadn't seemed at all fazed or horrified to find it was only as advanced as the human world had been hundreds of years ago.

"Suki seemed rather pleased with herself after you left." The cutting edge to her sharp tone told Tegan what he could already sense in her. Suki had been happy, but this female felt quite the opposite for some reason. "She regaled her sisters with tales of you and accepted their congratulations."

He frowned now. "Congratulations?"

"Yes." She nodded serenely, an edge to her smile that he didn't like, because from where he was standing, it looked as if he wasn't going to like what she was going to say, and she was going to enjoy that far too much. "I sent Suki to you because the poor girl was lacking confidence and wasn't contributing enough to the clan. She has been so desperate to prove herself worthy. I took pity on her. She wanted a challenge and I issued her one."

Her eyes narrowed with her cold smile.

"You."

Ice slithered down his spine. "Me?"

She nodded, so regal and calm she could be a queen. It hit him that this was the leader of Suki's clan.

"I failed to seduce you once. You rejected me and that stung." She practically hissed those words, her veil of calm failing for a heartbeat before her vicious smile returned. If she wanted him to be sorry that he hadn't fallen for her charms, he couldn't be. He didn't remember her at all. She glared at him and tipped her chin up. "So when Suki showed me how much she wanted to be a good clan member, accepted by her sisters and valued by the whole family, I pointed her in your direction. If she could seduce you, feeding the clan with your strength, she would finally believe in herself."

That ice invaded his blood, turning it to sludge in his veins as he reeled, struggling to take in what she was telling him. He didn't want to believe her, but Suki had told him herself that she loved her family and the way she had spoken at times had made him see that she desperately wanted to be accepted by them.

She had wanted it so badly that she had tricked him.

She had played him.

Rage surged, obliterating the ice as that feeling took hold and shook him.

"She used me?" He hated the sound of those words spoken in his voice, hated how his heart throbbed madly in his breast, pain spreading outwards from it with each beat, as if it pumped poison rather than blood through him now.

He couldn't believe her. He didn't know her. He knew Suki.

That line of reasoning faltered as his mind whispered that he did know Suki and that meant he knew how much she adored her sisters and family, and how devastated she was that they were cruel to her. She wanted them to accept her.

Had she really wanted it so badly that she had used him?

"I am surprised the young succubus succeeded so easily when you had been so resistant to my own charms."

He frowned at the black flagstones and muttered, "Suki never charmed me."

Her snide tone lashed at him. "Didn't she?"

He didn't want to be rattled but he couldn't stop his mind from running back over their time together, picking out all the moments where he had felt so close to losing control, when her beguiling eyes had been bright and enchanting, goading him into letting go.

No.

It wasn't her charms that had made him wild. It was the fact she was his mate.

His fated one.

"Suki has been struggling to fit in, poor dear. Now she has succeeded in seducing you, a demon king, she will be regarded as one of the strongest members of our family. I can feel the power of you flowing through my veins too, through the connection every member of the clan shares. Everyone will benefit from what Suki has done."

That rage he had tried to restrain broke its tethers again and he growled as the pain grew deeper, so intense that he could barely breathe as it assaulted him, ripping at his strength. He fought to deny the hurt, the thoughts that this female was speaking the truth and Suki had used him, but they cut him like a thousand blades and he couldn't stem the bleeding.

His ears rang as he struggled to figure out what was real and what had been a lie.

What they had shared was real.

Wasn't it?

The female moved closer and cooed, "That wounded look doesn't suit one born for war like you were. You're a warrior. A king. Are you going to let a female treat you with so little respect?"

No. He wasn't.

He launched at the succubus, grabbed her by her throat and hauled her off the ground by it, growling at her as pain pushed him deeper into his demonic nature, had his muscles straining against his skin and his bones aching to grow. He flashed enormous fangs at her and tossed her aside, breathing hard as he wrestled with himself.

But it was no use.

Because deep in his heart, he already knew the truth.

Suki had used him.

"Leave," he gritted and turned his back on the female, because he was damned if he was going to let her see how deeply this was hurting him.

She picked herself up and moved closer instead. "What Suki did was just in her nature. A succubus seduces. It's what we do. You mean nothing to her. You were a game to her."

He growled as that word struck him hard, sending his heart reeling this time.

"A *game*?" He turned on her as his rage got the better of him, his muscles expanding as his wings unfurled from his back, knocking against the table and columns, and his horns curled, twisting around on themselves.

She nodded.

"She set out to seduce you and feed from you to prove herself... to elevate herself. She knew you were a demon king and you were strong, and she knew I had failed at seducing you. It was the reason I chose you as her target." The female grazed fingers around her throat, over the marks he had placed on them when he had seized her, her expression cold and emotionless. "I gave her a chance to succeed where I had failed, and she took it, and you fell for it. Gods, for all I know, she might continue the charade until the crown is secured."

She laughed, the sound of it scraping out his chest, leaving him hollow as he snarled and staggered back a step, his legs weakening beneath him as his mind spun.

"What succubus wouldn't want to be a queen too?" She grinned at him, a vicious one that had him snarling and baring fangs at her because she was enjoying watching him suffer, driving a thousand more blades into his heart to rip it to shreds. "We do love money."

Money.

The way Suki's eyes had lit up when she had seen his collection of plastic flashed across his mind and drove another blade through him.

"It would go against clan law of course and we would have to exile her, but I wouldn't blame the girl if she wanted to make an attempt to seize hold of your kingdom."

Tegan sank against the table behind him.

He was a fool.

He recalled the other succubi who had been with her in Underworld when they had met. He remembered them talking, grouped together and glancing at him. Had they conspired to bring him to his knees all to help Suki prove herself?

Was that all he was to her?

Just a means of proving herself so her sisters would love her.

What about his love? Did that mean nothing to her?

He grabbed one of the wooden chairs beside him and roared as he hurled it across the room. It hit a bookcase and shattered under the force of the impact, and the female tensed, drawing his focus back to her.

He turned a glare on her and pushed away from the table as his body grew, limbs lengthening as the pain reached a new crescendo, obliterating everything but the rage that was now a living thing inside him, a writhing and vicious beast that demanded his absolute obedience.

He flexed his fingers, his claws like talons as he stalked towards the female.

She swallowed and backed away, fear flickering in her brown-to-blue eyes before she recovered and stood her ground.

She still reeked of fear.

"Leave," he snarled.

She bowed her head and edged backwards towards the open doors. When she reached them, she paused and he braced himself, waiting for her final blow, one he could see coming as her eyes lifted to lock on him, her smile cold and victorious.

"I must go. There will be a celebration for Suki."

Tegan roared at her and kicked off, hurtling towards her and filled with a black need to cleave her head from her shoulders as payment for twisting the knife she had already plunged into his heart.

She teleported before he could reach her and he slammed his fist into the door, sending it flying off its hinges and clattering along the broad hallway.

He breathed hard, fighting to calm himself even when he knew it was impossible. Nothing he could tell himself would change the way he felt, the rage that blazed inside him.

The succubus was a bitter old bitch, angry because Suki had succeeded where she had failed, and he was a fucking fool for thinking it was real.

When it had all been a game to Suki.

He roared again, grabbed the other door and ripped it from its hinges. He snapped the thick wooden panel in two and hurled it after the other door, his chest heaving as he watched one piece of it smash into the black wall on the left of the wide corridor and the other collide with it as it fell.

His senses sparked, warning someone was coming and they were coming at a pace.

Tegan teleported on a black snarl, because he didn't want anyone to see him like this and he definitely didn't want to see anyone. He landed in his bedroom in his private floors of the castle and seized the phone he had placed on the dark wooden bedside table.

He gripped it hard, the urge to destroy it blazing inside him, but all of it bled out of him as the screen came on to reveal the picture of him with Suki.

He stared down at it, dazed and hurt, unsure what to feel as he gazed at her beautiful face now.

He sank to his backside on the bed and opened the gallery, thumbed his way through all the pictures of her as he tried to convince himself that it had been real.

But he had seen the way the succubi had looked at him when he had wished Suki goodbye and promised to see her again.

He had seen the way those same succubi had smiled at her when he had stepped away, just before he had teleported.

Tegan leaned forwards, sickness brewing in his stomach for the first time ever, a feeling that felt as if it was going to destroy him as he clung to his phone and the fragile belief that it had been real.

She had called him fucking stupid once.

He stuck his head between his knees and half-growled half-groaned.

Had she meant that? Had the fact he hadn't been able to see through her ruse to the truth amused her?

Gods, he hurt so much.

He had never known pain like this. He had been wounded on the battlefield countless times, had been close to death several of those, feeling his life draining from him and sure he was going to die.

But it had never hurt like this.

Those wounds had never been as deep as the one on his heart.

That left him feeling as if he was broken in a way he would never heal.

He teleported on another pained and furious snarl, grabbed the nearest object as he landed in his study and hurled it across the room. Rage consumed him, a darkness that obliterated all awareness, all feeling but the black need to destroy. He unleashed it all on the room, smashing the furniture, tearing at the bookshelves, and battering the walls in a desperate attempt to vent his rage.

It gripped him harder instead and he was in the next room before he was aware of what he was doing, was ripping apart every book in his precious collection with his bare hands, until a mountain of paper lined the broken pieces of furniture that littered the floor and his hands were bleeding.

Until his sanctuary resembled the chaos whirling inside him.

He sank to his knees amidst the debris, threw his head back and roared as his heart broke.

Because the one who was meant to be his, never would be.

His life had changed when Edyn had died, and he had thought things couldn't get any worse for him, and then his life had changed again when he had met Suki, and for a brief, wonderful moment it had felt as if it couldn't get any better.

But this was worse.

So much worse.

Now, his life was over.

Because how was he meant to live without his heart?

CHAPTER 27

"There's a demon at the door for you, Suki."

Suki didn't even catch a glimpse of the succubus who poked her head into Suki's bedroom to deliver that message. She teleported immediately, heart racing, excitement rushing through her veins at the thought of seeing Tegan again.

Only it wasn't Tegan standing on the doorstep.

It was another demon.

His black horns and leathers, and onyx hair and eyes said the burly male was from the Second Realm.

"Is something wrong?" She stepped forwards, her heart stuttering to a halt in her chest as a thousand scenarios ran through her mind, reasons that ranged from terrifying things to completely possible and normal.

Like, maybe Tegan hadn't been able to get away from the castle today, but he wanted her back at his mansion and had arranged for this demon to take her there, where he would meet her.

Which was better than Tegan was in trouble, hurt or worse, and this demon had come to deliver a devastating blow to her.

The man just held his hand out to her, his eyes impassive, not giving anything away. She focused on him to reveal his aura. It was flat, muted shades of grey and other dark colours that gave her nothing to go on. He wasn't feeling anything as he waited for her to take his hand.

She slipped hers into it and squeezed her eyes shut as the world dropped from beneath her and she plummeted into the darkness.

When it receded, it wasn't the mansion looming before her.

It was an imposing black castle, like a Disney logo gone gothic mixed with a dash of Lord of the Rings. Sauron would be happy in such a dwelling.

The main bulk of the castle stood several storeys tall, but massive obsidian towers reached up from it, stopping at various heights, some of them capped with square or conical roofs, while others were flat. On the flat ones, golden light flickered and shadows moved around. Guards.

Beyond the castle, black mountains rose, cragged and sharp, perfecting the terrifying image of the building.

Her heart started at a pace again as the demon pushed her forwards. Her sneakers scuffed the black flagstones as she stumbled along, feeling dazed as she stared at the castle.

And a little frightened.

If she had known she was coming to such a place, she would have dressed. Her classic red Converse were worn and dirty, her blue jeans shorts rode a bit high for decent company, and she had tossed on a loose black T-shirt with a cute bunny on it and the words 'Go to Hell'.

She hadn't figured she would actually be going to Hell today and she wasn't sure the people milling around outside the castle would find it particularly amusing. Judging by the way they were all looking at her as she strode towards the massive arched entrance ahead of her, they didn't find anything about her amusing. They looked as if she disgusted them for some reason.

Probably because she was a succubus.

Two demons stationed on either side of the door, their hands resting in front of them on the pommel of the broadswords they held point down, glared at her as she passed.

She was tempted to flip them off, but a feeling suddenly hit her.

One that wasn't her own.

Pain.

Tegan was hurting.

The fragile bond that had been building between them over the last few days they had spent together, a cause of fascination she had enjoyed studying, relayed his pain to her, had her heart seizing again as she looked at the demon beside her.

"What's happened to Tegan?" It was strange saying his name for the first time.

She had avoided it, desperate to maintain some distance between them.

Now she couldn't bring herself to call him Solid Twelve.

Because she no longer wanted any distance between them.

The demon didn't answer. He marched her past the guards and dread built inside her as she walked down the imposing wide high corridor, heading towards a huge set of closed black wooden doors at the far end of it.

The closer she got to those doors, the stronger the pain beat inside her.

Had the demon brought her here because Tegan had been injured? Or perhaps he had been punished for something?

Her?

She hated the thought that he might have been punished because of their relationship. He hadn't talked much about whether demons were allowed to have a relationship with a woman who wasn't their fated one. They placed a lot of value on their fated one though, and her research on demons had turned up that they could only breed with that woman. With the fate of their species depending on breeding with their mates, it was possible that Tegan had gotten into trouble for wanting her.

Her research had also turned up some interesting facts about demon kings.

According to the history books at the clan, demon kings were notoriously brutal and vicious.

Extremely violent men.

The thought of Tegan at the mercy of such a man had her breath seizing in her lungs.

The doors opened, an ominous creak filling the stark silence as she swallowed her heart and braced herself for whatever awaited her on the other side.

A long black carpet lined the space between the towering carved obsidian columns that supported the vaulted roof of the enormous room. They led her eye to the far end of the grand hall and her step faltered when her gaze reached the raised dais.

Shock swept through her.

Her eyes widened.

Tegan wasn't on his knees before the throne as she had expected.

He was sitting on it.

The demon shoved her forwards and she stumbled, all the warmth that had hit her on seeing Tegan swiftly draining away as the distance closed between them and his cold gaze locked with hers.

His eyes were glacial as they held hers, dark irises bright with a violet-red corona that revealed his pupils, and his horns were enormous, twisted around on themselves and flared into deadly points on either side of his temples. He was enormous too, larger than she had ever seen him, his bare chest packed with muscle that tensed as he gripped the armrests of his black throne.

Her step faltered again as another emotion hit her.

She swallowed hard as flares of crimson shone through the black shadows of his aura.

Deep rage.

"What's wrong?" She tried to move towards him but this time the demon gripped her arm to hold her back.

Tegan's expression blackened, the dark slashes of his eyebrows knitted hard above his eyes as they brightened further, narrowing on her in a way that revealed he hadn't liked her choice of question.

Or the fact she had tried to move closer to him.

He slowly raised his right hand and the demon holding her pulled her back a few feet, positively dragged her, his grip on her fierce and unrelenting, so hard that it hurt.

She didn't understand.

"What's wrong?" She tried again, because she wanted answers. This whole thing was beginning to scare her for some reason.

Tegan's eyes remained cold as they drilled into her.

"I know what you really wanted from me." Each word was a rumbling growl and that pain she could feel in him grew stronger. He gave her a harsh smile as his pain burned deeper still. "I was wrong."

Tears lined her lashes, her throat constricting as she stared deep into his eyes and saw in them that she was about to lose him and she had never even realised she truly had him.

Or what that meant.

He hesitated, his brow furrowing, and she knew he could feel her pain too. She shook her head, silently pleading him not to do this. It had been wrong of her to target him, to view him as a means to an end, but it had all changed the moment she had spoken with him in Underworld.

He had to believe her. He had to let her explain.

She struggled to find her voice as her entire world started to fall apart around her, as she stared deep into his eyes and fought for the words she could say that would make him see he *was* wrong.

His face screwed up on a frustrated snarl, his voice a black growl as he bit out words that tore her world apart in an instant.

"You are banished from my kingdom."

Her heart lurched, pain ripping through her, and she launched towards him, teleporting out of the demon's grip to land closer to Tegan.

"You're wrong." She shook her head, her eyebrows furrowing as she looked up at him, begging him to listen to her. "Whatever you think you know, it's wrong."

He teleported, rising out of the darkness beneath her, his hand closing around her throat so swiftly that she didn't have a chance to block him or even think about attempting to flee. His grip tightened, his claws pressing in as he loomed over her, and her throat burned as fiercely as her eyes were as tears tumbled onto her cheeks.

He snarled and looked away from her, closed his eyes and gave another pained growl as he hurled her backwards, away from him.

She hit the flagstones and tumbled across them, pain exploding in her shoulder and hip.

As soon as she stopped, she pushed up and reached for him, refusing to let him do this and refusing to stop trying to make him listen to her. His brow furrowed, his pain hitting her in stronger waves that ripped at her heart.

"Please, T—" Darkness swallowed her before she could say his name and she slammed into the cobbles outside the succubus house.

She turned on the demon who had teleported her and grabbed his leg, looking up into his empty black eyes as he glared down at her.

"I don't know what I did wrong. Okay, maybe I do, but I'm not sure. Please, take me back to Tegan. I didn't know—"

The bastard teleported out of her grip before she could finish her sentence and she sank onto her backside, all hope flooding out of her as cold swept in.

"I didn't know he was a king," she whispered, tears burning her eyes.

Gods, it hurt.

She couldn't move, couldn't think clearly as pain consumed her, numbing her to the world as everyone stared at her. She didn't hear their muttered comments, didn't see their cold looks, didn't feel anything as she sat there on the cobbles, reeling and confused, feeling as if her whole life had suddenly come to an abrupt end.

She had never really risked it all, because risking it all had meant endangering what meant the most to her in her eyes—her clan.

But as she sat in the middle of the road outside the clan house, shell-shocked by what had happened, she couldn't help but think that Tegan had been worth the risk.

Only rather than filling her heart up by choosing her when she had definitely chosen him, he had smashed it to pieces instead.

And it was all her fault.

For the first time in her life, she might have had something wonderful, and she had destroyed it.

CHAPTER 28

Tegan paced in front of his throne, his heavy footfalls echoing around the expansive room. His heart thundered, each beat agony as his mind churned, his rage seizing on every dark thought that crossed it, keeping him permanently locked in his more demonic form.

The weight he had thought would lift upon dealing with Suki only pressed more heavily on his chest, until he felt as if he couldn't breathe. He growled and turned, stormed back the other way, fighting to get his fury under control and banish her from his mind.

Gods.

For the first time in his life, he had felt sure he had found someone who wanted him, not his throne.

Someone who had challenged him in so many ways, had stood up to him and made him work for her affection.

Someone he could be with forever.

But it had all been a vicious game to her.

Everything was a damned game to her.

She had called war a game. Love was apparently a game too.

That sickened him, cut him right down to his soul because while he was furious that he had been played, he couldn't convince himself to hate her as she deserved.

He loved her too damned much.

She was his mate after all.

She was meant to be his.

Or had that all been a lie too, a clever ploy to achieve the victory she sought?

Maybe she had lied about everything. Maybe the mistress of her clan had been right about her and Suki could use glamours and charm him, and had tricked him into reacting to her as if she was his fated one.

At first, he had felt sure it had been the effect of her charm.

Then, he had convinced himself that she was his mate.

Just as she had planned?

He breathed through the rage that rose in response to that, desperately clinging to control so he could retain his mind and resist the urge to go after her. It had been difficult to hold on to the ability to speak her tongue when he had seen her again, but somehow, he had managed it.

Most likely because pain had kept him locked in his larger, more demonic form since the night Suki's mistress had left him, and he was growing used to it now, was able to speak normally when his mind was calm enough.

Rage still took him at times though, had him destroying everything in sight and reduced him to nothing more than a beast, only able to utter a few words in the demon tongue.

The male he had sent to bring Suki to him returned, a grim look on his face that warned he wanted to speak.

Tegan didn't give him a chance.

"Bring me a powerful witch. The strongest you know." He had been fooled once and he wouldn't be fooled again.

The male didn't question him. He nodded and teleported again.

When he returned this time, a petite blonde dressed in a drab black long-sleeved dress was slapping at his chest, a thousand curses flying from her rosy lips.

"Fucking demon!" She battered his man, a fierce determined look flashing across her face. "I'm fairly bloody certain that witchnapping is illegal. Or it sodding well should be."

The fieriness of her temper and her British accent reminded Tegan painfully of Suki and he had to bite back another growl as fresh agony rolled through him.

The witch managed to get free of his man and turned on the male, silver stars flaring in her blue eyes as she planted her hands on her hips and her lips twisted in a cruel smile.

"My mate is going to eviscerate you."

She seemed to take great pleasure from that thought.

Tegan stared at her, finding only concern in what she had said. She had a mate? That wasn't good news at all. He wasn't sure who this female was, but he needed to calm the situation before this mate arrived for her or she decided to unleash the power he could feel building inside her.

"My apologies," Tegan said.

She whirled to face him, her hands flying up in front of her. Violet ribbons of light swirled around her fingers, sparking and crackling in places, illuminating her and the columns nearest her and competing with the light from the torches mounted on four sides of each column.

For such a small female, one who stood at least four and a half feet shorter than he was in his current state of close to ten feet tall, she had fight in her, a lot of strength and power that started to fill the room with a heavy sense of danger as she glared at him.

Enough power to cast the spell he needed?

"Who the fuck are you, and what bloody realm am I in?" She peered closely at him, a frown etched on her brow as she eased a step nearer, her long dress brushing the black flagstones to blend into them as she leaned forwards. "I've not seen your sort before... and have you been crying?"

"Leave," he barked at his man and the demon bowed his head and backed away.

When he was gone, the doors closing heavily behind him, and Tegan was alone with the witch, he bared his fangs and snarled at her for daring to belittle him.

The vicious sound echoed around the room.

She paled but was quick to rally, her chin jutting up as she flicked the soft waves of her golden hair over her shoulder and stared him down. "Do not dare lay a finger on me or my mate—"

He held his hand up to silence her. "I know. I know. Will apparently eviscerate me. I would like to see him try. Perhaps death would be better than living."

She smiled coldly, her blue eyes sparkling like the iciest abyss. "Vail would destroy you."

Tegan stilled right down to his breathing.

The urge to call his man back and eviscerate him shot through him.

Of all the witches to take.

He bowed his head. "My apologies again. Do not blame my man... although I am... but I asked for the strongest witch he knew."

She preened a little on hearing that, fluffing her pale hair. "Strongest witch, eh? Well, I can't say it will stop Vail from playing with your entrails, but I certainly forgive you. Now, you have business to discuss I presume?"

Odd little female. So quick to shift moods.

"I require a spell to stop someone from coming near me." One he was determined not to regret if she could cast it for him.

He needed to focus on his kingdom, and he couldn't do that when his mind was constantly on Suki, the urge to go to her beating inside him even now. She had said that he was wrong, but how could he be? She had used him. She had treated him like a game in order to score a victory with her clan, the ones who were truly important to her.

He needed this spell, not only to keep her away from him but to keep himself away from her too.

In time, he might heal and forget her.

A voice deep inside him laughed coldly at that, a mirthless chuckle that called him a fool. He would never forget her. He would never heal.

The witch frowned at him. "Like an old-world restraining order?"

He didn't know what one of those was. "I have a problem with a female and I need her kept away from me."

Her lack of respect was startling as she looked him up and down and said, "Is it for the woman who's responsible for those manly tears in your eyes?"

He scowled at her. "Do not try my patience."

She did just that by swirling her hand over a patch of the flagstones, sending green light spiralling down to touch them. When it connected, the black stone rose to form a throne that mirrored his, and she lounged in it.

"What will you do if I *try your patience*." Her voice deepened on the last three words, mimicking him in a mocking way that had his horns curling as he turned towards her. "Harm one hair on my awesome head and you're dead. Vail will hunt you to the ends of the Earth... or Hell."

He huffed, hating that all he could do was concede she was right. "True. Plus, Vail is brother to my ally, Prince Loren."

"Oh! Um... Second King!" Her eyes lit up like she had just won a prize at a fayre and wanted him to congratulate her. "I'm right, aren't I?"

He dipped his chin. "Correct."

"So, Second King wants a spell to keep a woman away. Cool. I can do that." She twisted on the seat, swinging her legs up so they rested over one arm of the throne while the other cushioned her back. "It'll have to be bound to your blood... so it's going to hurt like a motherfucker. Plus, I'll need some blood from her, or some hair."

"I have neither of those things." He wasn't even sure how anyone she cast such a spell for would happen to have some blood lying around.

He might be able to find some hair if he left with the witch and went to his mansion, but he wanted the spell done now.

This instant.

Before his rage subsided and the ache to see Suki and hear what she had wanted to tell him won him over.

She shrugged. "A name will probably do."

He growled, frustration getting the better of him as he paced towards her. "I cannot give you that either, witch. She is fae and closely guards her true name."

"The name is Rosalind. *Ros-a-lind.* I do get tired of people calling me Witch. Ask my husband what happens when you call me Witch too much."

He wasn't sure he wanted to know, but he could imagine it had been painful.

"He might have shed a few manly tears of his own." She grinned. "Our courtship was a blast."

His courtship had been a disaster.

Her lips pursed and she tapped a finger against her chin, her expression turning thoughtful as she stared at one of the torches mounted on the column she was facing. The flames flickered and distorted, turning blue in the heart of them before they settled again.

"You need to work with me here." Her eyes were brighter than ever when she looked at him, silver flakes spinning in her blue irises. "I need something to narrow down the target of the spell unless you want *every* female banished from your presence."

He paused as an idea came to him.

It was worth a shot.

If nothing else, it would prove whether or not she was what he believed her to be.

"Make the target of the spell my fated one."

That had her sitting up on her throne, coming to face him as shock rippled across her delicate features.

"A demon who wants to keep his fated one away from him?" She lifted both of her hands and a glowing square appeared in the air before her. She took hold of the square and flicked it over the top of another square, as if she was leafing through a book turned with its spine upright.

"What are you doing?"

She glanced at him. "Checking my calendar to see whether it's the apocalypse or something."

"Why?"

"Because no demon in his right mind would want to keep his mate away from him." She slowly shifted her gaze back to him and her eyes narrowed.

"Although, maybe you aren't in your right mind. I've seen the crazy look enough times to recognise it a mile off, and I've made tinctures for enough broken hearts to know yours has been shattered. Obliterated. Probably no longer exists in that oversized body of yours."

He snarled and pinned her with a black scowl. "Do you intend to make the spell or not?"

She waved her hand and the magical calendar disappeared.

"I'll make it, but only because I *really* want to see you regret it and my spidey-senses are tingling, telling me I'm going to be there when it happens." A slow mischievous grin curled her lips. "When you realise what a dick you've been, I'm going to make you naked wrestle my husband for the cure and I'm going to invite all my friends around to watch."

She had strange ways of speaking. They vexed him but he didn't let her see it.

"Make the spell." He stood his ground before her, even when her expression softened and she rose to her feet.

"Last chance." She held her hand out in front of her as she approached him, black and violet light chasing around her fingers. "You'll regret it if I do this."

He wouldn't stop now. He couldn't.

She was wrong about him.

He wouldn't regret this, because he wouldn't allow himself to feel that emotion, even when he knew that he was going to be miserable when his rage wore off and he was seeing things more clearly. It was better this way. Safer.

Being unable to see Suki was a torment he could endure.

Because seeing her again would be unbearable.

Just the thought of her with another male was enough to have his rage storming to a new level, rising again just as it had been starting to abate. If he foolishly went to see her as his aching heart wanted, if he witnessed her with another male, nothing would stop him from turning the black rage he would feel on the fae town where she lived.

Nothing would stop him from going to war.

And the entire world would be his enemy.

For the first time in his long life, he didn't want a war.

He wanted the peace Edyn had given his life for. He wanted to uphold the truce and he wouldn't be able to do that if he could see Suki. His strength would crumble, his resolve sure to waver without a spell to keep him from her and her from him.

War would be inevitable.

So he had to do this, to keep his people safe, to be the king they deserved, and to keep his word.

He stared the witch down and growled.

"Make the spell."

CHAPTER 29

Suki stumbled into the clan house, making it as far as the foyer before she collapsed to her knees again. Several of her sisters came to her as she sat there, ears ringing, mind swirling, struggling to grasp what had just happened.

Everything in her life had been looking up, filling her heart with light and hope, and now all she knew was darkness and pain.

She had to find a way to see Tegan again so she could explain. She had to make him see that he was wrong about her. It might have started out as a seduction, a way of gaining respect and acceptance from her clan, but by the time she had finally slept with Tegan, it had been something else.

It had been love.

"You're bad for business sitting there," one of her sister's grumbled and took her arm, trying to pull her off the floor.

Another sister helped her, muttering, "She'll drive the men away and I'm hungry."

Allura shoved them aside, breaking their hold on her. "Back off. Something's wrong with her, can't you see that?"

She had never heard Allura speak that way, with so much care in her voice. She wanted to cry when the black-haired succubus crouched before her and brushed her hair from her face, sweeping it back behind her ears as she looked at her with warmth flooding her violet-to-blue eyes.

"What's wrong?"

Suki wasn't sure she could find her voice to tell her what had happened. She fought for the words as other succubi surrounded her, driving back the ones who wanted to evict her from the foyer.

"Tegan," she muttered, fresh pain rolling through her as she recalled how cold he had appeared sitting upon that black throne, looking at her with eyes that had held no trace of softness, no warmth.

There had been only anger and pain, fury directed at her.

"The one who dropped you off the other day? Your trophy male?" Vidia eased to her knees beside her, her standard blue plaid skirt filling the edge of Suki's vision.

Sickness brewed inside Suki on hearing her sister speak of Tegan in such a crass way and guilt followed it, eating away at her because originally, that was what he had meant to be to her.

A trophy.

She had wanted him as her prize. There was no denying that.

And gods, she hated herself for it.

Vidia patted her knee. "Cyrena went to see him after he dropped you off. She looked pleased when she returned."

Another sickening wave broke over Suki, this one born of the horror that filled her as she listened to Vidia. It couldn't be coincidence.

"You're sure of that?" Suki lifted her head and searched Vidia's aqua-to-navy eyes.

Her friend nodded. "She told me she had gone to Hell to see for sure whether you had successfully managed to seduce the Second King. She's planning a celebration for you."

Was she the only one who hadn't known what Tegan was? Vidia didn't look surprised that he was the Second King. She looked at Allura, who didn't look shocked to hear that either.

A celebration? Checking she had seduced Tegan? Suki hadn't been born yesterday. Cyrena's reasons for going to Hell hadn't been so magnanimous.

Cyrena had gone there to destroy everything between Suki and Tegan.

Suki hissed and pushed to her feet, strength flowing through her as anger turned the blood in her veins to molten fire. Her short claws and fangs grew as her pointed ears flared. She felt her eyes brighten, the colours of the world growing more vivid and the auras of everyone around her appearing as her temper snapped.

She shoved past her friends and the other succubi, and stormed across the foyer, heading for a corridor that led to the eastern wing of the building. Rage built inside her as she picked up pace, the hallways passing in a blur as she focused on her destination. She rounded the corner at the T-junction, banking left and not hearing the noises coming from the rooms on either side of her as her gaze locked on the closed door at the end of the corridor.

Cyrena's office.

Suki didn't bother to knock. As soon as she reached the cream wooden door, she shoved it open and strode into the office, making a beeline for Cyrena as she shot to her feet on the other side of the wide dark oak desk in the middle of the red room.

"What is the meaning of this intrusion, Suki?" Cyrena swept her blonde-to-blue waves over her shoulder with a flick of her wrist, her brown-to-navy eyes flashing at her as she swiftly gathered herself.

Suki reached the desk and slammed her palms down onto it. "I think you bloody well know what this is about. Don't act dumb. Vidia told me you went to see Tegan and I don't believe for a second it was for the purpose you told her it was."

The fire blazing in her veins burned hotter as she stared Cyrena down, waiting for the bitch to admit she had intentionally messed everything up for her out of jealousy and anger.

Cyrena's red lips curved into a vicious smile. "You reap what you sow, Suki. You thought to undermine me by seducing the demon I had failed to win over. I only did what any respectable succubus would have in my position."

She had lashed out in a way that had saved face for her, making her appear like a caring and wonderful mistress to the clan, a woman who only wanted to check Suki truly had fed from the demon so she could officially congratulate her with a celebration.

"You conniving bitch," Suki spat and leaned towards her, breathing hard as rage began to get the better of her. She pressed her short claws into the wooden top of the desk, fighting for restraint as the urge to leap over the damned thing and attack Cyrena built inside her, stoked by a thought that left her cold and on fire at the same time. "Did you get what you wanted? Did he fuck you this time?"

Cyrena's expression soured and she jerked her chin up, doing her best to look as if Suki's rage and what had happened with Tegan didn't bother her, but Suki could see she was affected by both. She was afraid of Suki and she was furious with Tegan.

"He became enraged and I left." Cyrena looked down at her and her cruel smile returned, a flash of victory crossing her eyes, and Suki braced herself for the incoming salvo. "After I had told him about your game."

Her heart sank as that hit her like an atom bomb, obliterating the tiny seed of hope that had started to grow inside her again. Now she understood why he had been so cold towards her.

So angry.

So hurt.

He thought she had betrayed him. He thought she had been using him the entire time. It had started out that way.

But now?

She hurt so bad she wasn't sure she could recover from it. Her chest was raw, scraped out and hollow, and she couldn't bear it as sorrow pressed down on her, her anger giving way under the weight of it.

Cyrena stilled.

Stared at her.

Whispered.

"You're in love with him."

Suki scrubbed a hand over her eyes.

"No, I'm not. I'm done with this conversation. I don't want a celebration." She hiccuped on a hollow laugh. "Funny… I wanted to be part of this family… I wanted to be included… and now I just want to be left alone."

Cyrena rounded the desk, her long crimson dress flowing around her ankles with each step.

Her tone softened, all the cruelty and hardness leaving her expression and eyes as she stopped near Suki.

"You know he's in love with you too, that's all this feeling inside you is. You don't really love him, Suki. You love the idea that he's in love with you."

Suki rubbed the heel of her right hand against her eye, trying to stop the tears from coming as she thought about Tegan and what she had done, and how Cyrena had ruined everything.

"Stop trying to be nice to me," she bit out and pushed her hurt down, seized hold of the tattered shreds of her anger and turned a glare on the blonde. "Stop feeding me bullshit. What do you think is going to happen? I'm going to forgive you for what you did? Lying to me isn't going to make me feel better. I don't know if he's in love with me."

Cyrena threw her a confused look. "What do you mean? It was painted all over his aura."

Shock swept through Suki, sending a chill tumbling down her spine and arms. "How? His aura is shadowed."

The blonde stiffened. "Shadowed?"

Suki nodded. "Wasn't that the reason you failed to seduce him?"

"No," Cyrena spat, a flare of gold in her eyes that warned Suki she didn't like being reminded of her failure. "I can see his aura. The reason I failed was because he thought I was only interested in his throne."

It hit Suki that he thought the same about her now. He thought she only wanted to be queen.

But she hadn't known he was a king.

She had fallen in love with him, not the thought of being a queen.

Cyrena edged closer, her voice low and cautious and brown-to-blue eyes holding a flicker of curiosity. "You really see shadows when you look at him?"

She nodded again.

The blonde hesitated and then shook her head. "It doesn't matter now."

Suki didn't like the way she said that, as if it was all over and there was no hope of getting Tegan back. She wanted to give up, but she couldn't.

She wouldn't.

If Cyrena was right and Tegan was in love with her, then she needed to find a way back to him. She needed to make him listen to her and make him see that she hadn't betrayed him. She needed to set things right.

Standing here arguing with Cyrena wasn't going to achieve that, and neither would moping and nursing her broken heart.

She pivoted and stormed from the room, not listening to Cyrena as she called after her and not stopping when Allura and Vidia caught her in the foyer, demanding to know where she was going.

She was going to war.

And she wasn't going to stop fighting until Tegan was hers again.

When she hit the steps, she teleported, appearing deep in the witches' district in a narrow alley in front of one of the small two storey white houses. The violet door had seen better days, the paint flaking around the ornate gold knocker. She grabbed it and rapped it against the wood.

Tense minutes passed as she strained to hear whether someone was home.

"Please be home." She shifted foot to foot, unable to keep still as she waited.

Finally, the door opened, revealing a brunette witch. Suki arched an eyebrow at Julianna as she hastily tugged her long black dress down and then retied her shoulder-length hair into a high ponytail.

As if that would cover up what she had been doing.

"I can smell sex on you and you're throwing off energy like a power plant." Suki shrugged when Julianna glared at her, chocolate brown eyes narrowing with it as her lips compressed into a mulish line.

"I didn't know it was you." The witch huffed and gave up trying to fix her appearance. Instead, she leaned back slightly and hollered over her right shoulder. "You might as well leave. I have a feeling this might take a while."

A handsome blond male leaned over on the stairs, his head appearing at ceiling level. "You sure. I can hang out."

"She won't be able to concentrate while you're skulking up there." Julianna jerked her chin towards Suki. "You want her feeding on your unsatisfied lust?"

He looked disappointed and tasted it too as Suki caught a faint whiff of his scent and his energy flowed towards her. Whatever these two had been up to, they had been right in the middle of things when Suki had knocked. She shivered as he emerged, descending the stairs to stop on the bottom step.

Julianna crossed the room to him, placed her hands against his shoulders and tiptoed, her lips claiming his in a brief, passionate kiss. He groaned, that sexual energy rising, sending another wave of it rolling over Suki.

Delicious.

But not why she was here.

She battled the haze, dragging her focus back to why she had come to see Julianna. "It's urgent, Julianna. I'm never one to interrupt anyone's fun time, but I really do need to speak with you. Alone."

Because the witch was right and she was never going to be able to focus while the man was hanging around, waiting to resume things with her friend.

"Go on." Julianna patted him on his ass. "Grab me some of those caramel shortbreads from the café and I'll call in when I'm done."

The man dutifully nodded, slid Suki a disgruntled look that left her in no doubt of how much she had annoyed him by interrupting them, and pushed past her.

"What's this about?" Julianna waited for her to step into the room before closing the front door.

The living room was a mess as always, books stacked everywhere, all of them with pieces of paper sticking out of them at haphazard angles. The handwriting on the notes was masculine, and Suki had spent years trying to get Julianna to tell her who the books belonged too, because apparently they didn't belong to her.

They certainly didn't belong to the panther shifter who had just walked out of the door.

Julianna was covering for someone.

She let her curiosity go as she cleared a stack of books from the worn crimson couch and slumped onto it, coming to face Julianna as she neatly settled herself in the plum armchair opposite her.

"I need a talisman. One that can open the portal pathways to me." Because in this instance, being a fae sucked. She was one of a few species who couldn't teleport into Hell without assistance.

Most succubi convinced demons to escort them, charming them into doing their bidding. Suki didn't think asking a demon to teleport her to the castle of the Second Realm would go down well with either the demon or Tegan.

Julianna rose to her feet, crossed the room to a wooden crate on the cluttered sideboard near the TV and started rifling through it. "Do I need to ask why you want a return ticket to Hell?"

Suki shook her head and then sighed. "I pissed off a demon and I need to make things up to him. I need to make him see he was wrong about me."

"He fled to Hell?" Julianna glanced over her shoulder at her, a cute toy bat in her right hand.

"Not really. He was already in Hell. I screwed up and he had me brought to him so he could banish me."

Julianna tossed the bat into the box, twisted to face her and frowned. "You sure you want to confront him then? Demons love a good grudge and a good fight. What if he tries to hurt you?"

"He already hurt me... and I hurt him." She shook her head. "And he wouldn't physically strike me. I know he wouldn't."

She rubbed her throat. Although, he had held her tightly, his grip strong enough that she hadn't been able to breathe in the moment between him seizing her and tossing her away from him like garbage.

She shook off the hurt and the doubts, and focused on her mission.

Winning Tegan back.

Julianna pulled a tangled web of black string from the box and held it aloft, glaring at the various wooden, stone and crystal talismans hanging from the thongs. Her face twisted in frustrated lines as she untangled two of the stone talismans, small black pieces of rock that looked as if someone had chipped them off an old lava flow.

The brunette witch brought one to her lips and muttered words against it, her eyes brightening with each syllable she uttered. Flakes of gold swirled around the rock when she was done and she set the uncharged talisman down near the TV, crossed the room to Suki and placed the charged talisman over her head.

It felt warm as it settled against Suki's chest.

She took hold of the talisman in her hands, clutching it over her heart, closed her eyes and focused on her destination, but stopped when Julianna grabbed both of her wrists.

"Swear to me that if he looks as if he's going to murder you, you'll leave."

Suki looked up at her friend and nodded.

The moment Julianna released her, she teleported.

There was a brief moment of darkness, the rush of cold wind over her bare skin, and then she landed.

She opened her eyes.

Julianna arched an eyebrow at her. "That was quick."

Suki frowned at the room and then her friend. "I'm sure I did it right. I pictured the castle. I envisaged the point where I had landed before with the demon Tegan sent for me. I should be able to teleport there."

Julianna took hold of her upper arms and looked her over, gold sparks lighting her eyes as she checked her from head to toe and back again. A frown slowly knitted her eyebrows.

"What is it?" Suki searched Julianna's eyes when they finally settled on hers.

"I'm picking up a faint trace of a spell. You haven't been dabbling in magic, have you?" Julianna frowned when Suki shook her head. Her friend closed her eyes and stood tall, breathed slowly and steadily as she held Suki's arms, and Suki struggled to remain quiet, silencing the thousand questions suddenly burning on the tip of her tongue. When Julianna opened her eyes, they were grave. "When he banished you, he *really* banished you. There has to be a spell on him, or something is blocking you."

Suki tried again.

And met with the same result.

It was as if she was being bounced back by some sort of barrier. A spell just as Julianna had said?

Tegan hated her that much now?

Suki sank onto the couch, losing a battle against the sudden surge of despair that ran through her.

Julianna picked up the other talisman and charged it up before holding it out to her. "It's good for another two attempts if you want to make yourself more miserable."

Suki snatched the lump of black rock and glared at her friend. "What do you suggest I do? Just give up?"

The witch's warm chocolate eyes widened.

"Oh, mother earth, you're in love with him." Julianna didn't even flinch when Suki hit her with her best scowl, stood and stomped towards the door because she didn't need another person looking at her as if she had gone mad, or soft, to have fallen for Tegan. Just as she reached the door, her friend said, "So don't give up... get even."

Suki paused with her hand on the knob and looked back at her. "Get even?"

Julianna nodded and swept around the couch, closing the distance between them as she smiled wickedly. "He hurt you, so think of a way to hurt him back."

Suki looked down at the talisman she clutched in her right hand.

It was tempting.

But she had already hurt him.

She didn't want to cause him more pain.

But she wouldn't give up.

She would find another way.

She would win this war.

CHAPTER 30

Rosalind had been right about the spell. It had hurt when she had cast it upon him after performing some sort of elaborate ritual involving his blood. It had more than hurt. Pain so intense it had blinded him had wracked him, left him cold and shivering on the floor of his drawing room, sweating profusely as his blood had boiled and every instinct had fired. The most primal of them had damned him, feeling as if they were going to tear his body apart and fracture his mind as thoughts of Suki had flooded him.

He had somehow mustered enough strength to tell the witch to go to the door and seize the demon who guarded it. Upon seeing the state of him, the demon had attempted to attack her, and Tegan had been forced to find the strength to speak again, demanding he leave her and take her to the male who had brought her to him so she could be returned home.

Rosalind had left, but not before she had reiterated her vow that he would have to fight her husband for the cure in a dark and grave tone.

After which, she had added a rather cheery goodbye and good luck.

Tegan had waited for the door to close before dragging himself up the stairs to his bedroom.

He had reached the foot of the bed before succumbing to the pain and passing out.

When he had awoken, he had been moved to his bed, and three of the males who served as medics in the Royal Legion were watching over him.

Together with a rather angry looking Ryker.

The fever had still gripped Tegan, but he had assured them all it wasn't poison or an attempt to murder him, and that he would recover once the spell had settled. The medics had looked slightly less distressed.

Ryker had looked as if he was considering killing Tegan himself.

Tegan had sent both the medics and his brother away, and had rested on his bed for the entire day, drenched in sweat and restless as his body alternated between burning and freezing, and delirium threatened to take his mind from him, tormenting him with memories of Suki that had stirred his instincts into a frenzy.

She wasn't his mate.

The quicker his mind and his body got that message, the better.

After succumbing again to the fever, he had awoken this morning feeling brighter. Definitely stronger. He had been able to walk to his bathing room and wash, had managed to dress with only a few stumbles and one moment where he had fallen on his naked backside and drawn the attention of his guards. They had been sent away with a vicious roar, because he was damned if his men would see him weak and sick.

He had eaten the food the medics had brought to him, and digested the news that Ryker had returned to the border near the Fourth Realm to continue protecting the villages there from a potential attack. Apparently, his brother had left a message.

Tegan had read the note.

It had been one word.

Dumbass.

He wasn't sure what that meant, but if the look Ryker had given him before leaving his rooms was anything to go by, it was not a compliment. His brother was angry with him still, and he couldn't blame him. He hadn't thought about how he might appear to others and he hadn't even considered telling Ryker what he had intended to do.

"Are you sure you are well?" Eryt eyed him closely, concern flickering in his dark eyes as he twisted his hands in front of his black tunic.

Tegan dragged his wandering focus back to the four males assembled before him and managed a nod. "I think I simply need some air. The castle seems stuffy today."

When Balkan tossed him a sceptical look, he stared the male down.

"I will not leave the castle grounds. You have my word on that." Tegan pushed his chair back and stood slowly, not quite trusting his legs.

They felt stronger, but sometimes pain suddenly ripped through him. When that had last happened, he had collapsed to his knees in the hallway outside this room.

And Raelin had witnessed it.

The bastard had summoned Tegan's other advisers and he had been here ever since, listening to them chastising him as if he was a child but too tired to fight them today.

"You must go to the grand hall. Your presence there has been greatly missed recently." Raelin offered a gentle smile that lacked the warmth he presumed the male thought it had.

Tegan could see straight through it to the pleasure he was taking from seeing him weakened and worn down, so tired and miserable that he lacked the strength to fight back against anything the male said.

Including when the male had suggested scaling back the number of test areas for windfarms.

Tegan shrugged, because he was stronger today than the last time they had spoken, although he was just as miserable. "I will go there when I am done getting some air."

All four males stood and bowed their heads as he walked around the table, heading for the door. He didn't notice the corridors as he moved along them, paid no attention to the men he passed. His thoughts turned inwards again, towards his shattered heart, and he fought to keep them away from Suki and failed.

Why had she done this to him?

He pulled the phone from the pocket of his leather trousers, woke the screen and found the pictures of her that had become his personal Hell over the last few days. How many times had he stared at all of them trying to discern why she had betrayed him? He never found the answer to that question. He still didn't understand any of what had happened.

He had loved her.

He *loved* her.

Cool air greeted him as he stepped out into the courtyard of the castle, but he didn't take his eyes off the phone as darkness, oily and thick, swirled inside him, filling the cavity in his chest. It wasn't the first time he had felt consumed by it, driven to unleash the fury he had locked inside him, the despair and desperation, all the damned misery in the hope he could purge it all.

It was growing like a living, writhing beast inside him now, demanding he sate it, and every time he denied it and fought it back, it came back stronger.

Now, as he stared at her image on his phone, he felt as if he was spiralling out of control, deep into the dark abyss, and soon there would be no coming back.

The black urges that filled him, fuelled by his misery and fed by his pain, tempted him to surrender to them, to step into the darkness to leave the light behind. Several times he had been close to teleporting to the borders with the Fourth Realm, a terrible need to provoke that kingdom into fighting him boiling inside him. He ached for a fight, for the pain in his heart to become something physical, a battle that would wear him out and give him a way of venting all the darkness churning inside him.

His fingers closed around the phone as he ambled around the bleak courtyard of the castle, his eyes narrowing on the picture of Suki and him together, one he had cherished once.

Now it tormented him.

Or perhaps he tormented himself with it.

His grip on the device tightened, the urge to destroy it rising inside him for what felt like the millionth time, but just like all the times before, he eased the pressure of his grip before it could damage the phone. He couldn't bring himself to part with it.

Just as he couldn't bring himself to part with her.

The spell hadn't changed a damn thing. Her betrayal hadn't changed anything either.

He still loved her.

A sense of power surged around him, ringing alarm bells in his mind as his muscles tensed and he instinctively braced his feet apart, preparing for a fight.

Because it wasn't a demon who had just arrived through the portal in the middle of the courtyard.

Guards rushed from their posts, the sound of their heavy boots striking the black flagstones filling the air as Tegan turned to face the intruders, sure it would be Prince Vail come to eviscerate him because the scent of the two males was distinctly elf.

Demons crowded the circular stone where the portal exited, blocking his view of the intruders.

"Back off." A deep voice snarled, gruff and demanding. "As much as I would love to fight you scrawny runts, I'm here on the orders of Commander Bleu of the elf legions."

"Way to go, Dacian. You trying to start another war when we're meant to be recruiting for one already?" The lighter male voice carried an amused but exasperated note.

Dacian.

That name was familiar.

Tegan had met an elf called Dacian a long time ago, centuries back when the male had been hunting for a dragon and had sought permission to cross the Second Realm.

"Leave them," Tegan barked and every one of his warriors stiffened, looked across at him as if they had only just noticed he was there, and swiftly backed away to reveal the two elves.

The larger of the two, a shaven-headed male who rivalled the height of many of his warriors and was just as broadly built, packed with muscle beneath his skin-tight black armour, pressed his right hand to his chest and bowed his head as he closed his violet eyes.

"Second King," he gruffly muttered, and when his companion didn't salute him in a similar manner, he slid him a glare and cuffed him around the back of his head, sending the shorter male lurching forward, the threads of his long ponytail flying up from the force of the blow.

The younger male rallied, pressed his hand to his chest and nodded. "Second King."

Tegan recognised him too.

"What business have you with me? I heard war mentioned." And he had locked on to that word like a fiend possessed, the darkness inside him roused by the thought of a battle, hungry to split flesh and break bone, and feel the pain of his enemies' blows on his own body.

The warrior in him stirred too. The treaty between the realms allowed him to go to war if called upon by one of the others.

He tried to conceal how much he wanted them to tell him they had come to ask him to fight, but his horns flared a little despite his efforts.

Neither elf mentioned it, although both noticed as they stood before him, their steady violet gazes locked on him.

Dacian ran a hand over his shorn hair and down the line of the scar that cut across his scalp and Tegan frowned at the fresh cuts on his face and neck. He looked the male over, taking in the black scales that covered every inch of him. How many other wounds did the male bear? Had he been fighting recently?

His dark eyes flicked to the male beside Dacian, one who also had a long gash across his cheek and one on his forehead, and a bruise forming on his neck. It darkened as Tegan looked at it, revealing that it was fresh, still in the process of blooming.

"You received those injuries in this war you spoke of?" He took a step towards them, compelled to take a closer look, the sight of them giving his hunger for war a stronger hold over him.

The younger male stroked the knives strapped to his ribs beneath his arms, nerves flickering in his violet eyes. "Not quite. We were sparring."

Tegan grinned. "And enjoying it by the looks of things."

He loved to spar too, but his men took it easy on him, and if any of them cut him, they apologised profusely, to the point where it irritated him, and then they ended the session, which annoyed him even more.

It had been too long since he had been in a good fight.

His mind tossed the fight against the incubi at him and he growled and shoved it out again, his heart aching at the memory as it brought everything that had happened afterwards rushing back.

He wasn't sure he would ever be able to set foot in his private mansion again.

"Commander Bleu sent us. I'm Fynn and this is Dacian. We've been asked to relay a message to you." The younger elf, Fynn, fiddled with the knives again. "You probably don't remember us."

"I do. You sought a dragon several centuries ago." He nodded towards the castle. "Come, let us speak in comfort."

"We don't really have the time." Dacian's hard tone had Tegan easing back on his heels, a frown tugging at his eyebrows as he looked at the male. "It concerns the dragon again."

Tegan arched an eyebrow. "The dragon? You never caught it?"

Fynn shook his head. "You know he stole a sword from Prince Loren?"

Tegan nodded. "An heirloom that was precious if I recall… and powerful."

Dacian's grim expression only darkened. "This dragon, Tenak, still has that sword and now he's heading towards the elf kingdom. It's possible he will pass through your lands from the dragon realm. Word is, he's amassing an army along the way."

An army led by a dragon in possession of a powerful sword?

That sounded like a good war to Tegan.

"We are to request you consider evacuating any villages that might be in the path of his army," Fynn said.

Tegan hiked his shoulders. "Or I could fight him if he dared enter my lands."

But knowing Tegan's luck, the damned dragon would avoid his lands entirely, stealing a beautiful bloody war from his grasp.

"You could." Dacian squared his shoulders, his muscles tensing beneath the black scales of his tight armour. "But we were sent to tell you that the dragon's sister is with us in the elf kingdom and she has seen a vision of the Second Realm, First Realm and Third Realm fighting on the side of the elves in our kingdom… in a great battle against her brother."

A great battle.

Gods, Tegan liked the sound of that.

The last report from his brother at the border had stated that the Fourth Realm were showing no sign of attempting it, and that several of that realm's legions had withdrawn in the past day. Because of this new threat? Were the Fourth Realm preparing to battle the dragon?

If the two elves were to be believed, and he did believe them because dragon visions were rarely wrong, then the dragon would make it to the elf kingdom and the war would take place there.

Attempting to battle the dragon and his army in the Second Realm wouldn't stop that from happening.

Tegan inclined his head. "Relay to Prince Loren that the Second Realm will answer his call. I will gather my finest warriors and we will travel to the elf kingdom as soon as we are able."

"Thank you." Dacian pressed his right hand to his broad chest and bowed his head again.

Fynn followed suit. "Thanks."

Light traced over the elves and they disappeared, leaving only a faint outline of them in the air where they had been.

Tegan stared at it as it dissipated.

War.

It was everything he wanted come to him at last.

His thoughts turned to the slight, fae female who had stolen his heart and the darkness in him wavered as he realised that war wasn't the thing he wanted now.

It was her.

She was everything he wanted. All that he needed.

If he had Suki by his side, he could gladly live another thousand years ruling a peaceful realm.

But she was gone.

War was all he had now and he craved it more than ever. The need to do battle raged back to the fore to destroy the vision of a peaceful existence with her at his side. A fantasy.

He had been born for war.

Not peace.

It was time he remembered that.

CHAPTER 31

Tegan stared off at the horizon, his horns curling and fangs sharpening as awareness pounded in his veins, hunger drumming in his heart, and the darkness he had been fighting since Suki had betrayed him roared back to life inside him, stronger than ever.

Soon he would be on a battlefield again, cleaving bone and flesh as he unleashed the rage and pain that blazed inside him, and it would be glorious.

He might even find his end there.

The grim thought filled his mind before he could stop it and he didn't deny it, let it swim around his head, because he had never been one to shy away from death. He had danced with it more than once on the battlefield, outwitting it and somehow surviving.

If it claimed him this time, so be it.

Death would be a relief from the pain, an end to his suffering, and dying on the battlefield was a noble, honourable way to go.

He looked at his kingdom, at his castle, his mind turning to Ryker. Guilt flooded him, churning his stomach, but it was no match for the darkness and rage that lived within him, goading him into surrendering to it.

He needed an outlet for it, for the self-destructive and destructive urges that refused to loosen their hold on him, rousing a recklessness that he knew was dangerous, but he couldn't bring himself to care.

Nothing mattered now.

Suki was gone.

What they had shared had been a lie, even though his feelings had been true.

She had carved his heart out and crushed it before him.

So he would do the only thing he could to purge the pain, to satisfy his deep need to tear down everything and make everyone suffer as he was.

He would go to war, hurling himself into the fray and praying to his ancestors that he would find the relief he needed there.

He strode across the courtyard, through the archway in the black wall that enclosed it, and along the wide path between the three storey square buildings that acted as a garrison for each legion whenever they were at the castle.

At the end of the road, a four-storey building stood, guards patrolling the roof, appearing and disappearing in the gaps between the high broad merlons of the battlement. Golden light glowed from several of the narrow windows on each floor, and torches burned on either side of the arched entrance in the centre of the building.

Several warriors milled around outside. All of them hastily saluted him as they noticed him.

"Send word to the legion commanders to assemble." Tegan waited for each male to nod and disappear before he started to pace, his boots loud on the flagstones as he wore a trench in them.

After a few minutes had passed and no one had appeared, he growled and shoved his fingers through his hair, impatience getting the better of him.

Finally, two commanders arrived. A third followed, and then a fourth and a fifth. The commanders of every legion other than the first, his Royal Legion, were present and the itch to go to war would no longer be denied, even when he knew he should wait for Ryker.

"The Royal Legion and the Second and Third legions are to prepare for war. The elves have requested our presence in their kingdom. We are to fight a dragon and his army. I will know more about what to expect when I have spoken with Prince Loren." He looked at the two commanders to his right, both seasoned warriors he could trust. "The Fourth will pull back to protect the castle while I am gone."

Everyone tensed and he glared at them all, daring them to say something about the fact he was going to be leading their warriors in this war.

He looked to the remaining male to his right. "The Fifth will split their forces and protect the borders in the stead of the other legions, using the trainees to bolster their numbers."

Ryker arrived.

He felt his brother's gaze as a searing streak of heat across the back of his head.

"What the hell is going on here?" his brother barked, not even a shred of respect in his hard tone as he moved around him, coming to stand between him and the assembled commanders.

Tegan kept his cool. Barely. It wasn't wise of his brother to challenge him, not in his current mood.

"You will remain at the castle while I lead the legions."

Ryker just glared at him and Tegan waited, watching as his brother's black eyes gained a violet-red corona and his senses warned Ryker was about to lose his temper.

Before his brother could speak, Raelin and the rest of his advisers appeared.

"My king, word has reached us that you are speaking of taking the legions into the elf kingdom to fight a war there. We must advise against this course of action."

Rather than calming Tegan, Raelin's words and snide aloof tone made him want to punch the male.

"I take your advice onboard." Tegan turned to tower over him, Sylas, Eryt and Balkan. "And I am still leading my warriors. Ryker will remain here, as my next in line."

"I should go," Ryker put in.

Tegan growled at him, flashing fangs. "No. You will remain at the castle."

Ryker squared up to him, fire burning in his eyes. "I should go in your stead. Brother… listen to reason."

The soft look that entered Ryker's eyes tore another growl from Tegan's lips, because his brother was suggesting he wasn't strong enough to fight, that he was still weakened by what had happened to him, and he was sick of everyone questioning him at every damned turn.

"You *will* remain here and that is an order, Ryker. I will not let you answer this call. This one is *mine* to answer." Tegan glared down at him, his horns curling, flaring dangerously as his mood darkened. Anger that was part of him now surged to the fore, rage so black it clouded his thoughts and had him wanting to strike his brother for questioning him, even when he knew in his heart that Ryker was only worried about him. "I must do this. Know, brother, that it is not because I want war. I owe Loren and Melia, and I intend to repay that debt."

Ryker's expression shifted, morphing from anger, to resignation, to a clear need to say something.

Tegan stared down into his brother's eyes, willing him to see that he needed to do this. He needed to fight. He had to release the rage somehow.

"A word with my king." Ryker seized his arm and pulled him away, into the Royal Legion's building and through to the back, where he pushed Tegan into a room.

His brother's office.

Ryker had barely closed the door behind Tegan before he rounded on him. "Are you sure this is wise? Just think for a moment about what you are doing and if you can tell me that you are not doing this because you are hurting, then I will stand aside and let you go."

Let him go?

Tegan was the king, not Ryker. It wasn't up to his brother whether he went to war or not, just as it wasn't up to his advisers.

He stared Ryker down but couldn't bring himself to lie to his brother and tell him this burning need to go to war had nothing to do with Suki.

"This violent and heavy-handed male who looked ready to physically fight his advisers and is looking at me as if I'm next in line for a good beating is not you, Tegan." Ryker held his gaze, not flinching when Tegan bared fangs at him.

"What is me?" Tegan bit out and paced away from his brother, needing space before he did exactly as Ryker had suggested he would.

Ryker sighed and scrubbed a hand over his wild black hair. "You are a good king, and I know you feel you owe Prince Loren and the First King, but this war isn't about that, is it? You are angry, and you are hurting, and that is making you destructive. This is not you. The Tegan I know strategizes, considers all the angles and comes up with a plan... he does not go off half-cocked looking for a fight... looking for death."

Tegan stared out of one of the two windows that lined the back wall of the office, watching the warriors in the training arena as they kicked up sand and fought hard, battling each other when they should have been fighting an enemy. They were warriors. Demons. War was in their blood and it was time he gave them one.

It was time he fought in one again.

"I am tired of it all," he said quietly, unsure whether he really wanted his brother to hear that. He loosed a long sigh, ploughed his fingers through his hair and pulled it back as that weariness pounded down on him, beating in every fibre of his being. "I am tired of having to be someone else... someone I am not. I am not Edyn."

"You do not need to be Edyn—"

He turned on Ryker with a black snarl. "I do! Because I was not made for this... and Edyn was."

A flare of regret shone in Ryker's eyes, pity that had Tegan growling at him because he didn't want his brother looking at him as if he was weak, lost.

Even when he knew he was.

"I know things changed when Edyn died," Ryker started and Tegan bared his fangs again, warning him to be silent because he didn't need to hear this, not today. Not now.

His brother had told him too many times that he felt sorry for him, that he had altered the moment Edyn had died and he had been thrust into the role of king. One time, Ryker had dared to say that it was as if part of him had died along with their brother.

Tegan hadn't spoken to him for several months after that.

"You are a good king, Tegan, whether you pretend to be Edyn or not." Ryker cautiously edged around to the other side of the desk and stopped in front of the window beside the one Tegan occupied. "You know Edyn wouldn't be heading into war. He would uphold his vow of peace over the alliance that created it."

Tegan frowned at the warriors. "That is not true. Edyn believed in the alliance."

"Edyn believed in peace," Ryker countered, his tone even but unyielding. "He hated war. He had not been made for battle, not like you or me. He never had the stomach for it. It was the reason Edyn always let you do the fighting. He didn't want to get his claws bloody."

"He just knew how much I loved fighting." Tegan believed that, but as he listened to his brother, he started to believe him too.

"I speak the truth, brother. Once, I caught Edyn vomiting at just the thought of having to fight. Remember the time he was meant to lead the legion?"

Tegan did remember that day, because Edyn had ordered him to remain at the castle as heir to the crown, and Tegan had been as angry with him about that as Ryker had been with Tegan just minutes ago. Tegan had fought against his brother's decision and, in the end, Edyn had decided they should both go.

And then Edyn had changed the plan again at the last minute, mentioning that the kingdom needed him at the castle and the council had tied his hands by advising him not to have both him and Tegan, his next in line, on the battlefield together. He had told Tegan that he would let him go instead as he clearly wanted to be there.

Tegan had bought that excuse at the time.

Now, he could see it had all been a lie to cover the fact Edyn hadn't wanted to go.

"Sometimes, not everything is as the eyes see it." Ryker diligently kept his gaze fixed on the world outside, blatantly avoiding looking at him as Tegan scowled in his direction.

He was talking about Suki now.

"I am not so sure about that." Tegan pivoted to plant his backside against the black sill of the window.

"You know your advisers will try to make me convince you to let me go in your stead." Ryker leaned against the wall beside his window and folded his arms across his chest. Tegan knew that, was fully expecting it to happen and was already figuring out ways to counter them. Ryker grinned. "I won't do it."

Tegan was surprised to hear that.

His brother's dark eyes softened and warmed.

"I know taking the throne and running the kingdom has taken a heavy toll on you. I might not be home often because you give me so much freedom and you seem so annoyingly disappointed whenever I don't make use of it, but I am home enough to see how you are slowly slipping... coming to despise the throne that has been your shackle for a thousand years now." Ryker shook his head and growled, "The court could give you a little more freedom, before they drive you mad through boredom... so I will stay here like the dutiful brother I am so no one can deny you this chance to hit the battlefield... because you look as if you need to get your claws bloody."

Ryker shrugged when Tegan smiled, unable to hold it back as he realised how deeply his brother cared about him. His advisers would give Ryker hell while he was away, demanding he attend meetings and give them regular reports on proceedings, and he appreciated his brother for putting himself through that and for giving him the freedom the court refused him.

His brother clasped his shoulder, gripping it as a grave expression tightened his features. "Promise me you will come back though."

Tegan mirrored him, clutching Ryker's shoulder as he felt the gravity of that request and saw the love that had birthed it in his brother's eyes.

He nodded. It was hard to deny the darkness inside him, the thorny tendril of it that kept trying to snake around his heart to squeeze the life from him, but he would fight it and keep his head during the battle. He would do his best to survive because the kingdom needed him, and Ryker looked terrified of the thought of having to lead it.

"Thank you, brother." Tegan pulled him into his embrace and slapped his back as their horns struck each other. "I just need to be away from this place for a time... hopefully it will help clear my head."

And his heart.

Ryker stepped back when he released him and nodded. "Just remember that vow. No dying. Because this kingdom would go to shit with me in charge and we will be living in squalor before the season was out. No pretty windmills and fancy electricity. I would probably rip the truce up too. Maybe go to war with a few kingdoms. Probably get myself killed... and then I think our cousins would be in line for the throne. Imagine that."

Tegan's grimace tightened with each word Ryker spoke, with every image of his lands in ruin that they placed in his head. All of them helped purge that dark, desperate need that had been inside him. He had plans for his kingdom, and he would see them through.

Plus, he was damned if his uncle's line was going to rule. They were worse than Raelin when it came to ideas about taxing the people. Everyone would starve and Tegan had sworn his people would never suffer another famine.

He nodded again. "No dying."

Ryker slapped him on his bare chest and grinned. "Great talk. Have fun. Send daily reports. Do not forget to wash, because cleanliness is important, and always watch your back. If I do not hear from you every six hours, I will send men to bring you back to the castle."

He scowled at his brother. "You may leave now."

Ryker shrugged his wide shoulders and gave a regal, mocking bow, twirling his hand as he bent forwards. "My king."

He backed to the door while still bent over, straightened when he reached it and shot Tegan a grin before turning towards it and opening it.

Ryker paused to look back at him.

Hit him with one last blow, this one striking him right in the heart.

"For what it is worth, I truly believe she loves you."

CHAPTER 32

It had been so long since Tegan had set foot in the elf kingdom that he had forgotten how bright and green it was. He tried to keep his focus on the three-dimensional map of Hell that filled an enormous table before him, but the verdant outdoors drew his gaze to the rows of tall windows on his left and right that filled the space between each glittering pale grey stone column and allowed light to flood into the room.

To his right, green hills rose up beyond the pale castle walls, lush and alluring, beckoning him with the peace they offered. It had been too long since he had lazed amidst nature, letting the ripple of a stream or the rustling of a forest speak to him and calm him, stealing away all the stress and strain.

To his left, beyond the six windows there, the landscape was just as green, undulating and spotted with woods and forests that were equally as vibrant, some of which glowed with ethereal blue flowers. There was a village in the distance, one with three windmills that had been tugging at his focus since he had set eyes on them.

The elves often sold grain to his kingdom, including some of what they milled into flour. If he built such windmills, ones designed to mill rather than produce electricity, he could reduce the need to buy in grain and flour for his people. Some of the power produced by the windfarms could be used to light and heat fields of wheat and other grains.

He frowned as he felt someone staring at him and did his best to ignore them.

His gaze traced the map, studying lands he knew like the back of his hand as he listened to the chatter that filled the air, a nervous sort of talking that had the war room buzzing with energy as they waited for the last of the people to gather before proceeding with the meeting.

King Thorne's deep baritone rolled over the softer feminine voices, interrupting the conversation between his black-haired mate, Sable, and the blonde female on the other side of the table to her, on Tegan's right.

Rosalind.

The witch's eyes landed on him again.

And that dark sensation of being mentally eviscerated by someone followed it.

This time, a vicious snarl peeled from her mate's lips.

Tegan glared at the witch, silently pleading her to stop staring at him and provoking her mate. She didn't relent. She casually flicked her golden waves over her shoulder. Her blue eyes sparkled as they always did whenever he dared to glance at her, a wicked glint in them that said she was waiting for him to regret what he had done.

Or perhaps she was imagining him naked wrestling her mate.

Vail towered behind her, the black scales of his figure-hugging armour blending with her dress as he stood with both hands on her shoulders, a protective gesture that he backed up with a flash of his fangs in Tegan's direction as his ears grew even pointier and his violet irises gained a black edge, a sliver of the darkness he held within him showing in them.

"Vail," Prince Loren chided. While his brother had chosen to wear his armour to the meeting, Prince Loren wore black formal attire of an embroidered knee-length tunic, tight trousers, and polished boots. The two were similar in height and appearance, but Loren's blue-black hair had been neatly trimmed and styled, and Vail's was wild and tousled. Loren sighed. "Rosalind has assured us that King Tegan apologised for what happened and she was returned unharmed. I do not need war between my allies when I have a war with an enemy ahead of me."

Vail issued his older brother an apologetic look and Tegan breathed a little easier. It wouldn't stop Vail from threatening him forever, but it would buy him a few minutes without the elf looking at him as if he was one step closer to playing with his entrails.

"How much longer must we wait for your man?" Tegan did his best to keep the bite from his tone, but it was hard when the tension between him and Vail was building and he was beginning to fear they would come to blows if the meeting didn't begin, and end, soon.

"Not much longer." Prince Loren smiled tightly. "He is not always this late."

That wasn't a comfort.

Thorne smoothed his hand over his mate's long black hair, gazing down into her golden eyes in a way that had a restlessness coursing through Tegan. The female smiled up at her demon and settled her hands on the waist of his deep burgundy leathers before sliding them up over his bare chest.

Tegan had seen enough.

He paced away from the table, turning his back on the room to take in the view from the curved end of it, where the columns between the windows that stretched up towards the vaulted ceiling were narrower, allowing an almost uninterrupted panorama of green fields and the black mountains that rose beyond them where the sky began to darken towards grey.

Terrible things called that region of Hell home. Unspeakable things.

He shuddered and went to the window, stared out of it as his right hand drifted to the back pocket of his black leathers. He stroked the outline of his phone, his thoughts turning to Suki again. It was impossible to keep her out of his head when he was surrounded by so many males and their mates. Thorne had brought his fated one, Vail was constantly in contact with his witch, and even Loren had had his female with him at the start of the gathering.

Worse was the fact that Melia, the acting First King, was here, her sombre bright blue eyes still holding the pain that had been in them when he had seen her shortly after the night she had lost her demon mate on the battlefield. He glanced back over his shoulder at her where she stood with another female, deep in discussion and slightly away from the others. While Melia's corseted white dress was a sharp contrast to the cerulean leather trousers, knee-high boots and bodice the second female wore, their delicate features were strikingly similar.

Same long white hair, same milky skin, same ethereal blue eyes and same delicate bone structure, beauty designed to lure males to their doom.

Suki popped into his head. He shoved her out again and focused on the two females.

He had met Isla, Melia's sister, in the past. The female was intelligent and quick witted on the battlefield and a skilled warrior.

Having her here was a good thing, and not only because she was capable with a blade.

Having a phantom on their side, even one who had been made corporeal, was a great advantage. Isla could kill a man with little more than a thought or a kiss, draining his soul from him.

Suki danced back into his mind, the similarities between her breed and the phantoms making it impossible to keep her out of his thoughts.

As she pirouetted and tormented him, Ryker's words echoed around her, adding another level to the torture he attempted to endure.

Was his brother right about her and she did love him?

Would she try to find her way back to him?

She had wanted to say something to him and now that he was thinking more clearly, finally calming down again, he felt sure she had tried to say his name just as his man had teleported her away.

She had never spoken his name before. At least, never outside of his dreams of her.

He stroked his horn with his other hand, unsettled by his turbulent thoughts and the ache that bloomed inside him, a fierce need to go to his rooms in the elf castle and call her.

He shunned that need.

What he needed to do was focus on his business here.

For the first time in a thousand years, he had been given leave to venture outside of the kingdom's boundaries and was in charge of a legion again. Not a legion, but legions this time. He meant to make the most of it and the coming battle. It had been too long, and he hadn't realised how deeply he needed this until he had gathered with the other leaders. Every second that ticked by, he grew more anxious, eager to get going and hurl himself into the fray.

He moved back to the table, studying the map, charting the possible places a dragon might pick as a battleground.

The door opened and he sensed an elf male enter, together with a strong female. The dragon. Her nerves preceded her. Not only hers. The male was nervous too, but not for the same reason. Tegan could feel that her fear was born of the coming fight. Commander Bleu's fear was born of something else.

He glanced at King Thorne as the large male moved, lifting his hand to place it on Sable's shoulder, clutching it through her black top in a protective gesture. Because of the elf male who had entered and was now looking at her?

When Thorne turned his dark red gaze on the violet-to-white haired female stood beside Bleu, the elf bared fangs, and Tegan wanted to sigh. Another damned male with a mate, this one in the throes of a courtship if his behaviour was anything to go by.

Although Bleu wore a similar black tunic, trousers and boots as his prince, their behaviour marked the difference between them. Prince Loren remained the epitome of calm, his regal bearing commanding the attention of all those in the room. Bleu was too busy glaring at Thorne, his pointed ears flaring back against his wild blue-black hair as he stared the demon down.

Thorne finally backed down, tearing his gaze from the slender female Bleu was so intent on protecting and pinning it on the map as he tunnelled his fingers through his russet-brown waves, pulling his hair back from his dusky horns.

Tegan focused back on the map too, uninterested in the battle for dominance that was clearly an ongoing war between the two males. He stroked both of his polished horns as he studied his own kingdom and tried not to think about Suki or the phone that felt as if it was burning a hole in his back pocket, beckoning him to look at the pictures of her again.

To call her.

He leaned over the map, planting his hands against the edge of the table and bracing his weight on them.

A hank of his black hair fell down into his eyes and he huffed as he preened it back, clearing his vision.

Vail suddenly growled low in his throat and Tegan glanced at him, ready to issue a snarl of his own if the male was directing it at him because he hadn't looked at Rosalind recently and she definitely hadn't looked his way either.

Vail wasn't looking at him. He was glaring at Bleu, his violet eyes narrowed and oily darkness threatening to fill them as he slung an arm around Rosalind's shoulders and his armour swept over his hand, transforming his fingers into black claws that he curled around her arm, tugging on the black material of her long dress.

She sighed and looked up at her mate.

When her mate's eyes landed on the dragon female, Bleu bared his fangs on a hiss.

Another protective gesture.

One that had Tegan's focus returning to the map as that need to call Suki grew stronger.

What had she wanted to say to him?

"Shall we begin?" Loren's deep voice cut through the silence and there was a murmur of agreement.

Tegan kept his eyes locked on the map, on his kingdom in particular.

"The dragon skirted the Second Kingdom, passing along the other side of this mountain range." He tried to keep the bite from his tone as he ran his left hand along the curving spine of mountains to the north of his kingdom, his thighs pressing against the edge of the three-dimensional map as he leaned over it. "He remained firmly inside the border of the First Realm."

Something that had irritated him, even when he knew he was destined to fight here in the elf kingdom and not in his own lands. The room brightened slightly, a sign his eyes were changing as the hunger for battle gripped him once more.

He breathed through it. He would have the battle he needed soon enough. He just needed to be patient.

"He came through my land on this course, decimating all in his path." Thorne charted one that had everyone in the room falling silent. The enemy had cut straight through the heart of the Third Realm, a kingdom that was still recovering from a recent war. Tegan could only imagine how many warriors had fallen in the battles that must have taken place over the last few days. Thorne swallowed hard, his dark crimson eyes brightening to scarlet as he stared at his lands. "He has recruited an army along the way. Men from my ranks, traders in the countryside, even some demons from the surrounding realms. We managed to evacuate some of the villages in his path, but others were not so lucky. We have lost many warriors and subjects already."

Thorne sighed and preened his left horn, stroking his fingers along the dusky curve of it. Sable rested her right hand on his bare shoulder, worry warming her golden eyes as she gazed up at her mate. The demon looked down at her, pain etched on every line of his face. Losing so many warriors in such a short span of time was taking its toll on the large male, but vengeance would be his soon enough.

"We will make him pay for what he has done," Bleu said, voicing the thoughts of everyone in the room.

Thorne looked across at him and nodded.

Queen Melia drifted forwards, the long skirt of her white dress floating around her ankles as she moved closer to the map, gliding away from her companion.

"I have had word that the dragon's army has passed through our outlying lands and has banked towards the centre of my kingdom. Scouts have reported he is on a direct course with a point beyond the demon kingdoms, and yours. It seems he is intending to recruit more, possibly from the other realms that lie that way." Her soft voice floated around the room, the faint echo it held lending it an eerie edge as she ghosted her hand over the map, the motion strangely light and slow. "Tenak's army is strong, with many dragons among its ranks. My men are engaged with them now. My advisor Isla came to warn me and she has witnessed the battle, so I brought her with me as she has valuable information."

"Do you believe any from the free realm will be joining the battle on either side?" Tegan looked at the realm that bordered the elf kingdom and the First Realm in the direction she had motioned.

Isla stiffened.

Bleu's violet eyes narrowed on her, curiosity filling them as he studied her.

"No." The male canted his head, his eyes remaining locked on Isla. "We sent word but none of the sirens, nymphs, incubi and succubi, shifter species or furies offered allegiance and stated they would not side with a dragon either."

Tegan looked at Melia's sister. The elf was up to something, and he wasn't sure why. He was sure of one thing though.

It was unwise to upset a phantom.

The air around Melia was already chilling, a cold breeze caressing Tegan's right arm as her blue eyes brightened, locking on the elf. Bleu didn't notice the way she was looking at him, the tips of her white hair beginning to float in the air as the sense of power around her grew.

On the other side of Melia, Isla carefully lifted her right hand and tucked a braid that hung from beside her temple behind her ear, blending it into her long white hair. Her pale hand shook as she lowered it, flexed her fingers and then tucked her hands behind her back.

A wicked dangerous light entered the elf's eyes.

"Although, we did not come to an agreement with the vampires," Bleu said and Isla tensed. "I am sure the Preux Chevaliers would join us if we turned off the portal and stopped sunlight from entering our realm."

Isla paled, turning as white as her hair. That sense of power emanating from her sister grew stronger still, and Tegan rubbed his arm to keep the chill off it as he glared at the elf.

Whatever game Bleu was playing, it was liable to get them all killed.

Tegan shifted his gaze to Loren, capturing his attention before he looked at his man, a silent warning that he was playing with fire.

Loren's steady violet gaze leaped to Bleu, a flicker of confusion filling it as he frowned at his man.

Bleu didn't relent.

"Lord Van der Garde even requested we do so as he desired to join the battle." Bleu's eyes remained locked on Isla. She glanced at Melia and her sister drifted closer to her, her ice-cold blue eyes landing on the elf. He tensed now. Had he finally sensed the dark intent rolling off Melia? If he had, he was an idiot, because it didn't stop him from saying, "Should we put it to a vote?"

"We do not condone vampires near us," the First King said, her voice as calm and smooth as still water but holding darkness beneath the placid surface, a threat that even a fool would know to heed.

Bleu looked as if he wasn't going to back down.

Tegan sidestepped, moving closer to Thorne as the demon wrapped his arms around Sable to shield her from the frigid waves of cold now flowing from Melia.

Prince Loren glared at his man, grabbed him and pulled him away from the table, to the far corner near the door. Bleu turned a surprised look on his prince. Loren cut him down with a scowl and spoke in the elf tongue, a sharp edge to his tone that left Tegan in no doubt that the male was being scolded.

The amusement that had been filling Bleu's eyes drained from them as he listened to his prince.

He spoke with Loren, and Loren slowly relaxed again, a glimmer of interest and curiosity lighting his violet eyes now as he listened to Bleu.

Tegan had never even attempted to learn the elf tongue. Rumour had it, the elves had a tendency to deal with anyone who tried to learn it. They were fiercely protective of their language, and Tegan could understand why. Being able to speak a tongue that no one outside of their species could comprehend was an advantage in countless situations, including war.

Everyone stared at the two, and Tegan wasn't the only one who was curious about Bleu's motives judging by the look on Thorne's face. Vail looked interested too, was listening intently to his brother, and surprise crossed his regal features as he glanced at Melia and Isla.

What did he know that the rest of them didn't?

Loren glanced back at everyone and tensed, released Bleu and cleared his throat as he walked back to the table.

"Let us discuss our plan and see what we can come up with. Taryn will lead us by sharing information on a vision she witnessed." Loren looked to the violet-to-white haired female.

Bleu's expression darkened and he was quick to resume his position beside her. Another protective gesture. He didn't like the idea of the dragon telling them what she had seen, looked concerned as he stared at her, his brow furrowing as he waited for her to look at him.

She turned her face towards him, her unusual violet-to-white eyes soft and warm, no trace of fear in them as she slowly nodded.

The male didn't relax. He placed his hand against her back, where her white leather corset met her violet leather trousers, and remained close to her as she relayed what she had seen in her vision and fielded a few questions.

Tegan's focus drifted as he looked down at the map again, his gaze automatically seeking his kingdom. He lost track of the discussion as he stared at it, as he pinpointed the location of his mansion. He tried to be of use as everyone discussed a battle plan, but he couldn't shake the thoughts that filled his mind, crowding it.

Had Suki attempted to return to him yet?

She would have to find a way to use the portal pathways if she wanted to enter Hell. The thought of her approaching a demon in the fae town had his horns curling and fangs sharpening, claws emerging as a black need to fight surged through him.

If his brother was right, and she did love him, then the pain he had seen in her eyes and had felt cutting into his heart had been real.

He had hurt her.

Did he even deserve her after that?

Bleu's voice rose above the din of chatter filling the room. "Taryn is right and we should move away from the castle."

The room fell silent.

"The stronghold is ideal. It is a defensive position close to the free realm, bordering the First Realm of the demons, and we have supplies in place there." Bleu leaned over the map, coming into view as Tegan attempted to tear his eyes away from it and focus on the meeting. The elf planted his right palm against the edge of the map and pointed to the spot where the garrison was with his left hand. "It is away from any villages on both the elf side and the demon side."

Tegan studied it.

It was a small area, nestled close to the First Realm and the free one. A suitable position for a camp for their forces if all the intelligence they had gathered proved correct and the dragon did attack from the free realm.

Bleu eased back and rubbed the pad of his left thumb across his lower lip as he frowned at the map. "We will need to infiltrate the enemy ranks to steal the sword back. It is pivotal... whoever possesses it will win. There is no doubt about that."

Rosalind rocked on her heels, her drab black traditional witch's dress swaying around her ankles as she grinned, starlight sparkling in her blue eyes. "I have a cunning plan."

Everyone stared at her in silence, waiting for her to explain it.

Apparently, this was not the reaction she had wanted.

She huffed, folded her arms across her chest, and muttered, "You all need to watch more classic British telly."

Everyone continued to stare at her.

"Perhaps you should explain your plan, Little Wild Rose." Vail lowered his head and murmured the words into her ear.

Her cheeks coloured, the starlight in her eyes exploded into fire, and she leaned towards him. Vail's violet gaze darkened, heat filling it as he lowered it to her neck.

Tegan looked away from them and scowled at the map.

Loren cleared his throat.

"Um… I was going to address the dragon in the room and say that I will mask Taryn by changing the colour of her scales." Rosalind's voice wobbled, uncertainty lacing it as the scent of desire rose from her, need that had Tegan on the verge of growling at them to leave before his mood took a dangerous turn.

He cursed everyone in the room, damning them for finding their mates. It felt as if everyone was throwing it in his face and the torment was too much to bear. He needed space. He needed solitude. He couldn't take this any longer.

He needed Suki.

The witch cleared her throat again. "It's a simple spell really, and it should allow her to enter the enemy's camp and get close enough to steal the sword."

"No," Bleu snapped. "Taryn is not going in there alone. She needs backup."

"Perhaps we could convince Loke to help," Loren said.

Tegan didn't know and didn't care who Loke was. With his luck, Loke would be another happily mated male.

"We do not have time," Bleu countered. "Loke is great as a backup plan, but Tenak knows him. Rosalind would have to change the colour of his scales too."

Rosalind shook her head. "I won't have enough strength to cast two spells like that if I'm also expected to shield the garrison and the lands surrounding it as I did for Thorne in the battle in the Third Realm."

Darkness rose to swamp the room and Tegan lifted his head and looked across the map at Vail. Rosalind nervously glanced over her shoulder at him too. Tegan had heard from Thorne that Vail reacted poorly to magic being used near him, that a madness gripped him whenever he sensed it.

The fates were cruel to pair him with a witch.

Rosalind turned to Vail and Tegan watched the tender exchange between them as she sought to soothe her mate, one that had him realising that fate had perhaps been kind to Vail after all. It had given him a mate who could free him of the black stain on his soul, restoring him to the male he had been before he had gone to war with his brother millennia ago.

The room grew louder as everyone tried to figure out how to provide Taryn with backup without using another dragon.

Bleu held his hand up. "I will shift into a dragon."

Silence fell again.

Loren was the first to find his voice. "How?"

Bleu looked to his left, at his prince. "I will drink Taryn's blood."

The dragon female blushed hard.

Hunger filled Bleu's violet eyes.

Loren looked at Taryn.

Bleu growled low in his throat, a feral snarl that had Sable gasping and Loren's expression blackening, turning as dark as the one his brother had worn just moments ago. Loren narrowed his eyes on Bleu, anger brightening them together with something that surprised Tegan.

Amusement.

Tegan didn't see what there was to be amused about. Bleu had just openly threatened him for looking at his female.

Or was it because the elf had threatened him, his behaviour revealing that the dragon was clearly his fated female?

Loren held his gaze, not backing down even as Bleu scowled at him, his lips compressing as he frowned at his prince.

"I think we are done here for today. Relay the plan to your people and we will meet again tomorrow to go over the final details."

Tegan didn't wait around to see whether they were going to fight.

He stormed from the room, heading at speed towards the steps that would take him down into the heart of his castle.

To his rooms.

Because he needed to be alone.

He needed to call Suki.

He couldn't go on any longer without asking her the question that had been slowly destroying his sanity over the last few days.

Did she love him?

CHAPTER 33

Suki stared at her fifth shot of Hellfire, watching the way the colourful lights rotating above the bar area of Underworld reflected off the dark surface and the damp black counter beneath the glass. Music pounded in her ears, but she didn't hear it. People crowded her, but she didn't notice them.

All her focus was on that shot of liquor and the escape it offered if she dared to consume enough of it.

Allura and Vidia had brought her to London, forcing her to go with them on a hunt she wanted no part in. Apparently, it was better than sitting in her room, spending every waking hour trying to figure out how to win back a demon who had banished her sorry ass from his kingdom.

Suki hadn't had the energy to tell them they were wrong about her. She didn't care about Tegan anymore.

She really didn't.

She knocked back her drink, grimaced as it burned on the way down, and slammed the empty glass back onto the black bar top.

Fine. She did.

She cared about the bastard.

She cared about him so much that she wanted to go home, because this foolish attempt by her sisters to get her to get over him by finding another man was pointless.

It was never going to happen.

Tegan was the only one for her now.

She would sooner starve than seduce another man.

Kyter poured her another shot and slid it towards her, a worried and pitying edge to his golden eyes as she glanced up at him.

Things had to be bad if the jaguar shifter was looking at her like that.

The gaggle of females to her left suddenly perked up, growing louder and throwing off heat that had her frowning at them, wondering what had got them all riled up and horny.

A shiver skated down her spine as her senses lit up, screaming a warning at her.

She slowly turned to face the man who slid onto the stool to her right.

He raked long fingers through the soft spikes of his blond hair as he spoke with Kyter, his steel grey eyes bright in the flashing lights.

He was handsome enough, drew the gazes of more than just the horny hen party to her left, but he was dangerous.

She could feel it.

She focused on him, a struggle with several large shots of Hellfire in her system. It took a few attempts that gave her a headache and made the room wobble a little, but eventually his aura appeared.

Suki stiffened.

Blue tendrils rose from his wide shoulders and the haphazard spikes of his fair hair.

An incubus.

She reared back, almost falling from her stool as instinct screamed at her to get away from him. He cast a black look at her, his eyebrows dipping low as his lips compressed in a hard line, as if her reaction had irritated him. She had every right to react to him the way she had. He was a bloody incubus!

Her heart pounded as awareness of how tipsy she was, and how vulnerable that made her, shot through her. Flashes of all her previous fights against incubi rushed through her mind, interspersed with that dreadful day her mother had been stolen from her by one of his kind. She threw a glance around at the crowd that now hemmed her in, keeping her in close proximity to the bastard.

She swallowed. What could she do? She couldn't teleport with so many humans around, not without getting into a world of trouble. She debated whether to squeeze through the crowd or vault the bar and flee before the incubus could launch an attack.

Her gaze locked back on him and something else hit her.

There was something different about him.

Wrong.

When Kyter moved away to get his order, the man turned on her.

"You got a problem with me?" He narrowed his grey eyes on her. "Never seen a vampire before?"

Either he was trying to trick her, which really pissed her off, or that weird sensation she got from him was because he was a rare half-breed.

"Piss off. Just leave me the fuck alone and we'll be just fine. Got it? I don't want any trouble." Her eyes leaped to the humans pressing against her on all sides as they attempted to reach the bar and order more drinks.

Her throat closed, fear tightening it as she sought an escape route.

"That makes two of us. I don't want any trouble either." His smooth, deep voice had calm washing over her.

Was he trying to charm her? She glared at him. He glared right back.

His features remained tight for long seconds, and then he sighed and slightly shook his head.

"Look. I'm here to relax, not get into a fight. Got it?" He held her gaze, demanding an answer.

Suki swallowed hard. Was he telling the truth? Could she really trust an incubus, even one who was part vampire?

"How about I help you trust me? Ah. I could tell you my name. It's Payne. Hell, I'll even tell you where I work. Vampirerotique. Heard of it?" He leaned a little closer.

Suki nodded.

Who in the immortal community hadn't heard of the erotic theatre run by and catering to vampires? Her sisters had seduced several of the vampires who worked there, and sometimes they hung around outside when the performances finished to feed off the second-hand sexual energy the patrons gave off as they left the theatre.

She had never been brave enough to go with them.

Okay. Maybe it was more like they had never invited her. Maybe the one time she had asked to go too, they had refused to take her because they believed she would scare off the vampires and ruin things somehow.

Payne arched an eyebrow at her row of empty shot glasses. "What has you so down in the dumps anyway?"

Suki knew better than to speak to him, knew she should be trying to figure out how to escape his grasp, her mouth had different ideas. He was the first person to speak to her all night other than the bartenders, and she was tired and worn down, and maybe a little drunk.

"I fucked everything up with a guy." She shrugged when he swivelled on the stool to face her, all of his focus settling on her, and knocked another shot back to steady her nerves. If her sisters saw her speaking to an incubus, even one who was only part incubus, they would have her head, but she needed to talk. "I wanted to prove myself to my clan and he was the perfect target, a demon I met in this bar. It all started out as a seduction."

"And it ended with a broken heart," he offered, resting his right arm on the bar.

Colourful fae markings tracked up the underside of his forearm, disappearing beneath the rolled-up sleeves of his dark pinstripe shirt. Her markings had been done with ink, but his were natural, a record of his bloodline that confirmed he was an incubus.

The flare of red in his irises said he was also a vampire, just as he had told her.

She wasn't sure how she felt about him as he waited for her to speak, as she slowly relaxed and that urge to run for the hills faded. She hated incubi. They were all bastards, out to hurt her kind for no damn reason. But he seemed nice.

Genuinely nice.

She put it down to his vampire side.

She nodded and thanked Kyter with a smile as he poured her another shot.

That crimson corona shone brighter as the incubus-vampire stared at her. "I know a thing or two about seduction, and I know a thing or two about love. You have it bad for him, don't you?"

She forced herself to nod again. It wasn't as if telling him that gave him any power over her, and he didn't look interested in attacking her. Because he was only part incubus? Or maybe because he obviously identified more with his vampire side.

"Hey, at least you're not spouting that shit about not being able to love." Payne hiked his shoulders when she frowned at him. "A vampire friend of mine has a succubus for his mate. I get along with her well now."

"You didn't get along with her all the time?" She sipped her shot this time, maintaining the buzz.

He chuckled. "There was a time I was trying to get her away from my friend. She was a little obsessed with him... Maybe addicted is the better word. She couldn't leave him alone... all because his aura was shadowed. Silly succubus didn't know what it meant."

Suki's eyes widened and she almost dropped her glass. "You know about shadowed males?"

The look Payne gave her asked if she was crazy or stupid. "Of course I do. Incubi experience something similar when they meet their mate. I had one hell of a time with my one."

She got stuck on one word.

Mate.

He leaned closer, frowning into her eyes as she stared right through him. "So… you look like you're about to pass out. Do you need another drink, or are you having a revelation?"

"The latter," she muttered, reeling and feeling as if she was in danger of toppling from her stool as she swayed, unable to believe what was whirling around her mind.

Tegan was her mate?

She hadn't thought it was possible for her to have a mate. None of her lessons and none of the books in the library had ever mentioned them.

She stared at the incubus-vampire. "You're sure… you're sure a shadowed male means a mate?"

"I'm not yanking your chain or anything." His look turned serious as he tilted his glass of dark liquid towards her. "If the demon has a shadowed aura, then you're his fated one."

The bubble of feelings that filled her on hearing that Tegan was more than just a demon she loved, that he was her mate, suddenly popped as reality slapped her hard.

"He dumped me." She necked her shot, savouring the fire as it burned away her pain.

If Tegan was her mate, surely he wouldn't have ditched her like that? Although maybe he would have if he had been convinced she had been playing him. Gods, did he think she had used her charms on him? She hadn't lied about them. They were completely unreliable and mostly useless. There was no way she could have charmed him, not even by accident.

"I'm sorry to hear that." Payne swigged his drink and she pulled a face as it left a red smear on his glass. Blood. Definitely a vampire as well as an incubus then. He smirked at her. "But then I'm also sorry you're proving yourself to be as weak and pathetic as incubi believe your kind to be."

She hit him with her best glare.

His smirk widened into a devilish grin. "If my mate had tried to dump me, I would be fighting for her, not sitting in a bar drowning my sorrows."

"I can't fight for him," she snapped. "He banished me with a spell and now I can't get near him. He thinks I betrayed him… that I just wanted his throne. Gods, maybe Julianna is right and I need to get even somehow because this is driving me mad. I keep trying to think of ways to get him back and make him see he was wrong, and I'm coming up with nothing!"

"Sounds like a good idea." His grin faded, handsome face sobering as he sipped his drink again. She frowned at him and he shrugged. "I'm just saying maybe a little payback is good. He's a demon and you're his mate. He's probably going mad about now. A little push and you won't need to go to him... he'll come to you."

Heck, that was tempting.

She shook her head. No. It wasn't a good idea. Tegan was mad. He was mad with her. Taunting him was only going to make him angrier.

Payne set his glass down, pulling her back to him as it hit the black bar top with a hard thud. "All you really need to do is toss him a little incentive."

An incentive didn't sound too bad.

"What sort of incentive?" She leaned closer to him.

Before she knew what was happening, Payne had grabbed her phone from the counter, lifted it so it was facing them and had leaned in close, pressing his cheek to hers. She tensed, every instinct telling her to move away before he hurt her, but she stifled them and remained where she was.

If it meant seeing Tegan again and having a chance to explain, she could suffer being close to an incubus.

She looked up at the phone, right into the camera, and leaned closer to Payne as he pressed the button, snapping a picture of them together.

He was quick to break contact with her and toss her phone at her. She scrambled for it, managing to catch it as it arced towards her, and clutched it in both hands, bringing it down in front of her.

She stared at the picture, a vicious knot twisting inside her, tangling all her feelings together as she hesitated. It took her an entire song to find the courage to turn the image into a picture message. Another half a song passed with her thumb over the send button as she waged war with herself.

Maybe the incubus was wrong and Tegan wouldn't care. Maybe her demon was already over her.

She wasn't sure she could take knowing that he didn't want her anymore.

The damned incubus took the decision out of her hands.

Literally.

He snatched the phone from her hand and she gasped and lunged for it, her eyes widening as her hand flew towards him. Too slow. His thumb came down on the send button.

"Gods fucking damn you, incubus!" She grabbed the phone from him and fumbled with it, her heart pounding in her ears and fingers shaking as she tried to stop the message.

Too late.

It was sent.

She turned a murderous glare on Payne, an urge to claw him to pieces lashing at her. What was the point? Nothing she did now could change what he had done. The message was gone, flying through the ether to Tegan.

It was all in the hands of the gods now.

Either she was about to get her demon back.

Or he was about to break her heart forever.

CHAPTER 34

Tegan stormed out of the squat two storey pale grey stone building and across the courtyard of the garrison, his muscles rippling and aching as fury mounted inside him, a fire that boiled his blood in his veins and had his fangs emerging as his horns flared. He pushed past several elves and demons of the Third Realm, not caring if his brutish behaviour caused a fight.

Because he wanted one right now.

His soul screamed in agony, heart a shrivelled black thing in his chest as he glared at the high glittering grey walls that encircled the garrison near the mountains that acted as a border between the elf kingdom and the First Realm of demons. The lush green hills that undulated around him did nothing to soothe him today.

Several males from his legion saluted him as he passed. Their gazes tracked him when he stomped onwards without greeting them, turning his glare on those around him now as rage got the better of him.

His eyes betrayed him, picking out the mated couples scattered around the packed courtyard. Loren and his female, Olivia. Rosalind and Vail. Thorne and Sable.

He tightened his grip on the phone in his right hand, the image he had just received burned on his mind as he gritted his teeth and growled through the pain.

A photograph of Suki and another male.

A *handsome* male.

He snarled, barely biting back his urge to throw his head back and roar.

He needed to go to her, to snap the male's neck before she did anything with him, but he couldn't.

The war was about to begin.

He staggered to a halt as questions bombarded him, ripping at the tattered shreds of his heart and his soul.

Hadn't she felt anything for him after all? Was it truly over?

He scrubbed his left hand over his face and tipped his head back to stare at the blue sky. Gods, he had been a fool. Ryker had made him see that and he needed to tell her, he needed to know what she had wanted to say to him.

But he was needed in Hell.

The urge to go to her had darkness seeping outwards from beneath him, spreading across the ground, and a few sensible males edged away from him, giving him more space.

The thought of her with another male slayed him.

He had to go to her.

No. He had to remain where he was. He had no commanders to replace him and they were close to leaving the garrison, just minutes from heading to the frontline to meet the dragon's army.

He lowered his head and his eyes landed on Bleu where he was making his way towards the female dragon. Perhaps speaking with the elf about the battle plan would take his mind off Suki.

He cut across the courtyard and stepped into Bleu's path.

Bleu snarled at him.

It died away when the male lifted his violet gaze to meet Tegan's.

Tegan raised an eyebrow at the elf's threat and then looked over his shoulder at Taryn.

Rage burned through him as the reason for the male's behaviour hit him.

The pair had mated.

It was written all over the female as she blushed, and all over Bleu as Tegan slowly turned back to face him, catching the flare of anger in his eyes as Tegan stood between him and his female, blocking his path to her.

Tegan narrowed his eyes on the male, his blood on fire, seething with a need to fight as a mocking voice rang in his head, telling him everyone but him had their mate, and the phone he gripped in his hand felt as if it was searing him. He didn't care who gave it to him, not right now. Friend or foe, it was fine with him. As long as he got to fight and unleash this pain ripping him apart from the inside.

Bleu spread his feet shoulder-width apart, adopting a fighting stance that only goaded Tegan into following through and attacking him.

A heavy hand slapped down on Tegan's bare shoulder and pain pierced him as dark claws pressed into his muscles.

"Perhaps it is best we leave the little elf to his business, King Tegan? I am sure Prince Loren would be more than happy to answer whatever question you desired to ask the commander." Thorne's rough deep voice rumbled in Tegan's ears, penetrating the thunderous rush of his heart, and Bleu flicked a glance at the Third King.

Thorne's chiselled features softened into a smile as Tegan looked across at him. The elf loosed a breath and relaxed on Tegan's senses as Tegan gave a curt nod and allowed Thorne to lead him away, because he no longer wanted to fight.

He wanted advice.

When they were far from the crowd, near the thick wall of the garrison, he broke free of Thorne's grip and paced, his boots loud on the cobbles and packed dirt.

Thorne's steady dark crimson gaze tracked him as the male tugged on the burgundy leather cuffs that protected his forearms, checking them. Tegan had donned similar ones in black, a rigid pair of vambraces that had steel running through them, strong enough to block a sword blow. The male swept his unruly russet hair back from his face and waited, his expression placid as he continued to track Tegan.

Tegan swallowed. He was building up to speaking. It was just difficult to find his voice and to know where to begin. He had never really asked for advice before. Ryker normally just threw it at him whether he wanted it or not, and his advisers rarely bothered to check whether he wanted their advice, and he had definitely never asked for it.

He wasn't sure where he was meant to begin.

Asking for the male's advice was probably a wise place.

He stopped and faced the male. "I need... your advice... on a delicate matter."

Thorne's eyebrows rose and then he nodded. "Of course."

Tegan wrestled with the words, grimaced and looked down at his feet.

Perhaps it was best just to purge it all at once, get it all out there rather than doing it in pieces.

"You have a female... a mate," he started and clenched his fists, gripping the phone tightly as he thought about Suki. "I had a female. She means much to me... but I was told I did not mean as much to her and now she has shown me I meant little to her."

"Okay, I have *serious* doubts Thorne can help you with this. What on Earth does he know about women?" The sharp feminine voice startled Tegan, and he lifted his head, horror sweeping through him as he met the golden eyes of

Thorne's mate as she tied her black hair up into a neat ponytail. He had been so caught up in trying to rush everything out that he hadn't sensed her approaching. She grinned, her eyes glittering as if she was going to enjoy counselling him. "Let me get this straight. You found a nice girl, she may or may not have been playing you... and how did she show you that you meant diddly-squat to her?"

Tegan wasn't sure what diddly-squat meant. He guessed it meant 'nothing' in her strange language.

When he lifted his right hand and revealed the phone, she arched an eyebrow at it. He woke the device and found the picture, one he wanted to burn, but that meant burning his phone too.

"She sent me this photograph a few minutes ago." He revealed the image to Sable and Thorne.

Sable's black eyebrows shot high on her forehead. "A few minutes ago? Did you pop to the mortal realm or something?"

He shook his head. "I was here in my quarters."

Her eyes widened. "Wait. Wait. Wait... wait... wait... *wait*! You're telling me that thing works in Hell?"

He nodded this time.

"Phones that work in Hell!" She turned to her mate, grabbed his arm with both of her hands and bounced on the spot. "I needs it. I *neeeeeds* it. My precious."

Tegan was beginning to wonder if all females from the mortal realm were strange. "I will procure you one if you help me."

"Oh, that's easy." She jerked her chin towards his phone. "It's a payback picture, dumbass."

That dumbass word again.

She meant to insult him.

She continued before he could warn her against doing such things. "You obviously made her mad or something, because that right there is a classic revenge snap. She wants to wound you and make you jealous, and make you see what you're missing out on now."

Suki had certainly accomplished all those things with the photograph.

"So be honest. What *really* happened with her?" Sable flicked her black ponytail over her shoulder, planted her hands against her hips over her black top and leathers, and stared him down in a way that said she wasn't going to help him until he answered that question.

"Things were going well. I had to take her home to the fae town, the one near Fort William, and after leaving there, I was visited by the mistress of her clan who claimed Suki had been using me to prove her worth to her family. I was apparently nothing more than a game to her." He huffed and pushed the hurt back down inside as it tried to well up again, forcing himself to continue. "I was upset, and I had her brought to me so I could banish her."

"That is bad." Sable frowned and looked up at Thorne. "I'd probably castrate you if you act like him."

Thorne shrugged. "I am not that stupid, Little Female."

Tegan growled at both of them. Neither looked at all afraid.

Sable folded her arms across her chest. "I'm guessing you didn't give her a chance to explain?"

She sounded more and more like Ryker every passing second.

When he didn't answer, she shook her head, looking as if she was astounded, but at the same time not surprised.

"Why must demons always come on so strong? It's always black and white with you guys. She's a..." She leaned forwards and frowned at the phone, scrutinising the image.

He offered, "Succubus."

Her eyebrows shot up again. "Well... I can't imagine how she feels... queen of playing the field and suddenly there's a big demon demanding she be his mate?"

"I demanded nothing," he snapped and straightened to tower over her. His attempt at intimidating her did nothing. She just glared up at him, as if daring him to attempt to put her in her place. He huffed and glanced at Thorne where the male stood behind her, glowering. "She does not know she is my mate. I never said to you that she was... and I am not even sure of it."

The huntress rolled her amber eyes.

"Oh, come off it. You damned well know she's your mate. You're just in denial because you got your delicate feelings a little trampled. I'll never understand demons." She shook her head on a sigh and shrugged. "You got what you deserved I'm afraid."

She wasn't going to help him?

Rage curled through him and he took a sharp step towards her as he barked, "Tell me what to do. She will sleep with the male!"

Thorne snarled at him and stepped in front of his female.

She peeked around her mate. "See. Demanding! It's a payback picture. She probably won't sleep with him. It's a blatant attempt to provoke a response. She wants you to contact her."

Oh.

Tegan angled the phone towards himself and looked down at his beautiful female, feeling lost and hopeless. He had no experience of this sort of thing.

He looked at Sable. "What sort of response might be preferable?"

She stepped around Thorne and slapped a hand on Tegan's bare chest, so hard it knocked the air from his lungs, and grinned. "The sort that comes from in here, big guy. Prod and poke those delicate feelings that got hurt and see what bleeds out of them. What do you want to tell her?"

He looked down at the female and considered the answer to that question. When it hit him, he tucked the phone to his chest and frowned at her.

"Private things."

Disappointment flashed across her eyes. "Fine. Keep it to yourself. But you owe me a phone."

He looked down at the image of Suki, studying it more closely now that his anger had ebbed. There was pain in her striking green-to-blue eyes. Hurt he had caused. The light he had always loved seeing in them was gone.

"Whatever you need to tell her, now is a good time." Sable took her hand away from his chest. "Probably the best time. Don't leave for this battle with things unsaid. Let her know how you feel. Win her heart... don't demand it be given to you. And you've got some serious sucking up to do if she does take you back. Like... centuries of apology flowers, chocolates, wine and presents... although she is a succubus, so it'll probably just be centuries of hot sex."

He groaned and rubbed his free hand over his mouth. He could do that.

He frowned at his phone, flexed his fingers and fought through a reply that seemed to take forever to type because his thumbs were too big for the fiddly device and he had to correct words several times.

He pressed the button to send it as he read the message back.

I must speak with you. Do not do anything with the male. As soon as the war in the elf kingdom is done, I will come for you. I am sorry. I miss you. Yours always, Tegan.

The phone rang.

He fumbled with it as her image flashed up on the screen, trying to swipe the stupid circle to make it answer the call. He managed to do it and lifted it to his ear.

It was still several inches from it when she screamed down the line. "How the hell are you going to come to me since I can't bloody get near you!"

A chill swept down his spine and over his arms. She couldn't get near him. She couldn't get near him!

She had tried to reach him, and the spell had repelled her.

She *was* his fated one.

A very angry fated one as she hollered abuse down the phone line, slurring a few words in a way that had him worried. Had she been drinking? He had recognised the location in her picture. She was at Underworld.

Or at least she had been.

Had the male taken her somewhere private?

"Do *not* do anything with that bastard!" he shouted down the phone so she would stop berating him and listen to him, because he needed to know she would wait for him. "I am sorry. I should have let you talk. I should not have acted so rashly."

"Well you bloody did and it fucking hurt, and I'm sorry too! It was real… it was real to me… and I think… I think I might vomit." Suki's voice grew more distant and he heard her retching. She muttered something about Hellfire.

"Tell me you are not with that male."

She screamed down the phone. "No, I am not with that male… because your dumb ass is the only one I want. I know what you are… he told me. Incubus-vampire told me. Took one look at my miserable ass and announced a verdict. You have shadows."

She hiccupped.

"You're my bloody mate."

He reeled, blinking hard as all the tension that had been building inside him over the weeks he had known her, born of a fear of how he was going to break it to her that she might be his fated one, suddenly rushed out of him.

Sable's brow furrowed as she looked up at her mate, a sweet look on her face that made it clear she was melting over what Suki had said. Tegan scowled at her and waved her and Thorne away. He didn't need them listening in on him. This was a private conversation and there were things he needed to tell Suki that he didn't want anyone hearing.

When they were gone, he held the phone closer, heart thumping hard against his chest as he ached to have Suki in his arms again, to kiss her and tell her that he loved her, that he would do all in his power to make it up to her.

Across the courtyard, Prince Loren summoned everyone.

Tegan cursed. "I have to go… but wait for me, Suki. Please. The witch who cast the spell on me is here and I will get it undone once the war in the elf kingdom is over. I swear it."

Although, he had the feeling he really would have to wrestle Prince Vail while naked to make it happen and the male was liable to kill him, or at the very least injure him. Or he might die from the embarrassment of having Rosalind and her friends all watching them as she had promised.

"I'll wait. Just... be careful." As Suki's sweet voice curled through the phone, warming him and easing his heart, he realised something.

If it meant having her back in his arms, he would gladly naked wrestle every damned male in the garrison.

Because it would be worth it.

CHAPTER 35

Suki stared down at the lump of rock dangling around her neck, nestled in the modest cleavage her black leather corset gave her. She had tried to wait. She really had. But it was too hard. Patience never had been her strong suit, and Tegan had said he was going to war.

War.

She shuddered at the thought of him in the midst of a battle, fighting for his life. What if he fell? She would never see him again. She had to at least try to reach him. She wasn't sure how wide an area the spell covered but maybe she could get near enough to him to keep an eye on him until the battle was done.

Or maybe she could find the witch who had cast the spell and get her to undo it.

She looked at herself in the mirror of her vanity, checking her hair as she smoothed her violet plaid skirt she had paired with her favourite thick-soled black leather boots. She had picked them because they had looked the most kickass. Just in case she had to fight.

Gods, the thought of fighting terrified her, but she would do it if she had to in order to protect Tegan.

Suki clutched the fragment of basalt, closed her eyes and focused on the black castle.

Cold swept over her and receded, and she stiffened as she sensed males nearby.

A lot of them.

She opened her eyes and offered the group of eight demons a sheepish smile.

Good point, she had successfully teleported to the imposing black castle that apparently belonged to Tegan. Bad points, that meant he wasn't home just as he had said and she had eight guards who all looked ready to attack her.

She teleported as the first of them lunged for her, saying something in the demon tongue. Two more hollered what sounded like orders and the remaining five attacked at once. She teleported again, swiftly dodging them as they launched at her, evading their attempts to catch her.

Her heart lodged in her throat as more men poured from the castle and the arches in the wall that enclosed it.

Maybe she should have thought things through and considered all the possible scenarios before popping in uninvited.

She had been banished after all.

She doubted Tegan had explained why he had tossed her out of the kingdom, or maybe he had and that was why the guards were so furious.

She kept teleporting, pinging around the courtyard until she was exhausted. As she landed on the wall and the demons rushed her, bellowing and growling what she imagined to be obscenities, a spot near the main arched entrance of the castle opened up.

Needing a break, even if it was only a few seconds without a demon attempting to grab her, she teleported there.

And smashed straight into the bare chest of a male.

She hissed and leaped back, ready to teleport again even when it would drain the last of her strength.

Familiar dark eyes looked down at her and the urge to flee dissipated.

"Ryker," she breathed, relieved to see a friendly face.

She leaned forwards and planted her hands on her knees as she struggled to catch her breath.

"For gods' sakes female," Ryker snapped and grabbed her arm, pulling her upright. He scowled down at her. "My brother would kill them all if he knew what you had just done."

She looked over her shoulder as she realised all the demons had suddenly stopped trying to capture her.

Every male had frozen in place, their eyes on her backside.

She scowled at them as she held her skirt down. "Freaking perverts."

Ryker pulled her into the castle, barking something over his shoulder at the demons. His horns flared, the golden tip of his right one curling past his cheekbone as he glared ahead of them.

"You have some nerve showing up here," he growled and pushed her into a side room.

"I never betrayed your brother," she snapped as he slammed the door and rounded on her. "Well, maybe I did. No, I didn't. When I first saw Tegan, I wanted to use him to prove myself to my clan... it meant everything to me. Then I came to know him and... well... then I fell in love with him."

Ryker's black eyes softened, losing their sharp hard edge. "You are his fated one."

"I know." She braved a step towards him. "That's why his aura is shadowed to me and I can't control him. I need to see him and explain. He told me to wait but I can't. The thought that he's in a battle... it's killing me. I need to see him."

Ryker tunnelled his fingers through his tousled black hair and grimaced. "I will get into trouble for this, since I am not meant to leave this castle, but my brother is in a bad place right now and he needs to see you. He needs to know that you love him."

"So, you'll help me? I can't get near him. There's some sort of spell... but if I can find the witch... or maybe you can find Tegan and tell him I'm there."

Ryker shook his head, his expression pained. "I cannot enter the battlefield. The king and his heir cannot be on it at the same time. I want to help, but I will not place the kingdom at risk. We will try to find the witch."

She understood that, even as she wanted to rail at him and convince him to say screw the rules. Maybe they could find another demon who could relay a message to Tegan for them, calling him back to whatever safe place he had been when she had called him. She shook her head at that. Even if she did get a message to Tegan, he wouldn't be able to see her, not without her finding the witch and getting her to break the spell.

"Fine. We'll do it your way." She held her hands out to Ryker.

He took them and darkness yawned below him.

When it receded, shouts rang around her, footsteps rushing past her, and she stared at the busy courtyard of the pale grey stone building, marvelling at the huge mountains that rose to her right and the endless green that rolled to her left, and the infinite blue sky.

The elf kingdom.

She had never been here before, and it awed her, but she wasn't here to sightsee.

Maybe later, when she had Tegan back in her arms.

Men hurried around her and Ryker broke away from her to grab a trio who had black horns like him. He spoke with them, concern filling his eyes as they answered him. It lingered as he glanced at her, his brow furrowing, and finished speaking with his men.

When he came to her, he took her arm and led her up stone steps, onto the battlement. He pointed to the distance, where the sky was dimmer, almost grey, as if a thunderstorm loomed there.

"Tegan is there." Ryker turned to her, a flicker of regret in his eyes. "According to the warriors, the only witch on our side is there also... something about having to aid her mate."

Suki looked at that grim horizon, at the darkness that swathed the grass there, a black swarm that she realised wasn't rock as she had presumed.

It was people.

A war that was raging right now.

A war her mate was fighting in.

Nerves threatened to rise as Ryker released her and moved away a step, that regret lingering in his eyes, telling her what he couldn't bring himself to say.

She had to do this alone.

Suki sucked down a deep breath and mustered her strength.

She had never been in a war before, she had always preferred to run away from a fight than towards one, but Tegan was out there. He needed her. If it would help him survive this war, then she would fight by his side.

Her battle plan was sound.

Find the witch.

Undo the spell.

Tell Tegan everything.

Spend the rest of her life with the man she loved.

CHAPTER 36

Gods, Tegan had missed this.

The clang of blades clashing around him. The heavy reverberation as his own broadsword met the steel of his opponent. The agonised bellow and the victorious roar. The beauty of war.

He grinned and charged forwards, beating his black wings to swiftly cover the pockets of ground that opened in the midst of the fray. The scent of the churned earth mingled with the coppery tang of blood in the air, driving him on as his instincts as a warrior seized hold of him.

He dropped into a teleport as several demons from different realms rushed him and fell out of the air above them as they looked around, trying to guess where he would reappear. On a flash of fangs, he sliced the head clean off the demon on the right, one with the golden-brown horns of the Sixth Realm, landed and pivoted on his heel to block the blade of a second demon from those lands.

The male's golden eyes narrowed on him as he shoved forwards, attempting to drive Tegan back and gain the advantage.

Tegan grinned and pushed forwards too, pressing his hand to the flat of his blade to counter the male as he tried to exert more strength, a vain effort on his part. Tegan was stronger, larger, and deep in the grip of his fury, rage stoked by battle and the excitement that gripped him, had him chasing down one foe after the other without rest, much to the chagrin of his escorts.

The group of demons from the Royal Legion caught up with him and clashed with the other enemies that had arrived as Tegan gave a mighty shove against his broadsword and knocked his enemy back. He slashed with his sword and grinned wider as the male disappeared, swiftly dropping into a black abyss.

A better opponent.

So far, none of them had been much of a challenge. He had cut his way through more than three dozen enemies, and although some of them had managed to land faint blows on him that had drawn blood, none had come close to beating him.

His sharp senses issued a warning and he spun on his heel, leaned back as he spread his wings and watched the blade as it cut through the air just above his stomach. He planted his left hand against the dirt for balance as he twisted and kicked with his right leg, catching the male in his arm. The sword went flying, tumbling through the air to land with a soft thud and a scream.

The male made the mistake of looking in the direction it had gone to see who it had struck.

Tegan launched his left leg up as he pushed into the air, smashed it into the side of the male's head and took him down, twisting at the same time so he landed on top of him. He slashed his claws across the demon's throat and kicked off, ignoring the hollers of his men as he charted a course ahead of him, seeking a stronger opponent.

The throng opened up ahead of him, the end of the forces of his side just a few metres from him now.

Soon he would lead the battle.

He grinned at the thought and teleported, landing beyond the male at the front of his side.

Before him, an entire army swarmed the lands, waiting.

For him?

His grin widened.

How sweet of them.

He gripped his broadsword in both hands and roared as his muscles expanded, his black wings flared, and his horns curled.

He met two of them head on, demons from the Seventh Realm. They spread their dark grey wings, their blue-grey horns flaring as they pounded towards him across the churned earth, long blades aimed at him.

Blood sprayed over Tegan's chest as he cut the first male down, driving him on as he tasted it and scented the fear of the other male. He turned on a growl and swept his broadsword up, the silver blade a blur as it sliced through the air. The male blocked it with his own blade and parried, sweeping his sword around in a circle in an attempt to disarm him.

Tegan snarled and sidestepped, thrust forwards and forced the male to break off. The tip of his blade nicked the male's arm and crimson streamed down it. He dodged the male's next blow, beat his wings and shot backwards, luring the male forwards, away from the rest of the demons as they charged his side.

Three more joined the battle against him and he relished it as he danced with them, blocking and parrying, landing blows designed to slow them down. A slice through a calf here. A slash across a sword arm there. He battered the ones behind him with his wings, stopping their attempts to reach him.

Two of his men finally caught up with him, disgruntled looks on their faces as they breathed hard and began to fight, tackling the ones he had injured. He left them to it, focusing on taking down more of them. He wanted to fight five on one. He wanted the odds stacked against him. He craved the high of victory that came from such a battle.

Tegan spotted another incoming wave of demons and cut his way towards them, hacking and slashing at any who were foolish enough to stand in his way. His heart thundered, adrenaline pouring through his veins as he blocked and stabbed, slashed and sliced his foes. Those he didn't kill, his men dealt with as he pushed onwards, deeper into the dragon's forces.

He could see the tents now, the camp erected by the dragon for his men.

They were close.

Soon, the real war would begin.

He grinned at that.

Roared.

All around him, he sensed the enemy stiffen, smelled their fear as their courage wavered.

They were right to fear him.

Death had come for them on black wings this day.

He clashed with a large demon male, one who had been taken by rage just as he had been. The demon's golden-brown horns curled through his long chestnut hair, his amber leathery wings spread wide as he shoved forwards, forcing Tegan back.

Another worthy foe.

Tegan placed his right foot behind him, bracing himself, so the male could no longer move him. He twisted his blade and slashed upwards, aiming high. The male aimed low and Tegan adjusted his attack, bringing his sword down hard on the male's blade, sending it slamming into the earth. The male snarled and bared fangs, golden light flashing in his eyes as he swung his fist.

It caught Tegan hard in his jaw, sent his mind reeling and him staggering to his left. He shook off the blow and kicked backwards, evading the attack the male levelled at him while he was recovering.

The bastard dragon had been saving his stronger forces for the rear guard.

He meant to weaken Tegan's side by using sheer numbers to inflict injuries and deaths, and then he was going to send out his strongest fighters.

A sound plan.

But Tegan wouldn't let him carry it out.

He roared and attacked, landing several blows as he clashed with the male, some with his blade and some with his claws. The male blocked his sword and Tegan lashed out with his claws, slicing through the demon's forearm to spill blood down it. The demon snarled as Tegan backed off a step and came at him again. The male brought his sword up, but Tegan blocked it, struck the blade so hard with his own that the demon struggled to keep hold of it as blood slicked his hand.

Tegan didn't relent. He struck again, forcing the male to drop his blade, twisted his broadsword and brought it back up, slicing clean through his chest. The male looked down, panic and fear lighting his eyes as he stared at the blood flowing from him.

Tegan wished him a swift death.

The male fell and Tegan watched the light fade from his eyes.

He lifted his head.

Locked eyes with an enormous demon of the Sixth Realm as the male leaped over his fallen comrade on an agonised roar.

Pain erupted in Tegan's chest.

Everything went quiet.

Everything slowed.

Tegan sank to his knees and looked down at his chest, at the silver broadsword sticking out of it.

He roared in agony as the male grabbed the hilt and pulled it free, yanking him forward with it and sending fire and ice rushing through him.

The demon hefted the blade and spun on his heel, aiming it at his neck.

Two thoughts hit him at once.

He would never see Suki again.

Death had come for him this day.

CHAPTER 37

Suki's first thought on finally spotting Tegan on the battlefield?

Her demon was hot!

He cut a brutal path through his enemies, his broadsword a flashing silver arc as he ducked and slashed, felling his opponents with ease. A group of demons from his realm tried to keep up with him, dispatching any poor soul that Tegan left wounded in his wake in his charge to remain at the front of his side.

A side that were storming forwards to meet a force far larger than theirs was.

Her second thought?

The man she loved was in danger.

She had tried to find the witch, but picking her out in the throng of men had been impossible. The only woman she had managed to spot was a black-haired huntress who had been working in breathtaking unison with a huge russet-haired demon.

So she had settled on trying to find Tegan to lure him away from the fight.

She had picked her perch well, a rocky outcrop high on the mountainside above the battle, one that had allowed her to easily scan the fray for demons of the Second Realm.

Tegan hadn't been difficult to spot.

He towered above the others, his black wings enormous and his horns huge as he fought, the rage he felt echoing in her own blood as she watched him with ever increasing fear.

He had reached the frontline of his side and he hadn't stopped.

He charged forwards, headlong into the enemy.

Reckless demon.

313

She had been afraid for what felt like forever, teleporting around the battlefield, seeking the witch. Now she felt strangely calm as she rose to her feet and drew down a deep breath.

Tegan needed her.

She had to at least try to reach him, to test the limits of the spell and see whether she could get within earshot of him. She couldn't let him fight alone, not even when he obviously wanted to do just that, kept leaving his men behind to surge ahead of them and tackle multiple foes on his own.

She focused on him, her short fangs and claws extending as she drew her courage up from the pit of her stomach and clung to it.

And teleported.

She landed in the middle of the battle over eighty feet from him, shrieked and ducked as her senses screamed at her, narrowly missing the blade that cut above her head and sank into the male it had been intended for as she kicked off into another teleport.

This one had her landing among friendlies, a group of Second Realm demons and some seriously hot elves who all looked at her in astonishment. She disappeared again before they could utter a word, making another attempt to reach Tegan.

Perhaps if she bombarded the spell rapidly enough it would fail.

She kept teleporting, getting dizzy as her fuel tank drained, what little energy she had left from being with Tegan rapidly flowing from her. Every time she landed, she was a little closer to him.

She focused on him again and teleported, a blade slicing through the point where she had been, and landed even closer.

Within forty foot now.

Someone roared. A shiver bolted down her spine and fear flared.

She would know that roar anywhere.

Tegan.

She teleported again, landing in a clearing this time.

Her heart stopped.

Tegan was on his knees just fifty feet from her.

A sword sticking out of his chest.

Numbness swept through her as a huge demon landed in front of him, gripped the blade and pulled it free of his chest.

The whole world fell silent around her.

No.

Blood poured down Tegan's chest, pumping heavily from the wound, one that had been right in the centre.

314

Over his heart.

The demon lifted his blade, taking aim.

Tegan blankly looked at his foe.

Acceptance and regret on his handsome face.

"No!" Suki shrieked as tingles rushed over her arms and down her spine.

She teleported, putting every last drop of her energy into it, fighting the damned spell that was keeping her from her mate.

From the man she loved.

She crashed out of it right next to him, her fear rising as she realised it was because he was bleeding out, the spell that had been placed on him flowing out of him together with his life.

She turned on a pinhead and shoved her hands against the arm of the demon as he brought it around, stopping him from slicing Tegan's head off.

The demon snarled at her.

Suki hissed and leaped on him, wrapped her arms and legs around him as he staggered backwards.

And kissed him.

Energy flowed into her. Life.

A gift she would give to her mate once this bastard was dead. He would pay with his life for what he had done, attempting to take Tegan from her. She had never wanted to kill anyone through feeding, but good gods, she wanted to kill this man.

She kissed him deeper as he struggled, his movements slowing as the rate of his energy pouring into her increased. Dizziness swept through her, power welling in every fibre of her being as her fuel gauge went right past the white line, shattering the needle.

As the flow of energy dropped to a trickle, she nimbly leaped away from him to land on her feet beside him as he crumpled to his knees. She glared at him as he fell to the ground, hissed and levelled a hard kick at his head once he was down.

Dead.

She turned and froze.

"Tegan."

She hurried to him where he lay on the ground in a pool of his own blood, wrapped her arms around him and teleported him back to the garrison.

The rush of activity in the courtyard ground to a halt.

"I need help!" She looked around at all the faces of the elves and the demons, desperation gripping her as they all stared at her, shock shining in their eyes. "Fucking help me!"

Tears streamed down her cheeks, hot against her skin, and splashed onto Tegan as she looked down at him. His heart beat weakly in her ears, ripping at her strength, tearing pieces of her soul away to leave her cold inside.

A woman stopped near her, a pretty brunette wearing a T-shirt and jeans that were caked with blood.

"Let's get him inside." The woman signalled to the men and three elves marched forwards, setting aside their weapons. Suki clung to Tegan when they tried to move him and he groaned, his face twisting in a grimace, and more blood oozed from the wound in the centre of his chest. She hissed at the elves. The woman crouched beside her, placed her hand on her shoulder, and smiled in that way only doctors could. "I'm Olivia. I'm a medic here. We have to move him and get him stable."

Suki nodded shakily, but refused to let the elves take him from her. When they lifted Tegan, she remained holding on to him, helping them carry his dead weight into the infirmary. The beds that had been laid out inside the garrison's lower floor were full, several elves and demons tending to those who occupied them.

Olivia led the way to a bed, quickly changed the stained sheets and stepped aside to allow the elves access to it. They placed Tegan down onto it and Olivia drew up a chair. When she placed it beside Suki, Suki looked up at her.

The woman smiled. "I figure you'll want to stay. I don't recognise you, but I know him, and I'm guessing he needs you here more than he needs me. You're his mate, aren't you?"

She looked back at Tegan and nodded. "I can help."

Before Olivia could ask how, Suki leaned over Tegan and pressed her lips to his. He didn't respond, his mouth remaining slack against her, but then he didn't need to. She funnelled some of the energy she had taken from the demon into him.

He groaned.

She pulled back and stroked his cheek as fear swept through her again, a wave that battered her strength and had more tears falling. "Don't die. Dammit, Tegan, don't you die on me."

The corners of his lips twitched, and he opened his eyes with effort, locking them on her.

The pain must have made him crazy, because he was on the verge of slipping away from her and he was *smiling* at her.

"You said... my name," he croaked and grimaced. "I thought..."

She seized his hand, clasping it tightly. "Whatever you thought, you thought wrong. I can't lose you. I never knew you were a king, and while I had wanted to prove myself to my clan by seducing you... things changed so quickly. This was never a game to me. The stakes were too high from the moment you kissed me."

He frowned and wheezed as he breathed, his heart stuttering and tugging more tears from her. "What... did you stake?"

She blinked and those tears chased down her cheeks to fall from her jaw. "My heart, and I lost it to you."

He smiled, but it was strained, and doubts coloured his black eyes. The corona of violet-red around his dilated pupils glowed brighter and he grunted, squeezed her hand so tight as his jaw tensed that she flinched in pain.

She leaned in close, desperation seizing her again. "Live. Don't be a stupid demon and think dying on a battlefield is the right way to go when living is a much more glorious adventure... one we could share. I'll give you a reason to fight this battle against death and emerge victorious... a reason to believe me when I say that it was never a game... I'll give you proof of my love for you."

She dropped her head to his ear, careful to avoid his horns, and whispered her true name in his ear, surrendering all power to him.

When she drew back, his eyes were wide, searching hers, and he had to see the love in them and that she had spoken true because his heart beat harder and his expression grew determined.

"Give me one more thing," he mumbled, his voice hoarse as he struggled to breathe.

She nodded. "Anything to bring you back to me."

"Your blood."

She knew what that would do. It would bind them and he would have the ultimate power over her.

But it would also make him stronger and give him a reason to fight.

So she didn't hesitate.

She gathered her tangled colourful hair and drew it back from her neck, baring it to him. His eyes watered, warmed as he gazed up at her, love shining in them as she offered her blood.

Offered him forever.

She gently angled his head as she brought hers down, slipped her hand beneath his nape and raised him to her throat. Pain arced through her as his fangs sank into her and she expected it to continue, but as he pulled on her blood and it rushed into him, heat erupted in her, forged a connection that felt as strong as iron.

Unbreakable.

Feelings swept through her, her emotions and his. Fear. Pain. Hope. Love. It all collided and blended as he drank from her, as her strength flowed into him in another way, a gift of life she hoped would keep him with her.

She shivered as he pulled his fangs free and swept his tongue over the puncture marks, her head a little hazy as desire and fear swept her up and pulled her down.

She drew back and stilled.

Tingles rushed down her spine and over her arms.

She could see through the shadows.

Beautiful, tear-jerking colours swirled in his aura, shimmers of pink, gold and red.

Revealing the depth of his love.

She clutched his right hand as his eyes slipped shut and her momentary elation shattered as his cheeks paled again, the colours of his aura dimming as he sagged heavily on the bed.

She turned her gaze on the doctor.

Another female, this one a petite blonde in the unmistakable garb of a witch bustled over to them and ushered Olivia out of the way.

The witch huffed and scowled down at Tegan, her blue eyes sparkling as power rose around her. "You were meant to realise you were a dick and then I would lift the spell. You didn't need to bleed it out of you, silly demon."

Suki wasn't sure what to make of her, but what the witch muttered next had her blood blazing.

"No naked wrestling for me."

Suki shot to her feet, leaned protectively over Tegan and hissed at the blonde. "This demon is mine. Find your own man, witch."

The woman blinked. "Witch with a capital B again. I've heard that before. Oh, and I'm happily mated. I just wanted to see him wrestle my husband for the cure. It was going to be epic."

Heat rolled through Suki, fogging her mind as desire swelled inside her.

Tegan wrestling another guy while naked?

Oh gods, yes please!

She shook herself back to the room before she started drooling. Tegan was awake again and looking more than a little unhappy, his black eyebrows knitted hard above his pain-filled eyes.

"Your eyes are glowing," he croaked. "Will not wrestle… the elf. Do not… want… your eyes… on anyone else."

Fine. No watching him wrestle another guy while naked. Anything to make him happy. She would settle for imagining it.

She stroked her fingers across his brow, clearing the damp strands of his black hair from it as she held his gaze, willing him to heal. With the potent cocktail of her energy and blood in him, he was looking brighter and the wound was no longer bleeding.

He was going to make it.

He suddenly jacked up off the bed on a deafening roar, squeezing her hand so tightly that a few bones in it broke, but she didn't feel it.

All she felt was fear as Tegan thrashed, blood streaming from the corners of his lips to track down his cheeks, and Olivia and the witch rushed to help him.

Because she hadn't been able to.

She had given him everything, and it wasn't enough.

Her ears rang, the numbness returning as she stared at Tegan as Olivia raced to assess the wound and the witch closed her eyes and held one hand over his forehead and the other over his chest, a faint violet glow emanating from her palms.

Suki stared at Tegan, willing him to keep fighting.

He had to fight for her.

For them.

She touched the marks on her throat that were still bleeding and sore.

Because she wanted that forever he had just promised her.

CHAPTER 38

For the first time in forever, Tegan was bone-deep afraid.

He had craved war, ached for battle, but now he felt it had been a terrible mistake and a terrible yearning to indulge, because he feared that it was about to part him from the beautiful fae female watching him with tears streaking her ashen cheeks. Her lower lip trembled, fresh tears glittering in her striking eyes as she assisted Rosalind, rushing to do all that the witch asked of her.

Attempting to save him.

He gritted his teeth against the agony that tore through him. The scent of his blood grew heavier in the air, choking his lungs, and he swallowed hard, desperate to keep breathing.

Suki's eyes leaped to his and down to his chest, and she grabbed a wad of material and pushed it against the wound, her expression stricken as she applied pressure.

His beautiful mate.

Their bond pulsed deep inside him, relaying all her fear to him, incomplete but powerful.

"Live," she whispered, voice hoarse, and choked on a sob as her eyes darted back to meet his. "Fight. I need you. I'm sorry. I know what Cyrena told you... but I changed. I changed when I got to know you... when I fell for you. So you have to live... because I can't live without you."

He felt the same way. When he had thought she had betrayed him, when he had banished her in a fit of rage and hurt, it had honestly felt as though his life had been coming to an end.

And he had wanted to embrace it.

But now he needed to fight it.

For her.

320

His female needed him, and he needed her.

He shifted his fingers, aching to touch her, and she noticed. She grabbed his hand and lifted it, brought it to her face and kissed his bloodied knuckles, smoothing her lips over them as her tears hit his skin, stinging the cuts. She closed her eyes, tilted her head and pressed her cheek to his hand. Tears raced down her face and it killed him to see them. He wanted to brush them away and tell her not to fear, but he was weak.

Tired.

He had to conserve his strength.

So he picked the most important thing he wanted to tell her.

"I love you."

She smiled, but it was strained and wobbled on her lips as more tears fell. "I love you too. I don't want to live without you. You've made my life too colourful... too warm and good... filled with light. I need you... so you can't leave me."

Her words echoed his feelings perfectly.

The impish female looking down at him with all the love in the world in her green-to-blue eyes had brought colour and life into his dull existence, had made his mansion feel like a home in the short time she had been there, and had shattered the need he had felt for war.

She had lifted his curse.

He no longer felt as if ruling the Second Realm was a chore, a punishment, one he would trade in a heartbeat for a life on the battlefield.

If he could rule his realm with her at his side, he would gladly do it, and damn, he might even enjoy it.

He husked, "I was wrong... I did not need war... I only needed you."

She smiled and kissed his hand again as Rosalind moved to the wound on his chest, taking Suki's other hand from it and the material.

Suki cursed him in the fae tongue. "I came here to give you hell... to make you see you were wrong for pushing me away... and now I'm going to lose you."

"Oh, mother earth!" Rosalind bit out. "Will you both stop being so bloody melodramatic! You're not going to lose him. Demons are stubborn bastards. A sword through the chest is just a flesh wound. Give me five minutes and I'll have him fixed."

Prince Loren's mate didn't look as convinced as the witch. She hovered near the foot of the bed, concern in her dark eyes. Suki didn't look convinced either as she cast him a fearful glance.

They weren't alone in their doubts.

Tegan found it difficult to believe he was going to survive the next few minutes. He could feel his strength leaching out of him as cold invaded to chill his flesh and his blood, turning his mind sluggish as the room gently spun around him and sounds grew watery in his ears.

Distant.

He clung to Suki's hand, afraid that if he released it, or even loosened his hold, that death would take him from her.

The air in the room suddenly darkened.

Tegan braced himself for the end.

But then it lightened again and an elf was glaring down at him, his sharp violet eyes edged with black as he arched an eyebrow and brushed a rogue hank of his blue-black hair back. Blood covered half of his face. Not the male's own.

"The war is done. Loren has the sword. We shall leave soon," Vail ground each word out, razor sharp fangs flashing between his lips as he turned his gaze on his mate.

The witch didn't take her eyes off Tegan's chest as she continued her work. "I'm a little occupied."

She wavered, swaying as she closed her eyes and Tegan grimaced as she pressed on his chest, supporting her weight on him as the colour drained from her face.

"Stop," Tegan gritted. He wanted to live, but he didn't want to kill the witch to achieve it.

"I agree." Vail closed his left hand over her shoulder and his armour receded, the black scales rippling towards his wrist to leave his hand bare.

"You can't stop!" Suki barked and sharply leaned over Tegan, her eyes wild as she stared at Vail and Rosalind, fielding a glare from the elf. "I'll lose him. He'll die."

Vail eyed her and Tegan, and casually said, "No one mentioned anything about allowing him to die."

He gently guided Rosalind to beside him, assuming her position at Tegan's side, and held his hands over Tegan's chest. The armour covering his other hand peeled away too, leaving them both bare.

Tegan mustered his strength, a desire to know what the elf was about to do rising inside him as the male's violet eyes brightened.

He screamed instead as Vail placed his hands on him and fire and lightning arced through him, sending him shooting up off the bed.

Tegan shivered at the same time as he sweated as he fought to remain conscious, every nerve ending in his body sparking and burning, the pain ripping through him so intense that the corners of his vision grew dark and he lost sight of Suki.

The elf was killing him.

He swore it as the pain built rather than receding, as the darkness pushed harder and his body grew colder.

He mustered his strength and managed to tilt his head enough that he could see Suki, because he needed to see her one last time to take her memory to his grave and into eternity.

She was pale, stricken and fierce as she fought the witch, battling to get past her to stop the elf.

Tegan lifted his right hand, desperate to touch her.

To comfort her.

Light burst around him, inside him, and suddenly the pain ceased.

There was no ice or fire.

He was warm.

Felt strangely at peace.

Was he dead?

He lay in the endless white, adrift and confused, awaiting the answer to that question.

Something tugged at his chest.

He sought the source of that sensation as it built and grew clearer, feeling as if something was reaching into him, holding hands out to him.

Something that comforted him beyond words and filled him with a soothing sensation, as if he was floating in warm air, embraced by light.

That light began to sparkle, waves of bright bursts of pale blue and purple that rippled across his vision, and then green joined them.

A lush and verdant colour that spoke of life to him despite the existence he had led in a black realm.

The comforting hands touched him, on his chest, warm on his skin, pouring life into his weary body as it calmed his mind and eased his heart.

He blinked.

Looked up at the person to his left and frowned when he recognised the elf. The male was glowing, the bursts of light dancing around him, and beyond him there was a shimmering form, one that seemed to be reaching into the elf.

Tegan reached for her, desperate to connect with her too as the elf could, jealous that the male could be held by her so closely.

So lovingly.

The illusion shattered and darkness crashed over him, pushing him back down into the world.

Voices sounded around him again.

The witch. "Did it work?"

Vail. "Yes."

Suki. His sweet, beautiful Suki. "If it didn't, I'm going to kill the fucking lot of you."

Tegan coughed and grimaced, sore now that the light was gone. Suddenly, the warmth and softness of Suki pressed against him, her tears hot on his cheek as she pressed hers to it and held him tightly. He gritted his teeth against the pain as she squeezed him, not wanting to upset her.

He looked up at the elf.

Rosalind stood beside her mate, her blue eyes bright with admiration and her smile proud. "I was right. Your connection is growing stronger again."

Vail nodded, a pleased edged to his violet gaze as he struggled to breathe and brushed his hand over his forehead, clearing the sweat away as he tunnelled his trembling fingers into his wild dark hair. He attempted a smile, one that shook as Rosalind hugged him, and Tegan could see how important this moment was to him.

"What happened?" The strength of Tegan's voice surprised him, and not only him.

Suki pulled back, shock in her eyes as she looked down at the healed wound on his chest, together with relief he could feel flowing through their growing connection. She looked to the couple too.

Rosalind released Vail and stroked his arm. "Vail is connected to nature, and while my spell kickstarted your healing, getting it going along at a nicer pace, it was Vail's bond with nature that saved you. It's coming back, just like I said it would."

She turned her smile on her mate again.

Tegan frowned, his head aching as he struggled to recall what he had seen when Vail had been healing him.

Nature.

He remembered the light. The warmth. The green.

The figure that had stood behind Vail.

"I think I saw it," Tegan murmured.

The colour drained from Vail's face. "You saw her?"

Tegan nodded. "Beyond you... reaching into you... there was something there... almost as if she was embracing you."

Vail suddenly dropped to his knees, his fingers grasping the dark grey flagstones as he stared at nothing, his violet eyes wide. He muttered in the elf language, lyrical sounding words that Tegan couldn't understand, but he could feel the shock and disbelief in each one of them.

Rosalind crouched beside him and stroked her hands over his trembling shoulders, caressing the black scales of his armour. Her voice was soft, light and soothing as she spoke to him. "It's good progress."

The elf swallowed and nodded, and Rosalind wrapped her arms around him and held him.

Tegan looked away, giving them a moment even when he wanted to ask more questions. He had known elves had a connection to nature, but he hadn't realised they believed her to be a living being, a higher power. He had a connection to nature too, had been born of the earth of Hell and travelled through his link to that earth whenever he teleported, but he had never believed nature to be an actual living thing.

A goddess.

He supposed he had to believe in her now.

She had healed him through Vail.

She had given him a second chance.

One he wasn't going to waste.

CHAPTER 39

Tegan breathed a deep sigh of relief as he strolled out of the meeting, leaving his advisers bickering over the windfarm project he had put forward, a new one he and Suki had come up with together.

This one included the castle in the list of areas where the test would be conducted.

His advisers had kept him for an extra hour to go over and over the plan, attempting to change his mind because of the cost involved in not only constructing the windmills near the castle, building enough to provide a suitable amount of electricity, but also in modernising the castle, fitting electrical wires and lights, and things called outlets.

He suspected Suki wanted power brought to the castle because she had unofficially moved in with him, making herself at home on his private floors. She had complained more than once about his lack of a television and the fact she had to get a fresh power pack to charge her phone so she could watch something called YouTube and browse the internet.

During the meeting, his advisers had brought her up, and although he had brushed aside their attempt to discuss the formalities of her becoming his queen, it had got him thinking.

And he hadn't been able to stop thinking about her.

Which had made every second of the meeting feel like an hour.

Now, as he ascended the stairs, choosing to walk to his apartments rather than teleporting there, giving himself time to fight for calm and control, the need that had been building inside him since he had bitten her rolled to a dangerous boil.

He flexed his fingers, spreading them and then curling them into tight fists as he wrestled with the urges swirling inside him, hungers that he could no longer deny. He had been patient, had waited until he was feeling stronger because she worried about him, but he couldn't wait anymore.

He needed to make Suki his mate.

He needed to complete their bond.

Before tonight's feast to celebrate their victory in the elf kingdom, a feast that Suki insisted on attending.

The thought of her there, around so many unmated males, drove him wild and half-mad, had him taking the steps to the next floor two at a time, rushing to close the distance between them.

He growled at the two warriors standing guard outside the heavy wooden door to his apartments, flashing his fangs in warning. They bowed their heads and were quick to stride away, leaving him alone in the lamplit corridor.

Tegan breathed hard, fighting to calm himself again. The males weren't interested in his female. She was alone in his rooms, waiting for him. She wanted no other male.

She loved *him*.

He gripped the door handle and wrestled with himself, clawing back enough control that he wouldn't frighten his female when he found her. It was impossible. Whenever he thought he was close, an image of her surrounded by males flashed into his mind, tormenting him. His horns curled, rage and desire an explosive combination in his blood as he shoved the door open and slammed it behind him.

He stilled.

She wasn't in the drawing room where he had left her.

On a low, vicious growl, he stalked through the room, scenting the air to track her. The sweet warmly-spiced fragrance of her led him up the staircase to the bedroom, but she wasn't there either. He pivoted and stormed back out of the room, breathed deep to catch her scent again and followed it as his heart thundered, each step ratcheting his need up another degree, until he was straining for her, aching for her.

On the verge of dying if he didn't find her soon.

He reached the open door of his study and paused on the threshold, his steps arrested by the sight of her where she stood amidst the carnage he had wrought when he had thought he had lost her.

Her green, blue and violet hair tumbled around her bare shoulders, caressing the black velvet corset she wore with her blue plaid skirt. Her striking eyes were fixed on the mess strewn across the floor as she bent and rifled through it, plucked a book from the wreckage and sighed at it, sorrow crossing her delicate features.

"Suki," he growled, voice a rough snarl as hunger mounted, threatening to rip control from him.

She paused and lifted her eyes from the book, settling them on him. "Done with your meeting?"

He nodded and stalked into the room, each step clipped as he wrestled to remain in control, to deny the primal need screaming inside of him, demanding he claim her.

She stood slowly, coming to face him, awareness dawning in her green-to-blue eyes as he stopped close to her, his bare chest heaving as he fought his need, afraid of how she might react.

She had given him blood when he had been dying, but had she done it because she had wanted him healed or because she had wanted his bond?

She was fae, valued her freedom, and he knew what a monumental step it would be for her if she chose to become his mate. As monumental as her decision to give him her real name. He couldn't rush her.

But he couldn't wait either.

They had triggered the bonding process and he needed to complete it.

"Suki... I..." He clenched his fists and took a deep breath, held her gaze and put it out there. "Would you be my mate?"

She stared at him in silence that ate away at his courage.

And then she grinned.

"I thought you'd never bloody ask!" She teleported into his arms, wrapped her legs around his waist and grabbed hold of his shoulders as her mouth came down on his, rocking him with a kiss so fierce he was left in no doubt of how much she wanted him.

He groaned, enfolded her in his arms and held her to him, gentling the kiss until it warmed him, had all his fear melting away and desire rising to replace it, a need that urged him to claim her now, before she changed her mind.

She was way ahead of him.

Darkness swept around him and when it receded, he was standing at the foot of his four-poster bed and she was grinning wickedly at him, her eyes sparkling with excitement and the need he could feel in her.

"Give me your blood," she murmured and dipped her head, swept her lips over his throat in a maddening way that had a thousand achy shivers chasing over his skin and his cock hardening in his leathers. She rocked against it, driving him crazier still. "I want to see it again."

"See what again?" He sounded dazed.

Felt it too as she worked her body against his, stripping away his control.

"Through the shadows." She pulled back with effort, groaned and trembled as she skimmed her fingers over his shoulders. When he lowered his hands to her backside, it was his turn to moan. She wore no undergarments. Gods, the thought that she was bare against his caged erection.

It destroyed him.

Almost obliterated his ability to think.

But he managed to keep it together. "Shadows?"

She nodded, sighed as she rubbed against him, her breasts jiggling in her tight corset, threatening to shatter his ability to think after all.

"Your aura is black. I can't read your feelings... but when you took my blood... I could see your love for me." A blush climbed her cheeks, a flicker of nerves lighting her green-to-blue eyes.

She worried what she might see this time, but she wanted to see it regardless.

He would show it to her.

He adjusted his grip on her, so he could hold her with only one hand without fear of dropping her, and brought his right wrist up to his lips.

She grabbed it, stopping him.

"No."

No?

His heart sank. She wanted his blood, didn't she? She wanted his bond.

Didn't she?

Her eyes glittered wickedly.

Hungrily.

Thrilled him as they lowered to his throat and she licked her lips.

Whispered.

"I want to bite you. Like you bit me." She nibbled her lower lip, her short fangs teasing it as she gazed at his throat, heat filling her eyes.

"Gods," he uttered, breathless himself now as he considered that.

He could wear her marks as she wore his. The whole world would know their love for each other and that they were bound, that they belonged to each other.

"That sounds like a yes to me." She didn't give him a chance to answer.

She lunged and struck, sank her tiny fangs deep into his throat and tore a guttural moan from his lips as pain and pleasure detonated inside him. His head swum with her first pull on his blood, desire flaring so hot he was burning, sure he was going to turn to ashes. In the wake of the fire, intense emotions rushed through him, tearing his strength away as he realised they were hers.

Her love for him.

Her need of him.

She moaned and shook in his arms and his knees gave out and he hit the floor with her at the foot of his bed. She didn't stop, didn't miss a single beat. She kept drinking and writhing against him, cranking his need tighter inside him, until he was on the verge of snapping.

Her sucking grew fiercer, the rush of his blood faster, and he shuddered as she pressed her heels into the floor and rocked on him, as she grumbled something against his throat and wriggled back a few inches. She made fast work of his leathers, tearing through the laces with her claws, and he hissed when cool air kissed his cock and then her hot hand replaced it.

She gripped him hard, stroked him roughly as she tore away from his throat and kissed him, matching his desperation as the connection bloomed between them, tangled their needs and their feelings together into one incredible sensation.

He had never felt anything like it.

Suki grabbed him by his right horn as she pulled herself up, as she grasped his cock and fed it into her, stealing his ability to think as she sheathed him, her heat scalding him as she gripped him tightly. He groaned and shuddered, clutched her bare backside and pressed her back against the end of the bed as he seized control. She moaned and kissed him deeper, wrapped her legs around him and clung to him as he pumped her hard and fast, unable to hold back now that she had roused his primal instincts and he was on the verge of claiming her.

She moaned hotly into his ear as he lowered his mouth to her neck, angled her head away from him and whispered, "Bite me. Do it."

He growled and sank his fangs into her in the same spot he had bitten before.

The moment her blood hit his tongue, heat rolled through him, an inferno so intense it branded his soul with her name. The bond blossomed, growing stronger still, bringing tears to his eyes as he felt all of her love for him and became aware she could feel his for her too. She held him close to her, stroked his hair and his horn, rocked her body against his as she took them higher.

Words rose to the tip of his tongue as he felt her soaring and flew higher with her, as his body tensed and release rose to the base of his cock. He held them back, pumping her harder, deeper, longer strokes that had her crying for more, digging her nails into his shoulders as she sought the release she needed.

A climax that would bind them forever as mates.

Together with the words.

And her answer.

She cried his name as she came apart in his arms, as her body quivered and milked his, pushing him over the edge. He groaned into her throat as he spilled inside her, his entire body trembling, fire rushing through his veins, along with bliss, happiness that he could feel blooming inside her too as she clung to him and slowly came down.

He forced himself to wait for her breathing to settle, for his own racing heart to calm, and kissed her softly, reverently, with all the love that he held for her. And then he pulled back and looked deep into her eyes, ones that had enchanted him the moment he had met her and would always hold him under her spell.

"Suki." He brushed his knuckles across her flushed cheeks, and she blinked, her gaze softening with love as she held his. It was tradition to speak the words in the demon tongue, but he wanted her to understand them, wanted to know her reply now without having to waste time explaining what he had said. He needed to know her answer. "Do you consent to become my mate, to take all that I am and give all that you are, in the eyes of the gods and eternity?"

She slowly smiled and the new bond between them hit him with her reply before it even reached her lips, setting his heart and mind at ease.

"Abso-bloody-lutely." She stroked her fingers down his chest, her gaze growing heated again, passion and need flaring that he could feel in her. "What about you? Do you swear you'll take me?"

He groaned as she wriggled on him, as if he needed an explanation of what she meant with that question.

"Whenever, wherever and however you want it, my love."

"How about right now, right here, and right on this bed." She grabbed his horns and dragged him down for a kiss, a sweet reward that promised something more wicked at the end of it.

Tegan moaned and clutched her to him as he counted his blessings.

For the first time in his life, he was grateful for what he had been given.

A bond he would cherish.

A mate he would worship.

A queen to rule by his side.

He revised that last one as she teleported him onto the bed, landing on top of him, pinning him beneath her as she grinned saucily and raked her nails down his bare chest.

A queen to rule by his side in public.

And rule him in the bedroom.

One he was looking forward to serving.
For eternity.

The End

ABOUT THE AUTHOR

Felicity Heaton is a New York Times and USA Today best-selling author who writes passionate paranormal romance books. In her books she creates detailed worlds, twisting plots, mind-blowing action, intense emotion and heart-stopping romances with leading men that vary from dark deadly vampires to sexy shape-shifters and wicked werewolves, to sinful angels and hot demons!

If you're a fan of paranormal romance authors Lara Adrian, J R Ward, Sherrilyn Kenyon, Kresley Cole, Gena Showalter, Larissa Ione and Christine Feehan then you will enjoy her books too.

If you love your angels a little dark and wicked, her best-selling Her Angel romance series is for you. If you like strong, powerful, and dark vampires then try the Vampires Realm romance series or any of her stand alone vampire romance books. If you're looking for vampire romances that are sinful, passionate and erotic then try her London Vampires romance series. Or if you like hot-blooded alpha heroes who will let nothing stand in the way of them claiming their destined woman then try her Eternal Mates series. It's packed with sexy heroes in a world populated by elves, vampires, fae, demons, shifters, and more. If sexy Greek gods with incredible powers battling to save our world and their home in the Underworld are more your thing, then be sure to step into the world of Guardians of Hades.

If you have enjoyed this story, please take a moment to contact the author at **author@felicityheaton.com** or to post a review of the book online

Connect with Felicity:
Website – http://www.felicityheaton.com
Blog – http://www.felicityheaton.com/blog/
Twitter – http://twitter.com/felicityheaton
Facebook – http://www.facebook.com/felicityheaton
Goodreads – http://www.goodreads.com/felicityheaton
Mailing List – http://www.felicityheaton.com/newsletter.php

FIND OUT MORE ABOUT HER BOOKS AT:
http://www.felicityheaton.com

Printed in Great Britain
by Amazon